HEAVEN SENT LOVE

Unaware of the light, seeing only the dark scene playing in his mind, Daniel felt guilt grind his soul. An old guilt. *I shouldn't have stopped when I did. I should have killed him,* he told himself. Killed his father.

"I'll kill you yet, you bastard, so help me —"

"McQuinn!" Frightened for him, Madeleine grabbed his upper arms and squeezed as hard as she could. "Look at me, McQuinn. Wherever you are or think you are, come back!"

As Daniel slowly turned his gaze toward the woman distantly calling him, a great orange moon broke through the clouds. Beneath it, her skin shimmered; her mouth was soft and sweet. She was Heaven and she'd brought him back from Hell.

She still had her power, not to seduce a man, but to induce him, not to lead him astray but to lead him home. But he wasn't ready to go home.

Daniel turned away. "The moon's given you a good look at me."

"Yes, it has." Raising her hand to his cheek, she grazed her fingertips down one side of his face, feeling the hardness of his cheekbone and the softness of the corner of his mouth. "It showed a man at war with himself, a man who's yet to decide who and what he really is."

He certainly knew who she was. She was a woman who read him like a book she herself had authored. A woman who had the power to make a story of his life. The kind of woman he'd religiously avoided. And for the first time, he felt he was about to sin.

Crushing her to him, he brought his mouth down hard on hers.

"A tour de force! Valerie Kirkwood's best work yet. *Trace of A Woman* is a must read!"

— Sharon De Vita, bestselling author of
Lady and the Sheriff

"An extraordinary novel."

— *Rendezvous*

BOOK YOUR PLACE ON OUR WEBSITE AND MAKE THE READING CONNECTION!

We've created a customized website just for our very special readers, where you can get the inside scoop on everything that's going on with Zebra, Pinnacle and Kensington books.

When you come online, you'll have the exciting opportunity to:

- View covers of upcoming books
- Read sample chapters
- Learn about our future publishing schedule (listed by publication month *and author*)
- Find out when your favorite authors will be visiting a city near you
- Search for and order backlist books from our online catalog
- Check out author bios and background information
- Send e-mail to your favorite authors
- Meet the Kensington staff online
- Join us in weekly chats with authors, readers and other guests
- Get writing guidelines
- AND MUCH MORE!

**Visit our website at
http://www.zebrabooks.com**

TRACE OF
A WOMAN

Valerie Kirkwood

Zebra Books
Kensington Publishing Corp.
http://www.zebrabooks.com

ZEBRA BOOKS are published by

Kensington Publishing Corp.
850 Third Avenue
New York, NY 10022

Zebra and the Z logo Reg. U.S. Pat. & TM Off.

First Printing: October, 1998
10 9 8 7 6 5 4 3 2 1

Printed in the United States of America

*For Rachel, beloved daughter and promising
young author of her life.*

ACKNOWLEDGMENTS

Not for the first time am I indebted to Nancy Vinsel and Susan Irving, librarians *extraordinaire*, for their research assistance. I am also grateful to (and proud of, as she is a dear cousin) Chicago journalist Kathy Catrambone for her invaluable insight on the world of newspaper journalism and the women who, in times past, dared invade it. Lastly, love and gratitude to my Head Coach and teammates, St. Jude, St. Lucy, and sainted husband, Alan.

Overcoming me with the light of a smile, she said to me:
'Turn and listen, for not only in my eyes is Paradise."

Dante Alighieri
The Divine Comedy
Paradiso, Canto XVIII, I. 19

Part One

One

"Cheese it, Delaney! Monstrous Lucifer's at the door."

Holding the pose of intense study that had deceived Lucifer before—shaved head bowed over the tattered pages of a broken-spined reader, bruised chin beneath split lower lip on fist—Daniel Delaney grumbled. "That's not news, Benny. You don't wake a fella up to tell him what isn't news. If old Monstrous had stumbled over his cloven hooves and fallen on his pitchfork, then you could have waked me up."

As he drifted back to sleep, Daniel knew old Mother Grimm wouldn't have had to wake him at all if he'd slept more than three hours last night. God knew his overworked, underfed, and battered body had sorely tempted him to sleep the full six hours allotted. But he'd figured that the next day, it would only be overworked, underfed, and battered again. So, as had become his habit, he'd scrimped on sleep, risking napping in class and another beating to read newspapers and books he'd stolen and hidden; to write on scraps of paper he'd thieved and hoarded.

Daniel Patrick Amadous Delaney wrote out of need, out of fear. The fear that if he didn't wield the sharp point of his pen, he might brandish the sharper tip of the knife he'd lifted from the kitchen and concealed beneath a loose floorboard under his dormitory bunk. Even if they found the weapon and took it from him, and took their righteousness out on him, they couldn't take his fists. Although just one month remained of his sentence to this hellhole, Daniel wasn't sure he'd ever get out. He wasn't at all sure that before the month was over, he wouldn't kill someone.

"He just finished talking to Bunco and he's looking around," Benny said, ever sounding as though he had a sore throat. "Oh, oh. He's in the room now and he's looking around."

"The Prince of Darkness Surveys His Realm," Daniel mumbled. "Great headline."

A chorus of chair legs scraped the wood plank floor.

"For God's sake, Danny, unless you want to go back to cutting overalls fourteen hours a day, stand up!"

Daniel shambled to his feet, responding less to Benny's sharp cuff on his arm than to the threat of the sweatshop's grueling monotony. He'd been beaten yesterday because, after cutting the seventy-sixth pair of overalls without a break, he'd stuck the scissors in the cutting table and refused to work any further.

Now, with as much residual insubordination as lingering pain, he slouched beside his pockmarked desk in the last precise row of pockmarked desks in Father Bianco's grimy classroom. Nevertheless, he was still a head or more taller than the other boys, and as he grazed his surly gaze toward the front of the room, he easily spotted the man he'd dubbed "Monstrous Lucifer"—Monsignor Lucius Hale.

The very sight of the prelate turned Daniel's blood cold. Reflexively, he went on guard, his spine stiffening and his muscles tensing. From the corner of his left eye— the right one was swollen shut and ringed in black and purple—he kept close watch on the man. Ghoulishly gaunt in his black cassock, he stood just inside the side entrance to the room, once again conferring with Father Bianco. Despite the distance between them, Daniel felt the icy reach of the man's dark soul, a malicious phantom that bore in its skeletal fingers a reminder of his last private "lesson"—with the head of the reform school that, in two years, had yet to reform him.

Not that Daniel needed a reminder beyond his battered, barely recognizable face and the ugly bruise over his right kidney that was twice the size of the boot heel that had made it. Now imagining that his glance was a hot poker, he held it to the boot's owner as the latter turned from Father Bianco and opened the door, granting someone as yet unseen admittance to the dim room.

"As you already know, most of our boys are either convicted criminals or awaiting trial," Monsignor Hale said to a plump woman who passed in front of him. "But you will soon see that at St. Augustine's, we know how to break young hooligans of their wayward tendencies."

Or just break them. Daniel held his searing, one-eyed gaze on the hated priest, though all the other boys' gazes followed the woman. He'd seen her kind before, the Lady Bountiful kind. She came briefly to this Hades, usually no more than twice, bearing bundles of cast-off clothing or pin money equal to a mill worker's yearly wages to purchase her salvation without the inconvenience of soiling her kid gloves. This latest benefactress, however, earned an extra measure of Daniel's disdain as he watched Lucifer cup her elbow and lead her to the chair Father Bianco had placed in front of the chalkboard. A truly great lady would have sensed the evil in the man's touch, would have thrown it off.

No sooner had Daniel rendered this judgment than the woman halted and glanced over her shoulder at the doorway. His thin chest swelled with the hope that she'd caught an alarming whiff of the brimstone into which she had so blithely waltzed. Just once he'd like to see one of these angels of mercy take off her gloves and put up her dukes. Fight to change this purgatory instead of providing the dollars that kept it burning. Rather, in a Southern belle tone Daniel deemed artificially sweet, she called, "Come along, Madeleine dear. The kind monsignor has more important things to do than indulge your dawdlin'."

"Yeah, lady," Daniel muttered out the side of his mouth that worked. "You wouldn't want to keep the 'ki-i-i-nd moanseenyuh' from making his rounds with the strop."

"Shut up," Benny blurted in the permanent whisper that was a remnant of one of his own "lessons" with Monstrous Lucifer. "You want to spend your last month in solitary?"

Daniel shuddered at the mere thought of ever returning to that place of darkly cramped isolation. But even more disturbing was the prospect of walking into the light beyond these walls without his self-respect. Instead of leaving here free, he'd be taking his imprisonment with him. Lifting his chin, he brought his fists to his waist and answered Benny out loud.

"Let 'em throw me in the hole. It'll take at least four of them to do it, and when they're done, they'll look like I do now."

"Who said that?"

Daniel watched Monstrous Lucifer's gaze cut across the rows ahead of his like a scythe, mowing down his cover. When it reached him, he checked it with a one-eyed look of steely defiance.

"I should have known it was you, Delaney. Come forward."

Though his heart pounded as he made his way to the front of the classroom, Daniel fixed a bold if handicapped stare on the man who everyone agreed, even Father Bianco, took an especially perverse pleasure in tormenting him. For that reason and because his right eye was closed, as he passed the door, he did not see the boy he plowed into and knocked away like a rag bag. To the accompaniment of a collective gasp from the onlookers, he whipped around to face his victim with his fists instinctively raised.

"I'm sorry. I don't know how to box."

Daniel's heart stopped beating altogether. Before his gaze and against the wall stood a vision in blurred plaid-and-velvet. A girl. He blinked to bring her into better focus but she remained indistinct. Still, he could make out the royal blue of her cocked tam and, beneath it, her curls, more white than gold. Even if his sight had been whole, he knew her hair would still have appeared to shimmer like the halo around the head of the Virgin on the holy card his mother had given him the day the police brought him here. Unlike the Madonna's downcast eyes, however, this girl's looked unblinkingly and boldly up at him. Squinting, Daniel refined his hazy sight just enough to determine their color and size. They were nearly black and so large that he imagined they were wells in whose depths lie knowledge that, until now, he'd only surmised from books. He wished he could see her well enough to imprint her features on his memory, the features of a girl who, though only twelve or thirteen to his nearly sixteen years, had instantly and somehow rightfully taken command of him.

Daniel lowered his fists. "I could teach you," he said, then inwardly groaned. *Knucklehead!* What would this small pearl, this lady-in-waiting, want with boxing lessons? Or need with them? If she hadn't already, she'd soon have boys bloodying one another to defend her honor, win her favor. If he'd thought for a single moment she could ever look on him with anything but disgust, he'd be the bloodiest among them. Still, he imagined her gently cleaning his wounds. Then, he realized she could not wash away the dirt of his class, the stain of his guilt. Or the memory of the fright he must be giving her now with his shorn head, smudged with the prickly beginnings of growth, and his pummeled face. His head sank over his chest and his heart lower than the fists at his sides.

But it soared again when she did the most miraculous thing. She stepped very near to him, her presence lifting his head and his single-sighted gaze, and she smiled. An angel had seen past his grotesqueness, looked at his heart and soul, and smiled.

"*I* think that would be fun," she said in a voice that, despite its girlish tinkle, messaged a woman's willfulness.

Daniel stood conflicted, wanting both to bend a knee to her and challenge her to a race through Sherwood Forest. Instead of deciding which to do, if only to satisfy his imagination, he grew sick to his stomach. Belatedly and with horror, he realized that when he'd plowed into her, he had to have hurt her. He couldn't bear it if, accidentally or not, he'd raised just one bruise on her perfect skin. Tentatively, his hands reached for her shoulders beneath her blue velvet cape. "Are you all—"

A set of knuckles on the back of a hand Daniel didn't need two eyes to recognize appeared atop the girl's shoulder, interrupting Daniel and turning his horror of having injured her to rage. A rage he had known before. A blind, killing rage.

"My dear Madeleine, are you sure you're all right?" Monsignor Hale asked the girl, giving Daniel a look that was a blow for his clumsiness, for existing.

"*Quite* sure," she replied testily, wiggling her shoulder free of the priest's grasp. She looked directly at Daniel. "As sure as I am that this boy never meant to hurt me."

Receiving her sweet absolution, Daniel sighed. But his relief was short-lived. As the prelate led Madeleine to a chair beside the Lady Bountiful's, his rage flared. He wanted to run after her, to bring her back from the netherworld to which Lucifer had lured her. Instead, he laughed at himself for presuming even to think of rescuing her. Surely, angels had been appointed the task—the privilege—of keeping her from harm.

Daniel remained in limbo until, hearing Monsignor Hale's summons, he did the inconceivable. He thanked the man for granting him his heart's desire: to feel the warm nearness of Madeleine—his Madeleine—again. To enter the spell cast by her scent, to hear her breathe. As he walked toward her, she so monopolized his sensibilities that he was unaware of Monsignor Hale behind him until a bony pincers clamped the back of his neck, freezing him to a halt.

"Don't think I have forgotten the threat you made a moment ago, Delaney," the priest hissed in Daniel's ear. "I can see you are in need of more tutoring. I will meet with you after our guests have gone." Releasing Daniel's neck, he went to stand behind Madeleine. "Father Bianco tells me the class has prepared recitations on the evil of drink. You will be the first to recite, Delaney. Face the class and begin."

Daniel faced the class, but not to begin. To hide his fear from Madeleine.

Not seconds ago, when Monstrous Lucifer had squeezed his neck until his pulse throbbed in his ears, he hadn't worried he might flinch before her eyes. Pride and practice had kept him from cowering at threats like the fetid one the priest had just breathed into his ear. Just as they'd kept him, during his many "lessons" with the man, from ever once begging for mercy.

But now standing ordered to recite in Madeleine's presence, Daniel was dangerously close to doing just that. Not because the blood had already drained from his head, taking his wits with it. Or because his arms had turned to lead and his mouth to meal. He'd overcome these manifestations of fear often enough before. What he couldn't overcome was the conviction that if Madeleine heard him speak more than a few words, she'd laugh at him.

Daniel knew that his speech branded him the product of the hard, flat city streets that had spawned him, belligerent streets where immigrants and the sons of immigrants fought one another as they fought to survive. Madeleine's speech was a wide, tree-lined, gently rolling boulevard in the best part of a Southern town where her family's name was undoubtedly old and respected. She would laugh at him, all right, out loud. And for the rest of his life, he'd hear her mocking reminder of something he'd known but hadn't resented until he'd laid his one eye on her and perfectly saw himself. He'd been born no good and no damn good he would die.

Yet, recalling that she hadn't screamed when she saw him or laughed when he'd idiotically offered to teach her to box, Daniel found the courage to clear his throat. Then, he summoned the greater courage to face his fear, to look at Madeleine. Suddenly, he no longer needed courage. Though he saw her no better than before, he nevertheless could make out the fathomless depths of her eyes. From those depths came a blessing, an anointment. And a charge to bridge the divide between them.

"Oh my Lord, Madeleine. How frightening he looks. Like a-a monster!" The Lady Bountiful, her hand over her heart and her eyes wide, leaned close to the girl as if seeking *her* protection. "Monsignor Hale, you don't mean to tell me you've taught this ruffian to read?"

Daniel's left eye flashed at the woman. He'd choke her fat neck if he could find it beneath her chins. "Monsignor Hale's taught me plenty, ma'am. But my mother's the one taught me to read. Kathleen Delan—"

"That will be enough, young man!"

Taken aback by Father Bianco's uncharacteristic vehemence, Daniel gaped at the younger priest.

"We're not interested in who taught you to read," the

priest continued. "Do as you've been told and recite a passage from your reader."

But Daniel went on staring quizzically at the man he'd nicknamed Bunco, figuring that because he was so different from the other priests at St. Augustine's, so gentle— the only truly gentle man Daniel had ever known—he had to have been swindled into taking the assignment. Yet for the first time, he was taking the monsignor's side against Daniel, and in an unjustifiably severe tone. That tone cut deeper than the ring on Monstrous Lucifer's teaching hand, deep into Daniel's nearly exhausted reserve of trust. Though Father Bianco didn't have the power to stop Lucifer's "lessons," Daniel could count on him to come quietly to his bunk afterward, as he had yesterday, with ice for the swelling and sometimes whiskey for the pain. No more, Daniel thought, wondering what he'd done since yesterday to lose his only champion. On the other hand, maybe he'd done nothing. Champions tended to get lost at St. Augustine's.

Dejected, Daniel looked as best he could at Madelcine, expecting to find that she, too, thought him a rude, frightening imbecile. Instead, the dark brilliance of her eyes beseeched, then commanded him to ignore all such slurs. Then, once again, she smiled a healing smile.

But there were some wounds, Daniel thought as he slid his gaze to the Lady Bountiful, not even Madeleine could heal. Some insults she couldn't will him to forget. If he could, he'd tell her he didn't mind that her companion had taken fright along with a good look at him. He *was* monstrous-looking and, as she well knew, a criminal.

But when the woman had doubted he could read, she might as well have called his mother any one of the vulgar names his father had called her. Not that Daniel could ever forget that his mother had betrayed him, but she wasn't a whore and she wasn't common. A flame burned in Kathleen Delaney that not even his father could extin guish, a candle on the altar of literature that had beckoned Daniel there. Beckoned him to a place that was as far removed from the lifeless book on his desk as Heaven was from Hell. He'd die, on the inside, if he parroted any part of it. But what *would* he recite?

"This is your last warning, Delaney," Monstrous said. "You can recite now or repent later."

Suddenly, Daniel knew what he would recite. Knowing, too, that after he finished he'd never see Madeleine again, he stole a last, imperfect look at her. Light shimmered in her dark eyes like moonbeams on Lake Michigan. Taking a deep breath, he drew the light inside him. Then, he faced his classmates and spoke in a clear, steady voice:

Come, fill the Cup, and in the fire of Spring
Your Winter-garment of Repentance fling . . .
Drink! for you know not whence you came, nor why:
Drink! for you know not why you go, nor where.

Daniel waited but no sound breached the silence that answered his recitation. He could discern movement, however, because it rippled through the room in an exchange of glances between boys who could see what Daniel could only feel: Monsignor Hale's gaze, so hot it was deathly cold, on the back of his head.

But he could feel Madeleine's gaze there, too, like a sword of pure white light clashing with Lucifer's blade of retribution. That was all the talismans he needed to take his punishment, not as a boy straining beyond his years, but for the first time, as a man. Hearing the priest move toward him, Daniel threw back his shoulders.

"Monsignor Hale, I declare," Lady Bountiful said, her rustling skirts signaling she'd gotten to her feet to interrupt the priest's mission. "I came here because my husband wished me to report on your methods in the interest

of applying them in our fair city. But if this boy's shockin'
behavior is an example of the kind of reform you conduct
here, I'm not sure I wish to contribute to your work much
less propagate it."

The blithering woman might as well have passed a
death sentence on him, Daniel thought. Her threat to
withdraw her donation was all Lucifer needed to justify
an even more brutal punishment than the one he'd surely
meant to administer, starting with the sharp yank on
Daniel's right earlobe that caused the young man's nos-
trils to flare as he stifled a cry. By that same ear, the monsignor dragged Daniel past the woman to where Father
Bianco stood.

"From whom did Delaney get that shameful, pagan
verse? You? Is that what you've been teaching? . . . Answer
me!"

"Lay offa him," Daniel shouted, forgetting he now
hated Bunco as much as he hated the other priests. "He
had nothing to do with it."

Father Bianco stood close enough for Daniel to see that
he was peering directly at him, communicating first his
gratitude, then a warning to say no more. Then he leaned
close to Monsignor Hale and spoke in a hushed tone,
though not so hushed that Daniel couldn't hear every
conciliatory—and to Daniel, mortifying—word.

"Monsignor, most boys flex their muscles to impress a
lady. Knowing Daniel as I do, I'm sure he thought that
displaying his knowledge of *The Rubáiyát* would better ac-
complish that purpose."

Daniel's mouth gaped as his mortification gave way to
shock. How was it that this celibate, so removed from the
world that he lacked physicality, had recognized the most
carnal of poems?

"An unholy purpose, Father Bianco," Daniel heard Lucifer say. "You should have discouraged this young preda-
tor from it long ago. Since you have failed to do your

duty, I have no choice but to do it for you." Still pinching Daniel's earlobe, he pinned the boy's left arm behind his back and pulled hard. "Apologize!"

"No!"

Lucifer pulled harder, so hard Daniel thought the man would separate his arm from his shoulder to get what he wanted. But Daniel would be damned if he'd oblige. Damned if he'd apologize to satisfy Lady Bountiful that Monsignor Hale knew his business. That he could bend wills toward Heaven as easily as he could break arms. His only regret was that Madeleine, who'd probably never even seen a bird with a broken wing, had to witness the violent consequence of his refusal to recant.

"Apologize to the ladies, Delaney," Lucifer said through his teeth, "and we'll forget the entire matter." Putting the lie to his proposition, he applied a tourniquet to Daniel's wrist.

Daniel grimaced at the pain. He could stop it, for now. All he had to do was say he was sorry he'd recited from a forbidden work. But he wasn't sorry. He was many things, most of them—if not criminal—certainly not admirable. But he wasn't a liar. He wasn't the conniving bastard his father was, always promising to change and never changing. He panted three short breaths. "Never!"

"We'll see about that," the monsignor said, cranking another turn of Daniel's wrist. "Right now."

As the priest marched him toward the door, Daniel gritted his teeth against the wrenching pain in his shoulder and wrist, and the wrenching pain awaiting him in Lucifer's office. But though he'd expected it, there was nothing he could do to mitigate the pain of being wrenched from Madeleine, of knowing his last look at her had been his last for all time, of forever losing the child-woman whose eyes were pools of ancient secrets he wanted—needed—to know.

Madeleine!

"Stop!"

At her cry, Daniel's heart lurched even before Monstrous Lucifer jerked him to a halt. He stood facing the door, his chest riding crests and valleys of emotion: the hope that Madeleine would come to him, the fear that she would come to him. To see her form again was to endure the agony of being torn from her again. Still, he listened for the sound of her step.

It never came. In its stead, her scent announced her presence. Whether or not it was the fragrance of a flower, Daniel couldn't say. He knew flowers only from poems. But it was bright and clean, and so nearly complete an embodiment of her, it made him ache to see what he could of her once more.

"Let him go, please, Monsignor," he heard her say in a voice that, unlike the Lady Bountiful's, was both genuinely sweet and brave. So sweet and brave, not even Monstrous Lucifer could refuse her request. Released from the prelate's hold, Daniel wanted to rub his shoulder, if only to prepare it for the punishment waiting for Madeleine and her companion to leave. But even more, he wanted to do nothing that might break the invisible thread he felt drawing Madeleine before him.

As she passed along his left side, Daniel felt her skirt brush his leg. Its caress traveled higher up his calf and thigh to the place responsible for the steady business at the confessionals on Saturday nights. Even before she appeared, a vision not of parts but of purity, the impossible happened. Daniel felt his tawny skin blush. He desperately wanted to avert his face from hers, to avert his shame. But he had only this one chance to say something that might help her to forget his ugliness and that he'd offered to teach her to box, something from his heart. Something that would express, at the very least, his gratitude for the respite from pain her bravery had bought him. Though he'd steeped his imagination in the most lyrical passages in the English language, when he parted his lips all he could say was "Thank—"

Daniel never saw it coming. The flat of her hand. It crossed his left cheek with a ringing smack. He felt its imprint on his soul. For a long moment, as long as the gasps that sucked what little air there was from the room, he held the profile she'd fashioned with her blow. Then, dabbing the old wound she'd opened in the corner of his mouth, he slowly faced her, making his one-eyed gaze as hard as the shield he now held over his heart.

She looked back at him, the contempt in her gaze so blatant that Daniel would have seen it with even less than the little sight he had. Then she turned to Lucifer. "If you don't consider this monstrous boy sufficiently punished, Monsignor, I might have to think you don't hold much regard for a lady's scorn." She folded her arms imperiously. "I wouldn't like that. And neither would my cousin, Mrs. Palmer."

"Not *the* Mrs. Palmer?" the priest asked. "I didn't know she was a relation of yours."

"Oh, yes," Madeleine replied. Daniel watched her idly arrange the folds in her plaid skirt. "She just dotes on me. I don't suppose I'd *have* to tell her anything but how nice it would be if she sent you a little something to help with your fine work here."

With both revulsion and fascination, Daniel saw Madeleine lay her hand over the priest's forearm and smile up at him. It wasn't the sweet, open smile she'd given him, but a coy one. Daniel wondered which of the smiles was genuine, which of the Madeleines. The angel or the little witch who was flirting not just with a priest, but with the Devil.

"That would be *very* nice, Madeleine," Lucifer said as he released Daniel.

"I'm so glad we understand each other, Monsignor."

she replied with one last flash of coyness then turned toward the door.

Daniel pinned a menacing gaze on her. He wanted to make her turn and look at him. Even if he couldn't see her at all from where he stood, he wanted to give her something to remember him by, the hatred in his eye. Seeing her pause, then circle toward him, he had all he could do to keep from gloating out loud.

Until he saw, however imperfectly, her perfectly sweet face. The coquette's smile had vanished. Her eyes were once again quiet, understanding. There wasn't a thing he could do to keep her from disarming him for the second time. "Goodbye, miss," he said, his voice near cracking.

And for the second time, she struck him, not with her hand but with a single, disdainful "Hmff!" Then, with a blurry toss of her curls, a shimmy of her shoulders, and a lifting of her chin, she sashayed out the door.

The Devil followed her.

Daniel watched until their vague forms disappeared. Then, shoving his hands in his pockets, he bowed his head in prayer.

"And may the Devil keep her."

"Sakes alive, you *are* the most unexpected girl." Approaching the brougham that had waited outside the reformatory, Caroline Faurest chirped over her shoulder at Madeleine. "I asked you to accompany me to Chicago to visit my sister in the hope that we'd get to know one another better. But I'm inclined to think I will never understand you."

"Inclining toward anything must be a pleasant change for you," Madeleine replied, lagging behind her newest stepmother and mimicking the woman's duck waddle. "From *re*clining, for example."

"Well, that's very sweet—" At the door held open by

the coachman, Caroline turned to Madeleine. "I beg your pardon?"

Madeleine's eyes grew suddenly wide and innocent. "Knowing how easily you tire, Mrs. Faurest, I only meant that perhaps you ought to recline inside the carriage. I could sit beside the driver."

"You're very kind, I'm sure," Caroline replied, saving her hat from being carried off by a gust of wind. "But I won't hear of your sitting with the driver."

Madeleine hugged herself to contain her shivers. "Oh, I don't m-m-m-ind the cold!"

"It isn't the weather that concerns me, Madeleine. A lady does not sit beside her coachman. Do you want my sister to think you're ill bred?"

As Caroline climbed into the coach, Madeleine looked back at St. Augustine's. "I don't care what anyone but *he* thinks," she said softly. That was why she had wanted to sit beside the driver, to be able to watch to the last the place where *he* dwelled. And also, not to have to listen to Caroline's prattling.

"Hurry up and get in, Madeleine," the latter said. "You know we're expected at my sister's husband's first cousin Lucy's for luncheon. Whatever can you be thinking of?"

Settling into the richly appointed coach, Madeleine immediately turned to gaze out its oval rear window at the prison school. *Him.* She imagined him staring at her through one of the lusterless windows that were mere slivers in the turreted fortress's ugly brown brick facade the way he'd stared at her through the slit he'd made of his good eye. With hatred. As long as she lived, she would never forget the look that had told her that as wretched as his life in this place was, she had made it more so.

This place. Madeleine couldn't take her eyes from it, even after the coach had pulled away and it had begun to shrink from view. She was almost fourteen, nearly a grown woman, she told herself, yet had never seen anyplace like it. Like hell on earth. She'd never even known such institutions, such boys—more like old men in young but beaten bodies—existed. Now that she knew, she would never forget.

"For Heaven's sake, Madeleine, turn around and sit like a lady," Caroline said. "I don't know what you find about that vile place that's so fascinatin', though after the way you behaved this mornin', nothin' you think or do or say could surprise me."

The reformatory vanished; still, Madeleine sat watching out the rear window. A moment later, sighing, she faced forward and tucked herself into a corner of the coach, as far from her stepmother as possible. "And what did I do this time that so surprised you, Mrs. Faurest?"

"*Surprised* me?" Caroline clasped her hands beneath her bosom, wedging them into the small space between it and where her waist should have been. "You nearly gave me one of my fainting spells!"

"I'm awfully sorry." Madeleine arched a brow. *That I failed. Those poor boys could have stood with some amusement.* "Please tell me exactly what I did to cause you such discomfort?" *So I can practice.*

Caroline knitted her thick brows above a quizzical gaze at Madeleine, as though amazed by the girl's need to ask. "I'm sure you'll recall, Madeleine, that you slapped that perfectly horrid boy right across his horrid face."

Madeleine shuddered. *"Someone had to do something."*

"Naturally, but I thought the monsignor was handling the situation quite well. After all, such unpleasantness is better left to men." Smiling indulgently, Caroline patted Madeleine's hand, which the girl immediately withdrew. "I'm not criticizing you, my dear. Once I recovered from the shock, I was actually quite proud of you for giving the nasty thing what he deserved. Such a vulgar speech, and in the presence of ladies."

"He isn't a nasty thing!" Madeleine snapped a glowering look at her father's third wife. She was both younger and more dull-witted than the second, who'd been dull-witted enough to die from infection after having a tooth pulled. Madeleine's mother, the first Mrs. Faurest, died when her only child was two. She'd broken her neck after being thrown from her horse at full gallop. "Besides, I liked what he recited."

Gasping, Caroline covered her mouth with her hand. "Madeleine, don't say that."

"Why not? It's true."

Swallowing hard, Caroline pressed her palm to her forehead. "What will Judge Faurest say when he finds out that you were exposed to such wanton sentiments? That you actually enjoyed hearing them? He'll hold me responsible."

"No, he won't, because you won't tell him about that part of our visit to St. Augustine's." Madeleine gave her stepmother a wry smile. "There's a lot you don't tell Father."

Pouting like a child caught with fistfuls of gumdrops, Caroline latched on to the strap above her. After a moment, she said, "There's certainly one thing I'd like *you* to tell me. If that nasty—if that boy didn't offend you, why did you slap him?"

Madeleine rolled her eyes then gazed out the window. She felt the ghost of the shiver that had coursed through her at the priest's touch and again, at the coldly murderous way he'd looked at the tall, wretched boy she knew only as Delaney. Then, straightening, she angled toward Caroline. "If you read novels as I do, Mrs. Faurest, you'd know why I slapped him."

Caroline's head jerked back, her pale blue eyes wide with disbelief. "Madeleine, you're not still reading those things? After your father forbade you to even bring them into the house?"

"And if Father also forbade me to breathe, would you expect me to oblige him in that, too?"

Caroline meshed her fat fingers entreatingly. "He's only thinking of your health. Dr. Withers cautioned him that highly strung creatures like you and I simply cannot stand the strain of too much reading, let alone of reading those romantic adventure stories you find so enthrallin'." She clamped her hand over her heart. "Lord, all those maidens in distress."

"Sometimes," Madeleine said, averting her gaze, "gentlemen get into distress, too."

Caroline ceased fluttering her lashes. "What on earth are you talking about?"

"Not what," Madeleine snapped, impatient with her stepmother's obtuseness. "Whom. Delaney." *My Delaney.*

"Delaney? I don't know any—" Caroline gaped at her stepdaughter. "That horrid boy! *He's* your idea of a gentleman?"

Madeleine recalled the look of terror in his one open, eerily light eye when he'd thought he'd hurt her, a terror of having wounded a lady that sprang from a natural regard rather than from the rules of a polite society he'd obviously never known. "He most certainly is," she said.

"Well, isn't that fine indeed? And when I think of what it's costing your father to educate you at that convent school . . ." Caroline heaved a perturbed sigh. "Where did you ever get the notion you could save that boy?"

"In one of the novels I read. You see," Madeleine began in the storytelling inflection that came naturally to her, "Lady Gwineth Tremaine very cleverly saved a lowly peasant named Regan from being tortured to death by her betrothed, the evil Sir Mordred Oakes."

Caroline cocked her head inquisitively. "How could one woman do that?"

"Oh, she ordered one of her servants to take Regan

away," Madeleine said nonchalantly, "and cut off his hand, then deliver it to Sir Mordred."

"Oh, dear." Clutching her throat, Caroline fell back against the seat.

Unfazed, Madeleine continued. "But the wise and faithful servant knew his lady's heart. Unbeknownst even to her, the hand he brought back wasn't Regan's. It belonged to the servant's dear son, who'd died of the grippe that morning."

Caroline slanted a look at Madeleine. "You don't say?"

"Oh, I do," Madeleine replied, smiling Cheshiredly to herself. "But that's not all. It turned out that Regan wasn't a lowly peasant at all but a lord in disguise. In the very nick of time, he stormed the chapel on his white charger and saved Lady Gwineth from having to marry Sir Mordred, whom he had to kill, of course, after the wicked knight drew his sword." Madeleine sighed. "Regan married Gwineth then and there, lifted her onto his mighty steed, and rode off with her. And they lived happily ever after."

Closing her eyes, Caroline rested her head against the seat and fanned herself despite the chill in the air. "Violence, torture, passion!" She looked at Madeleine. "You didn't leave anything out, did you?"

Madeleine curled her finger over her lips, containing a smile. "Let me see . . ."

"Yes?"

Madeleine waited until she saw the buttons on Caroline's jacket appear about to pop. Then she said, "Oh, yes. I forgot the part about Lady Gwineth's sacrifice."

Caroline gasped. "Oh, yes, sacrifice."

"After she presented Sir Mordred with the hand that was supposed to have been Regan's," Madeleine went on even more melodramatically, "Lady Gwineth promised him that if he made no effort to find Regan and further harm him, she would marry him in a fortnight."

Caroline smiled. But after a moment, she sat up and gazed at Madeleine beneath a furled brow. "Something about that last part sounds vaguely familiar to me, young lady. Did I imagine it or did you really promise Monsignor Hale that you would ask Bertha Honore Palmer, the very queen of Chicago society, to make a donation to his school?"

Clasping her hands around one knee, Madeleine gazed at the tufted velvet roof of the carriage. "I think I may have made some reference to my mother's distant cousin."

Caroline snorted. "So distant, she hasn't responded to a one of our calling cards since we arrived from Louisville."

"We aren't returning for another week," Madeleine replied, not fooling herself that her chances of meeting her many-times-removed relation were anything but nonexistent. With a sulk, she twined her arms. "Well, I had to promise Monsignor Hale something not to beat Delaney, something I knew he wanted. Just the way Lady Gwineth saved Regan's life because she knew all Sir Mordred ever wanted was to get his hands on—"

"I don't want to know," Caroline said, holding up her hand. Slowly, she lowered it. "On what?"

"Her father's lands."

"Oh." Caroline tugged the lowest of her chins. "Why couldn't Lady Gwineth have done that without ordering Regan's hand cut off?"

Madeleine tsked, annoyed by her stepmother's lack of imagination. "Because if Sir Mordred suspected how terribly she was in love with Regan, he would have beheaded her beloved on the spot. Also, I suspicion . . ." Madeleine paused in thought.

"For mercy's sake, Madeleine, go on."

"Yes, that must be it," Madeleine told herself with a firm nod. "She needed to suffer."

Caroline blinked, shuttering a blank gaze. "Lady Gwineth ordered a man's hand lopped off and *she* suffered?"

"Oh, yes," Madeleine said, gazing at her own hand. She could still feel the sting to her palm as it struck Delaney's cheek, and the ache in her heart at the humiliation she'd seen in his one proud eye. "Lady Gwineth nearly died from the anguish of believing she'd maimed Regan. That's how much she loved him."

"Oh, my," Caroline murmured. Then her eyes widened with horror. "Oh, my! Madeleine, have you gone and developed an affection for that ugly hooligan? An affliction, I should rather say."

"He's not a hooligan!" Madeleine propped her fists on her waist. "And you'd look ugly too, if someone had cut off all your hair and beaten your face black and blue. For all we know, beneath those sad bruises, he's a nobleman."

"What *I* know is that he was sent to St. Augustine's for nearly killing his own father," Caroline retorted. "The monsignor told me so."

Madeleine pressed her hand to her abdomen, over her lurching stomach. She'd felt as though she knew all there was to know about Delaney. She'd learned from his fear that he'd hurt her and the way he'd let her gentle him with her smile. She'd learned from the offense he'd taken when Caroline had expressed surprise that he could read and from the conviction in his voice when he'd recited. Then, from his refusal to apologize for what he'd recited and his courage in facing his punishment for that refusal. How could she not have also learned that Delaney was capable of murder?

"I don't believe it!" Squaring her shoulders and setting her jaw, she stared straight ahead. "He wouldn't just one day decide to kill his father. He must have had a reason. Self-defense, perhaps."

"Don't be absurd, Madeleine," Caroline rejoined. "If he'd been defending himself, he wouldn't be in reform school. The plain and simple fact is that he's nothing but a vicious street criminal."

"He's not!" Madeleine sat forward, digging her fingers into the edge of the velvet seat cushion. "I'm so sure he's not, I think I may just marry him one day."

Caroline Faurest shrieked as though something with a long, slinky tail had just scampered across her feet. "Madeleine, you really are determined to give me the vapors, aren't you? If you persist in this nonsense, you'll leave me no choice but to tell your father you've been hiding those fanciful novels again."

"So that he can do what? Find them for *you*?" Letting go a determined breath, Madeleine fixed her stepmother with a calculating gaze. "You mention one word to Father of what I said and I'll tell him who's been filching his best brandy. And it isn't one of the servants."

With a snap of her head, Caroline Faurest faced forward. "You may have your books, young lady, for all the naught they will one day bring you."

Suddenly trembling, Madeleine wrapped her arms about her and once again nestled in the corner of the coach. What *would* her books bring her?

Delaney.

Two

"Madeleine, really, you simply will send me to my sick-bed before your weddin' day, won't you?" With an exasperated sigh, Caroline Faurest set her teacup down on the gift-laden mahogany table in the paneled library of the Faurest mansion. "You've put Senator and Mrs. Brecker's card with Congressman and Mrs. Carlisle's silver compote," she said peevishly as she removed the Breckers' card from the long-stemmed dish and switched it with another already propped beside a pair of porcelain candlesticks. "Now where does *this* card belong?" She turned to Madeleine, who was curled in a large leather chair beside the window, reading the front page of the *Louisville Record*. "If you'd kept a list as you should, this wouldn't have happened."

Knowing her stepmother wouldn't allow her a minute's peace until she responded to this latest prenuptial crisis, Madeleine set the newspaper aside and walked to the table. Taking the card Caroline was using to fan her flushed face as she searched the trove—English bone china, Irish crystal, French linen—she read the distinctive signature. *Mr. Christopher McCarron and Mrs. Eleanor Barlow McCarron.*

Seized with an inordinate pique, she tossed the card into an Italian marble urn.

"There," she said, dusting off her hands and starting for her newspaper. "Now every gift has a giver and the library can go back to being a library."

"Honestly, Madeleine," Caroline began, delving her pudgy hand into the urn. "I can understand why you dislike Mrs. McCarron. But her husband *is* my late second cousin Hermione's nephew by marriage. Besides, the McCarrons will soon be our neighbors. Even if they are of the merchant class, we must observe proprieties."

Pausing before the stone fireplace, Madeleine peered over her shoulder at Caroline. "Why do you say I dislike her?"

Caroline appeared surprised by the question. "I just assumed . . . After all, she is *the* most unsettling woman."

She was, Madeleine agreed, but not for the reasons Caroline imagined. Nor for any reason Madeleine herself had yet to discern much less have evidenced. "But in what way have I shown any ill feeling toward her?"

Still scouring the bottom of the urn, Caroline tsked. "For one thing, whenever she calls, you refuse to receive her. For another, you once loved shopping her store, but the last three times I asked you to accompany me there, you made feeble excuses not to go." She grew breathless with the exertion of retrieving the card. "And now, the very sight of her name appears to upset you."

Madeleine turned away and gazed out the window at the McCarrons' nearly completed home across the court. Lately, when she left her own home, she avoided looking at the dwelling, as though by doing so she could deny the disturbing if unidentified feelings its mistress conjured. Feelings somehow linked to her impending marriage. "Perhaps I'm more anxious a bride than either of us suspicion, Mrs. Faurest."

"Not anxious enough to make sure of keepin' the right

card with the right gift," Caroline replied as she clutched the urn, her right hand still inside it, to her bosom. "Upon my word, Madeleine, I should think you of all people would be more fastidious about etiquette. After all, you do write the society news for the *Record.*"

Madeleine folded her arms, digging her nails into her flesh. "Only because the editor won't let me cover real news."

"As well he shouldn't! I know what you mean by 'real news,' " Caroline shot back, her rings clanging inside the urn. "The very idea of a woman, let alone a judge's daughter, hangin' about filthy tenements and nasty ol' police stations and keepin' company with a lot of disreputable reporters is preposterous."

"So I've been told." Madeleine charged toward Caroline, her fists on her waist. "By every managing editor in Louisville. And by my father, my priest, *and* my physician. By every man I know, except Roger. At least *he* listens to me."

"They all listen to you until you take your vows," Caroline muttered sullenly. "Sometimes, I'm of the mind that once they hear you say 'I do,' they have no further need of your conversation."

Madeleine's jaw dropped. In ten years, she'd never heard her stepmother utter the slightest marital complaint. "Mrs. Faurest, you do astonish me," she said.

Caroline began a tug-of-war with the urn. "Oh, don't pay me any mind," she replied. "You'd do well to listen to your father and the other men, and forget about being a news reporter. Maybe then you'd show a little more interest in your own—" She grunted, her face reddening. "Wedding. How will you be able to thank people for their gifts if you don't know who sent what?"

"I'll show you," Madeleine said. Standing shoulder-to-shoulder with her stepmother, she began scrawling a note in the air. " 'Dear Mr. and Mrs. Cream of Society, Roger and I simply adore the—' " She slanted a look at Caroline, who had momentarily ceased struggling with the urn. "Where I should mention the gift, my penmanship will become artfully illegible." Swirling her hand, she continued. " '—the illegible gift you gave us. It will always have a prominent place, as will you, in our home and in our hearts. With deepest gratitude, Mr. and Mrs. Roger Mabrey.' " Adding a flourish beneath their names, she returned to her chair and picked up her newspaper.

For a long moment, Caroline stood staring at the imaginary note. Then, shaking her head, she resumed scrounging in the urn for the McCarrons' gift card. "I can't imagine Roger approvin' of such deception, Madeleine. Your father says he has a brilliant future in politics and he'll expect you, as his wife to—"

"To what? Smile through the speech I've heard him give twenty times? Pretend to laugh at his backers' dull jokes? Tell what little truth can be told, the way you do for Father? Roger wouldn't dare ask me to do such things." Madeleine scowled. She'd meant every word, but she regretted they sounded so superior, so cruel, if for no other reason than that the last thing she needed was to put her stepmother into one of her debilitating sulks. *Someone* had to see to the wedding minutiae that bored her to distraction. Rising, she approached Caroline with a perfunctory apology in mind. "Mrs. Faurest, I'm terribly sorry, really I—"

Caroline turned her face away.

Madeleine tapped her foot, mostly in vexation with her own reckless tongue. Thanks to it, one of Caroline's three-day snits was undoubtedly coming on. Then, quite to her disbelief, she heard a sound she recognized as soul-deep sadness. She circled her stepmother and saw a drop fall from her lowered eyes. "You're crying!"

Gazing up through the tears matting her lashes, Caroline laughed. "You'd cry, too, if your hand were stuck in a marble urn."

Madeleine looked at the urn, which indeed appeared to have swallowed the lower half of Caroline's arm. Still, she somehow knew it was not the cause of her stepmother's tears. "You really are stuck, aren't you?"

The two women's gazes met, and for the first time in a decade, the only child and the third wife of Judge Matthew Faurest understood one another. Taking hold of the urn, Madeleine helped Caroline to ease her hand—the gift card tenaciously pinched in her plump fingers—from inside it. Then she picked up Caroline's cup of tea, which she knew to be brandy-flavored, and traded it for the card.

"You rest, Caroline," she said, smiling softly. "I'll take care of matching the right cards to the right gifts."

As she set about the task, she hoped she'd been more careful about matching herself to the right man. Holding up a silver platter and seeing her reflection, she murmured, "Is any man ever the right man?"

The answer came from far and yet very near, both memory and thought, feeling and belief, yes and no. The answer was the question, and the question came from some hidden facet of her being that didn't belong to Roger. But it didn't belong to her, either. It was unclaimed and yet, strangely, purchased. Like the silver platter, someone had bought it, but she had no idea who.

No, that wasn't quite true, for the reason that this wasn't the first time Madeleine had felt the presence of a foreign power inside her, an island of otherness in her soul. She'd been aware of it since she was nearly fourteen and had returned with Caroline from a trip to Chicago. It had a face she recalled as battered and nearly unrecognizable as human and a name she couldn't recall at all without the diary that had been lost when the tornado of 1890 damaged a good portion of the Faurest mansion in an older section of the city. At times she found herself at war with it and vanquished it with ease. But at other times, it overran her like a marauding horde and she became insensible of the world. Even during periods of truce, when it withdrew to its own territory, Madeleine rarely forgot it was there. The few times she had, she panicked, sensing that when it finally did abandon her, she would have already abandoned her dreams, her ideals. Herself.

"What adolescent nonsense," Madeleine said, thinking perhaps she *had* read too many novels for her own good when she was young and impressionable. Surely, by now, her education by nuns, whose sole mission was to relieve young girls of adventurously romantic fantasies and prepare them for their places as wives and mothers, had taken. She should be free of fears for her own destiny. Free of the unseen, unnamed presence with whom her destiny seemed inextricably linked.

Why then, she asked, pressing her fingertips into the table and bowing her head over its treasures, *have I been so fearful these past months, knowing the presence was there but feeling it grow weaker? Why am I trembling now because, only a moment ago it was so weak I could barely sense it at all?*

Turning, Madeleine peered at Caroline, asleep on the sofa. Her fingers curled around the empty teacup on her lap, her head bobbed as soft snores escaped the oval of her mouth.

"Did you ever harbor impossible dreams and ambitions like mine, Caroline?" Madeleine murmured. "Did you ever suffer the sweet tortures of a reminding presence that was, in so many ways, your own true self?"

Madeleine turned back to the table and the gifts for the bride and groom who would commit their lives to one another in less than two weeks. For her and her father's political protégé, Roger Mabrey. A shiver coursed through her. "Don't answer, Caroline. I don't want to know."

* * *

While Caroline was in her dressing room below, berating her dressmaker despite the poor woman's assurances that her gown would be ready for the wedding in two days' time, Madeleine clacked at her typewriter in her attic "office." When she began writing for the *Record,* she'd claimed a corner of the library for herself. But her father so disapproved of her reporting for the paper, even for its society page, that the mere sight of the typewriter Roger had given her for her twenty-third birthday launched him into a campaign speech. Suffragettes, weak-willed men, and noisy newfangled contraptions all suffered his wrath. They were threats to the sanctity of motherhood and the serenity of the home—his home, in particular. Madeleine quickly discovered that her own serenity, not to mention her concentration, was better served by moving her machine to the attic, where she now ceased typing to read her finished story.

On Saturday last, Colonel and Mrs. Rupert Throckmorton gave a gala reception in honor of Count Laszlo Szaldorny, recently arrived from Budapest, Hungary.

"I wish I could be a fly on the wall when Mrs. Throckmorton finds out that Mrs. Howland Davis is about to trump her with another obscure, overly inbred, and totally parasitic European noble who nevertheless happens to be a prince."

One hundred guests attended the glittering affair at the Throckmortons' eighteen-room Romanesque-style home on Third Street near Ormsby. The sumptuous menu included Louisiana steamed oysters, Virginia baked ham, Maine boiled lobster, and Tennessee roast pheasant.

"And was served to Kentucky hogs."

Mrs. Throckmorton wore a stunning gown of amber-beaded yellow tulle and matching ostrich feathers in her head.

Madeleine's brows arched above hugely astonished eyes. Then, laughing at her slip, doubting its inadvertence, she regretfully penciled a line through "head" and scribbled in "hair." She resumed reading, but after a sentence more, stopped. Shoulders slumping, she sat back in her chair. "I can't do this any longer. I don't have any more words to give to this piffle."

She'd never had the words to begin with, Madeleine thought. She'd only borrowed them from her predecessor, whose articles the *Record*'s publisher and managing editor, Jackson Crowley, had given her to study and imitate. Her own words she hadn't even begun to use. She was saving them for stories she could only hope to investigate and write. Stories she hadn't known existed until she'd spent a cold, sobering afternoon in a Chicago reform school. Stories whose bitterness she'd tasted and fearfulness she'd smelled, and whose despair she'd felt around her like a tattered shawl. And one story, in particular, whose heroic struggle against bitterness, fear, and despair she'd seen with her own eyes. The story of a boy whose already pummeled face she'd slapped and pride she'd wounded, a boy whose name she'd tauntingly suggested to Caroline she might one day take and now couldn't remember to save her soul.

She'd often wondered if the reason she felt compelled to write stories like his was because she'd carried guilt for having wounded him, especially in spirit. She'd hated to think she'd scarred him. She'd hated to think that he still hated her for it. For nearly ten years, she'd prayed she would one day find him and have the chance to explain her seeming cruelty, to ask his forgiveness. She'd prayed and now she wondered if the answer to her prayer wasn't the command to remember him, if not by name, in her writing. Writing of substance. To remember him in that way *was*, perhaps, to save her soul.

"What difference does it make why you want to write such stories?" she chided herself as she tore the Throckmortons out of the typewriter. "No editor will ever give you the chance to write them or anything else that matters." She crinkled her nose at her own handiwork, slid the pages inside an envelope, then slipped on her blue linen jacket. She had just an hour to make her deadline.

As she stepped out the front door, pausing at the top of the stone steps to button her gloves, Madeleine couldn't help gazing across the usually quiet cul-de-sac at the bustle outside the McCarron home. Today, she saw, was moving day, and Eleanor Barlow McCarron was directing burly men twice her size to and from her front doors with the authority of a general.

Little to Madeleine's surprise.

Eleanor Barlow had come to Louisville from Boston in the late 1880s at the request of Josiah Bond, who'd employed her to modernize and manage his dry goods store on Twelfth and Market. Only a year later, old Mr. Bond made her his partner, and when he died, she assumed full ownership of the store. But by staking her claim in traditionally male territory, she had made herself the talk of a highly talkative town, scandalizing it and posing a threat to a social order that, in comparison to the flux in mores in Northern cities, was ossified.

Not all Louisvillains, however, had been discomfited by Eleanor Barlow's extraordinary independence. Her only major competitor, Kit McCarron, had so respected her talents that he'd emulated and bettered her innovations until the two established an intense rivalry they eventually took to court. Where, after numerous suits and countersuits, they were married.

The same day, a tornado destroyed both stores and Kit McCarron's home. The day after that, the newlyweds purchased land for a single, larger department store they called Barron's and hired an architect to design their home, which, as anyone who'd known them might have expected, was quite unlike any other on the court. When the couple wasn't overseeing its construction, they devoted their energies to their store or to their travels, though Mrs. McCarron had recently caused another stir by traveling alone to New York on buying trips for Barron's. Married or not, a woman loose on business risked being thought a loose woman.

And Eleanor McCarron couldn't have cared less. As Madeleine watched the woman lead two men carrying a wardrobe through the double doors, she couldn't help admiring her, even envying her. This envy, which was perhaps part of the reason for her recent agitation—at the mere mention of the woman's name, as Caroline had pointed out—quite baffled Madeleine.

Because for all that she was and had achieved, Eleanor Barlow McCarron was disfigured.

Rumors as to the cause of the dreadful scar on her face abounded, from a skating accident on the Charles River to a jealous lover. But none was ever confirmed. The fact remained that a deep white line bisected her left cheek, contrasting so breathtakingly with her classic beauty that one had no choice but to stare at it in utter and embarrassing fascination. Although Madeleine had conversed with Eleanor McCarron often enough to have trained her gaze not to fix on the wound, her embarrassment at simply knowing it was there inexplicably remained. An embarrassment that even more than envy, Madeleine knew, lay at the heart of her avoidance of the woman.

But why, she asked herself, should the evidence of another woman's misfortune cause her to feel anything but compassion instead of emotions she could only describe as shame and guilt? As Madeleine drew the envelope containing the Throckmorton story from under her arm and started for the trolley that would take her to the *Record,* one possible answer came to her. Not one she liked, but one she had to test.

Moments later, Madeleine handed her calling card to Eleanor McCarron's Irish maid and was admitted to a light, spacious vestibule rising two stories and crenelated with generous windows near the top. Instead of the dark, massive wooden staircase that dominated the entrance halls of most of the fashionable homes Madeleine knew, including her own, a graceful black wrought iron banister capped with a polished brass handrail tendriled the white risers. The treads were inlaid with a diamond pattern of black and white marble to match the floor rather than swathed in the typical scrolled carpet. The walls were plaster rather than wood-paneled or busily papered, and painted off-white to reflect the light. Though boxes and the odd table and chair littered the hall, Madeleine sensed that this home would break with the worship of clutter. She could breathe in a house like this, and so realizing, filled her lungs with the newness of the air.

"Miss Faurest, how nice of you to call."

Madeleine turned to face a tallish woman barely thirty. Her hair was a luxurious black and her eyes, an arresting shade of green. Her lovely complexion was flushed with the exertion of moving day, and against its rosiness, the white wound halving her left cheek was more startling than usual. "I'm afraid it wasn't at all nice of me to intrude today of all days, Mrs. McCarron," she said. "But I was passing on my way to the trolley and I thought I might be the first to welcome you to St. James Court."

"You are and you needn't apologize. You'll find that Kit and I have little patience with a good many formalities." Eleanor McCarron revealed a smile that Madeleine found rivaled her scar for its ability to mesmerize. "Come onto the veranda," she added. "We'll have some of Emma's cool lemonade."

"Oh, no, that really would be imposing," Madeleine replied, suddenly wishing she hadn't come. She had the distinct feeling Eleanor McCarron would take her not merely to the veranda, but to a place from which she might never return.

Laughing, Eleanor McCarron looped her arm through

Madeleine's. "I won't hear of your leaving," she said, leading Madeleine to the wide, covered porch at the rear of the home. "You've given me a good excuse to rest. Besides, I want to hear all you've planned for your wedding. And you may feel perfectly free to tell me how madly in love you are with Roger Mabrey."

Madeleine stiffened. She now had one more reason to envy Eleanor McCarron, to feel guilty in her presence. To want to run away from her. Only a woman who was madly in love with her own husband would have assumed Madeleine felt the same way about Roger.

To be sure, Madeleine loved many things about her fiancé. He was handsome, intelligent, ambitious. His kisses, if not ardent, were pleasant. He wasn't a Regan, the romantic hero of the novel that once fired her impossibly youthful imagination, but then, she was no Lady Gwineth and had no desire ever to become one. When a woman loved a man as desperately as the heroines of novels loved the heroes, perhaps as Eleanor McCarron loved her husband, some sacrifice was always required of her. No matter how readily Madeleine's mind accepted the pairing of love and sacrifice, she had, overall, grown accustomed to the ease and privilege of her class. Her marriage to Roger, as she had always known, would perpetuate both.

And yet, as she accepted the lemonade Eleanor McCarron had poured for her, Madeleine was suddenly so beset by guilt over the marriage bargain she'd willingly struck that she felt compelled to confess the defect in her own character that had led to it.

"Mrs. McCarron, I didn't come here solely to welcome you to St. James Court."

Eleanor McCarron set her lemonade down on the wrought iron table and sat back in her chair, draping her lovely tapered hands over the ends of its arms. "You know, Madeleine, every time we've met, I've had the feeling I unsettle you more than I do most people who can't quite accustom themselves to my face. It's not just my scar that disconcerts you, is it?"

Lowering her gaze, Madeleine shook her head.

"So why don't you call me Eleanor and tell me what it is about me that so disturbs you?"

Madeleine looked up. "You make me feel like a coward," she blurted.

Eleanor merely blinked. "Go on."

Emboldened, Madeleine set her own glass down, atop the envelope containing the Throckmorton story. "I know that before you came to Louisville, your brother bankrupted you. When you went to work for Mr. Bond and he so quickly made you a partner, I heard the talk myself. Everyone said that you and he . . ."

Eleanor lifted her chin. "Don't hold back, Madeleine. I'm perfectly aware of the malicious gossip about Mr. Bond and me."

"Not that I believed a word of it!" Meeting her hostess's candid gaze, Madeleine sighed. "That's not true. I did, with absolutely no justification. If it means anything, I don't believe it now."

"I'm glad," Eleanor replied, fingering the key she wore on a chain around her neck, the key to his store which Mr. Bond had left to her as he lay dying. "I won't say the talk didn't hurt."

"But you didn't let it stop you from realizing your vision for the store. Not even a tornado kept you from doing that. That's why . . ." Madeleine rose, walked to the edge of the porch, and gazed at gardens of wildflowers.

Eleanor came to her side. "You've come this far, Madeleine. Why stop now?"

Gazing down, Madeleine clasped the railing between her and the gardens and took a deep breath. "That's why I find your scar so disturbing. It reminds me of all the extraordinary obstacles you've overcome and all the ordinary ones I haven't."

After a moment's pause, Eleanor looked at Madeleine. "You write for the *Record,* I believe."

"Only the society news."

"But you're not happy doing that."

"I loathe it. I only agreed to do it because I thought that if I could just get my foot in the door, Mr. Crowley would eventually see that I can write and allow me to cover straight news stories."

"But he won't because you're a woman and such work is considered too dangerous, too unladylike."

"And he would feel too responsible for me."

"Madeleine, surely he's heard of Nellie Bly and her exploits on behalf of Joseph Pulitzer's *New York World?*"

Madeleine turned to her hostess. "I want to be a first-string news reporter, Eleanor, not a stunt girl. The public will soon tire of women getting themselves committed to insane asylums, but fresh news happens every minute of every day." She sighed. "In any case, *I* know that Jackson Crowley is no Joseph Pulitzer and *you* know better than anyone that Louisville isn't New York. Even if they were, some of my father's political backers are prominent business leaders who advertise in the *Record.* I suspicion he's informed Mr. Crowley that he'll suggest they withdraw their advertising if I should be assigned to anything more dangerous than an afternoon tea."

"I could threaten to withdraw my advertising if you're not."

Madeleine laughed. "Thank you, but fearless as you are, not even you can outintimidate Matthew Faurest. You haven't his leverage or his complete lack of scruples."

Eleanor made no reply, but gazed into the distance. Then she said, "There's something I want to show you, Madeleine. Wait here."

In a few moments, she returned with a simple, oval photograph frame. "You say I'm fearless. But I *have* known fear, Madeleine, and still do, even now. Especially now." She handed the frame to Madeleine.

Gazing down at it, Madeleine saw a full-face portrait of Eleanor and gasped. "How beautiful you look," she said, amazed that the scar, which might easily have been the focus of the photograph, failed to prevent her being instantly captivated by the subject's warm radiance, her exquisite grace, her remarkable strength. Whoever had made the likeness had truly captured the essence of Eleanor Barlow McCarron. She looked up at the original. "But I don't understand. I see no fear in you in this portrait, no hesitancy."

Leaning against a column, Eleanor twined her arms. "For years after my face had been cut by flying glass when a tree limb shattered my bedroom window during a storm, I shunned the camera. Then, I fell in love with Kit, who as it happened, was passionate about photography. When he asked me to sit for him, I grew sick with terror at the prospect. I begged him to ask anything of me but the one thing I was sure would destroy the very illusion he'd created for me, that I was beautiful. But he convinced me that unless I took that risk, I'd never know the fullness of his love. So, I allowed him to make a portrait of me."

Madeleine raised her fingers to her own cheek, felt fear gnawing at her own soul. Would she have had the courage to do such a thing? "You must have loved him very much."

"I did," Eleanor replied, taking the portrait from Madeleine and gazing at it. "But before I saw this photograph, I doubted *his* love and nearly lost him. Then, he sent this picture to me, and the instant I saw it, I knew I'd been horribly wrong to have doubted him." Clutching the portrait to her heart, she looked directly into Madeleine's eyes, her own moist and bright. "You see, Madeleine, my husband wanted me to see myself as he saw me, as beautiful and strong—not despite my scarred face but because of it. With his camera lens, he made my wound appear so much a natural part of the whole of me that I could no longer imagine being without it. Only an extraordinary man with an extraordinary love for me could have done that."

Abruptly, Madeleine turned and wandered toward the table, her chest heaving with doubts of her own, doubts that Roger's love would survive let alone celebrate so great an imperfection in her own appearance. Indeed, the small bump on the bridge of her nose elicited deprecations he'd couched in jokes she'd sportingly laughed at but found petty and cruel.

But Madeleine knew she could not blame Roger for her cowardice. She lifted her glass of lemonade, noting the ring it had left on the envelope destined for the *Record*. "I believe what you're trying to tell me, Eleanor, is that I must learn to turn my disadvantages into strengths."

Eleanor joined Madeleine at the table, setting down the photograph. "As an advertiser, I know more women than ever are reading daily newspapers. Before long, they'll demand that women write the news and some bright editor is bound to listen to them." She clasped Madeleine about the shoulders. "I don't know you well, Madeleine. But I know you're not a coward. It took courage for you to speak to me as forthrightly as you did today. I feel certain that, one day, one of those front-page women reporters will be you."

Madeleine was a great deal less sure. Nevertheless, she smiled, thanked her hostess, and announced she must leave or would miss her deadline. As she picked up her envelope, she took one last look at Kit McCarron's remarkable portrait of his remarkable wife. A woman she now gratefully considered her friend. Walking arm in arm with Eleanor, she retraced her steps to the airy vestibule and through the open double doors.

"One thing you mentioned still puzzles me," she said, gazing back at Eleanor from the top step and admiring, without a trace of irritability, her hard-won serenity. "You said you knew fear, even. Especially now."

An enigmatic smile formed on Eleanor McCarron's pink lips. "Since you were the first to welcome me to St. James Court, let me make you the first on the court to know that Kit and I are going to have a baby."

Smiling, Madeleine embraced Eleanor. "When the time comes, I know you'll be brave."

"So will you, Madeleine, when your time comes."

Madeleine felt a blush rise. "I'm not even married yet."

"Somehow, I think your time will come before then."

Madeleine frowned. "Time for what, Eleanor?"

Eleanor Barlow McCarron arched one exquisite black brow. "Risking your all, Madeleine. Nothing less will do."

Three

Bridgeport, Chicago
May. 1893

"To the Devil with you!" Daniel Delaney rolled onto his side, turning his back on the intruder bludgeoning both his door and his head, swelled by wine. And whiskey. And, if he wasn't mistaken, brandy.

"The company you keep, it's a sure ting you'll be makin' his acquaintance long afore I do!"

Daniel cocked a smile, triggering an explosion of pain between his eyes. Squeezing them tightly shut, he pulled his only blanket, which he'd pilfered from a swaybacked nag at Washington Park, over his left shoulder. "You don't fool me, woman," be said, suddenly aware that since he'd left the Whitechapel Club, his tongue had tripled in thickness. "You don't give a damn if I rot in hell so long as you get your back rent."

"Hah! And you can just bet I will, too. One way or ta other. Isn't that so, love?"

Hearing a series of bawdy cackles, Daniel cringed. Even if he were not temporarily devoid of the stamina he'd require to settle his arrears with the Widow Corrigan, he couldn't bear the thought of her suffocating bosom. At this very moment, it was ramming down his door, bulging throughout his cramped room, the crucifix upon it spreading and both of them overtaking him. He drew his blanket over his head. Finding the familiar hole made by a considerate moth just the right distance below the blanket's edge, he situated it around his nose.

"Leave me in peace, you she-monster. I'm working on a story."

"Don't you lie to me. The only ting you're workin' on is the aftermath of gettin' corned with them other reporters. You're a worthless lot, and you worst of all, Dan'l McQuinn."

The sound of his assumed name, his mother's maiden name, briefly took Daniel aback. Despite his having worn it since he began working for the *Chicago Clarion* as a copy boy nearly eight years ago, the fit was still uncomfortable. Delaney, however, was an altogether unwearable name. Father Bianco had been right to suggest, the day Daniel left St. Augustine's, that he change it.

"You've got talent, Daniel. You can make something of yourself," the priest had said. Then he'd pointed to Daniel's last name, stitched across the breast pocket of the blue shirt that, along with blue pants, comprised his inmate's uniform. "But you won't get the chance as long as employers can trace you to a reformatory."

On the other hand, Archibald Monroe, the *Clarion*'s managing editor, had considered Daniel's intimate knowledge of various police stations around town a definite advantage to an aspiring young newsman and his paper. Still, though he was only eighteen at the time, Daniel hadn't needed Monroe to tell him that a reporter with a criminal record was a reporter who could be outtrumped. He could be blackmailed by the very sources he was used to blackmailing. For that reason, his editor, his readers, the woman now breathing heavily on the other side of his door, had never known him as anyone but Daniel McQuinn.

He smiled irreverently. "Worthless, am I? That's not what you said the last time I caught up on my rent."

"Well, I'm sayin' it now . . . And I'll tank you to recall you're talkin' to a lady!"

A lady. Daniel quietly laughed at the illusions of Eileen Corrigan. But then, what right had he to scoff? He was certainly no gentleman. The slim chance he'd had of ever becoming one had vanished years ago, when *She* had vanished, without a trace. She, whose name he couldn't remember but whose bright halo of hair he couldn't forget. She, whose face was featureless except for dark, glittering eyes that haunted him still, eyes that held the secrets of all time.

And she slapped you, Daniel, remember? She humiliated you and you damned her to the Devil's keeping. "And what a pair they must make."

"What's that you're sayin'?"

Not even his landlady's coarse tones could dispel the lewd images of She and the Devil, images that, if he hadn't known better, he'd have said broke his heart. But he did know better. He had no heart. That had been cut out of him by another woman, one who had also vanished, without a word, without a trace.

Daniel inhaled sharply. "I said you'll have to settle for getting paid next week . . . One way or ta other."

"I'll look forward to it, Danny me boy, though I must tell you I didn't coom about the rent money." Eileen Corrigan's next words came in an urgent whisper. "It's him again, the one with the voice that puts me in mind of a black cat skulking through a graveyard at midnight. Says I'm to get you to the telephone if I have to drag you by them long limbs of yours."

Daniel shot up. "Confounded woman! Why didn't you say so from the begin—" He clamped his hands on either side of his head to hold it together.

"Dan'l? Are you all right? You ain't hurt yourself?"

Daniel barely heard the woman over the blood tide pounding the shores of his hearing. He willed it to recede. "I'm not your chick, Eileen. Quit clucking at me like some infernal hen and tell the man to wait. I'll be right there." *As soon as I pry open my eyes.*

Throwing back the blanket, he swung his legs over the edge of his thin mattress and planted his soles on the bare plank floor. He shuddered, feeling as though he'd just plunged feet-first into a chilly Chicago River, just beyond the tracks that lay a few blocks to the north. But at least his eyes had popped open at the shock. Only to deliver another, more chilling.

Daniel's eyes saw nothing, nothing at all.

He rubbed them, hoping they merely needed more time to adjust to the morning light. But when he lifted his lids, there was no light. For the first time since he'd awakened, something other than alcohol churned in his stomach. Fear. Maybe he'd finally done it, drunk himself blind. Maybe he deserved to. But without his sight, without the ability to see death in dark alleys and on the docks and Back of the Yards, and then describe it in the lurid detail the public craved, what was he? A former police reporter, that's what.

Slowly, he pushed off the bed and shuffled three paces to the one window in his room. He groped for the frayed bottom edge of the shade and, finding it, yanked. The shade recoiled then crashed down on his bare toes.

As he jumped back, Daniel lifted his forearm across his eyes. Light! He'd glimpsed a circle of soft light. Kicking the shade aside, he pressed his palms to the glass and peered down through rivulets of soot. Seeing the yellow glow from the lamp on the corner of Twenty-sixth and Canal, he suddenly understood why only a moment ago he'd opened his eyes to impenetrable blackness. A new night had fallen without his ever noticing the day.

"Dammit!" His hands still flattened against the dirty

pane, Daniel closed his eyes, lowered his head, and snorted a breath. He'd missed his deadline. Again. Monroe would fire him. Again. But if the man on the telephone had called for the usual reason, with the usual grisly information, Daniel knew he could hand in a story that would make the baseball-loving editor eat the words "You're out of the game, McQuinn!"

Provided he could rely on the usual. Provided that his old friend from St. Augustine's, the aptly named Detective Grimm, was tipping him off to a homicide the rest of the press wouldn't sniff out for hours. Provided that the body Benny was calling him to come view didn't belong to her. The woman he'd gone in search of the minute he got out of reform school. The woman who'd abandoned him for the man hell-bent on killing her. The other woman who had picked him up only to slap him down, then vanished without a trace.

But this woman would return, one way or the other. Dead or alive. More than likely, dead, and in a part of town where no lady would be caught in that condition. And despite all the pain she'd caused him, Daniel would spare her the final indignity in a life taken one day at a time by indignities. She'd loved words but he would spare her these:

"The body of an unidentified woman was found today."

Daniel would identify her. "She's the one taught me to read," he'd say.

Kathleen McQuinn Delaney.

Madeleine Faurest dropped her story on the Throckmortons' gala atop a mound of papers on Jackson Crowley's desk. The *Louisville Record*'s publisher and managing editor was out of his office, which was fortunate for him, Madeleine thought. On the trolley ride between Eleanor Barlow's house on St. James Court and the *Record* building downtown, she'd rehearsed a plea for a chance at writing hard news stories that was so rousing, it made one of her father's legendary campaign speeches sound like a bedtime tale. Madeleine felt as though the spirit were upon her, the spirit Eleanor Barlow had breathed into her, making her determined that before the day was through, Jackson Crowley would play Joseph Pulitzer to her Nellie Bly.

If he would have the consideration to show his face, that is.

Impatient, she paced, folding and unfolding her arms, practicing her speech, now and then pausing, finger thrust in midair to emphasize a crucial point in her argument. At length, she reached the grand finale. Placing her palms on Crowley's desk, she leaned forward, looking directly into the rapt gaze she imagined him fixing on her. "Mr. Crowley, you're wasting my talent by limiting me to writing society news and it's about time you realized it!"

"If you don't mind, Miss Faurest, I shall decide how to spend your self-described talent."

Aghast, Madeleine whipped around and came face-to-face with Jackson Dillard Crowley. A tall, Kentucky Colonel of a man with a full head of beautiful white hair and white mustachios to match, he offset his courtly elegance with an air of stern detachment. Madeleine often pictured him atop a mountain, handing down stone tablets engraved with the *Record*'s masthead. Now watching him move toward her, walking stick capped with a silver horse's head in hand, she swallowed hard. "Mr. Crowley, I didn't hear you come in."

"My dear Miss Madeleine," he replied, removing his hat and laying his walking stick across his desk, "I'd be surprised if you could hear thunder over that diatribe you were deliverin' just now."

Madeleine felt her cheeks go pink and silently cursed

them for giving him the advantage of witnessing her embarrassment. "I'm terribly sorry, Mr. Crowley. I didn't realize I was so loud."

Crowley gave her a paternal smile as he seated her in a chair beside his desk. "No need to apologize, my dear. I've always admired your spirit."

As he rounded his desk, Madeleine's heart pounded bruisingly against her chest wall. Nevertheless, clenching her fists, she steeled herself. She was going to have her say. "I'm afraid you don't admire it enough to put it to a test, Mr. Crowley."

Crowley fixed a father's sharp eye on her. As he took his own seat, he lay a sheaf of copy atop the Throckmorton story, burying it. "It so happens I've been thinking along those very lines myself," he said, folding his hands over the grave.

The gesture, which resembled the start of a blessing, coupled with his remark, threw Madeleine off stride. Dare she hope he was about to lay her career as a society writer to its final rest? "Mr. Crowley, am I to understand that you no longer wish me to write the society news?"

Tweaking the end of one of his mustachios, he gave her another of his from on-high smiles. "You are, my dear Miss Madeleine. I know you haven't been entirely happy doing so."

The weight of her anticipation stopped Madeleine's heart beating entirely. "But you do have another assignment in mind for me?"

"A very special one," he replied, picking up his stick and holding it horizontally in both hands. "I daresay I don't personally know of another woman in the country who now holds a comparable position."

Crowley's words sent Madeleine's imagination on a binge of possibilities, but she forced herself to remain skeptical. As godlike as he was as an editor, he was first a publisher and businessman, one who was increasingly dependent on his advertisers. "And what of the objections my father will most certainly raise?"

"Well," he drawled, swiveling in his chair, "I can't see that your father will have much to say about the matter. Not even Matthew Faurest can stop progress."

Laying her hand over her heart, Madeleine released a long imprisoned breath. Her head went light. She was witnessing a miracle, Jackson Crowley defying her father to bring women into journalism and the *Record* into the modern age. This is it, she thought, the chance of a lifetime. Her lifetime. The chance to write this town up as she saw it, as she wanted to see it, from inside city hall to inside tenement buildings. From the docks to the distilleries, the carriage houses on the estates along River Road to the courthouse. She trembled to think of the stories ripening in rooms above the glittering lobby of the Galt House and behind the worn facades of the overcrowded slum houses along East Jefferson. She trembled to think that she would soon ferret out those stories and write them, as she'd known she was meant to do from that moment ten years ago when the flat of her hand had struck the cheek of a boy fighting the odds to become a man, a young criminal struggling to protect his poet's heart.

"Mr. Crowley, forgive me. I heard every word you said and I know what you're offering to me, but I . . ." Madeleine shook her head disbelievingly. "I still can't believe it's true. You have no idea what this means to me."

"I think I do, my dear," Crowley replied, smiling with obvious self-satisfaction, as though pleased to have brought such joy to a beloved daughter. "After all, we're breaking new ground, you and I."

"Oh, indeed we are," Madeleine replied, unable to keep from crowing. "When may I start?"

Laying down his stick, Jackson Crowley rose and started toward Madeleine. "I see no reason why you shouldn't begin as soon as you and Roger Mabrey return from your honeymoon."

"Of course . . . My honeymoon." Madeleine sat back, hiding a two-pronged twinge of guilt and disappointment. She realized she'd not only forgotten about her wedding, but resented it for forcing her to delay what she'd already come to think of as her life's work. No, more than that. A rendezvous with her own soul. "Mr. Crowley," she said, biting her gloved thumbnail. "You're quite sure you won't change your mind while I'm away?"

As though laughing at an adorable puppy, Crowley patted Madeleine's hand. She frowned, unable to imagine him behaving so condescendingly toward Joe Kimmel or Haley Green or any other first-string male reporter. But she supposed she ought to give him time to adjust to a woman in the city room. As he'd said, they were both breaking new ground.

"Ah, Miss Madeleine, you do have a way with me," he said, taking her arm and raising her out of the chair. He retrieved his silver-handled stick. "Come. The least I can do is to show you the desk you'll find awaiting you upon your return."

As she walked beside "J.D.," as the front-page boys called Mr. Crowley, Madeleine fought the temptation to pinch herself. She was actually going to have her own desk, her own typewriter, not hidden away in some garret but right out in the open. In the city room, where she'd sit shoulder-to-shoulder with Joe and Haley and the rest of the gang.

Well, perhaps not shoulder-to-shoulder, she thought as Crowley led her down a short hall into the city room— deserted except for a few copy-editors—past the city editor's office and also past several desks she knew were unclaimed. When he arrived at the entrance to a tiny alcove in which sat one lone desk, she smiled to think of his exceeding and exceedingly unnecessary chivalry.

"J.D.," she began, laying her hand on his sleeve, "if by chance you're worried that I might not be prepared to work alongside the"—she cleared her throat—"gentlemen of the press, I just want you to know that I've heard about their"—*ahem*—"Colorful language and their taking a little nip now and then. And as for their smoking . . ."

"Why, my dear, how thoughtless of me," Crowley replied, looking chagrined. "I never stopped to consider that some smoke is bound to reach you from the city room."

"Please, don't concern yourself about it, J.D.," Madeleine replied, thinking that she would gladly learn to smoke if that's what it would take for her to earn a place among the men. "I expect that most of the time, I'll be out pounding the streets, searching for copy."

"Searching the streets?" Crowley looked at her not only askance but with a hint that he'd found something distasteful in her reply. One magnificent white brow arched. "Oh, I'm afraid you'll be chained to your desk from now on, Miss Madeleine."

Madeleine felt her stomach sicken the way it did at her father's fund-raising dinners, where she lacked a higher purpose to prevent her from gagging on the exhalations of pompous men blowing all kinds of smoke. Unless her new assignment to the city desk were so much smoke, Crowley's remark made no sense. "I don't understand, J.D. What will I be doing while I'm chained to my desk?"

Crowley's expression matched hers for apprehension. "Why, editing our new ladies' page, of course. Since you began writing the weekly society news, our circulation among women has so increased that I decided to establish a new department and put you in charge of it."

Pressing her palm to her abdomen, Madeleine turned away. Now she knew where newborn hope, once struck a fatal blow, went to die. The pit of the soul. "I see now," she said, her voice bated. "You thought that since I was unhappy writing about what Mrs. Pennington served for Sunday supper last and the color of the feathers in Mrs. Throckmorton's head, I'd need only to assign others to write such drivel to find contentment."

Crowley's blue eyes showed rare astonishment. "I thought no such thing. Naturally, you'll want to include recipes and advice on marriage and homemaking—"

"How dare you!" No longer able to contain them, Madeleine released hot, bitterly angry tears as she turned on Jackson Crowley. "Do you imagine Joe Kimmel or Haley Green would kiss your hand for the opportunity to edit a page filled with articles on how to mix a proper mint julep or what the men in Paris are wearing this season, when all they want to do is dig up and write the stories at the heart of this city?"

His eyes popping, his eminent white head trembling, Jackson Crowley stood speechless, whether with shock or rage or both, Madeleine neither knew nor cared. She'd cast her fate and she wasn't going back on it. She held her ground as Crowley, clutching his lapel in one hand and his stick in the other, stepped toward her.

"We have been through this nonsense about your becoming a news reporter before," he said. "How could you have thought for an instant that I had any intention of assigning you to . . ." A smile, cold as it was artful, lifted the ends of his mustachios. "Miss Madeleine, I have always abided by a code of honor and chivalry I simply cannot compromise. As a gentleman, I could never send a lady to cover a class of news that is, frankly, indelicate."

"Apparently, your code of honor finds no indelicacy in submitting to my father's blackmail." Madeleine folded her arms as fresh tears of rage stung her eyes. "You, Mr. Crowley, are a hypocrite!"

Crowley's face blackened like a storm cloud. The silver handle of his stick flashed like lightning as he raised it above Madeleine's head. She stood unflinching, holding his gaze. After a moment, he released a breath and lowered the stick. His voice came tautly controlled.

"And you, young woman, are a slanderer. Matt Faurest has never used such tactics to prevent me from assigning you to the city desk, nor has he needed to. The truth is that women are constitutionally incapable of writing a factual news story. There is nothing more to be said on the subject, except that only respect for your father could induce me to forget this entire episode. As far as I'm concerned, the position as editor of the ladies' page is still open to you. Think it over, Miss Faurest, and let me know in the morning. Oh, and I'd prefer you call me Mr. Crowley." With a formal nod of his head, Crowley left Madeleine to furtive stares from copyeditors who cowered as he passed them by.

Madeleine quickly drew a hanky from inside her sleeve to blot her tears, then, lifting her chin, summoned a voice as clear as the mission she refused to abandon. "J. D.! Why aren't we capable?"

Crowley halted, but didn't look at her.

"Are we not able to see with our eyes and hear with our ears and question with our minds, the same as men do?"

The editor turned. With both hands curving over the horse head handle of his stick, he planted it in the center of the city room like a flag claiming his territory. "Yes, but you are not at all able to report what you see and hear and learn *accurately.*"

"I report the society news accurately, don't I?" Madeleine charged past the astounded copyeditors to stand before Crowley. "I list every course at every dinner in such detail, I could throw up!"

"Well," he replied, glancing at the copyeditors, "your *language* certainly qualifies you to work alongside the men."

Hearing titters, Madeleine turned on the copyeditors. "Cowards! There's not a one of you who can fault me for accuracy, but you're all too yellow-bellied to say so."

"I rescind what I said about your language qualifying you to write for the *Record*, Miss Faurest," Crowley said. "I can, however, recommend you to a dime-novel publisher I know."

Madeleine looked at him. "Apparently, he bears no prejudice against women writers."

"On the contrary, he prefers them for their blatant sentimentality." Crowley raised his stick atop his shoulder. "As for reporting straight news, only rational beings who are free of the tyranny of their emotions qualify."

"In a word, men."

"Precisely." With an indulgent smile, Crowley patted Madeleine's arm. "Now, dry your tears like a good girl and let's have an end to this pointless discussion. There's work to be done here, man's work."

As he lowered his stick and walked away, Madeleine stared at her hanky and, on it, a wet ring of self-betrayal. She *had* given free rein to her emotions. Not that she hadn't been justified in feeling the gamut, from despair to outrage. Her mistake had been in allowing Jackson Crowley to see that panoply in the form of tears, which men mistook and pointed to as proof of feminine frailty rather than of a woman's unique strength—the linkage of her body to her heart, soul, and mind. She would never, she vowed, make that mistake again. Hurriedly and indelicately, she wiped her remaining tears, tucked her hanky in her sleeve, and stalked after Crowley. She'd appealed to him on every imaginable grounds, save one. The one thing the racehorse-loving Jackson Crowley couldn't resist.

"Mr. Crowley! I have a wager for you."

Stopping, he looked over his shoulder at Madeleine.

"Assign me to just one straight news story," she said.

"If you don't agree it's every bit as objective and accurate as any story Joe or Haley might write, then I'll accept your offer to edit the ladies' page." *Until I get what I want from you or some other editor at some other paper.* Until, as Eleanor Barlow had predicted, Madeleine thought, her time inevitably came.

As Crowley turned to give Madeleine his answer, the door to the city room burst open.

"Mr. Crowley! Gosh, where's Mr. Logan?"

Madeleine recognized Bobby, one of the copy boys, as he came skidding across the floor and lurched to a halt between her and Crowley. Obviously, he had something important to tell Logan, the city editor, who, Madeleine knew, was home with a bad cold.

"Easy, lad. Catch your breath," Crowley said, staying the boy's arm. What is it you want with Harry Logan?"

Between gasps, the boy blurted, "I just got a tip a woman turned up dead in Bug Alley." Another gasp. "Murdered!"

The word triggered both Crowley's and Madeleine's gazes at the city room. Each saw that a sports reporter and a financial news writer had wandered in, but neither of the two aces who could cover a crime story were anywhere to be seen.

Crowley wiped his mouth and chin. "Sometimes I think I'd see more of Kimmel and Green if I tended bar. Bobby," he said, gripping the boy's shoulder, "search the usual establishments, and when you find one of my star reporters, tell him I'm terribly sorry to disturb him, but if he doesn't bring me this story in time for the evening edition, this paper won't be troubling him for another. Ever!"

Madeleine only faintly heard the final word of Jackson Dillard Crowley's edict. Before he finished delivering it, she had slipped quietly and unobserved out the door.

Her time, she knew, had come at last.

* * *

"This time I thought I'd found her for sure." Standing beside Daniel on a dark, deserted corner as they both stared down at the body of an unidentified woman, Chicago homicide detective Benny Grimm spoke in his padded whisper. "She's about your old lady's age, same build, leastwise by your description." He spit out a wad of gum that landed beside the murder victim's hand, which reached over her head as though she'd been trying to crawl out of the gutter at the end of Thirty-fifth and Halsted before she died. "Course, a lotta years passed since your ma disappeared. She could have changed so's you wouldn't recognize her now."

Daniel crouched beside the strangled woman, his elbows resting on his thighs, his hands dangling between them. Without conceding that Benny had a point, he took a match from his pocket, struck it, and slowly trailed its light over the upturned right side of the woman's face. Over the years, he must have studied a couple of dozen faces like hers, allowing for the lines that had undoubtedly etched his mother's face since he last saw her. Allowing for death's theft of the intangibles—a sparkle in eyes it rendered blank, a sweet smile it replaced with a grimace—that distinguish a person from a corpse. This one had come closest to reminding him of the person Kathleen McQuinn Delaney had been ten years ago. But the evidence of his father's handiwork—the smashed right cheekbone that had mended poorly, creating a small lump of scar tissue—was missing.

As he got to his feet, Daniel shook out the match. "Thanks anyway, Benny," he said, tossing the match over the body. He pushed back the brim of his fedora and gave Benny a half-smile. "Again."

"Don't mention it. Actually, old pal, when you write up this story you *could* mention—"

"Don't worry," Daniel said, rapping the back of his hand against Benny's shoulder. "I'll cite the name of Benjamin B. Grimm so many times, the mayor will think he's going to be running against you in the next election."

Benny chuckled then, growing sober, motioned for the patrolmen to take over getting the body ready for transport from the crime scene. Taking Daniel by the arm, he led him to one side. "There's something I've been meaning to talk to you about, Delaney."

Daniel grabbed Benny by the lapels. "How many times do I have to tell you not to call me that?" After scanning for eavesdroppers and finding none, he let Benny go, smoothing out the lapels he'd crushed in his fists. "Sorry, Benny." Daniel meant it. When he'd pulled Benny close, he'd detected a faint whiff of rum on his breath. Again, and as before, only at the scene of some woman's murder. Daniel worried about Benny. He sometimes thought he was too softhearted for this kind of work. "Just try to remember Daniel Delaney doesn't exist anymore. All right?"

Gazing up at Daniel, Benny Grimm shook his perfectly round head. "I don't get it, Danny boy. I came outta the same reform school you did and whadayaknow? They made me a cop! A detective, no less."

"Maybe marrying the Chief of Police's niece had something to do with that," Daniel replied. "Besides, *you* don't have a record. Your only crime was getting orphaned."

"All right, all right," Benny said, holding up his hands in surrender. "You don't have to remind me I was at the bottom of my class."

The two men laughed. Then, propping his fists on his perfectly round waist, Benny said, "If you wanna call yourself Grover Cleveland, Danny, it's all right by me. But that won't stop me worrying about you."

"What for?" Striking another match, Daniel cupped his hands and lit a cigarette. Forgetting the body that lay sprawled behind him, he tossed the match over his shoulder. "You know me longer than anybody, Benny. You ought to know I can take care of myself."

"I'm not talking about the characters you do business with," Benny replied, "though you shouldn't oughta spend so much time on the Levee."

Daniel laughed. "Now, I understand. You're afraid I'll find out who's been murdering young prostitutes before you do. And I don't blame you."

Pulling in his girth, Benny hiked his pants. "I'll get The Red Rose Killer with no help from you, all right." All at once, he let his waist expand. "Listen, Danny, all I'm saying is how are you ever going to meet a nice girl to settle down with if you spend all your spare time with lowlife?"

"I don't know why I bother looking for my mother when I have you," Daniel replied, tapping Benny's cherubic cheek. "Come on, you know my interest in the ladies on the Levee is purely professional. If you knew half of what they tell me about who's doing what with whom in this town, you'd be as good a cop as I am a reporter."

"Good and dead," Benny shot back as he glanced at the shrouded body being loaded into the back of the patrol wagon. "No thanks, Danny. What I don't know can't kill me. I've got a wife and kids to think of."

Turning and watching the patrol wagon pull away with a new shipment for Cook County Morgue, Daniel rubbed his thumbnail alongside his mouth. "True, you'd win more popularity contests in this town if you weren't an honest cop. But nothing's going to happen to you, Benny. To either one of us. Twenty years from now, you'll be telling me you've got grandkids to think of." Turning back, he threw his cigarette to the ground and stamped it out. "Parting may be sweet sorrow, pal, but I've got to file this story. With luck, Monroe will take me back, with an advance, and then I can take myself down to the

Levee. Waiting for me there is the biggest, the pinkest, the juiciest—"

"See what I mean, Danny? You shouldn't talk that way, not even about—"

"I'm surprised at you, Benny." Shaking his head, Daniel tsked loudly. "Any impure thoughts at the moment are all yours because I was talking about a porterhouse steak." With a sidelong grin and a farewell salute for his old prison schoolmate, Daniel stepped into the street.

"Danny?"

Though Benny's voice had come as close to a shout as it ever could, Daniel smiled and kept on walking. "Aw, quit nagging me, you old woman, and go home to Alice," he called over his shoulder. "She's probably got hot apple pie and coffee waiting." At least he hoped so, especially the part about the coffee.

"She's not coming back, Danny."

"Finally had enough of you, did she?"

"I'm talking about your ma."

Daniel stopped cold. Slowly, he cocked his gaze at Benny. "Then you're talking to yourself," he said. Turning up his collar against the drizzle that had begun a moment ago, he walked on.

"She's the real reason I'm worried about you, Danny. Don't you think it's about time you let her go?"

When Daniel turned around this time, he found Benny standing opposite him in the middle of the street. Big drops of rain exploded at their feet. "Any particular reason why I should?"

Benny looked at the patrol wagon starting its journey to the morgue. "The way I figure it, Danny, she's already met her end . . . someplace. Like that woman."

Daniel watched the wagon until it disappeared around the next corner. "I used to think so, too. But lately, I've had a feeling . . ." He looked at the detective. "She's coming back, Benny. Here. To the old neighborhood. It's written, somewhere, like the final chapter of a book."

Benny relinquished a sigh. "If you say so, Danny." The rain was falling in torrents now, and when he spoke, his words spattered. "I guess you know books better than I do."

Daniel shoved his hands in his pockets. "I guess so," he said, wishing he knew women half as well. Or maybe just one woman, one who wasn't two-faced, like his mother, or grasping, like Eileen Corrigan, or pathetic, like the whores on the Levee. Or dead, like the one the police had just carted off.

Where was *She?*

"Miriam?" he asked, squinting at Benny. "Was her name Miriam?"

"Who? Oh. *She.*" Benny shook his head. "After ten years, don't tell me you still think *She's* coming back, too?"

"Call it wishful thinking. She slugged me, remember?"

"And you figure you owe her for that."

With a laugh, Daniel shrugged. "That's the way I am." A sudden frown pinched his gaze. "But you know, as often as I think how sweet it would be to make her beg my forgiveness, there are times I know I'd give my soul if she'd come back and slug me again. I must be crazy, huh?"

Benny paused, a look of strained pensiveness in his gaze that was interrupted when he was nearly run down by a passing carriage whose driver obviously hadn't seen the two men standing in the middle of the street. Taking out his notebook, he made a mark in it.

Daniel frowned. "What are you doing?"

"That's my seventh near miss," Benny replied. "I like to keep track of how much of my borrowed time I've spent."

Daniel cupped his hand over his friend's shoulder.

"Thanks for answering my question. *I* am not crazy. Say hello to Alice for me." Laughing, he walked away.

"When am I going to be able to tell you to say hello to *your* wife for *me?*"

Shaking his head, Daniel batted his hand over his shoulder. "Old woman," he said.

Her handkerchief pressed over her nose and mouth, Madeleine crept up a flight of rickety stairs toward the second floor of a tenement in the Louisville slum known as Bug Alley. She understood how the place had come by its name the instant she'd stepped inside the ramshackle dwelling, when a colony of roaches had scurried from the light she'd let in at the door. Her skin was still crawling moments after she'd heard the crunch of one of their backs, felt it cracking beneath her shoe. Nevertheless, she kept climbing. A story awaited her at the top of the stairs, in the flat pointed out by smudge-faced children who were like curious bugs themselves as they crawled over the hansom she'd arrived in. She would have found the flat without their help, though. She would only have had to follow the muffled sounds of grief-filled sobs too tired and worn to become wails.

Putting away her handkerchief, Madeleine knocked on the door whose little remaining paint was peeling. A pot-hatted policeman answered her knock. Obviously bewildered as to what a lady of her class was doing in this vermin-infested part of town, let alone at the scene of a murder, he stood in stunned silence as she crossed the threshold.

"Beg pardon, miss," he said at last, stepping in front of her. "You can't come in here."

"Oh but I can, Officer, and I will." Bolstered by her own bravado, Madeleine squared her shoulders. "I'm with the *Record.*"

As she had hoped, her announcement had rendered the man, once again, speechless just long enough for her to gain a firm foothold inside the flat. She quickly gathered there were but two rooms, the one she now stood in, containing a broken divan, a greasy stove, and a battered oak table and four splay-legged chairs; and a bedroom, from which emanated the soft moans she had heard earlier. She was amazed to discover that although she'd never before seen a slum flat, she'd pictured this same faded wretchedness—except for one detail. She had never imagined the stubby bunch of bright cut flowers sitting in a jelly jar in the center of the table. They held her gaze as she made her way to the bedroom.

Madeleine pushed the ajar door fully open. A woman who was probably no more than thirty, but looked to be half-again as old, sat on a chair beside a window hung with yellowed lace curtains. Hugging herself, she rocked back and forth, keening low. Then, seeing Madeleine, she stopped. "She was my sister," she said softly, her gaze reaching out with her hand.

Struck by the woman's grief, Madeleine clasped the outstretched hand. At that moment, a man wearing a somber brown suit drew her attention across the bed. When she turned to look at him, he scowled at her.

"I told that fool not to let anyone in," he said, his voice as jagged as Kentucky limestone. "You'll have to leave, miss."

Madeleine gently squeezed the woman's hand then, letting it go, moved past the foot of the sagging bed toward the man. Though she stopped at the blockade he made of his broad torso, she coolly and instinctively rerouted her gaze to the floor behind him where it limned the lower half of a woman's body. The legs were gently curved beneath neatly and modestly arranged patched skirts. The woman might have been sleeping, Madeleine thought. She wondered, too, whether the deceptively reassuring pose accounted for her own surprising detachment. She was seeing what most women of her breeding didn't even speak of, the corpse of a murder victim, and feeling remarkably in control of her wits. Or perhaps, they were in control of her, as though they knew that what mattered most now was getting the story and getting it right.

"I'm with the *Record,*" Madeleine stated matter-of-factly. "Who are you?"

"I'm with the city. The police department to be exact, and I don't care if your daddy *owns* the *Record.*" The detective's tone was belligerent, his gaze contemptuous. "So why don't you just run on back to your garden party. A crime scene is no place for a lady."

"So I've heard." Madeleine slanted a look at the woman's shoes. The soles had holes in them but the uppers appeared freshly polished. "Wasn't *she* a lady?"

The detective threw a glance down at the woman then looked at Madeleine as though she were as buggy as the tenement they were standing in. "All I know is you don't belong here," he said, taking her by the arm. "Let's go."

As he turned her toward the door, Madeleine's will discovered a powerful expedient in something he had said. She pulled free of his hold. "Since you brought up the subject of my daddy, perhaps it would change your opinion of whether or not I belong here to know that his name is Matthew Stapleton Faurest."

"Judge Faurest?"

Madeleine arched a brow. "You've heard of him, I see."

"You see nothing," the man shot back. "Yet." With a mock bow and a flourish of his arm, he stepped aside and gave Madeleine full view of the body. Of murder.

What had once been a face was now a pulp of blood and bruises and broken bones. Before she could stop herself, Madeleine inserted the knuckle of her forefinger into her gasp of horror, biting hard on it to keep from screaming or, perhaps, becoming ill. She wanted to do both. But she wasn't going to faint; that much she knew. She had fought a split second battle with faintness and won. Nor would she turn her back. The last thing she would do, she told herself, was turn her back on this woman.

Despite icy, trembling fingers, Madeleine removed a small notebook and pencil from her purse. "Who did this to her?" she asked the detective.

"We're pretty sure it was her husband," he replied. "According to our records, he's been out of work for over a year and hittin' the bottle pretty hard."

Madeleine turned a blistering gaze on the man. "You mean the police have been here before? You knew this might happen and yet did nothing to prevent it?"

The detective ground his square jaw. "It's not the law's place to come between a man and his wife."

"Maybe it should be," Madeleine said, jotting in her notebook. When another officer entered the room with a cloth to lay over the woman's body, Madeleine forced herself to take a last look at the face. She felt no less revulsion than she had when she first saw it but a great deal more anger. She was angry at the evil that had lain in wait for this woman and angrier still at the law that saw it lurking yet looked the other way.

"Mommy, Mommy!"

As the policeman covered the woman's face, a tike of about four, his head a mass of red-gold ringlets, crashed into the room. He was carrying a small tattered book. "Read me a story, Mommy!"

All at once, the detective shouted for someone to get the kid out of there, the boy's aunt scooped him into her arms, and another, older woman rushed in, apologizing in a German dialect that the little one had gotten away from her the one, brief moment she had turned her back on him.

Observing the scene, Madeleine stepped back against

the wall. But she felt as though she were crossing a bridge in time. A bridge built of echoes and perhaps, destinies. Flattening her palms against the thin wall, she distinctly heard a man's voice from far beyond it. A voice that was deep and proud. A voice she'd never heard before and, yet, found strangely familiar. Closing her eyes, she held the breath she'd inhaled, wanting the voice to stop. Exhaling relief when it came again.

When, with proud defiance, it said, "My mother's the one taught me to read."

Madeleine sat across from Jackson Crowley, reading his expression as he read her story on the Bug Alley murder and finding, to her utter frustration, a blank page. Convincing him to look at the piece had been no easy task, but awaiting his verdict was pure torture. If only, she thought, he would raise an eyebrow, frown, sigh, give *some* indication of what he was thinking, good or bad, then she could endure this torment. But as it was, anyone would have thought he was perusing an advertisement for hardware rather than the story of a woman's brutal death.

Removing his glasses and laying them on his desk, Crowley walked to the window. He stood peering out it, his hands clasped behind his back.

He's trying to think of a way to both let me down and uphold his precious code of chivalry, Madeleine thought. To tell me that in all his years, he's never read more terrible copy and wouldn't print it if Matthew Faurest paid him to. She should have expected as much. After all, she had no experience writing stories about people who hadn't been *willing* to die to be written about. Suddenly, she couldn't recall what had possessed her to attempt writing a breaking crime story. Something Eleanor Barlow had said, she supposed, though their conversation might as easily have occurred last month as this morning. Or not at all. Seeing Crowley turn from the window, pick up the story, and with a sigh, pinch the bridge of his nose, Madeleine cringed with profound embarrassment.

"Mr. Crowley, I'm terribly sorry for troubling you with—"

"You're quite right, Madeleine," he said, giving her a stern look. "You have troubled me, indeed."

Madeleine's breath caught. Her story may be pathetically amateurish, but he needn't be nasty about it. She rose and held her hand out for the pages she'd typed in the city room, sitting at Joe Kimmel's desk, when she should have been at the dressmaker's for a final fitting of her wedding gown. "If you please," she said, summoning what was left of her pride. "I'm late for an important appointment."

"I don't give a damn if you're late for an appointment with St. Peter," Crowley snapped. "I haven't finished with you, Miss Faurest. Sit down."

"There's no need to take that tone," Madeleine shot back. "Now, I'd like my story so I can be on my—"

"Sit down!"

Stunned speechless, Madeleine sat. She'd never heard Jackson Crowley roar at anyone but his ace reporters.

"Madeleine, this story," Crowley began, perching on a corner of his desk and tapping the pages with the silver tip of his walking stick. "This story is not only one of the best written I've ever read, but one of the most moving. That's why I said you troubled me. You made me realize that as a newspaper, we should have been clamoring for laws to protect battered women long ago. We might have saved this woman's life."

Suddenly, Madeleine understood why Crowley had chucked his chivalry and bellowed an order to her. He'd been telling her she was a journalist, in a class with Joe, Haley, and the rest of the boys. That one shout meant as much to her as all the words of praise that had followed.

Yet, none of what was now happening to her was easy to believe. Looking down, she touched her fingertips to her temples, as though to impress on her mind the incredible fact that she had achieved her greatest ambition, to become a first-rate journalist. Still, she was skeptical. Why is it, she wondered impatiently, that the psyche conjures dreams, then, when they come true, doubts their reality? She looked up at Crowley. "Will you run it in the evening edition?"

Drawing a very deep breath, Crowley stood and gazed down at Madeleine. "I'm afraid not."

"Tomorrow morning's edition, then."

Averting his gaze to the floor, Crowley drew a circle there with his walking stick. "No."

Her disbelieving psyche, Madeleine realized, had been wise. Rising, she stood before Crowley. "You're not ever going to run it, are you?"

Without looking at her, he wagged his head from side to side.

Madeleine didn't even try to control her indignation. Snatching her story from Crowley's hand, she shook it in his face, forcing him to meet her angry stare. "Are you telling me that a woman can be beaten to death by her husband while the police look the other way but another woman can't report the story?"

"That's not at all what I'm telling you, Madeleine!" Sighing, Crowley ran his fingers through his beautiful white hair. "I'm saying that I can't print *your* story."

Madeleine's shoulders sagged under the weight of her ultimate disappointment in Jackson Crowley. "I see," she replied coldly. "All that talk about wanting to change the law and save lives was just that, talk. My father really does own you, doesn't he, Mr. Crowley?"

Crowley looked at her, a vulnerability in his eyes she'd never seen before. "Madeleine, when I told you your father hadn't needed to blackmail me to prevent me from appointing you to the city desk, I was telling the truth. What I didn't tell you was that the reason he hadn't needed to was because someone else already had."

Taken aback, Madeleine cocked her head to one side. "Who? Who else wants to keep me from working as a journalist?"

Twisting the end of one of his white mustachios, Crowley stared at her as though debating whether or not to truthfully answer her question. Then, resting both hands on the top of his stick, he lifted his chin. "Madeleine, I'm a selfish, self-serving man. But I'm also a newspaperman and I can't stand the thought of a talent like yours going to waste. The man's name is Roger Mabrey."

"Roger?"

"He came to me about a year ago, saying he planned to run for Congress next election and wanted to be able to count on the *Record*'s endorsement. When I told him I would make that decision only after I'd seen his platform, he handed me a copy of information he'd obtained . . ." Crowley lowered his head and his voice. "Information that, if revealed, would ruin me both personally and professionally."

Madeleine felt as though she were careening between two cataclysmic shocks—Roger's treachery and Crowley's admission of some unnamed but scandalous behavior. She could absorb neither. "There must be some mistake," she said.

Crowley's stare was wide, feverish, even a little crazed. "Oh, there's no mistake, Madeleine. I *am* a wretch, a sinner of the first order."

Madeleine stared back, fixed by the chilling, fascinating sight of a man being consumed, body and mind, by a bad conscience. She tugged his arm, hoping to pull him from the brink of total incoherence. "What I meant was that I can't believe Roger would blackmail you to keep me off the news pages. He's always known about my ambitions and encouraged them."

"He took your father's advice to humor you, Madeleine," Crowley replied, his gaze cooler, as though the power of confession were already at work. "But he was afraid that humoring you wouldn't be enough. It was his idea, supported by your father, that I make you editor of the ladies' page. He thought that would pacify you, and then, once you were married—"

"He would lay down the law." Turning away, Madeleine pictured the woman in Bug Alley, her face broken, her life ended by her husband's hand. She saw her stepmother, unconscious on the sofa, numb with brandy, numb to the pain inflicted by a husband who had broken her self-esteem with his neglect. She wondered what she herself would look like after she'd married Roger and he'd done his best to break her spirit, her dreams, with his false authority. The law, she now understood, was silent about women and, in so remaining, acquiesced in their being silenced. Sometimes, forever.

But no more, Madeleine thought. Not while there was breath in her to speak, to put her words on paper, to fight to get them into newsprint. Story in hand, she walked to the door.

"Madeleine?"

Madeleine paused, her hand on the doorknob, but did not look at Crowley.

"Do you think that from now on, you could call me J.D.?"

The offer of a privilege she'd once coveted without the job that went with it brought Madeleine to a very real crossroads. Earlier that day, when she'd heard about the murder in Bug Alley, she'd thought her time had come—as Eleanor McCarron had put it, the time to risk her all. Although she'd gone after the story, she now realized that she'd risked nothing more than a rebuke from Crowley and the loss of a job she hated. So here she stood, neither rebuked nor fired, nor holding on to any illusion that she could remain in Louisville and become a front page reporter.

Only now had her time arrived, she realized, the time when nothing less than risking her all would do. She straightened her back, squared her shoulders. "Goodbye, Mr. Crowley," she said, and without looking back, marched out of his office, never, she knew, to return.

Part Two

Part Two

Four

"Less than nothing and it won't do," Madeleine said, clutching a well-traveled brown leather portfolio to her chest as she evaluated her career since she'd arrived in Chicago.

"I beg your pardon?" The woman who sat to Madeleine's right on a bench outside the office of the *Clarion*'s managing editor peered at her through a silver lorgnette. "Were you speaking to me?"

Madeleine gave her a quizzical look. "Have you eaten since yesterday morning?"

Behind her glasses, the woman blinked enormous owl eyes. "Why, yes."

"Then I can't imagine I was speaking to you. We have absolutely nothing in common."

Ignoring the woman's aghast "Well, I never," Madeleine looked past her to the two women to *her* right. Then she studied the women packing the bench to her left. Lastly, she gazed around the room filled to capacity with women waiting to see Archibald Monroe. She wondered if any of them had eaten since yesterday morning, and, if so, what. As she pictured two huge fried eggs, her stomach rudely gurgled.

Fifteen heads in feathered hats turned in her direction. "This place looks like a henhouse," she muttered.

"It sure does," the woman to her left whispered back. "Only instead of eggs, these brooders are hatching stunts they're desperate to sell to Monroe or the managing editor of one of the ten other major dailies in town." She gave Madeleine a streetwise but genial smile and her hand. "The name's Tess," she said aloud. "Tess Lawrence."

Laying her portfolio on her lap, Madeleine returned the smile with a handshake. "Margaret Flynn." After four months, she easily supplied the alias she'd chosen when she'd fled Louisville, leaving behind only Roger's ring, a note reassuring Caroline she was safe and, she hoped, no trail for the detectives her father would undoubtedly hire. "Tess Lawrence? Didn't you do a stunt for the *Times*? Yes, now I recall. You posed as an immigrant housemaid."

"Indentured servant, you mean. I didn't think anyone in town remembered that story. After all, it made the front page one whole week ago." Rolling her hazel eyes, the big-boned, broad-faced woman released a short but heavy sigh. "So, here I am, back in the coop, a few headlines to my credit but no security. One of these days I'm going to take the advice given to me by every editor in this city—go back to Peoria and marry Fred Thistle next door."

"You wouldn't do that, would you, Tess?" Leaning toward the woman whom she estimated to be a few years her senior, Madeleine lowered her voice. "You're not like these other stunt girls. You can write. You belong on some city desk."

"Tell that to Monroe and the other editors," Tess whispered back.

"I will," Madeleine replied with a firm nod. "When I tell them for the twentieth or so time that *I* belong on the city desk, too. And then, for the twentieth or so time, they'll tell me that they're not interested in my news-writing ability because—"

"They'll hire a woman to write the news when the Stockyards smell like lilacs in the spring."

The two women laughed. "What I can't understand," Madeleine said, "is how the *Tribune*'s editor, for example, can send Nora Marks into an insane asylum while refusing to subject the 'fair sex' to the lunacy of the city room."

"It all sounds crazy to me." When neither of them laughed, Tess slanted a look at Madeleine. "That wasn't very funny, was it?"

Madeleine slid a look back. "It would have been funnier if I'd heard it on a full stomach."

Tess glanced at Madeleine's portfolio. "Don't worry. My guess is that with as many stunt proposals as you have in there, a seven-course meal is in your near future."

Her brows shirring, Madeleine looked at the portfolio that contained her Bug Alley story, its location changed for the same reason she'd adopted an alias and a drab brown wig, and more than a dozen other minor news accounts she'd written hoping to exhibit her reporting skill. "Oh, I haven't any stunt proposals in here. Just a lot of unpublished news copy."

Tess's eyes widened. "Now *that's* funny." Pressing her shoulder to Madeleine's, she muted her voice. "But you're smart to play possum. You don't know me from the rest of these biddies, and believe me, they'd as soon steal a stunt proposal as worm a marriage proposal out of a Vanderbilt."

Looking around the room, Madeleine was amazed at the obvious shifty-eyed glancing and over-the-shoulder peeking that previously escaped her notice. "I believe you," she whispered back, then laid her hand flat on her portfolio. "Nevertheless, there really aren't any proposals in here."

Backing away, Tess gawked at Madeleine as though she

were a P. T. Barnum sideshow attraction. "You mean there's no plan in there to get yourself sent to a shelter for wayward women?"

"No."

"No scheme to pose as a farmer's daughter applying for a job in a men's haberdashery? You know, if you countrify that Southern drawl a bit, you could convince anyone that until you came to Chicago, you'd never been off the back forty."

Madeleine chuckled. "Thanks, but I have no such scheme in my portfolio or in mind."

"Not even one tiny suggestion for belly-dancing on the Midway at the World's Fair, like Little Egypt?" Tess glanced away. "Say, that's not a bad idea."

Still smiling, Madeleine shook her head. "You keep it, with my compliments. I'm afraid I don't have enough of a belly. Besides, I have no interest in becoming an ingredient in stories that are nothing more than a lurid brew of sex and violence, the sole purpose of which is to titillate the public into buying newspapers." Her eyes ballooning, she clamped her fingers over her gaping mouth. "Oh, I'm sorry, Tess. I didn't mean that you . . . that your stories are lurid or—"

"I know what you meant." Bowing her head, Tess twisted the strings of the purse in her lap. "And you're right about stunt journalism satisfying a morbid thirst for stories in which innocent young things face death or a fate worse than." Patting her purse, she looked up at Madeleine. "Still, it pays. For breakfast this morning, I had a two-inch stack of fluffy wheatcakes smothered in syrup, two fat sausages, and fresh hot coffee with cream."

Forlornly, Madeleine looked away. "And I had memories of them."

"There you are," Tess replied, tossing her hands. "Listen, kid, you know as well as I do that the city room isn't so much a place as it is a fraternity. No women allowed.

Not even 'little girl reporters,' as editors call us stunt gals. Why fight it?"

Madeleine winced at a hunger pang. "I have to admit—that's a better question now than it was four months ago, Tess."

Four months ago, she recalled, she'd left Louisville with just two things to sustain her. First, her principles regarding the important role of serious journalism and the right of women to participate in it. Second, the bequest she'd inherited from her mother's modest estate upon her engagement to Roger Mabrey, along with Margaret Charbonnay Faurest's initial ring and a far more precious message: "My Darling Daughter, Should I not be able to advise you upon your taking this irreversible step, may this small sum afford you the luxury of thinking twice about it."

Madeleine still wondered how she could have denied herself that luxury until just weeks before her wedding. Although she hoped she wouldn't have gone through with the marriage even if Eleanor McCarron hadn't heightened her doubts or Jackson Crowley hadn't revealed Roger's treachery, she could never know for certain. What she could do from now on, she'd told herself when she boarded the train to Chicago, was to live her life as any self-respecting woman ought to and as her mother would have wanted her to. Fearlessly.

Unfortunately, she was also having to live it hungrily. And when her inheritance ran out in a week's time—two, if she could avoid her landlady—homelessly. Principles, she'd discovered, were costly to maintain. A month ago, when she could still comfortably afford them, she'd refused an opportunity to join a composite of writers known as "Merry Haven" that churned out an advice-to-the-lovelorn column. If anything could more dangerously compromise her principles than writing for the society page, she'd thought at the time, helping old maids to reel in balding bachelors was it.

But now, her survival was being compromised. The Merry Haven offer had been accepted by someone else, which left Madeleine to choose—when the time came to take a steady job—among waiting tables, sewing in a shirt factory, or selling silk hosiery she couldn't afford at Marshall Field's. If any such jobs were available, that is. A deep economic depression was gripping the nation; Chicago, it was strangling.

That would leave her one final alternative, the one she dreaded. Stunt journalism. If she were ever to actually eat those two huge, sunny-side-up eggs she was picturing again, this time with two strips of crispy bacon and hot buttered biscuits, she might have to serve the public the sensationalism they demanded with their own breakfasts.

Her expression pinched, she bit her gloved thumbnail. "God help me."

"God help me, I oughta break your neck!"

The plumage atop fifteen hats, including Madeleine's, quivered as every woman in the room snapped her gaze at Archibald Monroe's door.

"Of all the shenanigans I've seen reporters pull in my time, McQuinn, this latest stunt of yours takes the cake. Hell, it takes the whole damn bakery!"

Madeleine trained her left ear on the door. She didn't want to miss a word of Monroe's tirade at the reporter whose name she'd recognized. As a rule, news reporters didn't get bylines, but by breaking all the rules, McQuinn had gotten a reputation. Madeleine had spent enough time in waiting rooms like this one to know that every managing editor in the city had once thought of trying to hire McQuinn away from the *Clarion*. Later, he thanked his stars he'd sobered up in time. As brilliant as McQuinn was, he was also brash, unpredictable, unmanageable, frequently dangerous, and rarely out of trouble with Monroe.

And Madeleine schooled herself on every word he wrote. Once before, while waiting—unsuccessfully—to see Monroe, she'd asked his secretary to point out one of McQuinn's stories. Ever since, she'd made a little game of trying to identify his work for its firm grasp of fact, inimitable style, and emotional punch. He was the only reporter who could make her see the real truth of a story behind the mere facts. With his stories on the Red Rose murders, for example, he'd opened her eyes to the preventable tragedy of young girls forced to prostitute themselves or starve. The way she'd opened Jackson Crowley's eyes to the preventable deaths of routinely battered wives.

"Wouldn't I just love to give Daniel McQuinn a run for his money?" she said, fantasizing out loud.

Tess leaned toward her. "Wouldn't I love Daniel McQuinn?"

Madeleine gave her a look of small astonishment. "Do you know him?"

"No, but I've seen him and one look was enough for me."

Intrigued, Madeleine cocked her head. She'd long wondered if McQuinn looked as he wrote, like a man who never walked but in shadows and who never stood still anywhere but on the brink of hell, observing a pathetic and sometimes tragic humanity he then rendered chillingly recognizable. She wasn't sure she wanted to learn he looked like Roger, for example. Perfect. Too perfect. Still, she couldn't imagine Tess being attracted to Roger's type.

"What *does* McQuinn look like?"

Taking a deep breath, Tess pressed her hand over her heart. "Like he writes."

Feeling a shiver, Madeleine slowly rose and walked toward Monroe's office. She wanted a close look at

McQuinn when he came out the door, at the face of a man she felt she already knew because, in his writing, she heard her own voice. Her own heart and mind and soul.

Strange as it seemed, she thought as she stood at the door listening, some part of Daniel McQuinn was a part of her.

Inside Archibald Monroe's office, Daniel Delaney, alias McQuinn, sat slouched, his legs outstretched, his hands folded on his abdomen and the brim of his fedora over his shut eyes. Given the hammering inside his own head, courtesy of the Whitechapel Club's impressive stock of diverse spirits, he was only vaguely aware that Monroe was on a rant. Nothing new there. Rawley would take care of things. He always did. Daniel hadn't started the rumor that the "G." in G. Vernon Rawlston stood for "God" for no reason.

At the time Daniel had, of course, the reason was that the *Clarion*'s city editor had sent him to cover a shooting that occurred *after* he arrived on the scene. Whether Rawlston truly possessed foreknowledge or just the keen instincts of an experienced newsman, to Daniel, he *was* godlike. Unquestionably, the greatest city editor in town. He'd made the *Clarion*'s news pages the new standard by which outstanding journalism was measured. Daniel couldn't imagine working under any other city editor at any other paper. Unfortunately, that meant that he ultimately worked *for* Arch Monroe.

"If you weren't two of the best damned newspapermen in this town, I'd see you both up on charges of arson myself!"

Daniel imagined the slap he'd just heard mere inches from his left ear was Monroe's fist pounding the flat of his palm. Laconically, he lifted his head, pushed back the brim of his hat, and fixed a hard stare on Monroe's fist.

"I wouldn't do that," he said, squinting up at Monroe. "Blame Rawley, I mean."

Taking the unlit stub of a cigar from his mouth, Monroe propped his fists on his waist. "Would you mind telling me, then, who or what possessed you to set fire to that warehouse?"

Slowly uncrossing his legs, Daniel shoved himself up to a sitting position. Reaching forward, he took the baseball and mitt sitting on Monroe's desk. He slipped the mitt on his left hand and began pounding the ball into its pocket.

"Rawley told me to get an interview with the killer hiding out inside the place, even if I had to set fire to it." He folded the mitt around the ball like a butterfly folding its wings. "So I set fire to it."

Snatching the ball from the mitt, Rawlston also snagged Daniel's gaze. He stared back at Daniel, a patch over the eye that was socked blind in a fight over a married woman—she was married to Rawlston—and mayhem in his good eye.

"Thanks for not letting me take the blame," he said under his breath.

Daniel shrugged. "You taught me to always report the facts straight."

Rawlston sneered. "After eight years, did you have to pick this moment to start doing what I tell you to do?"

Walking behind Daniel, Monroe bent close to Rawlston, his cigar circling the latter's ear as he spoke. "Rawley, this is Chicago. How could you even suggest setting fire to a building, let alone to this lunatic!"

Facing forward, Rawlston folded his arms. I guess he finally drove me as crazy as he is." He looked up at Monroe. "On the other hand, Arch, he did get an exclusive interview with the killer. And got him to surrender to the *posse comitatus.*"

Frowning, Monroe pulled his cigar from his mouth. "The *who?*"

Tucking in his chin, Daniel hid a grin. Rawley was single-handedly keeping Latin alive and he loved throwing Monroe off track with it. More than a few times, he'd derailed Daniel's firing.

"He means the police," Daniel said.

"Ah, yes. The police." Returning to his desk, Monroe perched on the corner nearest Daniel. "You two will be interested to know that I received a call from the chief this morning. He was wondering if we newsboys wouldn't mind letting his boys catch the crooks from now on. Seems he got a lot of calls from taxpayers who wanted to know why McQuinn, here, was having to do the department's job for it."

Feeling the heat of both editors' gazes, Daniel responded with wide-eyed earnestness and a wave of his hands. "Believe me, gentlemen, I tried to keep mention of my name in the story to a bare minimum."

Monroe sighed. "Thank you, Mr. McQuinn. Until this moment I didn't realize that at the *Clarion*, a bare minimum is twenty-seven."

Daniel gave a low whistle. "That many, huh?"

"Please don't take *my* word for it," Monroe replied. "Count them for yourself. You'll have plenty of time now that you're fired. This time, for good."

Getting to his feet, Rawlston put the baseball back on Monroe's desk. "Listen, Arch, if this is about McQuinn's promoting himself, I'll take part of the blame for that." He scowled down at Daniel. "I've warned him about it and I've tried to catch him at it, but every so often, a story gets past me."

"Don't worry about it, Rawley," Daniel said. "He's bluffing. He's always bluffing."

"*Am* I?" Rising from the desk, Monroe leaned over. Clutching one arm of Daniel's chair, he jabbed Daniel's chest with the V-ed fingers holding his cigar. "If I ever so much as see your face in this building, I'll have you sent up on charges of criminal trespass. If don't tear you to pieces first."

Rising, Daniel forced Monroe back. Eye-to-eye with the man, he pulled Monroe's mitt off his left hand, held it up for Monroe to see, then let it drop to the floor. *"That* will be the day."

Monroe glanced down at his mitt. He looked back at Daniel, his expression blank. After a moment and without warning, he knocked Daniel's hat off his head. "Today's the day."

Before Daniel could land his punch on Monroe's jaw, Rawlston restrained him. "You damn fool," he said, shoving Daniel to the center of the room. "Aren't things bad enough?"

Whipping around, Daniel pointed at Monroe. "I've put my life on the line for this paper!"

"Now my job's on the line," Monroe shouted back. "So don't bother to tell me how many times you've beaten the competition and that I don't have anybody else who can sell out editions like you do. If I don't throw you out of the game, I'm done managing this team."

Daniel felt a prick of fear. And fear, he learned a long time ago, was something he couldn't afford to show. He snorted a laugh. "Who told you that, that fortune teller you go to because you can't get another woman to hold your hand?"

"I'll overlook that remark," Monroe began, picking up both his mitt and Daniel's hat. He tossed his mitt on his desk, then walking to Daniel, handed him his hat. "Because I just realized that after today, I no longer have to stomach you. Orders, from the top. The *very* top."

Daniel gazed up at the ceiling, two floors above which was the office of the *Clarion*'s owner and publisher, William Royce Hart. And behind him was the real power ruling the *Clarion*, from whom he could expect no mercy and with whom there would be no negotiating.

"Hell," he said, putting on his hat and shoving his hands in his pockets. "Pamela Hart."

"Great Caesar's ghost!" Shoving aside a chair, Rawlston charged at Daniel, his good eye wider than Daniel had ever seen it. "With all the females pouring into this town every day, their sweet little hearts just palpitating with romantic notions, did you have to palpitate with the publisher's daughter?"

"But I didn't, Rawley, I swear!" Turning away, Daniel tore off his hat, raked back his hair, then beating the hat against his leg, whipped back around. "You've got to believe me, both of you. I can't stand the woman. She overestimates her charm and the charm of her father's money." He drew a deep breath and puffed it out. "Which is, word for word, what I told her."

Rawlston and Monroe looked at one another in gape-mouthed astonishment.

"Mac, I always knew you were reckless," Rawlston said, "but I never thought you were the type to blow out the light without turning off the gas. How could you do something so stupid?"

Daniel spread his arms wide. "What *should* I have done, Rawley? She was always after me to—"

"We know what she was after to you to do, McQuinn." Monroe stepped up to Daniel, his beefy arms akimbo. "So what was the problem? You couldn't have had a sudden attack of chastity."

Daniel stood molding the crown of his hat. Finally, he put the hat on. "Pamela Hart's not my type."

"Your *type*? She's a woman, isn't she?"

"With a wealthy and powerful daddy." Daniel rubbed his cheek, recalling the younger version of Pamela Hart who had scornfully slapped it ten years ago. "And that kind of woman never lets my kind of man forget that he's dirt under her feet."

"Is that so?" Monroe asked, rocking on his heels. "Well, before you threw cold water on Miss Hart, I wish you'd given the *Clarion* half the consideration you gave your male pride!"

"Arch is right, Mac," Rawlston said, stepping into Monroe's place as the latter stalked away. "There isn't another reporter in this city let alone on my staff who knows The Red Rose story as well as you or has your sources. I was counting on you to bring in another exclusive when the case is solved."

"If you're worried I'll take the story to another paper . . ." Sighing, Daniel turned away. "There is no other paper."

"You're damn right there's no other paper," Monroe said, bearing down on Daniel. "None of them will have you. You aren't worth the cost of your upkeep."

"Bastard!" With blurring speed, Daniel drew back his right arm, the white-knuckled fist at the end of it aimed at Monroe's jaw.

Grabbing Daniel from behind, Rawlston aborted the punch. *"Think,* Mac," he said, squeezing Daniel's upper arms. "For once in your life, *think* of the consequences before you act."

Lowering his fist, Daniel resumed his normal stance. Rawley was right. Monroe wasn't worth sore knuckles. Keeping his sights on Monroe, he lurched toward the door at Rawlston's shove.

"That's it, Mac," Rawlston said, clamping his left hand on Daniel's shoulder. "It's not so hard, thinking ahead," he added as he reached for the doorknob.

"You're a fool, McQuinn!"

Hearing Monroe's shout, Daniel straightened.

"Ignore him, Mac," Rawlston urged under his breath.

"All you had to do was give her what she wanted. You could have named your price!"

Inside Daniel's head, a bolt of lightning flashed. He went blind. When his sight returned, he saw Monroe on the floor at his feet, propping himself on his forearms, dazedly rubbing his jaw.

Coming to Daniel's side, Rawlston looked down at Monroe. "The die is good and cast, now," he said, picking up the hat that had flown off Daniel's head when he'd delivered his blow. Handing it to him, he shook his head. "He was right, Mac. You *are* a damn fool."

With her back to the wall beside Monroe's door, Madeleine had heard more anger than words, though she'd heard enough of both to know that the *Clarion* was now short its star reporter. McQuinn's departure from the paper, she felt certain, spelled opportunity for her. But before she could determine exactly how she was going to seize it, a heavy thud sounded inside Monroe's office telling her that McQuinn was on his way out, rubbing the knuckles she expected he'd planted on Monroe's jaw.

Hurriedly, she came away from the wall and staked a spot beside the desk Monroe's secretary had earlier vacated, ensuring that McQuinn would pass her on his way to the outer door. She wanted a good look at the man whose talent she revered and whose place she planned to take. Picking up a copy of that morning's *Clarion* from the desk, she lowered her head and pretended to read while, through the netting covering her face, gluing her gaze to the door.

"Come on, McQuinn," she murmured through tight lips. Seeing the doorknob turn, she felt her pulse quicken. She shot her gaze upward, as high as she imagined McQuinn was tall.

Hinges creaked. Madeleine held her breath, then

quickly released it when Vernon Rawlston stepped out the door. She'd been able to identify him because he'd been pointed out to her once before as the man with the eye patch. As he turned and looked back—she assumed at McQuinn—she turned in the same direction, peeking higher over the newspaper.

"Believe it or not, even without you I still have a front page to put out," Rawlston said, then strode past Madeleine, though her gaze never strayed from the door.

"Wait, Rawley."

The voice was deep, edgy, dark. A man followed it, in profile. Madeleine's heart caught. He was tall, so much taller than she'd imagined she had to look higher to see his face. And still, she couldn't make it out. Instead of rubbing bruised knuckles, the man was settling a black felt fedora atop his lowered head, his arms concealing his features. Even after he'd shoved his hands in his trousers pockets, his face remained obscured. He'd pulled his fedora so low over the right side of it, she saw nothing but the chiseled line of his jaw.

But she knew he was Daniel McQuinn. Something inside her recognized him, was glad to see this telegraph wire of a man crackling above long legs, transmitting a jolt of defiance along the broad stretch of his shoulders. Though standing still, he was far from at rest. Even the thick strands of black hair on his coat collar tangled, both with one another and the current close-cropped fashion.

"*Turn*, McQuinn." She willed him toward her, willed him to show her the other side of his face.

When he did turn and walk in her direction, Madeleine felt a surge of elation and a strange new power. But she still couldn't see the left half of his face, at least not without stepping directly into his path. *Or* she might make him turn and look at her. When he paused just past her, lit his cigarette with a broad-backed, long-fingered hand, then tossed the still-burning match over his shoulder, striking her newspaper, she saw her chance.

"From what I just heard, McQuinn," she said, blowing out the match, "that's the only way you'll be hitting the front page from now on." She flicked the smouldering match back at him.

Feeling something hot graze his neck, Daniel quarter-turned to his right. From beneath the brim of his fedora, he saw just enough of a young woman reading a paper to know that she was plain and drab, so plain and drab he'd swear she worked at it. And she was much too thin, most likely from not having worked at all.

"Did you say something to me, sister?"

The edge to his voice was so biting, Madeleine thought, she expected to look up and find he'd chewed off the tip of the cigarette he'd spoken around. It had certainly taken a chunk out of her composure. Not that she was afraid she'd betray herself. After four months of living alone in a violence-prone part of the city, she'd learned to put a defiant face on fear. Besides, now that she was looking directly at McQuinn, she wasn't about to reveal the effect he was having on her any more than his hat was revealing the other side of his face. It allowed her to see only the shadow of its own brim and below that, half his mouth and all of his arrogance.

"What if I did? *Brothuh.*"

Plucking a bit of tobacco from his tongue, Daniel looked at Madeleine. She'd taken him aback with her tangy Southern tongue that reminded him of an even tarter one that, ten years ago, had called him "monstrous." And intrigued him with her eyes. Even behind the netting that obscured the rest of her features, they were remarkably large and dark—nearly black—and luminous. He stood, penetrated.

But then, he supposed they owed their effect on him more to their owner's prolonged hunger than to any feminine mysteries lurking behind them. Very likely, the little mouse was just another of the twitteringly annoying females always cluttering Monroe's office, imagining herself a journalist and willing to starve to prove that she was.

"Even if you didn't," he said, taking the cigarette from his lips and blowing out a long stream of smoke, "let me give you a piece of advice that won't cost you anything but the price of a train ticket. Go back to wherever it is the magnolias bloom and marry Homer. He may be dull, but at least he'll keep you fed."

Madeleine cast a long, slow glance at Monroe's door. Then, looking back at Daniel, she crossed her arms, holding the *Clarion* to one side of her. "Is *she* dull?"

Daniel glanced at the door and back. "Who?"

"The woman Mr. Monroe said would have paid your price, just before you hit him."

Tightening his gaze on her, Daniel took a step closer. "Very, in a sharp sort of way."

Madeleine further narrowed the gap between them. "But if you'd given her what she wanted—and I'm not so backwater that I can't imagine what she wanted—you could have kept your job."

Gazing down at her, Daniel strained to see past the netting to her eyes. But he really needn't have. No veil could have prevented him from noticing that they suddenly teemed with feminine mysteries he hungered to know. And knew better than to reach for. He'd get his hand slapped. Or his face. "Point taken, Magnolia. *You* mind your business and I'll mind mine." He turned away, paused, then looking at her over his shoulder, gave her half a grin. "But if you were raised in some backwater, I grew up on Fifth Avenue."

"*Really?*" Madeleine stepped back, suddenly so angry with him she wanted to slap away what she could see of the careless grin that epitomized his self-destructiveness. Any chance he'd had of salvaging a brilliant career that, in time, might have become legendary, he'd destroyed when he'd struck Monroe. No other editor would ever hire him now. She was a fool to worry about him. After all, she fully intended to turn his loss into her gain. Nevertheless, she couldn't help shuddering at the thought of what might become of him if he couldn't work at what he was so clearly born to do. As she was.

She sized him up and down. "You're not grown up, McQuinn," she said. "You're just tall."

The gone-to-the-devil grin cocking one side of his mouth disappeared. "But I cast a long shadow." He ran his gaze over her, from the tips of her brown shoes to the tendrils of her plain brown hair. "Remember that."

He knows what I'm after, Madeleine thought, watching him walk away. *He knows I'm after his territory, his place at the* Clarion. That made her quest all the more challenging, and would make it all the more satisfying when she attained it. With an intent gaze, she followed him to the outer door, where to her surprise, Rawlston stood waiting. From the bemused glance Rawlston sent her, she gathered he'd been observing McQuinn's and her conversation.

"Thanks for holding me to just one punch, Rawley," she heard McQuinn say. "I'm not in the mood for the menu at Cook County Jail."

"I wasn't doing you any favors, Mac. You'd have killed Monroe and I'm too set in my ways to change them for some new s.o.b. of a managing editor."

"All right, so you weren't doing me any favors. But let me do one for you. Let's go to the Press Club, get good and drunk, on me, and figure out how you're going to get me my job back."

Rawlston shook his head. "Not this time, Mac. For your own sake, you've got to learn that this newspaper can get along without you. As good a newspaperman as you are, you aren't bigger than the news itself. Nobody is."

Madeleine saw McQuinn's chest lift, as though he'd taken a blow. Then, "You say that now, but in three days you'll be begging Monroe to take me back."

"If you really believe that, then I feel sorry for you." Despite his pirate's patch, Madeleine thought Rawlston looked fatherly, or as she imagined a caring father ought to look. He put his hand on McQuinn's shoulder. "Let me give you a last bit of advice. You've got a vengeful streak in you, Mac. If you're not careful, one of these days it's going to land you someplace that will make the county jail seem like a hotel. It's going to land you in Hell."

Madeleine shivered. She knew an omen when she heard one. Strangely, Rawlston met and held her gaze as though he knew she'd heard it, perhaps, as though he'd intended for her to hear it. What passed between them in the brief moment before he walked out the door, she thought, was nothing short of bizarre.

But if Rawlston had meant for her to overhear his conversation with McQuinn, McQuinn himself seemed unaware of her as he leaned to his left and stubbed his cigarette out in a standing ashtray. She could see his entire left profile, now; the slope of a thick black brow, dense black lashes that—half-lowered—softened the dangerousness riding on the hard ridge of his cheekbone and in the dark, pebbled plane beneath it. The way he stood there, looking past the ash tray and absently mashing the cigarette, she knew she was catching him in a rare unguarded moment. Once, he paused, and staring up without focus, appeared so genuinely uncertain, Madeleine's heart went out to him.

Then he must have glimpsed her from the corner of his eye because coming to his full height and shoving his hands in his pockets, he looked at her, a mask of reckless cynicism replacing what she thought had been genuine self-inquiry.

"Feeling like this may be your lucky day, sister?"

At his taunt, Madeleine took her heart back. Rawlston had been right. McQuinn needed a lesson, several at least, starting with his inflated opinion of his worth, however considerable, to the *Clarion*. She supposed she'd imagined it, but she sensed that Rawlston believed she was the teacher to give McQuinn that lesson. But how?

Glancing down, she saw the headline of a story she'd read earlier that morning. RED ROSE KILLER SNUFFS FOURTH YOUNG LIFE. McQuinn's story. And he'd lost it. But as she'd already decided, what he'd lost was hers to find.

With a message in her eyes, she lifted her chin. "It just may—"

He was gone. McQuinn was gone, for good. But Margaret Flynn was here to stay. Seeing Monroe's secretary walk in the door, a stack of files in her arms, Madeleine charged at her. "Tell Mr. Monroe that Margaret Flynn wants to see him."

"You'll have to wait your turn with—"

"Now!"

Swiping the files from the woman's arms, Madeleine plopped them on her desk. "Tell him if he's interested in returning the favor McQuinn just did for his jaw, I have a proposal *and* a proposition he'll want to hear."

Five

Behind the offices of the *Daily News* in "Newspaper Alley," several nights and several hangovers after Monroe had fired him, Daniel stood looking at a door that was never locked. Behind it was a dimly lit room. Most people, observing the ropes and knives and blood-stained blanket on the walls, would suppose the place were inhabited by the county hangman or Jack the Ripper. Indeed, the club's members had named it for the London district in which several *filles de joie* met the Ripper and forever lost their joy—along with various body parts.

But the patrons of the Whitechapel Club, all men, were neither executioners nor the perpetrators of grisly crimes. They were writers—reporters, mostly—at home with the macabre. At the end of a day covering stories like that of the assistant coroner who died from formaldehyde poisoning after dining at work—on his work, actually—drinking around a coffin-shaped table bearing human skulls was merely a rite of their profession.

Rather, of their brotherhood. As Daniel stared at the door, which had never separated him from his brothers for want of a key, he knew it wouldn't do so now for want of a job. Among the fraternity's most memorable gatherings, according to the few who could remember them, were those it had spent cheering their own newly jobless. And as never before, Daniel needed cheering. He was actually beginning to think that when he'd walked out of the *Clarion* that day, it really had been for the last time. He'd thought Monroe was too shrewd a newspaperman to let a punch in the mouth stand between him and the credit for the *Clarion*'s beating the other papers on the Red Rose stories. Knowing he needed Daniel McQuinn for that, Monroe, according to Daniel's logic, would find some way around Pamela Hart's scorned woman act then send Rawley to beg him to come back. But after four days, Rawley still hadn't called, not even to see if he'd found another job.

He hadn't. Monroe might be able to forget that sock in the jaw, but all of Press Row, including every other managing editor on it, was still talking about it. At least there was one place in town he was still welcome, he thought as he entered the Whitechapel Club.

The room was as black as the grave. Still, Daniel heard the shuffling of feet, the creaking of chairs, and smelled the distinctive breathy mingling of whiskey and smoke. He smiled. Leave it to Eugene Field, easily the most oft-fired reporter in the city, to plan a surprise party for him.

"Daniel McQuinn?"

The voice wasn't Gene Field's but that of the man with whom Daniel had more in common than any other club member, Finley Peter Dunne. Of Irish descent and close to the mother he'd lost when he was seventeen, Peter Dunne was an ingenious, sometimes manic prankster. He'd certainly fanned the flames that fueled the Whitechapel's most notorious escapade, their cremation of a member's body on the shores of Lake Michigan in fulfillment of his last will and testament. But Peter was also the most prominent of the club's "sharpshooters." When he aimed ridicule at a member, he never missed. His pillory of Field for having written the child's verse "Little Boy Blue" had made more than one grown reporter quiver. Suddenly, Daniel had the feeling that Peter had something in mind for him that would make Field's ordeal look like an award ceremony.

"This is McQuinn. What's going on here?"

"Your trial," Dunne said. "How do you plead, McQuinn?"

"Plead?" Daniel chuckled. "All right. What am I supposed to be guilty of? Certainly not knocking Monroe on his—"

"Silence! Mr. Field, please state to the defendant the charge against him."

Daniel heard a glass hit the table then Field's voice, remarkably sober. "Daniel McQuinn, you are charged with abandoning your journalistic duty."

"Abandoning my—? Listen, boys, I'd like to play along with the joke, but I'm afraid I just don't get it. Maybe if I had a drink . . ." Stepping farther into the darkness, Daniel approached the table.

"Stay where you are," Dunne warned.

Daniel halted. "What's the matter with all of you? I got fired, nothing most of you don't do on a weekly basis. I don't mind discussing it, but do we have to do it in the dark?" He no sooner struck a match than someone blew it out and snatched it from his fingertips. Whipping around, he reached out for a body, but felt only air.

"Reporters who quit in the middle of a story are doomed to darkness."

At Dunne's pronouncement, Daniel whipped back around. Insofar as it could be said that the Whitechapel Club had a conscience, Dunne was it. Through his essays written in the dialect of a shanty Irish barkeeper, he railed against every manner of corruption, public and private. But to put Daniel in a class with the lot of boodlers known as the city council, simply for getting himself fired before finishing his investigation of the Red Rose murders, seemed a bit extreme.

"Forgive me, Father Dunne," he said, recalling the

penetrating blackness of the confessional, "but I fail to see how I've sinned."

"You're here, aren't you?"

Daniel frowned. "Where should I have gone?"

"To the Levee," Dunne said.

"Tomorrow," Daniel replied. "At the moment, I need a drink. I need more than a few drinks, in fact."

"And while you sit here drinking," Dunne's voice of doom said, "another forsaken young creature perishes."

"Yes," Field said, then made the sound of a knife cut across a throat, reminding Daniel of the method by which the Red Rose victims had all perished. "Take that to bed with you tonight, McQuinn, as you contemplate the knowledge that our illustrious constabulary couldn't find the killer if he gave himself up."

"Nor can you console yourself," Field added, "that citizens will gladly pay for a Pinkerton to stop the fiend who's been disposing of a few young women whom they regard as highly disposable."

Daniel heard chair legs scrape the floor then saw, or perhaps felt, the figure of Finley Peter Dunne loom in the darkness. "You must search him out, McQuinn. Unless you do, that door is locked to you."

Daniel glanced over his shoulder at the portal he couldn't see but had entered more times than he could count. No matter how outrageous his past behavior, on either side of it, it had never denied him access. And why not? Because of his sparkling wit, his companionableness? No, he realized now. The door had always opened for him because he'd always lived up to the only code any reporter worth a damn ascribes to: Follow all leads. Most of all, never quit on a story, even when you've been thrown out of the city room on your ear. That he'd so easily abandoned a story, let alone one in which young girls whose lives had been miserable were being dealt unimaginably horrible deaths, appalled him.

Making his way to the door, he paused. "Thanks, Brother," he said, thinking of Dunne and Field, and the rest. But as he stepped outside, he suddenly recalled the woman he had seen in Monroe's office the morning he'd been sacked. He saw her dark, arresting eyes and heard her voice, as revealing of life among Southern gentry as a cotillion.

"Brother," she had shot back when he'd called her "Sister."

He remembered he'd liked that, her tangy rejoinder. But there had been more than admiration for her spunk in his reaction. By the end of their exchange, he'd felt that, somehow, they really were related. Not by blood, of course, but under the skin. The way he was related to Dunne and Field. That was how he'd known she thought she could replace him at the *Clarion.*

Daniel laughed aloud. Monroe would hire *him* back before he hired a woman, even if she could write rings around him.

Lighting a cigarette, Daniel realized what he'd just suggested. A woman reporter the equal of Daniel McQuinn. "That will be the day they hold an honest election in this town," he said. Tossing his still-flaming match to the ground, he headed for South Dearborn Street, the heart of Chicago's infamous Levee.

And the hunting ground of The Red Rose Killer.

For nearly the end of September, Madeleine thought, the night was warm, reminding her of home, where fall came late and stayed long. But as she strolled the plank walk, what really brought the South to mind wasn't the weather. It was the name of this place. The Levee.

Not that she'd ever seen the vice dens on docks along the Mississippi that had inspired the gamblers who'd fled the Confederacy like ship rats to so name the place. Still, not every novel she'd smuggled into the house in her adolescence had featured maidens fair and knights on white horses. Nevertheless, whether due to timid authors or constraints upon her convent-bred imagination, she had never dreamed such sights and sounds and smells as these—part carnival and part Hell—existed.

As she observed it, Dearborn Street was a garishly lit arcade of gambling houses, dance halls, tintype galleries, voodoo doctors, and of course, brothels. Scores of them. To incessantly plinking pianos and tuneless banjos, on the aroma of onions from hamburger stands, revelers careened from one pleasure to the next. If their appetites exceeded their means, they hadn't far to go to find a pawnshop to trade gold for tinsel. In all her life, Madeleine had never watched anything with so much revulsion and, yet, so much fascination.

And fear. Ahead, a distinguished-looking man of about fifty wearing a gray chesterfield coat stood negotiating with an old woman—quite stooped for all her plumpness—who was one of the many vendors plying the Levee traffic with flowers, candy, trinkets. Regular patrons of prostitutes, Madeleine had learned from McQuinn's reporting on the Red Rose murders, often had favorites among the girls and liked to present them with gifts, as though they were suitors come courting.

Though he'd been fired before he could complete a profile of the killer, McQuinn had written that the murderer was most likely one of these romantics, a gentle, even chivalrous man by day. By night, a fiend who chose his victim from the newest of the girls who walked the streets, then lured her to a back alley where he gruesomely ended her young life, placing a single red rose in her limp hand. Beyond that, McQuinn knew nothing, and from his stories, Madeleine had gleaned his frustration when his few leads had all taken him to dead ends.

Watching the man in gray purchase a single bloom

from the old woman then slip it into a pocket in the lining of his coat, Madeleine pictured it lying in some poor young woman's lifeless hand.

In *her* lifeless hand.

Suddenly, she didn't know who had been crazier, she for proposing to Monroe that she pose as a streetwalker in the hope of catching the Red Rose killer or Monroe for approving so insane a stunt. Whoever won the prize for insanity, they were each getting what they'd wanted. She wanted to eat and the job on the city desk she'd gotten Monroe to promise her if she got both the murderer and an exclusive for the *Clarion*. Monroe, his jaw smarting throughout their bargaining session, had made it clear he wanted to return McQuinn's blow. She, too, wanted to hurt McQuinn. Abandoning himself was one thing, but abandoning his story and the Red Rose victims was unforgivable. For both Monroe and her, the most painful retribution they could wrest from McQuinn was to claim the story he'd owned and do with it what he'd failed to do. Resolve it.

Assuming, Madeleine thought, that she lived to do the resolving. When she saw The Man in Gray turn and walk toward her, her heartbeat became a ruckus. Glancing to her right, she peered into the open penny arcade she'd been told to station herself in front of and prayed that Monroe's foolproof plan to protect her wouldn't prove just plain fool.

"Good evening, miss," the man said as he removed his hat with a gloved hand. His voice was deep and his tones cultured. His teeth were white and even, and gleamed nearly as brightly as the diamond stickpin in his silk tie.

A murderer if ever she saw one, Madeleine thought. She swallowed hard, realizing how little she'd ever appreciated the yeoman's work her throat had done. "Good evenin', suh," she said, exaggerating her mint-julep tones.

"Ah, you're from Dixie," he said, giving her a killer

smile. "I should have known. Nowhere else could so fair a flower bloom."

A murderer and a liar. In the getup she'd concocted with Monroe's hard cash and "professional" advice, she looked so much like a strumpet she was afraid of catching some unspeakable disease from herself. She threw a glance at the arcade then, taking two deep breaths, looked back at the man and smiled. Batting her lashes, she cocked a hip and draped an arm over his shoulder. "You're too kind, suh."

"And you're too modest," he replied, wrapping his arm around her waist. Drawing her into an embrace, he breathed into her ear. "I'll bet you taste like honey all over. How much?"

Madeleine looked up at him. "Honey?"

"Yes, Sugar?"

"Aren't you amusin'?" Madeleine said, faking a giggle. "What I meant was, how much what?"

A shadow clouded the man's expression then quickly vanished. "Oh, I see. You're new at this. That's all right, Sugar. The fresher they are, the better I like them. And when they're unspoiled, I don't care what they cost."

Madeleine wracked her memory of Monroe's plan, but there was definitely no contingency in it for extreme nausea unless it was the reminder to keep the customer talking, find out as much about him as she could. That he could be The Red Rose Killer was bad enough; that he could try delivering that bloom in his coat, fail, and get away, worse. "The way you talk, suh," she said, stroking his cheek and thinking that now she knew what a snake felt like. "I'll just bet you're a grocer man or a butcher—"

The word was out before she knew it, and her nausea was back, stronger than before. "Why, I just don't know what's the matter with little ol' me. Anyone can plainly see that you're dressed too mighty fine for a market man." Wrapping her hands around his arm, she squeezed it. "I'll just bet you're somebody real important. I know! A doctor."

"No, but I'd like to examine you just the same."

Madeleine laughed the way she'd heard the other street-walkers laugh, without humor. She wet her rouged lips. "Let me see," she said, running her fingers up and down his shirtfront. "Are you one of those—what are they called?—oh yes, captains o' industry like that Mr. Rockefella?"

Clamping his hand over hers, he squeezed so hard she winced. "No, Sugar. But you'll like it when I play captain and you beg me not to make you walk the plank. Which way?"

Craning her neck, Madeleine shot a desperate backward glance at the arcade. A hulk of a man, six feet tall and built like a tugboat, stepped from inside it onto the sidewalk. He paused to light a cigarette, looked to his right then to his left. He winked at Madeleine.

"Thank God," she murmured, then turned back and pointed up the street. "Just a few blocks that way. As the man locked her arm in his and led her away, she looked back at the bruiser, who could only be Davis, the bodyguard Monroe had promised would never let her out of his sight. She hoped his sight was keen because there was a good chance she was on her way to some back alley, where she'd later be found with a blood red rose in her very cold hand.

Actually, there was a better than good chance, she thought, seeing the man she'd thought was Davis walk in the opposite direction. Her heart leaped to her suddenly precious throat. She looked down at her still warm hand, the hand The Man in Grey was now crushing in his.

From across Dearborn Street, for the last twenty minutes, Daniel had stood outside one of the better opium parlors on the Levee, watching the flaming redhead in front of the penny arcade. He'd noticed her even before he'd gone into the place to collect the latest hearsay from the trade—several aldermen and a judge. As always, he'd found them founts of gossip, just more philosophical about it than when he ran into them at Lizzie Allen's brothel farther up the street. But much to his disappointment, they'd been able to shed no light on the identity of The Red Rose Killer, even though they had declared as reasonable his theory that the murderer was someone who imagined himself doing a mercy, or perhaps meting out justice. What disappointed him further was that they hadn't a clue as to who the girl in front of the arcade was. They knew every girl working the street. Daniel had thought he did, too. But since neither he nor his sources had ever seen this one before, they agreed she must be new in town.

And if the way she was parading herself was any indication, Daniel now thought, new to the business. If she'd hung a sign advertising her rates around her neck, she'd have more allure. Not that her hips lacked the right amount of swish and sway. And the pose she intermittently struck against a lamppost, one knee slightly raised, her arm over her head and her breasts uplifted, was sufficiently enticing. But her movements spoke more of quick practice than of long experience. He'd like to see her again in about a year, he thought.

Then again, maybe not. The longer he watched her, the more he realized that her awkwardness resulted from more than inexperience. It came at least as much from her body's struggle to undo a lifetime of discipline, as though she were asking it to perform an undulating dance when it had been trained to march. When she propped her hands on her hips and thrust her pelvis forward, her back remained so ramrod straight she looked like a composite of two entirely different women. Of course, she wouldn't be the first cultivated woman to make her way and her fortune on the Levee. Usually, though, the ones who'd come with a finishing school diploma found fast employment in the best brothels, where they entertained in paneled libraries and gilded music rooms as well as in silk-and-satin bedrooms. If this one was as well-bred as he suspected, he asked himself, what was she doing pounding the pavement instead of pouring tea while dressed like a Turkish concubine at the request of an eccentric millionaire?

Suddenly, he knew. If every fallen woman came to look like her, no devil-stomping tent preacher would ever again be able to titillate a crowd right out of their last dollars with that delicious term "fleshpot." The woman was just too damned skinny for the average millionaire's taste. The rich, after all, were used to getting more than they paid for.

On an impulse, Daniel looked in his wallet, as thin as she. He hadn't much to spare, none really. But he was accustomed to letting tomorrow take care of itself. Tonight, he wanted to buy the woman a sumptuous meal. He wanted to sit back and enjoy watching her eat with abandon, watching her hunger disappear. That was because he knew what hunger felt like, how it robbed not just the body but the soul. For tonight, at least, maybe he could give her back a little bit of her soul.

But as he started toward her across Dearborn Street, he saw that for one man's taste she wasn't at all too thin. He winced as she made a pathetic attempt at flirtatiousness. The way she was stroking the man's face, he'd no doubt been more deftly handled by his dentist. Soon, he saw the man lead her away. Daniel felt sorry for her. She kept looking back as though expecting someone to save her. Before long, she'd give up that fantasy.

Sighing, Daniel slipped his wallet back into the breast pocket of his jacket. "We all give up a fantasy or two, sooner or later," he said. Sliding his hands into his pockets, he kicked an empty beer bottle and walked in the direction opposite hers.

"Say, we've gone a lot farther than a few blocks. You aren't lost, are you, Sugar?"

"I hope not," Madeleine replied on shaky breath. Here, Dearborn Street was dark and deserted except for herself and, possibly, a murderer.

The Man in Gray stopped and roughly turned her toward him. "Time to walk the plank, wench." He glanced behind him at a narrow passageway. "I know the alley behind these buildings well."

Despite the darkness, Madeleine saw his gleaming teeth and a grin that was the essence of evil. Her mind detached a bit, she noticed. All she could think was that, despite his lacking the eye patch Vernon Rawlston wore, he looked exactly like her image of a murderous pirate. With startlingly clear, cold reason, she realized she was very likely going to die.

As Black Beard dragged her toward the passageway, she glanced once more behind her. There was no sign of Davis and every indication that now was the time to launch a contingency plan of her own. She thanked God that Roger had earlier confirmed her belief that the only thing most women could truly depend on most men for was to let them down. Despite Monroe's assurances that she could well leave her safety in his hands, she had decided to strap an assurance of her own to her thigh. A small, potato paring knife wasn't much of a weapon, she supposed. But then, she didn't want to dice the killer, just peel him a little. Enough to disable him long enough for her to get away and summon the police. All she had to do was get at the knife.

"Ow!" Limping, Madeleine pulled up.

Wringing her wrist, the cutthroat halted. "What's the matter?"

"I think I've picked up a pebble in my slipper," she replied. She glanced behind her at the edge of the wooden sidewalk. "I'll just sit there and remove it. Then we can get along to that sweet little ol' alley of yours."

"Make it fast," he snarled, then let her go.

Madeleine perched on the edge of the sidewalk, her feet below her on the dirt and cinder pavement. She raised her skirts above her knees and, bending forward as though to remove her shoe, reached for the scabbard she had fashioned from a scarf. She felt for the knife's handle and, finding it, slowly slipped it upward from its sheath. Suddenly, she frowned. Even for a short knife, it had come free awfully quickly. She moved her fingers along the handle toward the blade. Now, she froze. There was no blade. The knife had been the cheapest she could find, so cheap the blade had somewhere, somehow slipped from the handle. Her mind was slipping, too, she realized, because she found herself thinking that she couldn't wait to find the street vendor who'd sold her the knife and demand her money back.

Suddenly, she heard cinders crunch and saw a pair of shoes come toe-to-toe with hers. Until now, she never would have guessed that murderers wore spats.

"Allow me, Sugar."

Abruptly, Madeleine slid the handle beneath the wooden slats of the walk, lowered her skirts, and sat up. With horrified fascination, she watched the return of the gentlemanly Man in Gray as he got down on one knee before her. Sliding one hand beneath her red petticoat, he felt his way down her calf as he lifted her heel with the other hand and removed her pump.

"Such sweet toes," he said softly. Then, he shook out the shoe. No pebble fell out. "You're playing games with me, Sugar," he said, jamming the pump back on her foot.

"But not the kind I like." Rising, he lifted Madeleine by the underside of her arms, set her on the sidewalk, then hoisted her over his shoulder. He started toward the passageway, a pirate with his plunder.

Madeleine saved her breath. Her only hope now was to scratch and claw. As she tore at his coat, kicking and groaning, she saw the sidewalk give way to the dirt floor of the passageway. What remained of her life, she realized, was better measured in yards than in years.

Then, in years again as she heard another man's voice. "Carry that baggage into the alley if you want to, but don't say I didn't warn you."

As her captor came to a halt, Madeleine arched her back and stared incredulously at the man whose serrated baritone and insufferably arrogant inflection sounded like Daniel McQuinn's. Fear for her life had obviously unhinged her mind. To conjure a rescuer was understandable. But why not a policemen or the U.S. Cavalry? Why McQuinn? For one thing, he certainly wasn't her idea of a hero. For another, his suddenly coming on the scene would be a coincidence so fantastic, it could only happen in a novel.

Unless it wasn't a coincidence. Unless, despite losing his job, he'd decided to stay on the Red Rose story, after all.

Madeleine studied the man on the sidewalk, rather his silhouette. In the thick, smoky darkness, she couldn't make out his features. But if it were broad daylight, she couldn't have said for certain that they belonged to McQuinn. All she'd ever clearly seen of his face was his profile, and that largely concealed by the angle of his hat.

A hat shaped very much like this man's hat, which he wore the way McQuinn wore his, cocked over his right eye. Moreover, the man was as tall as McQuinn, a good inch over six feet. Not many men were, nor as broad in the shoulders and as narrow in the hips. This man was, and standing there, he gave as good an impression as

McQuinn did of a coil about to spring. Just when she thought he would, he lowered his head, cupped his hands, lit a cigarette, and dropped the still-burning match to the ground.

McQuinn.

Grinning as much because his being here must mean that he hadn't abandoned the story as because she was going to live, Madeleine strained to hold sight of him as her abductor turned her away.

"I don't see what business it is of yours," he said to McQuinn.

"None at all. I just thought I'd do you a favor." Propping his cigarette between his lips and shoving his hands in his trousers pockets, McQuinn shrugged. "Of course, if you're not interested in knowing who she really is . . ."

Madeleine's grin imploded as her eyes grew wide. Disguised as she was, how could he possibly have recognized her as the woman he'd met outside Monroe's office? He could if he'd known well in advance about the stunt she and Monroe had planned. He must surely have friends at the *Clarion* who would alert him that Monroe intended to humiliate him by replacing him with, God forbid, a woman.

So now, McQuinn was going to expose her as a journalist. But why to the killer he'd been trailing for months? Why didn't he just sock him the way he'd socked Monroe, send for the police, claim credit for helping to capture a madman, and offer it to Monroe. Seeing an opportunity to once again trounce his competitors with an exclusive and a sell-out extra edition, Monroe would forget his grudge. McQuinn would get his job back, and after Monroe tossed her a bone in the form of ordering McQuinn to mention her name—Margaret Flynn's name, anyway— in his story on the capture, she'd be out on the street.

Suddenly, Madeleine realized why McQuinn wasn't moving to apprehend The Red Rose Killer. He wanted more than his job back. He wanted *all* of the credit for the capture. At the moment, the murderer had no idea that he was toting one reporter and looking at another who'd been looking for him for months. But once McQuinn informed him that the trollop on his shoulder was really one of those meddlesome women journalists who were always preaching reform and spoiling everybody's fun, the killer would drop her like the baggage McQuinn had said she was. Grateful, he'd go off with the man he thought a kindly fellow debaucher, who would call the police only after he'd gotten an exclusive interview some copyeditor would headline INSIDE THE MIND OF A FIEND and Monroe would splash over the *Clarion*'s front page. The only thing that wasn't completely clear to Madeleine was whose mind was more fiendish, McQuinn's or the killer's.

"If it's so damned important that I know who she is," the killer said, taking a step forward, "why don't you tell me?"

"Wait!" Madeleine clutched fistfuls of his coattails. "What I have to tell you is more than important, it's urgent. The man you're talking to is a reporter."

"What's so urgent about that?" the killer replied. "I already know he's a reporter."

"But . . . if you know he's a reporter, then . . ." Madeleine's arms hung limp. *He probably knows you're a fiend.* Maybe, when McQuinn had said he wanted to do the fiend a favor, he really meant it. She'd heard of reporters who would arrange to have their own grandmothers snatched to get a story on granny-napping. But that McQuinn had been protecting the identity of a monstrous killer to ensure front page copy for himself was unthinkable.

Then again, maybe it was quite thinkable. How was it that McQuinn, according to his own reports, often reached the scene of a crime even before a patrol wagon arrived? Of course, all city reporters had friends on the police force. Perhaps McQuinn had them among criminals, as well. Fiend friends. Or perhaps they were all just one, big happy family. This was, after all, Chicago. Armour and Swift dominated its stockyards but its tenderloin districts, like the Levee, couldn't have existed without the protection of Mayor Carter Harrison.

The question Madeleine now asked was whether McQuinn would go so far as to allow her to become the next Red Rose victim to maintain his hold on the story and win back his job. He had to know that if one of the "little girl reporters" were murdered in the course of a stunt, the public would first lick its chops then demand that the mayor, the police, and the other papers trawl the entire city for her slayer and bring him to justice.

On the other hand, McQuinn *could* simply let the murderer have his way with her. Then, when the public's rage reached fever pitch, he could bring in the killer and promptly march down State Street at the head of a parade in his honor.

For this last scenario to play out, however, the Man in Gray alias Black Beard alias The Red Rose Killer would have to cooperate. He would have to cart her off to the alley and do her in instead of toting her, as he was now, in the opposite direction, toward McQuinn. She propped her hands on his shoulder blades and pushed up as far as she could. "Excuse me. But what are you doing?"

Emerging from the passageway onto the sidewalk, the man nodded toward McQuinn. "I know who *he* is," he said. Then, flipping Madeleine off his shoulder, he looked down at her as he held her across his chest. "What I *don't* know, Sugar, is who *you* are. But if McQuinn says I should know, what he really means is I should change my plans."

With that, he lobbed her through the air into Daniel McQuinn's arms.

Six

Catching the little redheaded wastrel, Daniel found her lack of heft unsurprising. But that her scent lacked the candied tawdriness trailing most girls in her line of work intrigued him. From his observation, the more delicate a woman's fragrance, the more expensive it was and the less she could be had for any price. This young woman, he imagined, had wrested the air of dignity surrounding her from the last drops in a perfume bottle she'd brought from a gentile Southern home. She'd also carried pride and indomitability in her gaze. He could feel, if not clearly see, the remnants of both through the sooty darkness.

He'd been right about her. Somewhere in her past, she'd been a lady. A born lady. He was glad, now, that he'd come back for her, though suddenly, buying her a steak and listening to her tale of woe no longer seemed enough. Now that she was in his arms, he just might carry her away from here, forever away from men like—

"Percy, Percy, Percy," Daniel said, whistling around the cigarette in his mouth. "I'm surprised at you being taken in by this skinny piece of goods."

Her right arm over McQuinn's shoulder, Madeleine gaped at The Red Rose Killer. What kind of name was "Percy" for a monster? Even more to the point, if McQuinn was still so concerned about her diet, why was he trying to hog the credit for capturing The Red Rose Killer and steal a job off her plate?

"Perhaps I am a mite on the slender side, suh," she said to him, further expanding her vowels to accommodate her dudgeon. "But by doing me out of work you certainly aren't helpin' to put meat on my little ol' goods."

"I was *coming* to that." Daniel wondered whether girls like her ever thought about anything but food, even on the job.

Madeleine looked askance at him. "Meat or my goods?"

Whichever of the other hookers had pointed him out to her earlier tonight, she'd neglected to tell her that he came to the Levee for just one thing, information. And occasionally, whenever he ran across a novice like her, he'd buy her a meal then take her on a tour of cribs so filthy, not even the rats would go near them. He'd actually rescued a few of these slightly tarnished damsels in distress. And whether she liked it or not, he fully intended to save this one.

"Meat," he replied to her question. "My guess is tongue. Southern fried."

"Oh, *goody,* " Madeleine shot back. "I'm getting so tired of *ham.* "

Chuckling, Daniel looked at Percy. "Don't you just love the way Southern gals talk, Perce? I'll bet that's what hooked you, those long, honeyed vowels of hers. But no matter what she told you, her name isn't Sugar." Drawing on his cigarette, he looked askance at the tart in his arms. "Take this thing out of my mouth, will you, Sadie?"

"S——?" Madeleine was stunned. Just how long, she wondered, was McQuinn was going to keep up this act? And for what purpose? He could end her bid for his job right now, simply by telling Percy she was a reporter and asking her what her real name was, not that it mattered to him.

On the other hand, suppose McQuinn wasn't as self-serving as she'd imagined? What if despite his knowing Percy, he'd only discovered that the man was The Red Rose Killer when he'd seen him with her tonight? In that case, he might be concocting a scene to catch Percy off guard before taking him down and sharing the credit for his capture with her.

And that meant, she'd better play along.

Smiling, she slipped her V-ed fingers beneath his cigarette and took it from his lips. As she did, she accidentally touched them, and suddenly, she was helpless to understand how a man who was all rough edges and hard angles could possess a mouth that was so warm and fleshy between clearly defined but pliant lines. How he was holding her more securely captive with the feel of his lips than with all the strength in his arms.

Questioningly, she met his colorless but penetrating gaze and made a startling discovery. McQuinn held her not just in his thrall but in his destiny. If she could have, she'd have trembled. But for a moment that felt like eternity, nothing moved. Not the earth, not The Red Rose Killer, not McQuinn. And certainly not his gaze on her own lips. It felt like a kiss. She closed her eyes.

Daniel stood motionless, staring down at the woman who had taken more than his cigarette from him. With her touch, she'd taken away a layer of the veneer he wore so that no woman would ever again take a piece of his heart, his soul. Two had and both had vanished like the smoke curling between him and the fallen angel in his arms. That was why she'd get no more from him than veneer. And a decent meal. *After* he'd not only made her unattractive to Percy but also, to at least a few future clients whom Percy would warn to stay away from her. *Then,* he would forget he'd ever laid eyes on her.

"Drop the cigarette, Sadie," he said. "Remember, you're not long out of the sanitorium."

Eternity, Madeleine knew, had moved on without her. She opened her eyes. "Sanitorium?"

"Oh my. What's wrong with her?" Percy asked.

"She didn't get this wasted from rushing off to work without breakfast, Perce." Daniel shook his head. "Consumption."

"But I haven't heard her cough once," Percy protested.

Daniel heaved a sigh. "Lucky for you. You don't want to be around her when she hasn't had her morphine. Believe me, the coughing isn't the worst of it."

"You mean . . . she gets violent?"

What a yarn, McQuinn! Tuberculosis *and* drug addiction. Percy was bound to become distracted. "Sometimes even *with* the morphine," she said, helping McQuinn along. For good measure, she yanked a lock of hair at the nape of his neck.

"Ow!"

"Has she attacked you, McQuinn?" Percy's voice quivered with alarm.

"Don't worry. I know how to handle her." Daniel looked down at his little Camille. "Take a puff on my cigarette, Sadie."

Madeleine's jaw dropped. "Is that really necessary, McQuinn?"

"Yes, McQuinn," Percy said. "Can that be good for her lungs?"

"No!" Madeleine answered, puzzling over Percy's tender concern for her lungs when he'd been about to slit her throat.

"Oh but Sadie," Daniel insisted, "you know how tobacco keeps you from turning into a drooling lunatic."

"McQuinn," Madeleine said, hoping he could see the grin she was wearing. "You do have a way with words."

"And with drooling lunatics," he replied. "Take a puff."

Madeleine entwined her arms. "No. I don't like *your kind.*"

His kind? Apparently, she hadn't looked in the mirror lately. "All right, Sadie, you asked for it." Daniel carried her off the sidewalk, sat down with her, turned her over, and ignoring her kicking and screaming, raised his hand over her backside.

"McQuinn, you wouldn't dare!"

"No more than you'd pull my hair."

"I was doing it for you," she whispered. "I thought you'd like it."

Apparently, this damsel was a little more tarnished than he'd thought. She was already specializing. "Then, you should like this," he whispered back, raising his hand higher.

Madeleine quickly put the cigarette between her lips and took it away.

"Again, Sadie girl. For real, this time."

Madeleine clenched her teeth. "I hate you, McQuinn."

"Inhale!"

Madeleine took a deep draw and held it for a long moment.

"Sadie?" Leaning over, Daniel saw the cigarette lying beside the limp hand that had held it. "Exhale!"

Madeleine did and coughed so hard, she could have convinced *herself* she had consumption. She was still wracking when McQuinn stood her in the street. And reeling. Her skin, she imagined, was the color of pea soup.

"You see, Perce," Daniel said, slipping his arm around her waist, propping up her slumping body. "Gentle as a lamb."

Groaning and pressing her hand to her abdomen, Madeleine lifted her head. "Must you persist in bringing up food?"

"If I felt the way you do, Sadie," Daniel said in her ear, "I wouldn't be talking about bringing up food."

Her eyes bugging, Madeleine slapped her other hand over her mouth.

Percy came to Daniel's side. "What else ought I to know about this doxy, McQuinn?"

"What *else?*" Daniel puffed out his cheeks. If TB and a morphine habit weren't enough to permanently discourage Percy's ardor and destroy Sadie's surprisingly promising career on the Levee, what was?

A slow grin broke the set of Daniel's concentration. "Of course," he said. "I mean, the alley, of course, was the worst place you could have taken her."

"The alley?" Percy glanced over his shoulder at the passageway. "But as you know, McQuinn, the alley happens to be one of my favorite spots to sport."

"And when Sadie spotted you," Daniel replied, taking Madeleine's hand from her mouth and waving it flirtatiously, "she favored you to be included in tonight's sport. Percy, my friend, you were about to be become pickings for one of the best little panel thieves on the Levee."

Percy gasped.

Raising her head, Madeleine gaped. She had no idea what a panel thief was.

"I simply can't believe it," Percy said.

"That makes two of us," Madeleine replied, straightening her knees and trying to peel McQuinn's hand off her waist. She wanted him to know that she was all right now and was ready to duck away from his punch the second he caught Percy sufficiently unawares.

She must really be in bad shape, Daniel thought, the way she was trying to pull his arm more tightly around her. Slipping his left arm through hers and around her, he whispered, "Don't worry, I've got you." Then, for Percy's benefit, he said, "That's right, Sadie. It takes two of you. You and your brother."

"Not her *brother.*" Bringing his hand to his mouth, Percy covered yet another gasp.

"Why not?" Madeleine said. McQuinn had added another arm to his hold of her—he might as well add another chapter to this ridiculous story. If he'd just let her go, she'd be glad to go at Percy.

"Why not, indeed, Perce," McQuinn said. "After all, blood is thicker than water and all that. Would you rather Sadie split the profits with a perfect stranger who might take advantage of her?"

"Well, no . . . I mean . . . What I don't understand, McQuinn," Percy said, pinching his lower lip philosophically, "is if she's a panel thief, why didn't she take me to a room with a panel for her brother to hide behind so that he could pop out and rob me?"

In the dark, Daniel and Madeleine exchanged blank looks.

"It's being redecorated," Madeleine said, still marveling at the sheer genius of panel thieving. She'd hate to be a real Sadie, though, with McQuinn for a partner. A girl could exhaust herself before he decided it was time *he* went into action.

"That's right, redecorated," Daniel echoed, marveling at Sadie's sheer genius. "In the meantime, she's been bringing her marks up here, where it's totally dark and deserted."

Leaning forward, Madeleine craned her neck and her gaze up at McQuinn. "My marks?"

"Not to worry, Sadie. I'm sure they've all been high," Daniel replied. "At least until your customers discovered that they'd been had instead of the other way around."

"Thank you." Madeleine turned back around. "I think."

"Well, I don't know what to think, McQuinn." Slapping his hand over his heart, Percy paced in front of Madeleine and Daniel. Coming to a halt, he looked at them and said. "All I know is that I feel quite dashed."

"That's because you very nearly were, Perce." Clamp-

ing his right hand around the back of Madeleine's neck
and raising her left arm, Daniel put Sadie on display.
"You might not think it to look at her, but her brother's
a real bruiser. He followed you from the arcade, and if I
hadn't come along when I did, you'd be lying in that alley
right now with a knot the size of a baseball on the top of
your head."

To which Percy's hand flew, crushing the crown of his
bowler.

"When you came to, Perce," Daniel said, throwing his
entire arm around Sadie's neck and pulling her to him,
"you'd have been lucky if this little trollop had left you
the pockets her brother had picked right down to the
lint."

"Junior always was—" Tugging on the arm McQuinn
held around her neck, Madeleine grunted. He was worse
than flypaper. "A hard worker."

"McQuinn," Percy began, coming to his full height,
smoothing his tie, and thrusting forth his hand. "You've
saved my wallet, perhaps even my life. How can I ever
thank you?"

Releasing Madeleine, Daniel clasped Percy's hand.
"You *know* how."

Hearing a new tone in McQuinn's voice, a darkly con-
spiratorial one, Madeleine's heart lurched with terrifying
suspicions. Perhaps McQuinn was totally self-serving after
all, monstrously so. Perhaps he and The Red Rose Killer
did have an agreement whereby one beast gave another
the exclusive right to report his heinous crimes in exchange for the freedom to go on committing those
crimes. Madeleine was filled with disgust, not least of all
for herself. She'd once revered Daniel McQuinn.

"I'll be running along now, McQuinn," Percy said.
"Miss Sadie." Tipping his crushed bowler to her, he
walked back up Dearborn Street toward the lights of the
Levee, a hunter in search of fresh prey.

Madeleine darted after him.

"Whoa," Daniel said, clasping the inside of her arm. "I'm not finished with you yet." He had a dinner to buy her and a rousing sermon to deliver on the evils of . . . evil.

"Well, I'm certainly through with you," Madeleine cried, pulling and tugging to get free. "What kind of a man lets a monster get away from him?"

"A real smart man?" Latching on to both her wrists, Daniel turned her toward him. "Listen, if you're referring to Percy—"

"*If* I'm referring—"

"All right. Percy. Isn't it enough that I rescued you from the man? Do I have to challenge him to a duel, too? After all, he is a pal."

Dumbstruck, Madeleine ceased struggling. "*A pal?*"

Letting go of her wrists, Daniel shoved his hands in his pockets. "Well, only in the sense that he makes for good copy and always lets me know when and where he's going to strike."

Madeleine's heart sank. "You admit it, then. You've been protecting him for the sake of your career."

"I wouldn't call it protection. Let's just say he has a secret and I'm keeping it."

Feeling faint, Madeleine lowered herself to the sidewalk. Her father and Roger and all their cronies together couldn't rival McQuinn for lack of conscience and simple, decent humanity.

"Dear God," she said, and letting out a single, mournful sob, partly for herself in her disillusionment but and mostly for mankind, she hunched over her knees.

Hearing her cry, Daniel sat down beside her and drew her into a one-armed embrace. "Listen, I know you've been through a lot. And Percy *is* odd, but—"

"*Odd?*" Madeleine burst into tears.

"All right, then. *Very* odd."

Madeleine wailed.

Taking her by the shoulders and turning her toward him, Daniel gave her a shake. "Stop that!" To his surprise, she did. Heaving a relieved sigh, he said, "What I've been trying to tell you is that if you stay in this business, you'll run into characters a whole lot worse than Percy."

Sniffing, Madeleine pushed on McQuinn's chest. "And you just can't wait for me to get out of the business, can you? Well, I have a news item for you, McQuinn. I'm not quitting. In fact, I'm going to expose you."

"Oh-h-h no you're not!" Daniel drew her so close, he could feel her sweet breath on his mouth, teasing him with the warm succulence it gathered from her lips. His heart began beating a stern reminder that the only reason he was here was to keep other men from doing the very things he wanted to do to her now. He closed his eyes and swallowed.

"As of this moment, Sadie, you're out of the exposure business."

The nearness of McQuinn's lips overpowered Madeleine with a heat to rival the swelter that rose from the sun-beaten Louisville shore of the Ohio in August. And God help her, but she wanted him to kiss her, this man who was threatening her in every way a man could threaten a woman. Closing her eyes, she inhaled his dangerous, smoky scent.

"And just how far will you go to see to it that I stay out?"

Just how far *would* he go? Daniel asked himself as he grazed his mouth over one corner of hers and across her cheek. What would he do to keep her skin—and her soul—this unblemished? He could take her home with him, take her in. Take her in his arms and— Break two of the few rules he lived by: Never take the only thing a woman thinks she has left to give. Never let a woman take a piece of your heart.

Opening his eyes, he held her away from him. "Only as far as a little place I know about two blocks from here, where we can get a hot meal." Rising, he held his hand out to her.

Rejecting the offer of his hand, Madeleine pushed off the walk. "Even if I still had an appetite after what you just told me, do you really think I'd share a meal with you? Percy's accomplice?" Making a sound of revulsion, she turned her back on him and marched off, not knowing where she was headed and not caring as long as it was away from McQuinn.

Daniel stood stunned. *"Accomplice?"* he muttered. "Wait a minute!" Catching up to Madeleine, he fell into step beside her. "I know I told you I went along with Percy on his little forays, but I'd hardly call that criminal!"

Madeleine walked faster. "If you don't call aiding and abetting The Red Rose Killer criminal, then may God have mercy on your—"

With one swipe, Daniel grabbed her wrist and yanked her toward him. "Did I or did I not just hear you mention Percy Teasdale and The Red Rose Killer in the same breath?"

Wresting her freedom, Madeleine stumbled backward. "You know you did," she snarled. "Because you know he is!"

Starting with a small chuckle, Daniel crescendoed to loud guffawing.

Folding her arms, Madeleine impatiently tapped her foot. "What, may I ask, did I say that so amuses you?"

After the moment it took him to ease the laughter that had bent him in two, Daniel peered up at her. "What half-wit gave you the idea that Percy is The Red Rose Killer?"

Madeleine pointed a shoulder down at him. "You did."

Daniel shot up. "Me?"

"Yes, you. He fits the profile you drew of the murderer

in your stories. Kindly, gentlemanly. His victims are usually new, inexperienced prostitutes." Propping her hands on her waist, Madeleine lifted her chin. "He picked *me*, didn't he?"

"That doesn't make him the killer, luckily for you."

"You can't fool me, McQuinn. I saw him buy a flower from an old woman and slip it inside his coat just before he approached me."

Behind his hand, Daniel suppressed a chortle. "Obviously, no one told you that, by night, Percy is known to every prostitute on the Levee as Captain Carnation."

"Car—? Madeleine lowered her arms to her sides. "You mean the flower he bought from that old woman wasn't a rose?"

"Not even by another name."

Biting her thumbnail, Madeleine turned a circle. "Why *Captain* Carnation?"

Clearing his throat, Daniel stepped closer. "Well, you see, my dear whatever your name is, Percy likes to play pirate. And for your information, he's never killed anything but a fifth of rum. As for what he does with the carnation, I'm told he likes the girls to wear it between their—"

"Stop!"

"Toes," Daniel, said. "Something to do with a woman he met somewhere in the Caribbean, I think."

Lowering her head, Madeleine pressed the tip of her middle finger to the crease between her brows. "You *said* you go along with him on his forays, as you so quaintly put it."

"Yes, forays. As in raids on gambling halls, brothels, opium parlors. The usual dens of iniquity."

"Well, I guess that eliminates his being on the police force." Abruptly, she looked up at Daniel. "Don't tell me he's a preacher?"

"Better than that," Daniel replied. "He's the President

of the Citizens' Committee to Suppress Vice and Protect Public Morals. The mayor appointed him."

"The *mayor?*" Madeleine pressed her palm to her forehead. "The same mayor who's on the Christmas list of every madam in the city?"

"That's some tie collection he has, believe you me."

"Don't change the subject."

"I couldn't be more on the subject." Daniel pushed back the brim of his hat. "Listen. All the big vice peddlers in town naturally want Harrison to stay in office. They know that to keep him in, they have to help him occasionally toss a few bones to the reformers."

"That's where Percy Teasdale comes in."

"Don't forget yours truly." Taking her arm, Daniel started for the opposite side of the street. "You see, Percy tips me off to the times and locations of his raids. I get a front-page exclusive, which makes *me* happy. Monroe sells more papers, which makes *him* happy. In return for the exclusive, I make Percy look like an avenging angel, which makes the reformers happy. The mayor stays in office, which makes him happy. And the vice merchants stay in business, which makes *them* happy."

"Oh, McQuinn," Madeleine said, throwing her arms around his neck with elation. He wasn't The Rose Killer's accomplice, after all. She could set Daniel McQuinn, white knight reporter, back on his steed, and enjoy jousting for his job all the more for it. "You don't know how happy that makes *me.*"

With her soft, bare arms clinging to him, her suggestive curves pressed against him, and her mouth so delectable, beckoning his, Daniel didn't know what to do with his hands. Actually, he knew what to do with them, but also that he'd be a fool to let them begin a journey his own code wouldn't let them finish. He was supposed to be discouraging her from this sort of behavior with men she'd just met. Reaching to the back of his neck, he took her arms from around it. "I admire you enthusiasm for your work, but—"

"Wait, McQuinn." Suddenly, Madeleine wondered if she didn't owe him gratitude. With his story about consumptive, drug-addicted, dangerous "Sadie," which he knew Percy would spread throughout the Levee, he'd thwarted her plan to take his story and his place on the *Clarion*. But he could have eliminated all future plans she and Monroe might devise simply by leaving her to Percy's plundering. That experience, he could be certain, would cause her to reevaluate her choice of profession, assuming she recovered from it at all. Many a newsman would have done so. As a lot, reporters were an unchivalrous, often outright woman-hating bunch.

Reaching through the darkness, she put her fingertips to his rough, dear cheek. "Thank you, McQuinn. You saved me from having to walk the captain's plank. I only wish I could say the same of Mr. Monroe."

When Daniel felt her touch find that soft, damnable spot in the region of his heart, his breath caught. And then he choked on it. "Mr. Monroe?" He'd never liked the sound of that name, but if "Sadie's" Monroe turned out to be *his* Monroe, he was going to hate it. "*Which* Mr. Monroe?"

Madeleine tsked. "Archibald, of course. Who else?"

Grabbing her by the shoulders, Daniel drew her close. "Say 'brother.' "

Madeleine gave an incredulous laugh. Apparently, McQuinn was both chivalrous *and* crazy, though why she should find that so astonishing eluded her. "Say 'sister' the way you did the other day and maybe I will."

Sweet Jesus. Daniel's shoulders sagged as he released her. His mouth went dry and his stomach sickened. He was having his worst morning-after in the dark of night. "Sadie" was the young woman he'd seen in Monroe's office. She wasn't beautiful, he recalled, but bright, with dark, penetrating eyes that had haunted him ever since. Mysterious eyes. Hungry eyes. But why hadn't she starved first? Why did she have to resort to lying down in back alleys with men like Percy?

Suddenly, the thought of Archibald Monroe slithered through Daniel's mind. Why couldn't the snake have seen she'd come to the end of the line? He could have found something for a smart, quick-thinking girl like her to do. Filing in the morgue, maybe, or even fact-checking. "I want you to know that I blame Monroe for what almost happened to you tonight."

Madeleine snorted a breath. "You can just bet I do, too. He broke his promise to me!"

The conniving bastard. He'd promised her a job he probably never intended to give her. Then he recalled that Monroe never promised something for nothing. Suddenly, he grew sicker, ill with the urge to smash Monroe's face.

"Son-of-a—" *Thwack.*

Madeleine started. "McQuinn, did you just punch your fist into your other hand?"

"I only wish that hand had been Monroe's nose."

Madeleine cupped her hand over his, the one that was still fisted. "Don't think I don't appreciate your chivalry, but haven't you learned your lesson yet? That temper of yours sealed your fate with Monroe."

"And you sealed yours with him, as well." He gazed up and around the atmosphere of grime and degradation.

Madeleine, too, looked around her. Some fate she'd chosen for herself, she thought. Living in shadows, never certain what unseen danger lay in wait. Or untold story that needed telling. "I did, that day in Monroe's office. But believe me, there's no going back for me now."

Daniel gave his head a violent shake. Had he heard right? "You mean that you and he— In his *office?*"

Madeleine rolled her eyes. "Of course, in his office. Where else? I was standing in front of his desk and—"

"You *stood?*"

Madeleine wondered if she'd broken some regional protocol of the profession. Perhaps one didn't stand when negotiating with the managing editor of a Chicago paper, though she thought it highly improbable that McQuinn had the vaguest acquaintance with etiquette of any kind. Nevertheless, she replied, "Not the entire time I was with him. At first, I was seated."

"At *first?*" Daniel propped his fists on his waist. "How long were you with him?"

"Several hours, I suppose." As dangerous a stunt as she'd proposed and Monroe had agreed to required meticulous planning. Unfortunately, Monroe hadn't been as meticulous in his choice of bodyguard for her. "But what difference does it make how long I was with him?"

Madeleine no sooner asked the question than she realized McQuinn hadn't heard it. In the dim light that was just now filtering through a thinning of the clouds, she saw he'd withdrawn into himself and a silence so ominous, she was loath to breach it. She resolved to watch, warily, as in a world of his own not reached by the growing light, he repeatedly slammed his fist into his palm as he turned a slow circle.

Unaware of the light, seeing only the dark scene playing in his mind, Daniel heard his steps grind cinders as he felt guilt grind his soul. An old guilt. *I shouldn't have stopped when I did. I should have killed him,* he told himself. He should kill his father, he thought, the man whom he now saw staggering from the bedroom where for hours, sometimes, he imprisoned Daniel's mother. He was sweating and red-faced, and ugly. Always so damned ugly. Like the mark of his big, rough hand on his wife's face and body.

"I'll kill you yet, you bastard, so help me—"

"McQuinn!" Frightened for him, frightened because he looked like a man who'd landed himself in Hell, as Rawlston had warned he would, Madeleine grabbed his upper arms and squeezed as hard as she could. "Look at me, McQuinn. Wherever you are or think you are, come back!"

As Daniel slowly turned his gaze toward the woman distantly calling him, a great orange moon broke through the clouds and shined down a harvest of pale amber light. Beneath it, her skin shimmered; her mouth was soft and sweet, like a just-ripe peach. And her eyes, sparkling and warm and compelling. She was willing him back from that familiar place inside him where there was no heat or light and yet he burned to kill the monster he saw there. She was Heaven and she'd brought him back from Hell.

And Daniel knew that despite herself, she was no harlot yet. She still had her power, not the power to seduce a man but to induce him, not to lead him astray but to lead him home. That was the most seductive of all the feminine powers. And the one he fought at all costs. He wasn't ready to go home, to make peace with himself and with those who deserved the retribution he'd been storing for them.

He took a few steps from her. "The moon's done you a favor. It's given you a good look at me."

"Yes, it has," she replied, walking to him. Raising her hand to his cheek, she grazed her fingertips down one side of his face, feeling the hardness of his cheekbone and the softness of the corner of his mouth and, in between, a patchwork of dark bristle and smooth skin. "It showed a man at war with himself, a man who's yet to decide who and what he really is."

Lowering his eyes, Daniel slowly turned away. For a man who didn't yet know who he was, he certainly knew who she was. A woman who read him like a book she herself had authored. A woman who had the power to make a story of his life. The kind of woman he'd religiously avoided. And for the first time, he felt he was about to sin.

He whipped his gaze over his shoulder. "Sister, say 'brother.' "

Madeleine listened to her heart's drummed warning. Then she ignored it. "Brothuh."

Daniel lunged to his side and pulled her opposite him. Cupping her chin in the V of his hand, he lifted her mouth to his. "Whatever you call me from now on, it won't be 'brother.' " Crushing her to him, he brought his mouth down hard on hers.

Madeleine sank into him. His kiss was strong, relentless, too feral to be pleasant, too good not to please. But she wasn't pleased because she wanted more. Suddenly, she became aware of another hunger, one she'd always suspected she had but never dreamed any man outside the pages of a novel could provoke. She wrapped her arms around his neck and kissed him back as hard as she could, though not nearly as hard as he deserved. Then, when he circled both arms around her waist and lifted her up to him, she did something she never could have done with Roger, something that came with McQuinn's kiss as naturally as heat came with fire. Parting her lips, she tasted his own with her tongue. They were hot and succulent and smoky. If they'd been a barbecue, she could have written a whole column on them. But no society editor would print it.

Feeling her tongue's shy exploration, Daniel lightened his kiss. He could almost swear she was a complete innocent. In some ways, so was he. Innocent not of passion, but of love. Certainly guilty of living for himself alone. So maybe, for just a moment, under a moon that brought the tides of a man's life to the shores of his soul, he could pretend she'd never before kissed a man the way she was kissing him now. He could pretend that he loved her.

Maybe he could even pretend that the woman in his arms was She. He'd tried before, with others, and failed every time. He'd tried because he'd needed to even the score with her, to humiliate her as she'd humiliated him when she'd slapped him and branded him her inferior. For ten years, he'd needed to make her love him as much as he still loved her. And when she did, he'd leave her the way she'd left him. Empty. Unable to have her, unable to love anyone else.

Daniel parted his lips on hers. "For tonight," he whispered, "you *are* She." Without testing or probing or coaxing, he plunged his tongue inside her mouth. But it was he who was plundered, by her sweetness, her moans, her going limp in his arms. Ending his kiss, he looked down at her. Her eyes were closed and on her lips was the kind of smile he usually didn't see until much later in the proceedings.

Madeleine felt as though she were floating, above the moon, through time. This, she knew, was what a kiss was meant to do, vanquish time and space, and considering what surrounded her, conquer Hell itself. If McQuinn was the right man, she'd gladly remain in Hell with him because without him she'd be condemned to a place she considered far worse. Limbo.

But he wasn't the right man. He wasn't anything like the presence that had guided her through these last ten years, the living memory of the proud, brave boy she'd humiliated with the flat of her hand. A boy who was now, somewhere, a man. So why hadn't she searched for that man, asked him for the forgiveness she needed? Because she was afraid that if she found him, the reality of him could never match her idealization of him. She wasn't ready to give that up, not yet. She needed its sustenance. But she needed to be kissed, too. And McQuinn had fulfilled that need with a vengeance, the only vengeance she'd never begrudge him.

"Sadie?" Gently setting her down, Daniel patted her cheek. She smiled wider. He frowned. He found it difficult to imagine that after she'd been with Monroe for hours, a simple French kiss had turned her into a life-sized rag doll. "Ah well, that's the trouble with athletic types. No gift for subtle persuasion."

Madeleine popped open her eyes. Not only was McQuinn not the right man, but half the time he didn't even make sense. *"What* are you talking about?"

He grinned, admittedly pleased that he'd introduced her to *something,* if only the knowledge that her tongue was a versatile entity capable of doing more than savoring roast. "Fast-ballers, like Monroe," he replied. "I'll bet he never put a smile on your face like the one I saw just now."

Madeleine took a step back. What unmitigated conceit the man had, to compare his kiss, pleasant interlude that it was, to Monroe's fulfilling the dream of a lifetime. "You're right, McQuinn, I didn't smile," she said, enfolding her arms. "I grinned the biggest grin of my entire life."

"Ho-ly Moses!" The woman has no shame, Daniel thought, clamping a hand on either side of his head, flattening the brim of his hat. "Tell me you didn't let Monroe catch you grinning like a ninny."

Madeleine brought the pommel of her fist to her chin. "I see your point. Not good business practice to act as though he was doing me a favor, even though I was terribly grateful at the time."

Speechless, Daniel drew his hands down his face, pulling down his lower eyelids and fixing Madeleine with the nonplussed stare of a basset hound.

"You think *that's* bad," she said, slapping her forehead. "I just realized that I was so excited, I forgot to ask him how much he was going to pay me."

Lurching, Daniel opened his mouth to speak but only managed a croak. He thumped his chest.

"Don't gawk at me as though I were a carnival freak," Madeleine said, feeling like a complete rube for not bothering to ask how much she could expect for doing the stunt successfully and, then, as a staff reporter. "You have to understand that I had no experience and was so desperate for work, that I suppose I thought I shouldn't make an issue of money."

Gazing up and clapping his hands to his sides, Daniel shuffled a circle he broke when he looked over his shoulder at the biggest babe-in-the-woods he'd ever come across. "Listen, Babe, you're just not cut out for this business and I can't let you go on trying to make it. I'd spend my days wandering alleys like the one you almost ended up in tonight, expecting to find the sanitation department collecting you with the garbage—though as often as it comes around, I might not be able to tell you from the garbage."

Madeleine felt chills on chills. In his inimitable way, McQuinn had graphically depicted the gruesome risk she was taking. But the picture she couldn't get out of her mind was of him, searching Hell's back alleys for her, afraid of finding her. Perhaps, even afraid of losing her, of losing himself.

"Why should you care what happens to me?"

Looking at her now, Daniel felt as though he were looking in a mirror that reflected not his image but his soul. "I don't know," he said, curiously touching her cheek. "I only know I can't let you get hurt. I can't take a chance that the next time you catch some flower-lover's eye, he won't be carrying a red rose instead of a carnation."

"But *I* can," Madeleine said, curiously feeling his touch compel her to defy him for his own good as well as her own. "And I hope he is."

"Carrying a red rose? Wait a minute here." Holding

both palms before her, he closed his eyes, then after a moment, he looked narrowly askance at her. "You *want* the killer to find you?"

Madeleine rubbed the back of her neck, her gaze matching his for uncertainty. "Why do you ask me that when you knew all along that I came here specifically to—" With a sharp gasp, she abruptly turned away and, wide-eyed, gazed at her hands to confirm that they were trembling as violently as she suspected they were. Tucking them into her armpits, she glanced at Daniel. "McQuinn, if this is your idea of a joke—"

"I'd be laughing."

Madeleine lunged at him, grasping his lapels. "Laugh! Then tell me you knew all along that Monroe hired me to pose as a prostitute to catch The Red Rose Killer. Tell me you didn't think I really was . . . that he and I—"

"Of course, I did!" Daniel stepped back. From her red wig to the five-and-dime baubles dangling from her ears, to the swell of her breasts above the low, square bodice of her cheap saloon hostess's dress, he scalded her with his gaze. "I took you for exactly what you look like, a—"

Madeleine's hand stung from the blow it struck his cheek. "You just took," she said, then with back of the same hand that had cut a path across his face, wiped all trace of his kiss from her mouth. "Now it's my turn. I'm taking your story, the Red Rose murder story. I'll wear a different disguise so Percy won't recognize me, find the killer, and claim the job Monroe promised me. *Your* job."

Daniel glinted at her, his face smarting and his pride blistering. "You really do want to make me laugh, don't you?"

"No, I'm going to make you regret every wrong conclusion you jumped to tonight." Shoving him out of her path, Madeleine started up the street.

"There was nothing wrong with my conclusions, Babe," Daniel called. "Monroe's a bastard but he's not a stupid bastard. It never occurred to me he would hire a woman to pull a stunt that could get her murdered. He wasn't risking just your life tonight, he was risking the *Clarion*."

"That's his prerogative!"

"Is it also his prerogative to break his promises?" When she halted with her back to him, Daniel walked toward her, stopping at arm's length. "Not that I believe Monroe ever intended to hire you in my place. He doesn't think a woman's place is in the city room. But for the sake of argument, let's say he did make that promise. What makes you so sure he'll keep it? After all, you said yourself he's already broken his word to you once."

Madeleine half turned. "I'm sure it wasn't his fault that Davis didn't follow me from the arcade as he was supposed to."

"Davis? Not *Howard* Davis? The only thing that so-called sports reporter ever follows is the scent of a dice game." Daniel shoved his hands in his pockets. "Face it, Babe. You gambled with your life tonight, and for what? The chance to see your story on the front page of a newspaper?"

Madeleine faced him. "Not *my* story," she said softly. "*The* story. As Vernon Rawlston said, nobody's bigger than the news. Not you, not I. In the end, the only thing that matters is the story, and the only thing that matters about the Red Rose story is that it ends." She laughed. "But I'm still going to love seeing my words in place of yours on the front page of the *Clarion*."

Daniel snorted. "And whose words would those be?"

"Flynn's." Madeleine squared her shoulders. "Maggie Flynn's."

"Well, *Babe* . . ." Daniel paused, lit a cigarette, and cast the still-burning match at her feet. "They'll have to be damn good words to take the place of mine."

Madeleine glanced down at the now smoldering match

then up at Daniel. "Read 'em and weep," she said, then walked away.

Daniel watched her make her way back toward the lights of Dearborn Street. When he lost sight of her, he at last raised his fingertips to the cheek she'd struck and felt the moist gash he'd guessed she'd made with a ring turned around on her thin finger. He stared at the blood smear on his fingertips then looked up, a whisper escaping his lips.

"Madeleine!"

Seven

Thankful for the moon's disappearance behind a new veil of clouds, Madeleine climbed the back stairs of the Halsted Street row house that provided her with shelter if not comfort. All she had to do now was remember exactly which areas on which treads produced creaks and groans, and she just might make it to her flat without alerting her landlady.

Of all the accommodations she'd looked at when she arrived in Chicago, Madeleine had chosen the tiny kitchenette-bedroom apartment parceled from an already cramped tenement flat because it afforded her the luxury of an indoor bath—shared—and the necessity of an outside entrance. At any cost, an extra two dollars a month to be exact, she knew she had to avoid familiarity with her neighbors. Neighbors asked questions; so did detectives, and she was ever on guard against inadvertently divulging information that might lead to her father's agents to her.

That morning, a notice in the *Clarion*'s classifieds chinked her armor and chilled her marrow. She tried telling herself that her father couldn't be certain she was in Chicago. That the advertisement was only one of many placed in cities around the country. Nevertheless, it haunted her. She recalled it now, word for cold word:

*Madeleine. Return to Louisville. All is forgiven. Roger still
willing.*

She had no doubt that Roger was. He'd loved her since
they'd danced at her debutante ball. But he was politically
ambitious and certainly not unaware that a marriage to
Matthew Faurest's daughter was a fast rail to a career it
otherwise might take him years to build.

As for her father, how like him it was to issue a command rather make a plea for her to return, not home,
but to Louisville. He had no concept of home, only of his
jurisdiction. Moreover, all was not forgiven because she
could never excuse the arrogance through which he saw
his wife and daughter as mere appendages of himself, the
arrogance which assured her of a forgiveness she didn't
seek, and never would. Neither would she forgive him for
the way he'd signed the notice. If only he'd written, "Your
Worried Father," or even just "Father," she might have
felt a twinge of remorse for the anxiety she would like to
believe she had caused him when she disappeared. Instead, he'd chosen to sign with his initials and the title he
used as a license to intimidate: "M.S.F., Judge." She'd feel
sorry for him if it weren't for the memory of the tears in
Caroline's eyes as she stood with her hand stuck in a marble urn and her life entombed by her husband's ambition
and corruption.

A fate she'd been fortunate to escape, she thought, fingering her mother's ring and feeling the sharp edges of
empty prongs. Several stones were already missing when
she received the ring, which had made her cherish it all
the more. She believed they represented Margaret
Faurest's stolen years, stolen dreams, which she, her
daughter, was somehow to live out and fulfill. That was
one of two reasons why she had dared to wear the ring
and take the name "Margaret Flynn," though both might
provide clues to her true identity. The other was that, liv-

ing alone in a city that was as dangerous as it was sprawling, she needed to feel the nearness—and often had—of a woman she barely remembered except for the feeling of being dearly loved and protected whenever lavender scented the air.

Still, as she reached the second-story landing outside her door and realized that, at this very moment, Percy Teasdale might have been forcing her to do God knew what with a carnation between her toes, she had a hard time believing her mother had sent Daniel McQuinn, the lowlife, to her rescue. He'd saved her from Percy's wenching only to call her a whore.

Or would have if she hadn't smacked the crude, unspoken word off his tongue. But oh, that tongue. Why couldn't she stop thinking about the taste of it, the way it whetted her appetite for deeper pleasures? She cringed, realizing the kiss had meant nothing to him. He'd arrogantly thought he had the right to take what he'd unforgivably assumed other men paid for. But if that were true, why had he stopped at a kiss?

Eyes closed, leaning against the wall beside her door, she could feel McQuinn's arms holding her aloft long after Percy had discarded her like so much refuse. He was hugging her to him like a man who had stood in the cold a very long time and needed her warmth. And as they stood beneath a truthful moon, he made her feel like fire to his ice-bound heart, a flame to his darkened path, a guide from his personal hell. Whatever he'd taken with his kiss, he'd given back as much and more, awakening her to her feminine powers. Sacred powers she knew she possessed but had exercised only in a dream world with an ageless boy whose name she still couldn't recall.

Only now did she fully understand why she had slapped him. He'd broken that ideal lover's spell over her, bringing her out of fantasy to live as a real woman as Roger never could have done. That had been a dangerous thing for him to do, call forth a woman only to reveal he'd all along thought her a purchasable commodity. If she could have struck him with lightning instead of her hand, she would have.

Coming away from the wall, Madeleine looked at the hand that, ten years ago, had slapped a boy who had been partly a man and, tonight, a man who was partly a devil. If she could have remembered the former's name, she'd have invoked it against McQuinn in her defense.

The way she intended to invoke every saint's name she could recall against Monroe in the morning for what his phantom bodyguard had put her through tonight. Taking her key from the bodice of her dress, she let herself into her room, walked to her shabby dresser, and turned up the gaslight on the wall beside the tarnished mirror. Angry but not knowing whether more so with Monroe, McQuinn, or herself for having trusted the one and kissed the other, she plunked her key atop the dresser. Atop it, she threw down the cheap earrings she pulled from her lobes. Reaching over her head and working her fingers beneath the red wig, she looked in the mirror.

Her scream was short and piercing. So piercing, it roused the stout figure sitting in the chair on the wall opposite the mirror.

"So, you come home. I was ready to send for police."

Madeleine braced herself against the mirror while she caught her breath and talked herself out of strangling her landlady. "Mrs. Panazapoulos, I assure you the police won't be necessary. I expect to be paid soon and then you'll get all the back rent I owe you."

The widowed tenement owner, her glasses atop her gray head, looked wide-eyed and hurt. "Miss Flynn, you wrong me. I not say I call police because of rent." As she stood, the newspaper that had lain in the wide gully of skirt between her knees slipped to the floor without her notice. Clasping her hands to the bosom lying on her belly, she took a step toward Madeleine. "I was afraid something bad happening to you. So late and you not return."

Madeleine walked away from the light and behind the near-sighted woman. She didn't want to have to answer questions about her appearance when she had a few important ones of her own. Such as when Mrs. Panazapoulos, who had evicted her own son and his wife after he'd lost his job and missed a few rent payments, had started taking a personal interest in her.

"It's most kind of you to worry about me, but I promise not to let anything bad happen to me until I've settled my account." Stooping to pick up the paper and seeing that morning's classified page, a section torn away, Madeleine suspected the reason for her landlady's sudden, overwhelming concern. "Although, I've been thinking that this place really is beyond my means. Once I've paid you my back rent, perhaps I ought to find a more affordable room elsewhere."

"No! You no leave!" As though she'd realized she'd protested too much, the woman plastered her hand over a heart. "Where you go, a poor young girl with no mother to look after her? You stay with Mrs. Panazapoulos. She will take care of you."

From the corners of her eyes, Madeleine watched the old woman waddle to the door. The instant she left, Madeleine took the newspaper to the light. As she'd expected, she discovered that the item her landlady had torn from the classifieds was the notice her father had placed. Obviously, she had an idea that the tenant she knew as "Miss Margaret Flynn" was the "Madeleine" named in the advertisement and would be worth a lot more to her father, a judge, than the sixteen dollars Madeleine owed her.

Dropping the newspaper on the dresser, she took from under the bed the two cloth valises she'd bought with the

paltry sum a pawnbroker had given her for her expensive
leather cases. Quietly, she began filling them with the contents of the dresser drawers—fraying undergarments,
stockings many times mended. Finding the small jewel
case Caroline had given her for her sixteenth birthday at
the back of the bottom drawer, she set it atop the dresser,
turned it over, then slid out the false bottom. She shook
out the contents, all that remained of her mother's inheritance, and counted it. Eight dollars and odd change.

"That *can't* be right," she said, counting the heap again
and arriving at the same figure.

And a terrifying prospect.

What if she couldn't convince Monroe that he'd been
responsible for the failure of her stunt? He might cancel
it and their agreement without paying her a dime.

She looked at the loose pile of money again and felt a
stab of fear. It might be all that stood between her and
living her life on her own terms, maybe even between her
on one side and her father and Roger on the other.

She looked in the mirror. Removing her red wig, she
brushed out her own pale blond hair. Still, the reflection
she saw wasn't entirely that of Madeleine Faurest, a
woman who had nearly allowed herself to be lulled by
luxury into extinction. Nor was it totally that of Margaret
Flynn, a journalist who'd never dreamed she'd walk the
streets of a notorious vice district, posing as a prostitute
to get a story.

"Maggie," she said. That was the name she'd given
McQuinn, the name of the woman looking back at her.
At last, a woman to be reckoned with. Shortly before
dawn, Maggie Flynn would rise, slip permanently away
from her flat, and exact her due from Monroe if she had
to hold him at the point of a decent paring knife.

But as she climbed into bed, she was sure she wouldn't
find kitchen tools or threats of any kind necessary
McQuinn may have been right in believing that Monroe

never intended to hire a woman reporter, but only half right. He should have added, "But then he met Maggie Flynn."

"No! Come back. Tell me who you are."

Bizarre though her dream was, Madeleine fought to hold on to it. But it refused to linger, to give up its secrets, secrets that struck her as vital. Sitting back against her pillow, she recalled it from the beginning.

She was barefoot aboard a ship flying a skull and crossbones from the mast and pitching in a terrible squall. Her own long blond hair flew in the gusting wind as McQuinn, a bandanna tied around his head, a patch over his right eye, and a gold earring in his ear, carried her beneath one arm toward the plank. He set her down and, pressing the tip of a potato paring knife between her shoulder blades, ordered her to the edge of the plank. There, she gazed down over her toes, which sprouted carnations, and shivered at the sight of shark fins circling in a sea of blood red roses. She opened her mouth to scream, but no sound came out.

McQuinn prodded her with the knife. "At last, my revenge. Jump, wench!"

With the middle fingers of her right hand, Madeleine touched her forehead, breastbone, and shoulders in the sign of the cross. Then, folding her hands prayerfully, she prepared to obey McQuinn's command.

"Let her live, McQuinn," another man said. His voice was low, matter-of-fact but clear with intent to enforce his order.

Madeleine turned around. The man who had interceded for her had thick black hair but no face. He wore what she took to be a kind of uniform, dark blue trousers and a lighter blue cotton shirt, buttoned at the collar. Something was sewn across one of the shirt's two pockets—what, she couldn't tell, not even after McQuinn dragged her off the plank and, with his arm around her waist, held her in front of him as a shield. She looked down at the other man's right hand, expecting to see a gleaming sword. Instead, she saw he was carrying a book.

The only book that had ever interested McQuinn, she thought, was probably kept by some oily little man who took bets on horses. The only way her faceless, literature-loving knight was going to overcome him with his book was to hit him on the head with it. Nevertheless, he joined McQuinn in circling a prelude to a fight-to-the-death. With her own fate resting on the outcome of this struggle between two men, one vengeful and one heroic, the dream ended.

But the faceless man continued to haunt her. *If only I knew his name,* she thought, yawning and soon feeling the undertow of her exhaustion.

As she was about succumb to it, her eyes popped open. Sitting straight up, she breathed the heavy breath of a sleep stolen by the blinding light of sudden revelation. The revelation of the blue shirt worn by the man in her dream, a name label on its one breast pocket with lettering she could plainly see. Her lips parted on a sigh.

"Delaney."

Peeking through the curtain over the narrow window beside her door, Madeleine saw the tenement behind hers take shape against the sky. Dawn. She'd finished packing her slim wardrobe into her two valises in the dark, careful to make no sound that would wake the baby in the flat next to hers. She couldn't chance his waking Mrs. Panazapoulos to her greed.

Tiptoeing to the door, she set her valises down. Then she went to the dresser, whose drawers she had emptied of the little she still valued except for what she valued

most of all. The brown leather portfolio containing her
Bug Alley and other stories. She'd left that with Monroe
at the conclusion of their meeting. Earlier, before agreeing to her proposed stunt, he'd perused its contents ap-
provingly then promised to send it to the man she would
be working for if her stunt succeeded. The man whose
opinion mattered to her most. Vernon Rawlston. All that
remained for her to collect, then, was her last eight dollars and change, which still lay atop the dresser. She
stuffed the money into her small purse, leaving her key
in its place, then stepping toward the door, paused.

Taking a dollar from her purse, she tossed it onto the
dresser next to the key. A dollar was all the conscience
and dignity she could afford and all the back rent her
mercenary landlady deserved. Returning to the door, she
gently eased it open then picked up her bags. As she
stepped out of the Halsted Street room that for the past
four months she'd loosely called home, she wondered
where she'd sleep that night.

Still, she knew exactly where she was headed this morning. Before she traveled to the *Clarion* and a showdown
with Monroe, she'd make the trip she'd avoided making
since she arrived in Chicago, preferring an ideal to reality.
But that ideal was no longer an abstraction. It had a
name. Delaney. And if Delaney was going to duel
McQuinn in her dreams, holding a book in one hand and
her fate in the other, she needed to know he was a man
who, in reality, had a fighting chance.

She needed to return to St. Augustine's Reformatory
for Boys.

In Vernon Rawlston's cramped cubicle of an office,
Daniel paced while he waited for the *Clarion*'s city editor,
his *former* editor, to arrive. He smoked and fingered the
spines of Rawlston's most cherished books—mostly about

or by ancient Romans—and worked up a charge from the noisy current outside, in the city room itself. How familiar it all was and how right, except for the sunlight streaming through Rawlston's window.

Rawley mistrusted extremes like day and night. "Go after the truth behind a story the way you'd make your way home at the edge of dusk," he'd say to his reporters, "when you can't be sure that anything is what it appears to be. That's when you ask yourself if the woman you're seeing up ahead is really Mrs. Goldberg bending over her baby carriage, or some other woman selling apples from a cart, or another picking through trash. Or whether you're seeing a woman at all."

Last night, through eyes that had grown accustomed to viewing the world at dusk, Daniel had lain awake thinking about the woman who with a smack of her hand had jarred his memory of a long-forgotten name. The creature he'd come to call simply "She" was named Madeleine. But who, he asked again as he peered out the window, was Maggie Flynn and why had *her* slap—she was only the most recent female he'd inspired to strike him, after all—resurrected a name that had eluded him for years?

The answer to that question, of course, was that she was the only female since Madeleine who'd had the power to shame him. She'd made him see what Rawley had tried but couldn't, that the only thing that matters is the story. Those weren't just words to her. She lived by them and she might have died by them. But so might the *Clarion*'s news pages.

"Maggie Flynn will be the death of Rawley," he said.

"That's funny. I've always thought *you'd* be the death of me."

Turning from the window, Daniel faced Vernon Rawlston, his gray hair uncombed, the familiar patch over his right eye. He stood with his arms folded across his chest over a tie that was a canvas for every lunch he'd eaten this week and a shirt that looked as though it hadn't been laundered in a month after only a few hours' wear. Daniel smiled. Rawlston was like a well-traveled letter from home. The city room of the *Clarion* was home.

"How are you, Rawley?"

"According to you, about to die." Unfolding his arms, Rawlston pointed to the brown leather portfolio he held at Daniel. "Worry about yourself, McQuinn. You're still *persona* very *non grata* around here. Monroe's installed a punching bag in his office, with your mug on it." As he walked behind his desk, reading papers he'd taken from inside the portfolio, he added, "But on your way out, tell me what you know about Maggie Flynn."

"What makes you think I know anything about her?"

Rawlston looked up from his reading. "She gave you that cut on your cheek, didn't she?"

Instinctively, Daniel touched the small gash she'd made with her ring, then poked back the brim of his hat. "I know this is probably a stupid question, but how did you know that?"

"You're right, that was a stupid question considering you're the wiseacre who figured out what the 'G.' in G. Vernon stands for." Rawlston put the papers and the portfolio on his desk. "Besides, any woman you think could be the death of me is the kind not only to let you have what you deserve but also to get you out of bed in the morning to talk about her."

Smiling wryly, Daniel shoved his hands in his pockets. "Sometimes, Rawley, that one eye of yours is downright scary."

"It's a curious fact, McQuinn," Rawlston said, pulling out his ancient oak desk chair to sit down, "but after a man loses half his sight over a woman, the remaining half sees a whole lot more of the truth about what goes on between men and women. Let's leave that aside for the moment, though. What's the story on Maggie Flynn?"

Daniel perched on a corner of Rawlston's desk and tried not to think about all he knew about her and didn't want to admit to Rawley. The way she fit in his arms, for example, as though she'd been made for him to hold and never let go. And the way her tongue had tasted after she'd parted her soft, pliant lips—shyly at first, then hungrily—smoother than that first sip of the good bourbon he'd rarely been able to afford and infinitely more exhilarating. Feeling the part of him it had exhilarated last night respond to the very thought of it, he picked up a blue pencil and commenced flipping it end-over-end.

"Monroe tried using her to get back at me for that right cross I laid on him," he said. "He sent her to the Levee looking like a cross between a convent school girl and a circus pony to lure The Red Rose Killer. Try not to die laughing, but according to her, Monroe promised her a job in the city room, *my* old job and *your* city room."

Rawlston grabbed the pencil in midair. "For once you have my permission to stop acting like a reporter. I know the facts."

"You don't know this one." Daniel leaned toward Rawlston. "Davis never showed up to protect her as Monroe had promised her. Fortunately, I got to her before Captain Carnation could swash her buckler. But you and I both know she could have met with something just as florid and whole lot deadlier."

"You don't say?" Throwing down the pencil, Rawlston stood up. "Hold on a minute, Mac. I just remembered something I need to take care of."

Casually, Daniel watched Rawlston step outside his office, collar one of the copy boys, giving him instructions of some sort, then return, leaving his door open.

"So, you followed the girl," he said, resuming his seat.

Daniel nodded. "From the arcade on Dearborn Street."

"Now if somebody had asked me last night where I thought you were, I'd have said the Whitechapel Club, drinking to Monroe's imminent demise." Rawlston's chair creaked as he leaned back and fixed Daniel with his one-eyed gaze. "What were you doing on the Levee?"

"What do you think?" Daniel asked as though Rawlston should have known better than to ask. "Working the Red Rose story."

Rawlston sat forward. "That's impossible. It's not Lent. No editor would hire you unless he were giving up his sanity for Lent."

"I'll remember that in case I'm still out of a job on Fat Tuesday," Daniel shot back.

Frowning, Rawlston looked askance at Daniel. "You're really working the story on your own? With no guarantee of getting your daring exploits splashed all over some front page?"

"The killer's not going to quit just because I do."

Rawlston tugged his earlobe. "Maybe I ought to listen to my wife, after all, and take a few days off. You won't believe what I thought I just heard you say."

"Listen, you cynic," Daniel said, picking up the pencil and rising. "Nobody has to tell me that the only thing that matters is the story, and the only thing that matters about the Red Rose story is that it ends." Someone *had* told him, of course. Maggie Flynn.

Leaning back in his chair, Rawlston clasped his hands behind his head. "Well, well, well. Daniel McQuinn is struck blind on the Damascus Road." His one visible brow arched. "Or did you see the light on Dearborn Street?"

"Actually," Daniel said softly, "the moon *was* shining when she . . ." Tossing the pencil back on Rawlston's desk, he walked to the window overlooking the city room and pressed his palms to it. "You know something, Rawley, I really do miss this place."

"Maybe you miss it so much you came to ask me to beg

Monroe to beg Pamela Hart to give you another chance. After all, she's not hard to look at."

Daniel whipped around. "No, just hard to take." Returning to Rawlston's desk, he leaned over it. "Listen, Rawley, I came here for just one reason, to warn you that last night, Monroe and Maggie Flynn nearly buried the *Clarion* as you and I know it. If anything had happened to that girl—"

"You don't have to tell me what would have happened to the *Clarion*, Mac," Rawlston said. Rising, he lowered the shade over his outside window, blocking out the bright, brittle light, then walked back to Daniel. "Every reform group in town would be here right now, screaming that the press was to blame. They'd say we'd gone too far in pursuing lurid crime stories, that we'd sacrificed an innocent young woman merely to sell papers. By tomorrow, no city editor in Chicago would be able to put any story on his front page that couldn't be read from the Sunday pulpit."

"Believe me, you don't know how close you came to that." Daniel sat down, leaned back, and crossed his legs atop the desk, placing his heels on the pages Rawlston had been reading. "If you could only have seen her in front of that arcade. Skinny, dressed like the kind of hooker you find only in dime novels, wearing a frowzy red wig and looking as green as grass. She was a joke."

Leaning over, Rawlston gazed down at Daniel. "Did you laugh at her, Mac?"

Daniel shifted in the chair, his brows shirring. "No. No, I didn't."

From the first moment he saw her outside that arcade, Daniel had known she was no laughing matter. Neither was she just some poor hooker he might later recall in a few column inches of newsprint then promptly forget. From that first moment, she'd mattered to him. And to the last, after she'd brought him back from the brink of

Hell and kissed him, and rightfully shamed him, she'd haunted him. She was haunting him now as he pictured her lying in some back alley, her lovely throat gashed, her lifeless hand cupping a red rose. As determined as she was to stay on the story, he feared she might haunt him the rest of his days.

"You asked me for the story on Maggie Flynn; well, here it is," he said. "She won't quit the Red Rose story until she finds the killer, in which case she'll get her heart broken when she finds out that over your dead body would you allow a woman in the city room even if Monroe wanted her. Or . . ." Daniel exhaled a long breath. "The killer finds her first."

"That thought disturbs you, does it?"

It slays me. "Only because if she goes six feet under, so do the news pages of this paper." Lighting a cigarette, Daniel threw the match on the floor. "I'm telling you, Rawley, you've got to take care of Maggie Flynn."

Rawlston slid his papers from beneath Daniel's heels. "Don't worry, Mac. I intend to."

Eight

Lugging her valises, Madeleine slowly climbed to the *Clarion*'s second-floor city room. Any other morning, if a copyboy had met her at the receptionist's desk with a message that G. Vernon Rawlston wanted to see her immediately, she could be lugging anvils and still take the stairs by twos. On this particular morning, however, not even the prospect of an interview with Mr. Rawlston could lighten her step. Indeed, nothing could make her forget what she'd learned when she visited St. Augustine's less than an hour ago.

"It hasn't changed," Madeleine said as she stood looking at the building she'd last seen ten years earlier. Of course, with its ugly brown brick façade, turrets, and narrow windows. it was never going to appear to be anything but what it was, a kind of prison.

Once inside, however. she saw that electric lights had been installed, relieving the gloom that once dominated the place. In addition to the old religious statuary and pictures, she noticed bright chromos—chromolithographs—depicting landscapes and homey scenes of the kind of domestic life the inmates had probably never known.

Even more telling of enlightened new leadership was the new library. Stopping and peering through a large window, she saw that it was well lit, well stocked, and well used by boys who, except for their sturdy blue shirts with name labels on the pockets and blue trousers, little resembled their abused predecessors. Walking further along to the library's entrance, she stopped to read the plaque beside it. Her heart lurched.

"Delaney Library," she whispered. "My Delaney?"

And if so, had the library been named for a living benefactor or in memory of a dead former inmate? The inmate who'd appeared in her dream to rescue her from McQuinn with nothing but his honor and a book.

Slowly, she moved along the wall, studying the photographs lining it, hoping to find a picture of the library's namesake. She saw landscapes, portraits, boats on the river, all labeled with the name of the boy who had taken the picture. But there was no Delaney. Puzzling, she followed the directions to the principal's office she received at the front entrance.

When she read his name on his office door, she thought little of it other than it represented the broad ethnicity of Chicago's population, an ethnicity Louisville lacked and she had found fascinating. The instant Monsignor Ralph Bianco greeted her, however, she recognized him. Despite his wavy black hair having thinned and grayed, his gray-blue eyes were still kind, though now behind spectacles. His voice was still strong yet warm, gentle. She hated having to deceive him. But since he obviously didn't recognize her, she'd be foolish to volunteer that they'd met in his classroom ten years ago, foolish to unnecessarily leave a tidbit along her trail for her father's agents to retrieve.

"My name is Maggie Flynn, Monsignor," she told him, counting her first lie to him as she held out her hand. His clasp was manly but tender. "I'm doing a story for the Clarion." Not exactly a lie, but misleading. "I'm interested in interviewing some of the men who spent time here, say ten years ago, to see how they've fared."

"You mean, to find out whether or not they've become useful citizens," the monsignor replied, offering her a seat. "I can tell

you that many of them have. Several of them, in fact, would be only too happy to talk to you. Detective Grimm, for one."

Jotting the name in a small notebook, Madeleine felt she'd seen or heard it before, but she had a more important name to trace. "And the Delaney for whom the library is named . . . might he be a former inmate as well?"

Monsignor Bianco's eyes narrowed. He lowered his head, revealing a bald spot, then removed his glasses and wiped them with a handkerchief he'd taken from the pocket of his black cassock. "Yes," he said. "But I'm afraid you won't be able to talk to him." Hooking the arms of his spectacles over his ears, he looked up. "He died shortly after leaving here. He was working for the railroad and . . . there was an accident."

Madeleine felt the room spin. Closing her eyes, she gripped the arms of her chairs desperately clinging to the presence that had lived inside her. After ten years, she'd discovered its name only to discover she'd been living with a ghost.

"Are you feeling all right, Miss Flynn?"

"No, Monsignor, I'm not." she said softly. "If you don't mind, perhaps I'll come back another time." She would, too, if only to stand outside and watch. Watch for a ghost. "I'm sorry to have troubled you."

"Not at all," the priest replied, then walked Madeleine to the door. "Forgive me, Miss Flynn," he added as he opened it, "but since the moment I saw you, I've had the feeling we may have met before. Is that possible?"

Madeleine touched the nape of her neck. Fearing that strands of her own blond hair had escaped her brown wig. "I don't see how, do you, Monsignor?" Her second lie to a man who deserved the truth.

"No, no I don't," he replied, smiling wistfully. "Perhaps you only remind me of someone I knew. Yes, I'm sure that must be it. Goodbye, Miss Flynn, and may God bless you."

"Goodbye, Monsignor." Starting toward the main entrance, Madeleine realized just how much she needed that blessing. In the last twenty-four hours, she'd posed as a prostitute, cheated her

landlady, lied to a priest, and lost a cherished hope. The hope that somewhere, a man by the name of Delaney lived prosperously and loved well.

But the boy who'd carried the heart of a man inside his lean, battered body had never achieved full manhood. Moreover, he'd died with the mark of her scorn on his brave heart. Stopping outside the library, she looked at the plaque bearing his name. "My mother's the one taught me to read," she heard him say.

"Forgive me," she whispered. Then, as she touched her finger-tips to her lips, a tear touched both. She placed it on his name like a flower on a grave.

Still, as she turned to leave St. Augustine's, she did not say goodbye to him. She knew she could never say goodbye to Delaney.

"Hello, McQuinn."

Madeleine stood on the threshold of Rawlston's office. Dim as it was with the shade drawn, she couldn't mistake the man sitting with his long legs outstretched and his feet crossed atop Rawlston's desk, his fedora cocked to one side of his head and a plume of smoke wafting above it. She was actually glad to see him. His being here meant that he thought she was more of a threat to him than he'd led her to believe. She might not have to sleep in the Polk Street Station tonight, after all.

The sound of Maggie Flynn's voice had knocked Daniel's feet off Rawlston's desk. Now, at the bidding of some long-forgotten instinct, he tumbled out of his chair, crushed out his cigarette, and turning, gazed at her as she stood in the doorway. Her silhouette was slender and straight, her bearing one of feminine command. Damn, but if she didn't look like a woman to be reckoned with. As he thought how much he'd enjoy reckoning with her, he was unaware that he'd removed his hat.

"You've got the wrong office, Babe," he said, leaning

back against the desk. "Monroe's the man whose head you want."

"Among others," Madeleine replied. "For your information, Mr. Rawlston sent a copyboy downstairs with a message that he wanted to see me the minute I arrived."

Daniel laughed. "Either you or the copyboy heard wrong because Rawley doesn't allow women in his city room much less in his office. But if I know you—"

"You don't know me."

"You won't take my word for it."

"True."

"See? I told you I know you. So why don't you come in and wait for the word? Rawley said he'd be back in a minute."

Madeleine stepped to her right and picked up the valises she'd left outside the door. She entered the office halfway, then paused. "On second thought, a minute alone with you is sixty seconds too long. I'll wait out in the city room, if you don't mind."

"Why should I mind what you do?" Daniel said, spotting a valise in each of her hands and suddenly minding very much where she was going. "I see you've taken my advice."

"To forget the newspaper business, go home, and put up preserves for the county fair? I told you last night, the only thing I'm taking from you is your place at the *Clarion*."

"Did you, Babe? I don't recall," Daniel said offhandedly, tossing his hat and wishing Rawley were here right now to set her straight on that particular score. The sooner she did leave town, the better for him, not because he feared for the job he knew he'd find a way to get back, but because he feared for his heart. Catching his hat, he settled it on his head, molding the brim over one eye. "But then, so much passed between us last night, *Sadie*, you can't expect me to remember every little ol' detail."

No, just the one you won't let me forget, Madeleine thought. When he'd called her "Sadie," he'd purposely reminded her of exactly what *had* passed between them last night. Her tongue. And her hand, she reminded herself, because she wasn't sure she could restrain it now any more than she had then. She despised him even more now than she had then. Because Delaney was dead. And though it made no sense, she held Black Daniel McQuinn, the pirate in her dream, responsible.

"If you'll excuse me," she said, "I begin to detect the unmistakable odor of swine." Taking a step back, she turned around and walked right into—

"Mr. Rawlston!"

"Miss Flynn."

Seeing the patch over his eye, Madeleine shivered a little. She was already cold from a long-time lack of a hot meal. "I didn't know you were . . . that is when I said I smelled swine—"

"You meant McQuinn. I understand perfectly. Please, come in and sit down." Rawlston stooped to pick up Madeleine's bags but Daniel got to them first.

"Just how long were you out there spying on us?" Daniel whispered.

"Since Miss Flynn walked in and you fell all over yourself standing up and removing your hat." Rawlston grinned. "You scared me, Mac. I was afraid my one good eye was going on me, too."

"Yeah? Well, you scare me, too, Rawley." Daniel sniffed the editor's suddenly slick hair. "Since when did you start ducking down to the barbershop on the corner in the middle of the day for a shave and hair tonic?"

"Since you walked in this morning and reminded me of the low standards I planned to raise around here. Now let go of the lady's bags."

"Uh-uh. The way you're acting, I'm afraid you might offer her tea and scones instead of getting rid of her. By the way . . ." Daniel leaned closer to Rawlston. "How *are* you going to get rid of her?"

"Gentlemen," Madeleine said, bending over, bringing her face to theirs. She glanced at Daniel. "I suppose I should have more accurately said 'Mr. Rawlston.' Since I carried my bags to the *Clarion* without assistance, I'm sure I can manage to get them from here to that chair."

Raising eyebrows at one another, Daniel and Rawlston released the bags.

Madeleine took her belongings to the chair in front of Rawlston's desk, set them down, then seated herself. Pressing folded hands against her abdomen to quell a sudden nausea she'd like to attribute to McQuinn but knew was due to acute hunger, she waited for Rawlston to join her.

He did, half-sitting on the desk in front of her. "Miss Flynn, let me tell you why I asked you to come—"

"I think I'll go out and see what the rest of the boys are up to, Rawley." Knowing firsthand how brutal Rawlston could be when he needed to, Daniel headed for the door. As much as the reporter in him would love to witness the kill, he just didn't have the stomach to watch the heart torn out of a woman who, all in all, had a lot of it.

"Stay where you are, McQuinn!" Rawlston's bark brought Daniel to a halt. "I may need to talk to you, after I've spoken to Miss Flynn."

Daniel translated Rawlston's order, which went something like, *After I destroy this little girl's dreams and make her cry, steer me to the Press Club and see to it that inside of an hour I no longer feel like a son-of-a-bitch, or feel much of anything, for that matter.*

Reluctantly, Daniel turned. "Sure, Rawley." Shoving his hands in his pockets, he leaned one shoulder into the wall behind him, crossed one foot over the other, and wished he'd heard something in his translation about Rawley doing the buying. He was broke and figured that when this was over, he'd need to down about a pint of forgetfulness himself.

"Mr. Rawlston, before you begin," Madeleine said, taking advantage of McQuinn's rude interruption—as if he'd interrupt politely. "I'd like to present my side of the story."

"Oh?" Rawlston folded his arms. "And what story would that be?"

Beneath the glare of his one steely eye, Madeleine shifted her weight. If she couldn't convince Rawlston that she was a capable reporter, even if Monroe did hire her, this tough city editor would make her wish she were back in Louisville writing up Fourth-of-July picnics. "The one I'm sure Mr. McQuinn told you about my . . . little mishap last night."

"Which started with a big mistake," Daniel said, just loudly enough for the Babe to hear.

Draping her hand over the arm of the chair, Madeleine turned aside, shifting her eyes and a murderous glint in his direction but not meeting his gaze. "What he couldn't have told you because he didn't know about it," she went on, "is that I was prepared for the possibility of Mr. Davis's not keeping our rendezvous." She told him about the paring knife. "I assure you, next time I'll be sufficiently armed."

"With what? An eggbeater?" Shoving off the wall, Daniel charged toward Maggie Flynn. He gripped the arm of her chair and fixed a hard stare on her. "You still don't understand, do you? If you stay on this story, your next *rendezvous* will be Death, and believe me, he'll keep it." He sighed. "Miss Flynn, go home."

Making slits of her eyes, Madeleine ground her jaw to one side. "Chicago is my home," she said, then looked at Rawlston. "I don't wish to appear rude, but is Mr. McQuinn's presence really necessary considering that he's no longer employed by the *Clarion*?" She slid a glance at Daniel. "Or by anyone else, for that matter."

Rawlston folded his arms. "Well, that may or may not be the case. That all depends on you, Miss Flynn."

Daniel shot to his full height. "I don't like the sound of that, Rawley."

"Neither do I," Madeleine said.

"Yes, Miss Flynn," Rawlston said, clearing his throat. "I did gather from the conversation I overheard between you and McQuinn a moment ago that you have an interest in his continued absence from the *Clarion*'s news pages."

Madeleine felt her skin flush, partly with embarrassment and partly with a fresh hunger pang. "I know what I said about my taking McQuinn's place sounded brash, Mr. Rawlston—"

"On the contrary, it sounded good."

"I like the sound of that even less," Daniel said.

"Then you're just going to hate what I have to say next, Mac." Reaching behind him, Rawlston picked up the papers he'd carried into the office with him earlier. He handed them to Daniel. "Go to school."

Beneath a gathered brow, Daniel began reading. He'd only had to finish the lead to the story of a woman's death at the hands of her husband to know that the reporter had the instinct for the shortest path between the heart of a story and the hearts of readers. His heart. He held the story out to Maggie Flynn. "Did you write this?"

Madeleine took the pages, recognized them, then giving him a triumphant look, turned grinningly to Rawlston. "Mr. Monroe kept his promise to give my portfolio to you."

Puckering his chin, Rawlston shook his head. "I'm afraid not. His secretary brought it to me after finding it in his waste basket. You must have made quite an impression on her."

Madeleine felt McQuinn's gaze on her but didn't dare meet it. She couldn't bear to see him gloating, or to let him see her humiliation. He'd been right when he said that Monroe had never intended to uphold his end of his bargain with her. She'd offered him a chance to both get back at McQuinn and get an exclusive on the capture of The Red Rose Killer, and he'd taken it. If she got the story, he could deny he'd ever promised her a job as a city reporter. There had been no witness to their agreement. If the story got her, he'd lost nothing. Oh, there'd be a public outcry over her death that might crimp the *Clarion*'s style for a while, but the public would forget her sacrifice about the same time it noticed its morning paper was blander than its soft-boiled eggs.

Feeling a little faint at the thought of any kind of eggs, she nevertheless rose. "Mr. Monroe isn't the only managing editor in town," she said to Rawlston. Then, upturning her palm, "May I have my portfolio, please?"

"I haven't finished reading it yet," Rawlston replied.

Madeleine blinked with astonishment. "You *want* to finish reading it?"

"If there are more stories like that one in it." He smiled, not broadly but genuinely. "It's good, Maggie. In fact, it's damn good." While Madeleine tried to coax a "Thank you" from her speechlessness, he shot a look at Daniel. "She's almost as good as you were, Mac, before you'd gotten the idea our readers find your derringdo in gathering a story more fascinating than the story itself."

Cocking his head to one side, Daniel met Maggie Flynn's bright gaze. "He said 'almost,' Babe." Then, with a skewed smile, he winked.

Madeleine gaped, slain by that wink, slain by what McQuinn had said with it better than he could have said with words, even his patented words: "You, Babe, are a news reporter."

Shaking her head, she smiled at him. "McQuinn, there

wouldn't be any 'almost' if could learn how to be good even when I'm bad."

"Oh, but Mac's not going to be bad anymore," Rawlston said, leaning back and hugging one knee. "He's been telling me how he's seen the light. Go ahead, Mac. Tell Maggie what you told me about how the story is the only thing that matters."

Clearing his throat, Daniel pulled the brim of his hat lower. "I wouldn't want to bore the lady, Rawley."

"Oh, but you could never bore me, McQuinn." Putting down her story, Madeleine batted her eyelashes and a dare at Daniel. "I'm simply dyin' to hear your little ol' philosophy of journalism."

"I thought you would be," Rawlston said, chuckling. "Go on, Mac. Philosophize."

Through a clenched jaw, Daniel let out a long breath. "I said that the only thing that matters is the story and the only thing that matters about the Red Rose story is that it ends." Jamming his hands in his pockets, he slid his gaze at Maggie. "Like it?"

"I love it," Madeleine replied through her teeth. "May I borrow it some time?"

Daniel shrugged. "It's all yours, Babe." Turning to Rawlston, he pushed his hat to the back of his head. "What's the point of all this, Rawley?"

"Just this." Standing up, Rawlston pinned Madeleine with his one-eyed gaze. "Maggie, how would you like to work on the *Clarion*'s city desk as a full-time reporter?"

"No she wouldn't!" Taking her by the shoulders, Daniel moved Maggie Flynn aside. Ignoring her protests, he rounded on Rawlston. "Think, Rawley. I know you want to keep her off the streets, but do you have to keep her in the city room? After all, she won't find the company out there much of an improvement over what she ran into on the Levee."

"I agree, Mac," Rawlston said, walking behind his desk.

"But she's obviously determined to continue working on the Red Rose story and I don't want to read on some other paper's front page that she trapped the killer and led to his arrest. Since Monroe's already failed to protect her, I don't see that I have any choice but to look after her myself. Besides, I need a good reporter."

Stepping to Daniel's side, Madeleine leaned in. "I told you I'd take your place," she said beneath her breath. Then, to Rawlston, "You're too kind, Mr. Rawlston. I know there's much I have to learn—"

"I'll say," Daniel muttered.

Ignoring him, Madeleine continued. "From *you*, Mr. Rawlston, and I'd be terribly grateful if you'd teach me."

Daniel rolled his eyes. "Did you hear that, Rawley? Did you hear what she just said?"

Propping her fists on her waist, Madeleine faced Daniel. "What is *wrong* with what I just said?"

"Oh nothing," he replied, flinging his hands in the air. "Only if you go out in that city room and start saying things like 'Mr. Rawlston, I just can't hardly still my beatin' heart waitin' for you to teach me every little ol' *thang* you know about the newspaper business—"

"I never said any such than—thing!"

"You will. And when you do, you'll empty the place faster than if you'd yelled 'Let's go, fellas, the drinks are on me!' No self-respecting reporter would work in an atmosphere like that. Its . . ." Daniel filled his lungs. "Harassment!"

"Harass—? In the first place, McQuinn, when applied to you the term 'self-respecting reporter' is an oxy—" Suddenly, Madeleine's vision went black. Lowering her forehead to her fingers, she swayed.

"Babe!" Catching her by the waist, Daniel sat her down in the chair behind her. "Rawley, open that window," he shouted. Then, gripping the arms of the chair, he caged the woman whose face was going chalky white under the light Rawlston was admitting. "What is it, Babe? Didn't you eat breakfast?"

Madeleine nodded. "Yesterday morning."

"Haven't you eaten since?"

"Not unless you count the lip rouge I got on my teeth last night."

Daniel gently lifted the veil from her eyes. "Let me finish what you were about to say applied to me. *Moron.*"

Madeleine smiled wanly. "I am kind of sorry I didn't make you buy me dinner instead of slapping you."

Daniel smiled back, taking one of her cold hands in his warm ones. "So am I, about dinner, not the slap."

"Tell me you think you deserved it and I *will* faint."

"You won't need smelling salts. I only meant that for some reason, that slap made me remember a name—"

"I'll get her something to drink," Rawlston said, creating a flurry of papers as he dashed from the room.

Their hands joined, Madeleine and Daniel made no response. Nor did they take their gazes from one another. Each realized he had never seen the other, full-face, in bright daylight before.

McQuinn's eyes were surprisingly lucent, Madeleine thought, silver gray with blue-black irises. Fringed by thick, charcoal lashes and over-arched by equally black brows, they first startled then mesmerized. Strangely, there was an ancient light in them, a timeless purity she had seen once before, in Delaney's one-eyed gaze, and would never have expected in any feature of McQuinn's. And did not see in the others. His nose, fine but at least twice broken, his mouth, as fleshy as it had felt when he'd kissed her last night, his coloring, like Southern clay beneath shadows, all conjured many things, none of them pure.

Then, she saw something that brought her other hand to his cheek. With her fingertips, she traced over the half-inch cut, seeing both it and the sharp, empty prongs on her mother's ring. "Did I do this?"

Captivated by her eyes, soft and dark and filled with unguarded tenderness, Daniel felt a lump rise to his throat. Though he'd tried, in ten years he had yet to find the eyes that recreated his memory of Madeleine's. The Madeleine who had forgiven his clumsiness with a miraculous look and a madonna's smile. Maggie Flynn's eyes were coming close. Close enough to remind him that a woman with the power to save with a look has the power to condemn with one.

Attempting to corrode her power, Daniel gave a caustic laugh. "And all this time I thought you'd meant to."

Madeleine stared at him, her eyes wide, entranced, and seeing someone else. "No. I *never* meant to. Forgive me."

How can I, Daniel thought, *when you look at me like this?* With eyes so suddenly innocent and searching, she made him feel as though she were seeing in him a feast for her deepest hunger. Worse, with pale lips tilted up at his and softly parted, she aroused a hunger in him that made him want to truly be her salvation, as he'd wanted to save Madeleine from the touch of evil so many years ago. Curving his fingers, he laid them tenderly alongside her mouth, Maggie's . . . Madeleine's.

At Delaney's forgiving touch, Madeleine smiled, drawing his lips closer. She clasped her arms around his neck. "Kiss me," she said softly.

Daniel's heart tripped; his breath grew ragged and his palms clammy. He was a lovestruck schoolboy and Madeleine, to his utter joy, had just asked him to kiss her. Placing his hands on her waist, he gently raised her, never taking his eyes from hers. Then, setting his head to one side, he bent down and kissed her, lightly, tentatively. And when that first kiss torched a bonfire inside him, he took her into his arms, pressing his closed lips against hers, feeling a rapture he'd never known.

Madeleine prayed Delaney's arms would never grow tired of holding her because now that he'd given her her first kiss, she never wanted him to stop kissing her and making the earth drop from beneath her feet, the heavens spin above her head.

"I scrounged up a doughnut and a few crackers, none of them fresh, I'm afraid," Rawlston said as he reentered the room. "But they'll tide you over until—"

Quickly separating, Madeleine and Daniel dodged Rawlston's and each other's gazes.

"That's very kind of you, Mr. Rawlston," Madeleine said, feeling so exposed, she nervously checked the nape of her neck for blond hairs peeking out from beneath her dull brown wig. "But I'm feeling much better now, thank you."

"So I see." Walking between Daniel and Madeleine, he set the doughnut and crackers down on his desk. "Hot coffee then," he said, offering Madeleine a steaming mug. When she accepted it, he gripped the desk behind him and looked from one to the other. "All right, you two. I don't have time to play chaperone so here's my proposition. Maggie, as I said before, I want you on my staff and on the Red Rose story, but—"

"For God's sake, Rawley," Daniel said, suddenly angry with a man he'd always thought had better sense. "Why don't you just put her on a cattle car to the slaughterhouse? You said you'd take care of her."

Rawlston laid a hand on Daniel's shoulder. "By which I meant that you're going to take care of Miss Flynn. You two will be a team. Everywhere she goes in covering this or any other story, you'll go."

White-faced, Madeleine and Daniel exchanged white-eyed stares.

"Let me get this straight," Daniel said, flinging his hat on the chair behind him. "You're saying that I can come back to work at the *Clarion*, but only if I work with the

Babe here? Not on your life, Rawley. I'm a first-string reporter, not a nanny!"

"Don't flatter yourself, McQuinn," Madeleine said, plunking her mug down on the desk then walking to Daniel. "Even if I needed a nanny, you'd be the last person I'd let tuck me in at night."

"Don't flatter *yourself*, Babe."

Rawlston pushed them apart. "How about flattering me with a final decision? Mac? Maggie?"

"Count me out, Rawley."

"I couldn't possibly work with this man, Mr. Rawlston. I'd rather starve—" Gurgling like a draining sink, Madeleine's stomach disagreed.

"Fine. Just thought I'd ask." Rawlston walked to Madeleine's valises, stooped to pick them up, then straightened without them. "I was just wondering, Maggie, in the unlikely event Mac changes his mind, where can I reach you?"

"Well, I . . . I'll have to let you know. You see, my previous apartment was entirely unsuitable—"

"And unaffordable," Rawlston said. "Did you sneak out?"

Maggie nodded. "I left a dollar."

"What did you do that for?" Daniel asked, his expression disbelieving.

"For my conscience's sake, McQuinn," Madeleine replied. "But I don't expect you to understand that."

"Why should I? My conscience never did anything for my sake."

"It might do something for your thirst, though," Rawlston said. "I heard no bartender in town will give you so much as the time until you pay your tab."

"*That* is a matter of credit, not conscience." And who would have guessed, Daniel thought, that he'd ever have less credit than conscience? Sighing, he looked at Maggie. Could he really work with her? If he did, would he ever be able to hold his head up at The Whitechapel Club again if Peter Dunne and the others found out he was playing nursemaid to a female cub reporter?

On the other hand, his credit had worn as thin with Eileen Corrigan as it had with barkeeps around town. So thin that his insatiable widowed landlady had started hinting that a marriage proposal might fatten it up. Her husband might have died with a smile on his face, but he'd been almost eighty. Daniel wasn't yet thirty.

"All right," he said, looking away. "I guess I don't have a choice."

Except to hit me with a fresh dilemma, Madeleine thought. All she had to do was echo McQuinn's assent to Rawlston's proposition and she'd realize her one great ambition: to cover the news for a great newspaper under a great city editor. But could she work with Daniel McQuinn? If he didn't drive her mad, he'd surely drive her to drink. On the other hand, if she didn't accept Rawlston's offer, there was a good chance that with seven dollars in her pocketbook, she'd be driven to dire straits.

She heaved a sigh. "Neither do I."

Daniel snapped his fingers. "But Monroe does!" Grinning like a reprieved man, he looked at Rawlston. "It won't work, Rawley. Monroe hates me. He'll never go for it."

"He will," Rawlston replied. "There are still a few skeletons in his closet that I haven't rattled."

Daniel gaped at Rawlston in disbelief. "Why couldn't you have rattled them the day he fired me?"

"Aside from the fact that I thought you needed a lesson," Rawlston said, "I distinctly recall that Monroe made a fairly persuasive argument for your termination."

"A slight case of arson?"

"Pamela Hart."

"A major case of arsenic poisoning," Daniel said, scowling aside. Suddenly, he brightened. "I told you this scheme of yours won't work. After the way I treated her, if she finds out you and Monroe brought me back to the *Clarion*, she'll see the three of us sent to the stockyards and funneled out as sausage."

Madeleine chortled. "McQuinn, what is it about you that just naturally brings pigs to a woman's mind?"

Daniel gave her a snide look. "If you knew how good you're starting to make my landlady look—"

"I've seen your landlady, Mac," Rawlston said. "I suggest you start figuring out how to appease Miss Hart. You'll have to convince her that you had a good reason for spurning her affections."

"I have a suggestion," Madeleine began. Twining her arms and laying her head to one side, she peered at Daniel beneath raised brows. "You could tell her that you just happened to be in the neighborhood looking to get your face slapped."

Closing one eye and sticking his tongue in his cheek, Daniel stared at her for a moment. "Yep. I'm through," he said, grabbing his hat and heading for the door.

"You're not through, McQuinn," Rawlston called. "You're married."

Daniel did an about—quite thunderstruck—face. "I'm what?"

"*Married!*" Pumping her arms, Madeleine marched on him. "I should have slapped the other cheek, too."

Hat in hand, Daniel pointed past her at Rawlston. "Now that *would* have made me mad because as he knows damn well, no woman's ever gotten me to the altar!"

Madeleine arched a wicked brow. "Only because it's so hard to get good help making ritual sacrifices these days."

"Save it for the honeymoon, you two."

In duet, Daniel and Madeleine turned and gaped at Rawlston, who had joined them.

"Let me take this rare opportunity to get a word in edgewise to explain," he said, and started a circle around the pair. "Mac, you struggled with all your might to resist Miss Hart's considerable charms—"

"Not unless all my might is in my little finger," Daniel said, looking at Rawlston in total bafflement.

"Nevertheless," Rawlston went on, you nearly succumbed."

"I did?"

"You did," Rawlston said, pacing and pulling his lower lip.

"McQuinn, you didn't," Madeleine said, shaking her head.

"Of course he didn't, Maggie," Rawlston replied.

"Well, Rawley, you sure explained things," Daniel said. "So, if you don't mind, I'll just be going—"

"Listen, you blockhead," Rawlston said, staying Daniel's arm. "The only place you're going is to Pamela Hart and tell her that just as you'd found you could no longer deny your passion for her, you reached into your pocket, and lo and behold, there was a love note from your sweet little wife, Maggie."

"Me?" Madeleine shrieked. "This lunatic's wife?"

"He said *sweet* wife, Babe."

"And secret wife," Rawlston added. "Mac, you'll tell Miss Hart that Maggie insisted on keeping the marriage a secret because she was trying to get work writing for the *Clarion,* and when she did, she didn't want anyone thinking you'd used your influence on her behalf."

"She'll see right through that," Daniel said.

Madeleine folded her arms. "You mean because no one would believe that the mention of your name could influence anyone to do anything except hide the silver?"

"No," Daniel said, folding *his* arms "because she'd never believe that I would marry a skinny pain in the neck like you."

"Let's just say, children," Rawlston began, drawing them into a huddle, "that there's a good chance she won't buy a word of it. Pamela Hart's no fool. But she's also vain. She won't mind saving face, and in the bargain, we can all save our jobs. And perhaps the life of the poor prostitute who would have become The Red Rose Killer's next victim." Picking up his blue pencil and tapping it, he faced them. "How about it, you two? Will you act like man and wife? For the sake of the story, of course."

Straightening, Daniel looked into Maggie Flynn's eyes. They were hungry, not just for a decent meal but for the chance to do what she had it in her blood to do: pound the streets in search of the story then pound it through a telephone wire to a rewrite man on the other end or on a city-room typewriter in the dead of night. Pound it once more, this time from her mind with sleep that comes too hard and stays too briefly. Then, wake up and start pounding all over again, searching for some new story, some different angle of view on the petty crooks and big-time grafters, the surprising sinners and the unlikely saints. How could he deny her the chance to do the very thing he loved more than anything, sometimes even more than himself?

"All right, Rawley. I can put on an act," he said, still gazing at Maggie. "For the sake of the story."

"Since you put it that way, Mr. Rawlston," Madeleine said, gazing at McQuinn and wondering what it would be like to truly be his wife, lie in his arms, make love with him. Whatever it would be like, it wouldn't be boring. "I'll go along with the ruse."

"I don't think you two understand." Rawlston drew their stunned gazes. "Mac, you know how Pamela Hart is. Do you really think she's going to take your word for it that you're married?"

As Rawlston's words struck terror in him, Daniel tore his gaze from Maggie to the city editor. "My God, she'll want proof. She'll come snooping around my place, looking for lace curtains and doilies and something besides beer in the icebox." His hat slipping from his numb, icy fingers, he croaked, "She'll come looking for Mrs. McQuinn!"

Rawlston walked to the window, closed it and lowered the shade, once again casting the room in a dusky half-light. Turning to Madeleine and Daniel, he fixed them with his shiver-me-timbers gaze.

"Then she'll just have to find her, won't she?"

Nine

Later that afternoon, Madeleine and Daniel walked out of City Hall through separate doors. Facing La Salle Street, they stood several feet apart and in tense silence. At length, Daniel said, "I wonder what happened to Rawley. I thought he was right behind us."

Giving Daniel a scathing look, Madeleine angled away from him then set down her bags.

After another long moment, Daniel gazed up at the sky. "I wonder what happened to the sun. I thought it was up there half an hour ago."

Madeleine looked up at the ominous, pewter-colored clouds that indeed had not been there when they'd entered City Hall. She might have expected them, though, warnings from heaven. Yesterday at this time, the weather had been almost balmy. Since then, however, she'd offered herself as bait to every man on Dearborn Street, felt desire in the arms of another she hated, run out on a debt, lied to a priest, and now, this.

Turning to Daniel, she released a breath of resignation as she thrust her arms from her sides. "I'm going to Hell."

"You've seen my neighborhood, huh?" After lighting a cigarette, he flicked the match to the pavement. "Well, you know what they say, Babe. Beggars can't be—"

"Catholic."

Daniel squinted through wisps of smoke. "Does that mean they can beg for meat on Fridays?"

"Scoff all you like," Madeleine said, her shoulders slumping. "But I'm Catholic, and when you're Catholic, marriage is forever."

"Even when you're not." Daniel checked his pocket watch. "We've been married only seven minutes and already it feels like an eternity."

Madeleine stared at him. "I can't do this," she said at last, then picking up her bags, started for the streetcar on the corner.

"The only thing that matters is the story and the only thing that matters about the Red Rose story—"

"Don't you dare throw that in my face!" Madeleine walked back to him. "For the sake of that story—"

"And your stomach," Daniel said, patting his. "Do you realize you set a record at Henrici's for the most helpings of sauerbraten at one sitting."

"If all I cared about was my stomach, I'd have walked out on you and Rawley once it was full. I'd have found a job, any kind of job. Scrubbing floors would have been preferable to—"

"Marrying me?"

"To making a mockery of everything I believe regarding love and marriage and the sanctity of promises."

Drawing on his cigarette, Daniel gazed into the distance. "That word 'sanctity' . . . it reminds me of another." He looked Madeleine fully in the face. "Do you think it could be 'sanctimonious'?"

Madeleine drew in a deep breath. She did have a nerve sounding so righteous when only four months ago she'd nearly married Roger Mabrey without wholeheartedly believing in any of the things she'd espoused to McQuinn. But then, at the time, she hadn't believed in herself. Now that she did, she believed in so many things, big things and little things, that she had no patience with cynics like Daniel McQuinn.

"Could be," she said. "But tell me, if you can, what did *you* sacrifice to marry *me*?"

The question echoed in Daniel's mind, where the answer was the image of a beautiful young girl. There had been moments in his life, the bone-deep loneliest moments, when he'd imagined that girl grown up and standing beside him as Maggie had today. Only, the judge had been a priest and the judge's chambers a cathedral and the plain, brown-haired woman in her plain brown dress had been golden-haired and radiant in white satin-and-lace. Closing his eyes, he desperately tried to recreate the fantasy. He pictured the cathedral, with its stained glass windows and candlelit altar. He even saw the priest in his white and gold vestments. Then, he looked to his left, seeking his bride, and though he repeated the effort several times, each time he saw not Madeleine, but Maggie Flynn.

Opening his eyes, Daniel sighed. "You'd be surprised what marrying you cost me, Babe," he said. Then, "*Your* soul, at least, is safe. We got married in City Hall, not Holy Name Cathedral. In the eyes of the Church, we're not married at all."

"And you find that comforting, do you?" Madeleine stepped closer. "Listen, I know this isn't a new experience for you, living in sin, but—"

"Whoa! I think you have the wrong idea." Daniel rubbed the back of his neck. "Of course, I realize you haven't seen my flat yet, but a more accurate description of what we're going to be living in is squalor."

For the second time, Madeleine stared unblinkingly at her husband. "I *really* can't do this," she said and walked away.

"*Veni, vidi* the Sweethearts of the *Chicago Clarion!*"

"For Pete's sake, Rawley, why don't you just yell 'Extree!' " Daniel said as he and Madeleine turned toward Rawlston.

"Well, here's an extra for you." Rawlston held out a folded piece of paper. "You forgot your marriage certificate." When neither of them moved to accept it, he stuffed it in Daniel's breast pocket. "So, how *are* the newlyweds?"

Stamping out his cigarette, Daniel turned up his collar against a sharp wind. "Newly separated, according to Mrs. McQuinn."

"Oh, that name." Closing her eyes, Madeleine pressed her palm to her forehead. "If only I'd stopped to think that my name would be Margaret Flynn McQuinn, I would have never gone through with this." She gave Daniel a look sharper than the wind. "Why couldn't your name have been Hackenbush or Rumplemeyer or—" *Delaney.*

Why couldn't yours have been Madeleine? "Believe me, Babe, if I'd known I was going to give you my name, I'd have changed it to mud."

"I like the sound of that, Mac," Rawlston said.

"Mr. and Mrs. Mud?"

"I think," Madeleine put in, "he means Daniel and Babe McQuinn."

"Yes. Has quite a ring to it, don't you think?" Rawlston tugged his chin. "With a byline like that, you two should sell quite a few papers."

"Rawley, I've been asking for a byline for years," Daniel said, "but if you put my name in print next to hers, so help me I'll—"

"Speaking of rings . . ." Setting down her bags, Madeleine removed the glove from her left hand then slowly slipped a plain gold band from the third finger. She could feel love embedded deep beneath its worn and scratched surface, not a perfect love but a lasting one. "It was sweet of you to remember a ring, Rawley," she said, gazing down at it.

"*I* thought so," Rawlston replied. "Besides, before I could get Monroe to agree to this scheme, I had to assure him we'd do everything possible to avoid raising suspicions about your marriage. Not even my wife suspects the truth, thanks to Mac."

"I'm glad *someone* appreciates me," Daniel said in a surly tone.

"Indeed I do, Mac." Rawlston clamped a hand on Daniel's shoulder. "If you didn't have a reputation for betting on nags, I'd have had a hard time convincing her you were too broke to buy your bride a ring."

"And you said I was throwing my money away," Daniel replied, rolling his eyes.

Shooting him a disapproving glance, Madeleine handed Rawlston the gold band. "Thank her for me, Rawley, will you? It must have been difficult for her to part with it."

"Naturally," Daniel said. "That's some inscription in it. Sheer poetry."

Madeleine laid her hand on Rawlston's forearm. "Pay no attention to him. I think YOU'RE MY LEAD STORY is a perfectly beautiful sentiment."

Daniel snickered. "It's a sentiment."

"And Clara's a sentimental woman," Rawlston said. "I couldn't get her to loan you the ring, Mac, until I suggested the alternative, loaning you the money. She's very sentimental about money, my Clara."

Madeleine and Rawlston broke into laughter.

Abruptly, Daniel straightened. "Enjoy it while you can, you two, because I'm now going to remind you that Pamela Hart will want to meet my bride. And you can bet she'll be looking for a ring."

Tucking her thumb beneath the third finger of her right hand, Madeleine felt her mother's ring beneath her glove. Even if Rawley hadn't borrowed his wife's wedding band, she wouldn't have suggested making Margaret Faurest's initial ring an accessory to her sham marriage. She'd felt, after losing her true name and identity as well as her scruples, that her mother's ring was the only genuine article she still possessed. Still, she might actually like to wear it on her left hand as a reminder that she was married not to McQuinn, but to her own destiny. Removing her right glove, she transferred the ring. "See? if I turn the initial around, like this, no one will know it isn't a wedding band."

Daniel rubbed the cheek the ring had cut the night before. "I will."

Madeleine shivered. "Don't speak those horrid words to me ever again."

Certain he was breaking out in hives, Daniel scratched his abdomen. "As long as you promise never to repeat 'By the authority invested in me by the State of Illinois I pronounce you—"

"Reporters," Rawlston said. "If you two are done feeling sorry for yourselves, I'd like to remind you of what you really said 'I will' to." He turned and gazed at La Salle Street. "See those tall buildings? They remind me of a loom, like the one my grandmother had. And all those people passing through them? They're weaving a piece of this city's fabric." He swept the skyline with his ink-stained hand. "Take a good look at it, McQuinns. Chicago. It's tough as hide and tawdry as Jezebel's garters. It's every newsman's dream. It's been my dream for over thirty years." He turned to the couple, his one eye gleaming. "And now it belongs to the two of you."

Angrily, kicking his cigarette across the pavement, Daniel said, "Listen, Rawley, I never said 'I will' to any dream. I agreed to marry the Babe so we could end the Red Rose nightmare. And when that ends, so does our nightmare of a marriage,"

"But *I'll* go on, McQuinn," Madeleine said, "because I do have a dream. Will *you?*" Walking to Rawlston's side, she slipped her arm through his. Together, they stood gazing out at the city.

Daniel stood gazing at his wife and his editor. After a moment, he jammed his hands in his pockets and his toe into the pavement. "Anybody would think the two of you were the newlyweds."

Placing his hand over Madeleine's, Rawlston looked back at Daniel. "Anybody would think you were a jealous man."

Daniel laughed. "That will be the day."

"In the meantime," Rawlston said, "I assume you won't mind if I kiss the bride."

"This wedding was your idea. It's about time you shared the load." Daniel watched Rawlston take Maggie by the shoulders and smile down at her. He saw Maggie smile up at Rawlston as the one-eyed pirate bent down to kiss her on the cheek. For a kiss on the cheek, it was lasting a helluva long time. "All right, I'll admit it. I *am* jealous," he said.

Madeleine looked at him with a mixture of disbelief and alarm. *"Why?"*

Daniel shrugged. "After all, Babe, I've been working for Rawley a lot longer than you and he's never kissed *me.*"

Madeleine clutched Rawlston's upper arms. "Take me home with you, Rawley. *Please.*"

"On your wedding night?" Rawlston gave her a sidelong smile. "Don't you think Clara will find that strange?"

"I don't see why," Madeleine replied. "She knows McQuinn so she should find my not wanting to be alone with him perfectly understandable."

"My blushing bride makes an excellent point, Rawley," Daniel said, backing away. "So why don't you take her home to Clara. You know how she's always wanted a daughter to have one of those woman-to-woman chats with. And I'll call for the Babe in a few days . . . or weeks . . ."

"Or months!" Picking up her bags, Madeleine backed away from Daniel. "We could tell Miss Hart that McQuinn and I *were* married but now we're separated and I'm living with you and Clara. In the meantime—"

"Babe and I can still work on the story, but in shifts," Daniel said.

"A brilliant little ol' idea," Madeleine replied. "We'll be doubling the coverage."

Grinning anxiously at one another then at Rawlston, Madeleine and Daniel turned and ran in opposite directions. They didn't get far before a shrill whistle brought them to halts.

"You're forgetting one thing," Rawlston said, coming up behind them.

Slowly, they faced him.

"Neither one of you works without the other." Crooking his fingers at them, he drew them near. "Maggie, you don't work without McQuinn to keep an eye on you, and McQuinn, you don't work without Maggie to keep you in line and *on* deadline." Loudly, he clapped his hands. "The honeymoon's over, folks. Now get the hell to work. Together!"

On the corner of Twenty-sixth and Canal, Daniel stopped and looked back at the woman trailing behind him in the dark, struggling with the weight of her valises and the treacherousness of the road she was crossing. She'd wanted to work in a man's world so let her work like a man, he thought. He'd promised he'd protect her fool neck, not her feminine privileges. Not that it had been easy for him to do nothing to help her. But after a few days of the same treatment he'd give any male colleague, she'd realize she wasn't cut out for journalism. No woman was. She'd get over her ideals and he'd get on with his life, such as it was, or had been until this afternoon. A bachelor's life, which was the only kind any reporter should live. For now, he wished only that she would hurry up. The temperature must have dropped twenty degrees in the last twenty minutes.

"This is America, Babe," he called. "You don't have to walk thirty paces behind me, though personally, I have no objection to the custom."

Madeleine drew to a halt. She'd lugged her valises on and off four trolleys and down streets without sidewalks and so deeply rutted, they'd have challenged a plow horse. Her feet and ankles screamed for mercy, her arms quivered with strain; the rest of her was merely numb with cold. And disbelief. She was married to a man who'd been content to watch her do the work of a pack mule—not that she would have allowed him to carry her bags if he'd offered. At least he hadn't lied, she thought, taking a look around his neighborhood and a whiff of the nearby Illinois and Michigan Canal. They were, indeed, going to be living in squalor. In fact, she wouldn't be surprised if they'd be living in a boxcar or on a garbage scow.

Hiking her valises one more time, she trudged toward McQuinn. "The only reason I'm following you is that I'm hoping you'll fall into one of these canyons in the road. Then I can walk on your head. What's . . ." She puffed, all but exhausted. "What's holding you up? All tuckered out?"

"Slightly tuckered out. Also, this is where I live."

Drawing to a halt beside him, Madeleine looked at the moonlit silhouette of a small two-story frame house with a pitched roof and sagging on one side. It reminded her of the pre-Civil War shanties she'd seen in Louisville's Bug Alley, so weary and worn no one gave much thought to who lived inside them. How many women, she wondered, had entered such houses and, though living, were never heard from again?

However many, she thought, she wasn't going to be one of them. Not this house nor the man with whom she would share it would defeat her, though he, at least, was already trying his best. But Daniel McQuinn would soon discover, she thought, looking at him, that his best had more than met its match.

"Then, I live here, too, McQuinn. Remember that." Without waiting for his reply, she walked up the path and climbed the stairs to the front door. McQuinn followed, and when he took a key from his pocket, she said, "I'll want my own key, of course."

"Of course," Daniel replied, pushing open the door. "But *you* should remember that some doors are better left locked."

"The door to the *Clarion*'s city room, for example?" Madeleine stepped across the threshold. "I know that as a woman I won't be welcomed, but I'm not afraid."

"That's not the only place you won't be welcomed," Daniel muttered, staring past her, "and I'm scared to death."

Suddenly, Madeleine felt a presence behind her, large, predatory and breathing heavily. Slowly, she turned around and came bosom-to-bosom with a florid-faced, red-haired, middle-aged version of "Sadie." And *this* is the woman McQuinn claimed looked good compared to her?

"Good evenin'. You must be Mrs. Corrigan," she said, offering her hand. "My husband certainly thinks"—Madeleine glanced down at the woman's chest—"about you a lot."

"Your hoosbund? Dan'l?" With a cackle, Eileen Corrigan overlooked Madeleine's hand, looking her over instead. "Don't you be thinkin' I was born yesterday, ya young tart. I'm a respectable widow woman and I run a respectable house—"

"You're a widow and you run a house, Eileen," Daniel said.

"You get this hussy out of here, Dan'l McQuinn, or I'll have the police after ya for th' rent you owe me."

Stepping inside, Daniel shut the door. From the side pocket of his jacket he removed an envelope containing a "wedding present" from Rawley, took out several bills, and handed them to the widow. "It's all there," he said. "And a month's rent in advance."

The woman counted the money, then stuffed it into the cleavage above the bodice of her dress and below a large cross. "Your doxy still has to go. I'll have none of that here, livin' like man and wife when you ain't."

Daniel took his and Maggie's marriage certificate from his breast pocket. Unfolding it, he held it up to Eileen Corrigan's eyes.

"You know I can't read none of them big words yet, Dan'l. You ain't taught me that far."

Madeleine turned a look of surprise on McQuinn. He'd been teaching his landlady to read?

"It's a marriage certificate, Eileen," he said.

Bending forward, she scrutinized the paper. Then she straightened. "It doesn't look like the one the priest gave Terence and me."

Daniel put the certificate back in his pocket. "We were married by a judge."

"Then you ain't married in my book."

Catching a glimpse of a pucker in the woman's otherwise obstinate chin, Madeleine gathered that reading may not have been the only subject she and McQuinn had studied together. This was all she needed, a spurned landlady who'd as soon see them both freeze to death as fix a broken windowpane. "Now that your rent is paid up," she said to McQuinn, "perhaps we ought to spare this good lady's conscience and find rooms elsewhere."

"No!" The widow pressed her hand to her bosom. "I mean to say, stay or go, it's nothin' to me." Turning, she walked to her own door, past the phone and opposite the staircase. "Only if you stay, Dan'l, your wife can call me 'Mrs. Corrigan'!"

"If I were you, Babe," Daniel said after Eileen had slammed the door, "I'd call her as little as possible."

At the top of the stairs, Madeleine had no choice but to stand close to Daniel in the dark. The landing was barely large enough for one, let alone four, counting her valises. She pressed her back to the wall that was at a right angle to the door, trying to avoid contact with him as he fumbled with the lock. "What's taking you so long?"

"Frankly, Babe," Daniel said, gazing down at her, "I'd expected more modesty of my bride."

"I can't imagine why, given the type of woman you attract." Trying to move the valise that was digging into her thigh, Madeleine groaned. "Will you please just open the door."

"Like *some* people I know, this lock has always been temperamental. If I don't jiggle the key at exactly the right angle . . . Do me a favor, Babe, take a deep breath."

"Pardon me?"

"Only if it will help me open this door. Now breathe in so I can attack this problem from your side."

Madeleine took a deep breath and held it as Daniel pressed against her. "That would be refreshing, your being on my side."

"Not to mention highly unlikely."

"Who needs you, any— Ow! Your elbow's jabbin' my ribs."

"Do forgive me, Magnolia Blossom," Daniel replied,

then wrapped his left arm around her waist. Pulling her against him, he felt his heart—and time—stop. "Aw come on. I've always wanted to make a woman say, 'Unhand me, sir.' "

With her breasts crushed against his chest and aching to be petted, and his scent, a cold smokiness warming to a solid masculinity thawing her resistance, the last thing Madeleine wanted him to do was unhand her. He was doing a far better job unlocking the door to her long-guarded passions than the one to his flat. A door which, as he'd said, was better kept locked.

"I imagine there wasn't enough time before they had to slug you." She pointed at the doorknob. "Difficult as it is for you, do try to concentrate."

I am concentrating, on you. Not that he wanted to, Daniel thought. But feeling the delicacy of her frame and the strength of her spine, she left him no choice. The kinds of women who'd crossed his threshold before were either softly feminine or as unmalleable as rock. Maggie was both, which made her the kind of woman who could make him open to her not only his door, but his life. The kind, he reminded himself, to take his hands off of while he still could.

"I could have picked it by now," he said, applying both hands to the stubborn lock.

"I'm sure," Madeleine replied. "Why don't you?"

Daniel glanced at her over his shoulder. "You'd only accuse me of showing off and trying to make you feel bad because you don't know how pick locks like all us experienced reporters do."

"Oh, but you're wro-o-ong, McQuinn," Madeleine said in a ringingly insincere Southern belle tone. "I'll be asking you to teach me sometime, the way you taught Mrs. Corrigan how to read."

"Not *that* way, you won't," he replied. He gave the lock an angry jiggle, again to no avail. "Dammit."

Take advantage of this offer to enjoy Zebra's newest line of historical romance novels….Splendor Romances (formerly Lovegrams Historical Romances)- Take our introductory shipment of 4 romance novels -Absolutely Free! (a $19.96 value)

Now you'll be able to savor today's best romance novels without even leaving your home with our convenient and inexpensive home subscription service. Here's what you get for joining:

- 4 BRAND NEW bestselling Splendor Romances delivered to your doorstep every month
- 20% off every title (or almost $4.00 off) with your home subscription
- FREE home delivery
- A FREE monthly newsletter, *Zebra/Pinnacle Romance News* filled with author interviews, member benefits, book previews and more!
- No risks or obligations…you're free to cancel whenever you wish…no questions asked

To get started with your own home subscription, simply complete and return the card provided. You'll receive your FREE introductory shipment of 4 Splendor Romances and then you'll begin to receive monthly shipments of new Zebra Splendor titles. Each shipment will be yours to examine for 10 days and then if you decide to keep the books, you'll pay the preferred home subscriber's price of just $4.00 per title. That's $16 for all 4 books with FREE home delivery! And if you want us to stop sending books, just say the word…it's that simple.

4 Free BOOKS are waiting for you!
Just mail in the certificate below!

If the certificate is missing below, write to: Splendor Romances, Zebra Home Subscription Service, Inc., P.O. Box 5214, Clifton, New Jersey 07015-5214

FREE BOOK CERTIFICATE

Yes! Please send me 4 Splendor Romances (formerly Zebra Lovegram Historical Romances), ABSOLUTELY FREE! After my introductory shipment, I will be able to preview 4 new Splendor Romances each month FREE for 10 days. Then if I decide to keep them, I will pay the money-saving preferred publisher's price of just $4.00 each... a total of $16.00. That's 20% off the regular publisher's price and there's never any additional charge for shipping and handling. I may return any shipment within 10 days and owe nothing, and I may cancel my subscription at any time. The 4 FREE books will be mine to keep in any case.

Name _____

Address _____ Apt. _____

City _____ State _____ Zip _____

Telephone ( ) _____

Signature _____ SF1098
(If under 18, parent or guardian must sign.)

"Maybe you're not going at it from the proper angle," Madeleine said dryly.

"Good point. The proper angle is the one I'm leaning at when I come home at four in the morning." Hand braced against the wall beside Maggie's head, he did his best to leer as he crowded her with bodily innuendo. "Like this."

Madeleine arched a brow at him. "It doesn't seem to be working," she said, referring as much to his pathetic attempt to frighten her off as to the still-locked door.

"Right," Daniel said, taking her meaning. Then, pushing up his sleeves, he pointed his shoulder at the door.

"McQuinn, what do you think you're doing?"

"Better stand as far back as you can, Babe. Hardware might go flying and knock you cold, or possibly splinters of wood might hurl your way like thousands of tiny daggers and stick you in the eyes and under the fingernails and—"

"Dream on," Madeleine said, stepping between him and the door. "Now I'd suggest you stand back." Facing the door, she took a deep breath and reached toward the key that was still in the lock. As her hand neared, a click sounded, followed by a long, slow creaking as the door swung open. Dusting off her palms, she gave Daniel a "top that if you can" look.

"That must be the woman's touch I've been told this place could use," he said, then with a rapidity that stole Madeleine's breath, he scooped her up. "Ready to begin married life, Mrs. McQuinn?"

"Don't call me that odious name," Madeleine snapped. "And put me down!"

"And bring bad luck to our happy home?"

"In the first place, we're not really married so we don't have a home. In the second place, I don't believe in silly superstitions."

"In the first place, I have a marriage certificate in my

pocket that says we are really married, and in the second place," he said, carrying her into the flat, "to be a really good reporter, you have to question everything you see and see the possibility of everything you question. Things that lurk in shadows and—"

"Go bump in the night?"

Pulling the key from the lock, Daniel kicked the door shut. Bringing Maggie's lips close to his, he whispered, " 'More things in heaven and earth than are dreamt of in your philosophy.' "

Madeleine pulled back in astonishment. "You know Shakespeare?"

"Yes. But aren't you making much ado about nothing?" Daniel set her down. "Stay here while I light a lamp."

As the odor of kerosene reached Madeleine, she saw McQuinn's belongings emerge from darkness into shadows. For a seemingly interminable moment, they appeared to float like the ghosts and ghouls he'd conjured, the specter of all that the rational mind could not grasp. Shuddering, she put her bags down and hugged herself, partly for warmth and partly for something real to hold on to. Still, she was grateful when he passed behind her with the light and dispelled the shadows, turning the demon hunched in one corner into a chair, the gremlin beside it into a typewriter atop a small trunk, the great arched entrance to an underworld cave into a massive bookcase.

Intrigued, she walked to it. Her fingers trailed her gaze across the spines of books that showed the wear of use, books she never would have imagined McQuinn possessed much less visited like old companions.

Or *had* she imagined it? Suddenly, she wondered if the pirate in her dream, who'd forced her to the edge of her existence, and the faceless man who'd come to her rescue with nothing more than his courage and a book were the same man, at war with himself. Perhaps, she thought, the civilized man who had built this library had already prevailed and now lived in this home. Her new home.

Smiling, she turned around. "McQuinn, I can't wait to see the rest of—" As she saw the flat in the light, her theory imploded and her face fell. "How long have you lived here?"

Daniel shrugged. "Five, six years."

"You couldn't have," Madeleine said, walking to the center of the room. "It's so . . . bare."

"Bare?"

"Bare, as in no rugs, no pictures on the walls . . ." Madeleine turned a circle. "And except for your books, which I admit are impressive, no personal touches."

Daniel looked around then hastened to a spot a few feet behind him. "What would you call this?"

"A crate standing on end."

"It's a dining table, Late Nineteenth Century Functional, which I personally carried up here and touch all the time."

"There's only one stool beside it."

"I always eat alone."

"Why? Do you drool?"

"I may start." Daniel tossed his hat on the bed. "All right, I'll get another stool or something."

Madeleine stared at the bed. "Make that *and* something." Propping her hands on her waist, she looked at Daniel. "Where do you expect *me* to sleep?"

Glancing at the chair in the corner, Daniel winced with imagined discomfort. "I guess you can have the bed."

"Are you sure the fleas won't mind a new tenant?" Madeleine expected a brisk retort. Instead, McQuinn gave her a soft smile that was vaguely haunting in the glow of the lamp he held.

"They should find the scent of lilacs a nice change from the smell of whiskey and tobacco," Daniel said, not knowing exactly why he had.

Unless, of course, he'd done so because ever since he'd carried Maggie into his home, he'd realized it wasn't a home at all. It was just a place to sleep, or to be exact, sleep it off. The moment he'd lit the lamp and saw her standing in the midst of his one spare room, he felt the spareness of his life. Strangely, he'd begun to think of what he might offer her in welcome, as though she were a guest, then as proof of his worth, as though she were an appraiser of souls. He'd panicked because he could think of nothing. Then he watched her touch his books, admiringly, he thought, and he'd felt relieved. No, more than that. He'd felt proud. But when she'd turned and, seeing the rest of the place, had wordlessly expressed not disgust, but the kind of mystified horror he'd felt himself the first few times he'd viewed a body without identity or life, his pride gave way to shame. He'd had no right to bring her here. Worse, he had no hope of making her stay. Worst of all, he wanted her to stay.

Madeleine stood momentarily stunned. She'd expected McQuinn to deliver a quick and equally scathing retort to her scathing insult. Instead, he'd handed her a single flower of a compliment with a sprig of surprisingly frank self-appraisal. Despite the stark anonymity of his quarters, she suddenly felt, not welcome, but as though she belonged. As though she were meant to probe behind the anonymity she believed was as much a disguise of McQuinn as her brown wig was of Madeleine Faurest. Perhaps even more. But she couldn't let him know he wasn't as opaque as he thought. She couldn't risk putting him on guard, eliminating the chance of another inadvertent slip of his mask.

"Don't try to sweet-talk me, McQuinn," she said. "If you want me to make you something to eat, why don't you just ask?"

For once, Daniel was grateful for the sharp edge of Maggie's tongue. If she'd sincerely thanked him for complimenting her, he didn't know what he would have done. Run out the door, probably. Eileen Corrigan was scary, but the Babe was fatal. "All right," he said, setting the lamp down on a battered pine hutch, its yellow paint faded and peeling. "There's a frying pan in here, a cook-stove over there, and eggs in the icebox. How about scrambling some?"

"On second thought, I'm too tired," Madeleine said brusquely, simply because she'd found herself wanting to do something nice for him. Walking to the bed, she sat down then bounced on it a few times. "It's lumpy."

Crossing to her, Daniel took her by the shoulders and drew her off the bed.

"Now what are you doing?"

"Removing the lump." He picked up his hat, newly flattened, and showed it to her.

Madeleine chuckled. "Did I do that?"

"As if you didn't mean to," he said, making a jibing reference to the cut on his cheek. He put the hat on.

Madeleine frowned. "Going somewhere?"

"Yeah, somewhere." Anywhere, Daniel thought as he walked to the door, where Maggie wasn't.

"Wait, McQuinn! I'm going with you."

Exasperated, he turned on her. "There are still, thank God, some places a man can find privacy."

"You wear your hat to the necessary? How dashing."

He was dashing all right, Daniel thought, out the door. Opening it, he said, sarcastically, "Don't wait up for me, sweet."

Madeleine grabbed his arm. "You can't leave. We have work to do, remember?"

"It's my wedding night, Babe. I'm entitled to some pleasure."

Picturing McQuinn stuffing money into the bodice of some prostitute's corset cover, Madeleine pushed his arm away. "You disgust me."

Daniel chucked her chin. "That, Babe, isn't exactly front-page news."

After McQuinn left, Madeleine fumed at him for as long as she felt he was worth fuming over, about a minute. Then she fried eggs and a bit of bacon, fished a brown wool cape with black trim from a valise, and headed for the door. Let McQuinn find dubious comfort with prostitutes on the Levee; she'd find out who was killing them. True, Rawley had assigned her to cover the story on the condition that McQuinn accompany her. But she imagined it was going to be a while before McQuinn was in a condition to cover anything but his eyes from the harsh light of day. Besides, what harm could come to her in simply talking to the denizens of the Levee, any one of whom might provide a clue to The Red Rose Killer's identity?

Realizing she'd forgotten to turn down the lamp, Madeleine turned back. As she did, she caught sight of McQuinn's typewriter and the trunk on which it sat. Until now, she hadn't wondered what secrets, if any, the small trunk might hold; what clues to his identity, the true one she was now convinced he was hiding.

Convinced, because two men lived in this all but barren flat, the one who'd just walked out the door bent on a night of carousing and the one who'd read his copy of Dante's *Divine Comedy* so often, the binding was loose, the corners of the pages creased. As Madeleine bent over the typewriter, she wondered if there had been a Beatrice in McQuinn's life, a great lost love who would one day guide him through Heaven.

"He'd have to get there first," she said, doubting the likelihood of that ever happening. Still, the thought of McQuinn's idealizing any woman let alone loving one with a singular, undying passion spurred her to lift the heavy machine and set it on the floor. Puffing, she knelt before the trunk and hoped only that she wasn't about to open McQuinn's version of Pandora's box. She rubbed the clamminess from her palms and grasped the lid.

"Dan'l! You're wanted on the telephone!"

Hearing Eileen Corrigan's voice shouting from below, Madeleine jerked her hands back. Getting to her feet, she went to the door and paused, thinking what to say. Even if she weren't a real bride, there was no need for her lascivious landlady to know her husband had walked out on her on her wedding night. She opened the door a crack. "My husband's busy, Mrs. Corrigan."

She gave Madeleine a chillingly resentful look. "And at what you don't have to tell *me*."

"Please take a message," Madeleine said. *And a cold bath.*

"Tell him 'tis that man again, the one with a voice like a black cat's breath. That Detective Grimm."

"I don't care who it is. Tell him—" Madeleine pictured the name she'd written in her notebook this morning, the one Monsignor Bianco had given her. He'd said Detective Grimm had been an inmate at St. Augustine's ten years ago and would be happy to speak to her. At the time, she'd thought the name sounded familiar. Now she knew why. She'd read it often enough in McQuinn's stories. Obviously, he was McQuinn's source inside the police department and someone she ought to know, but not for what he could tell her about the Red Rose murder investigation alone. For what he might tell her about another a boy he surely must have known at St. Augustine's.

Delaney.

"Ask Lieutenant Grimm to hold the wire, Mrs. Corrigan," Madeleine said. "And tell him Babe McQuinn is on her way."

Within minutes of speaking to the whisper-voiced detective, Madeleine was indeed on her way, to meet him in the alley behind Dearborn Street. The same alley toward which Captain Carnation had been stealing her when McQuinn came along. There was a bloom in the alley tonight, but according to the detective, not a carnation.

In the alley tonight, in the limp hand of a lifeless young woman was a single red rose.

Of course, she'd had quite a time extracting the information from Grimm, and then, only on the assurance she would pass it along to Daniel, who he clearly doubted was truly her husband. Getting him to share the preliminary facts in his investigation when she arrived on the scene might prove impossible. Even if she could convince him she truly was McQuinn's wife, policemen were as hostile to women covering their beat as city editors were.

But then, she'd won the confidence of no less an editor than G. Vernon Rawlston. She saw no reason why she shouldn't eventually win the confidence of the Chicago Police Department, starting with Lieutenant Benny Grimm. And she wouldn't need McQuinn's influence with Grimm.

She had Delaney.

Ten

At the macabre coffin-shaped bar inside the White-chapel Club, Daniel downed his third shot of whiskey, poured a fourth, then rejoined a crossfire of speculation about The Red Rose Killer. Word had reached the club's members that Daniel had been on the Levee last night, probing for information leading to the identity of the killer. And so, back on the story, he'd been welcomed back into the fold by everyone but Finley Peter Dunne, who'd yet to arrive. Daniel expected that Peter would first impose a "penance" on him, to drink from one of the silver-lined human skulls, perhaps, though that was part of a ritual normally reserved for honored guests. But then, what guest was traditionally more honored than a returning prodigal?

Still, the prospect of a revel, during which there was a good chance they'd all end up at the Stockyards to literally slay the fatted calf, left Daniel flat. His flat, and the woman he'd left there, was the reason. He couldn't stop thinking about Maggie. He couldn't stop wondering what she was doing at this very moment, alone in his apartment and maybe afraid. Nah, she didn't have sense enough to be afraid, he told himself. And suddenly, Daniel was very, very afraid. What if she was neither in his apartment nor alone?

"Aw, she's probably sleeping," he muttered to himself.

After all, she'd said she was tired and he hadn't blamed her. She'd lugged those damn bags of hers all over the city since before she'd walked into Rawley's office a single woman until he himself had carried her into his flat a married woman crime reporter. When he'd left, he'd simply assumed she'd stay there and, after exhausting herself soundly cursing him or perhaps slashing his ties with a paring knife, go to bed. But he'd assumed stupidly because he'd stupidly forgotten what he'd discovered in Rawley's office that morning, when he'd read her story. Although the Babe wasn't an experienced crime reporter, she had an experienced crime reporter's instincts. And those instincts would tell her to forget about sleep and head for the scene of the crime.

"My God, she's gone to the Levee," he said, shoving his glass away. He shot up, turned to the door, and headed right into Finley Peter Dunne.

"I didn't expect to see you here tonight, McQuinn," Dunne said. "Let me buy you a drink." He reached for one of the two silver-lined skulls on the table, reputedly the one of Frances Warren. Known as "Waterford Jack," she'd claimed to have earned a million dollars in a decade of streetwalking.

"Some other time, Peter. I have to find my—"

"Wife?"

Daniel stood stunned. "How did you know?"

"One of the boys from the *Herald* saw you at City Hall this afternoon, walking out of Judge Kelly's chambers with a woman. He heard the judge's clerk congratulate a Mr. and Mrs. McQuinn." Dunne chuckled. "Did you hear that, Gentleman? McQuinn is a bridegroom."

Daniel listened to the eruption of whistles and ribald jokes. "I had no choice. I swear!"

Spying a folded piece of paper in McQuinn's breast pocket, Dunne whisked it out then read it. "And we know why," he said, laughing. He showed the marriage certifi-

cate Daniel had forgotten about around the table. "Who
got the clerk to date the certificate back six months, Mac?
Vern Rawlston?"

"Hey, Mac," Gene Field called from the end of the table. "What are you going to do if the kid looks like the
milkman?"

"Shut up! All of you." Daniel's shout silenced the
room. "The next one of you who talks like that about
Maggie will answer to my fist."

"Oh, a love match!"

Bounding to the end of the table, Daniel hauled Gene
Field to his feet. "If you weren't so drunk I'd—"

"Easy, McQuinn," Dunne said, pulling Daniel away
from Field. "Gene's still trying to make up for writing
'Little Boy Blue' by accusing any of us he can of sentimentality unbecoming of a reporter. Obviously, if you'd
lost your reason out of all proportion and given your
heart to the lady, you wouldn't be here on your wedding
night."

Daniel knew he couldn't have lost his reason and given
his heart to Maggie if he'd wanted to. He'd already given
it to Madeleine ten years ago. Relaxing, he laughed genially. "Mrs. McQuinn *is* a lady, gentlemen, but she won't
be for long. You see, my wife is the *Clarion*'s newest crime
reporter." Daniel knew he could have said she was a Sia-
mese twin and not elicited more astonished expressions.

"You're joking, of course," Gene Field said. "There's
no such thing as a woman on the crime beat, and God
willing, there never will be."

"God," Daniel began, "as in G. Vernon Rawlston has
already willed otherwise."

Quickly summarizing the circumstances of his marriage, he took heat for agreeing to play nursemaid to
some fool woman who fancied herself a reporter. But
when he replied that, as much as he hated to admit it,
his ward was a damn good writer, he touched off a

firestorm. There was loud indignation over women trespassing on solidly male territory, firm pronouncing of
their inability to do the work, and speculation about Rawlston's sanity. None of the arguments against women covering crime—the scene; the morgue; the capture, trial,
jailing, and execution of the criminal—were new to him.
He'd made them all himself at one time or another.
Women were too frail, too fearful. They'd faint at autopsies.

The problem Daniel now had as he listened to the others deriding women was that he saw just one woman. Maggie. He saw her on Canal Street, struggling with two heavy
bags at the end of the long journey from downtown and
an even longer day, and knew that what she lacked in
strength she made up for in sheer willpower. He saw her
strutting pitifully in front of the arcade on Dearborn
Street, offering herself as bait to a vicious killer, and knew
that she wasn't so much fearless—no one was—as determined and able to conquer her fears. And as for the likelihood of her fainting at autopsies, he recalled the one
time he'd seen her near fainting, in Rawley's office this
morning, not because her stomach was weak but because
it was empty. As he'd caught and held her, she'd felt like
a steel filament wrapped in the softest velvet. Besides,
he'd once seen a rookie cop keel over at the first autopsy
he'd viewed.

The only objection to Maggie's working the crime beat
that Daniel couldn't overcome was that for all her will,
courage, and stamina, she was still physically vulnerable.
A crime reporter didn't keep the best company and often
attracted the worst. At times, he'd had all he could do to
keep himself alive. In similar circumstances, the Babe
wouldn't have a prayer.

"A woman covering crime news is obscene," Field said.

"It's intolerable," Dunne replied. "Before we know it,
city rooms all over town will be wallpapered and hung

with chintz curtains. McQuinn, the woman's still your wife. You have to do something about her."

"I intend to," Daniel said, snatching his marriage certificate from Dunne and returning it to his pocket. Then he walked to the door, paused, and looked back at the brotherhood, his brotherhood. "I'm going to protect her."

Madeleine stood in the alley behind Dearborn Street, back from the policemen around the body of The Red Rose Killer's latest victim, whom she'd just viewed. At the sight of the girl's blank, staring eyes, her hideously gaping throat, and the incomprehensible red rose in her hand, Madeleine had felt a convulsion of horror. Then, abruptly, as though a curtain had descended between her and the brutally slain girl, she no longer saw her. She felt a detached calm possess her. She was so in control of herself, in fact, that when Lieutenant Grimm had spotted her and angrily shunted her to the spot where she now stood, anyone would have thought *he* were an hysterical woman.

Now, he approached her, conspicuously chewing a wad of gum.

"Who is she, was she, Lieutenant?" she asked.

"That's none of your business," Benny Grimm replied, hiking his trousers.

She'd never get used to his breathy voice, Madeleine thought, especially if that breath were tinged with alcohol as it was now. If his appearance weren't so disarmingly round and grandmotherly, she would have said there was something about him that, if not quite sinister, unsettled her. One thing she wouldn't allow to unsettle her, however, was his attitude.

"I told you, Lieutenant, I'm a reporter with the *Clarion*. I've been assigned to this story."

"I'll believe that when I see it."

"You're seeing it."

Crackling his gum, Benny Grimm pushed his hat back from his face. "I mean when I see your press credentials."

"Oh." Madeleine paused. "Well, you see, Rawley—"

"You mean Vernon Rawlston?"

"I *mean* Rawley," she said. "He was so busy arranging a wedding for McQuinn and me, he forgot about my credentials."

"That's impossible."

"That he forgot to get me a press badge?"

"That you're married to Daniel," Benny said, walking her farther from the crime scene. "Not only is he one of my best friends, I've been after him for years to settle down. If he was getting married, he'd'a told me. Now I don't know who you are, lady, but you're not Mrs. Daniel McQuinn."

"For better or worse, Benny, I'm afraid she is." Through the small crowd that had gathered at the scene, Daniel approached, glad to see Maggie safe and gladder to see her on her feet. He'd viewed The Red Rose Killer's work and it wasn't pretty. "I'm sorry there wasn't time to let you know," he said, clasping Benny's pudgy upper arm. "I'll explain later."

"Where have you been, Danny?" Benny asked. "Or don't I want to know?"

"You don't want to know," Madeleine replied, noticing she'd had some difficulty forming her words. Noticing, too, that when she saw McQuinn, a tiny fissure marred her monolithic calm. Through it, she glimpsed the image of the murdered girl's hand cupping the rose the killer had placed in it.

"I've been at the Whitechapel Club," Daniel said.

Madeleine had heard wild stories about the fraternity of writers and journalists. Fractious as it was, it wasn't a brothel, and to her surprise, she was relieved to discover McQuinn had been there instead of in some other woman's bed. "How did you get word of the murder there?" she asked, her words, for no apparent reason, slightly slurring.

"I didn't. I only heard about a minute ago, on Dearborn Street."

Madeleine lowered her eyes, following the direction of her heart. McQuinn had been headed for the Levee and a lover all along.

"It's a good thing I figured out," he continued, "that not only wouldn't you wait up for me, you wouldn't wait at all."

Madeleine looked up. Lord, but McQuinn was handsome and something even more compelling at the moment. Familiar. "You realized I'd come here."

Daniel nodded. "That wasn't smart, Babe."

A familiar know-it-all, Madeleine thought. "No it wasn't. You should have figured it out a lot—" As a vision of the dead girl's eyes flickered before her own, she couldn't get out the word "sooner."

Daniel frowned. He'd noticed a trace of alcohol on Benny's breath, but Maggie was the one who looked and sounded as though she'd been at the still. "Babe, you've been a reporter less than day. Isn't it a little soon to start hitting the bottle?"

Not if it's over your head, she heard herself reply, but only in her mind. Her mouth had never opened. Until McQuinn arrived, she'd had no trouble talking. Now, she was feeling increasingly less detached from the gruesome scene behind her and more so from her own body.

Daniel moved closer to her. If she'd heard him, she'd have pulled the trigger on her tongue and fired back. "Babe, are you all right?"

His voice was like the cape she wore, Madeleine thought, soft brown wool, warm and accustomed. So why wasn't it keeping out images of slaughter the way her cape kept out the cold? "I won't be all right until we find the man who did that." She tried to look around at the victim, but all she could manage was a sluggish nod in her direction.

"We will, I promise you," Daniel said softly, relieved to hear the bravado that told him she was in possession of her faculties. He turned to Benny. "From now on, Babe and I are on this story together. Anything and everything you would tell me you can tell her."

"Not everything, Danny. Not—"

"Yes, even the sexual aspects." Daniel looked at Maggie. "The autopsy on one of the victims showed she was still a virgin. Whatever the killer's motive, it isn't sex."

"What could his motive be, then?" Madeleine asked. When both McQuinn and Benny Grimm ignored her question, walking to the body instead, she became furious. Then she realized she hadn't posed it out loud. Something strange was happening to her, something she had to stop. Closing her eyes, she prayed. Not in form, but for the first time, in true supplication. Rawley had risked putting her to the test. She couldn't fail him. She couldn't fail herself. She couldn't fail that girl lying dead just a few feet behind her.

Standing beside Benny, Daniel looked down at the body delineated by a police blanket. "Tell me about this one," he said.

"Fully clothed, no signs of sexual assault." Benny glanced back at Madeleine. "Danny," he said, his whisper suddenly strident, "are you out of your mind marrying a woman like that?"

Daniel lit a cigarette. "Like what?"

"The kind you don't mind talking to about such things as no man who respects a woman would talk to about?"

Turning to Benny, Daniel dropped his match to the pavement between their feet. "If you're trying to say my wife isn't a decent woman, I wouldn't if I were you."

Benny tugged his belt buckle. "I didn't mean she

wasn't decent, only that she's one of those 'new women' who's always making trouble for a man instead of a home." Benny spit his gum out, landing the wad on the covered corpse. "You deserve a good home, Danny, considering the one you grew up in."

And the one you grew up in. Daniel recalled the night at St. Augustine's when Benny had confessed what he'd never told another soul since, not even his own wife. Especially not thoroughly wholesome Alice. Benny had never known his father, and perhaps, not even his mother knew who the man was. Even as she'd raised Benny, she'd been a prostitute.

"Thanks, Benny," he said, then smiling, patted his friend's belly. "But I don't put as much stock in homemade apple pie as you do."

"Maybe," Benny replied. "But I know what you do put stock in, and believe me, that lady reporter over there is nothing like—"

"Madeleine," Daniel said in a hush. "I remembered her name, Benny."

Benny took a long, hard look at Maggie McQuinn. "Danny, you haven't gone and fooled yourself that just because she talks like her—"

"That she *is* Madeleine?" Daniel gazed at the woman who was as drab as Madeleine had been radiant. "I might be crazy but I'm not blind. Still, do me a favor and don't give her a hard time. If the day ever comes I need your help getting her out of my hair, I'll let you know."

Benny paused. "Anything you say, Danny boy."

"I say we talk about *her,*" Daniel said, squatting beside the body and lifting the blanket covering her face. Lowering his head and closing his eyes, he sighed. They were getting younger, the victims. Rising, he took his notebook and a pencil from inside his jacket, questioned Benny, then approached the man who had discovered the body.

Benny approached Madeleine. "Sorry if I went rough

on you, Maggie. It comes with the job, I guess. Believing that nobody's who or what they seem."

Madeleine's instinct was to search for telltale blond hairs escaping her brown wig, but seeing a picture of the dead girl's own soft, golden hair, she found she could lift her hand no higher than her shoulder. After hovering there for a moment, it fell to her side. She felt her head begin to loll.

"You sick, Maggie? Maybe you shouldn'a come here, like Daniel said."

Yes I'm sick, she thought, not knowing why. Knowing only that she couldn't reinforce McQuinn's and Benny Grimm's prejudice against women reporters. Fighting to hold her head up, she managed one shake of it. "It's been a long day," she said. Then, "Early this morning, I talked to a Monsignor Bianco—"

"You went to St. Augustine's?"

"I thought a story about what became of some of the boys who were there, say, ten years ago, might be interesting. One, I understand, was killed in a railroad accident, a boy named—"

"Come on, Babe," Daniel said, taking Maggie by the arm and hauling her away. "We have work to do."

"But I just want to ask Benny—"

"He's already told me everything he knows about the girl. We have to call in what we know and find out as much as we can of what we don't."

Madeleine relented. McQuinn was right. They needed to get to a phone and call the story of this latest murder in to the *Clarion*'s night city desk. The competition wasn't going to wait for her to question Benny about Delaney. For the moment, she'd have to contain her craving to know more about him, to know if he'd ever loved anyone, hated anyone. A young girl, perhaps?

A young girl. Suddenly, the curtain that had descended between Madeleine and the murdered girl lifted, bringing her face-to-ghastly-face with the full horror of the crime. Inwardly, she became hysterical. Outwardly, she went so numb that she couldn't feel McQuinn's grasp of her arm as he propelled her away from the scene.

"There's a whiskey mill called Jake's in the next block," he told her as they made it out of the alley. "We can phone the paper from there."

The very next thing she knew, she was standing next to McQuinn in back of the bar in a cheap saloon. She had no idea how long it had taken them to get there nor any memory of what she might have seen or heard on the way. She supposed that was because she was losing her mind.

Still, she knew that the instrument McQuinn was holding out to her was a telephone, its stalk in one of his hands and its receiver in the other. What did he want her to do with them? she wondered.

"You got to the scene first, Babe," he said. "You give the story to rewrite."

As she looked at the phone, all she could think was how cold she was, cold and frozen even though inside her, panic was heating to a boil. "I . . . I don't think I can."

"Of course you can," Daniel said, shoving the phone at her.

"But—" Madeleine looked aside, at the specter of that poor girl with her white, startled, dead face. Who could have committed so unspeakable a crime? *A monster,* she thought. She had to report that a monster in the guise of a man was still on the loose. "The police wouldn't give me any information. You have the notes."

Switching the receiver to his other hand, Daniel took his notepad from his pocket. He opened it on the ledge behind the bar. "Can you read my writing?"

Madeleine looked at the notepad, then nodded. Not only was his lettering clear and surprisingly elegant, for some inexplicable reason the very sight of it warmed her, quashed the last of the rebellion against her sanity. She reached for the receiver. McQuinn placed it in her curved fingers.

They betrayed her. Completely numb and unable to grasp, they let the phone slip through them. She met McQuinn's gaze, and, seeing alarm in it, knew she had every right to the fear gripping her.

Seeing fright in her eyes, Daniel took Maggie by the shoulders. "What is it, Babe? What's wrong?" When she didn't answer, he gave her a shake. "Talk to me, dammit!"

Madeleine slowly blinked several times. "My hands, McQuinn," she muttered. "They're paralyzed."

"Jake, pour us two whiskeys," he shouted down to the proprietor at the far end of the bar. Then he turned to Maggie. "I thought something was wrong back there in the alley. Why didn't you say something?"

"The story."

"The hell with the story!" Daniel was angry with himself, not her. He should have recognized the signs of shock. Grabbing her wrist, he hauled her toward the door. "I'm taking you home."

"Not until I call in the story!" Madeleine wedged herself in the corner of the bar, yanking Daniel toward her. "Hold the receiver for me, McQuinn. Please."

Narrowing his gaze on her, Daniel saw the breadth of her courage and determination. There was no use arguing with her. "All right, Babe." He walked her back to the phone, pulled over a stool, and sat her down on it. Then he took one of the whiskeys Jake had deposited on the bar and put it to Maggie's lips. "But drink this first. We have to get your blood flowing again."

Madeleine took a sip, grimaced, then shuddered as the crude concoction scorched a path to her stomach.

"Not exactly wedding night champagne, is it?"

Madeleine looked askance at him, not sure what to

make of his remembering that it was their wedding night, especially since she'd forgotten the fact the instant she saw that girl's face. She supposed he was so callused to the sight of violent death that it no longer intruded on his reality, the way his nearness was now intruding on hers, altering it, becoming a part of it.

"No, it isn't," she said, softly. "But then champagne is for whispering sweet nothings into your beloved's ear, not for dictating a murder story into the phone."

Suddenly, Daniel wanted nothing more than to hear her whisper in his ear, feel her full, pale lips on it and her sweet breath in it. No, he wanted more. He wanted her to breathe her spirit into him. Apparently, it was a night for shocks. Putting down Maggie's glass, he downed a swig from his own.

"All right, Babe. Get ready to dictate," he said, slamming down his glass and picking up the phone. After reaching the *Clarion* and asking for the city desk, he came behind Maggie's left shoulder. With his left hand, he held the phone's mouthpiece to her mouth, discovering he was jealous of it. Then, bending and bringing his right ear close to her left, he held the receiver so that they could both hear.

Madeleine closed her eyes. She'd expected her heart to trip with the anxiety of calling in a story for the first time, but with McQuinn so near, it was threatening to burst. Still, she couldn't bear for him to move so much as an inch. She could feel his faith in her. And God help her, she could feel his lips.

"City Desk, Johnson," Madeleine heard.

"This is Babe McQuinn. Get me a rewrite man."

"You got one, lady, and you might as well know now, we've heard all about you and there isn't one of us who'll take a story from a woman."

Daniel yanked the phone from Maggie's mouth to his own, bringing her lips to his. "Listen, Johnson," he said, his cheek pressed to hers, his breath and hers forming a single exhalation. "Unless you'd like for your wife to know that the mugger who relieved you of your pay envelope two weeks ago had four legs, a mane, and a helluva swayed back, you'll take this story from *my* wife exactly as she gives it you!"

Johnson called Daniel a name which neither he nor Madeleine heard over the drumbeat summoning their passions. "McQuinn," Madeleine whispered against his lips, hungering for them. "Saying we're married is one thing, but calling me your wife—"

"Isn't that what you are, Babe, my wife?" His lips parted, Daniel breathed over a corner of Maggie's mouth. Touching the tip of his tongue to it and tasting its sweetness and texture, like the flesh of ripe fruit, he instantly hardened and pulsed and ached for her. Ached unbearably for his wife.

Yes, I'm your wife, Daniel. Probably for worse, poorer, and in sickness, she thought, but also for this, the ecstasy of his kiss. Turning her mouth openly and eagerly to his lips, she took McQuinn's tongue into it. Flicking her own tongue against its whiskied warmth, she torched a blaze in the core of her womanhood, a gorgeous, ravenous conflagration that would consume her until McQuinn—until her husband—took her in his arms and to his bed and quenched it.

"What the hell are you waiting for, Babe? I got other stories to work on, you know."

Hearing Johnson's impatient call, Madeleine groaned. Daniel trailed his tongue from her mouth, leaving soft kisses on her lips as he touched his fingertips to her cheek. For a moment, they stared at one another, their chests heaving slow deep breaths, their gazes sharing both puzzlement and pain.

"Come on, Babe," Johnson snapped. "Do you want this story on the front page of the next edition or not?"

Madeleine inhaled sharply. She turned from McQuinn, shivering at the loss of the intimacy they'd shared. "All right, Johnson, here it is," she began. And sitting behind a bar with a whiskey and a tall drink of undistilled man at her side, his raw notes before her, she dictated her story. Their first story, Daniel and Babe McQuinn's.

When she'd finished, McQuinn hung up the phone. Standing before her, he lifted her chin and her gaze. "I couldn't have done better myself."

Tears sprang to Madeleine's eyes. "Oh, McQuinn," she murmured. She strained to lift her hand to his face, but as it neared his mouth, it dropped to her side. Her head slumped as the events of the most incredible day of her life weighed around her.

Wrapping Maggie in his arms, he walked her to a booth in a dark corner and slid her to the far end of a hard bench. As a Creole banjo band struck up a bawdy tune, he began vigorously rubbing first one of her hands between his, then the other. When, at his signal, Jake brought their whiskeys to the table, he made Maggie finish all but a swallow of hers.

"Feel anything?" he asked.

"That depends. Are you trying to get me drunk?"

Daniel laughed quietly. "Try making a fist."

Madeleine curved her fingers but couldn't tightly curl them. She gazed worriedly at Daniel. "What's wrong with me, McQuinn? After all, I've seen what murder looks like."

He took back her hand. "But not the kind of evil you saw tonight. At first, your mind refused to believe it even exists, then, after a while . . ."

"I saw you," Madeleine said, and laid her head against the back of the booth.

Daniel paused. "I know I'm no saint, but . . ."

Madeleine chuckled softly. "I mean, for some reason

when I saw you, I began to let it in, the horror of what I'd just seen, and as you said, the evil of it."

He laid his head next to hers. "Maybe you felt safe."

Madeleine peered into the coal dark centers of his silver eyes, the eyes of a pirate who loved *The Divine Comedy.* She smiled. "Don't ask me why, but I think I must have."

Daniel stopped grazing his fingers over the back of her hand. Looking at Maggie, he suddenly found himself falling into her mysterious well of a gaze, the way he once had Madeleine's. And as he had then, he desperately wanted to tap it.

"I'm glad you feel safe with me, Babe."

Madeleine looked away. There were some things not even McQuinn could keep her safe from because there were secrets she couldn't entrust even to him. She held too many unanswered questions about who he really was to divulge who she really was. Besides, as reassuring as he'd been tonight, last night in her dreams, he'd been a pirate who'd driven her to the edge of her existence.

"If I did," she said, sitting up, "I made a mistake. I can't afford to feel safe with anyone."

Abruptly, Daniel let go of her hand. Any mistake was all his, especially the urge he'd had to tell her that he could willingly die for her. "We need to get going if we're to have any hope of finding someone who might have seen the girl earlier tonight. See if you can pick up your glass."

Hearing the ice in his voice, feeling his body grow chill, Madeleine gripped the glass with cold, hard resolve. She lifted it, her confidence renewed. But halfway to her mouth, her hand trembled violently and the glass fell to McQuinn's quick retrieval.

"Dammit." She looked at Daniel mistrustfully. "I imagine you can't wait to tell Rawley about this."

"I'll say. You swore."

"I meant this damn paralysis." Propping her elbows on

the table, she lowered her head to her hands, her fingers tingling as though thawing after long exposure to freezing cold. "Why don't you just say it? I couldn't take seeing that poor, butchered girl. A woman isn't fit for crime reporting."

Daniel lowered her arm then, lifting her chin, turned her face to his. "The first story I covered was about a drowning in Lake Michigan. The man's body had been in the water about a week when I saw it. And that's about how long it was before I could hold down three meals a day again."

Madeleine grazed the backs of her fingers down Daniel's cheek, noting that the only thing they tingled with now was the feel of his skin. "McQuinn, that's the nicest thing you've ever said to me."

Smiling, Daniel took her hand, rubbing his thumb over her palm. "I wasn't trying to be nice to you, Babe. I was just trying to warn you that you might not want to cover drownings."

"Or the Red Rose murders?" A smile sidling up her face, Madeleine tapped his cheek. "Let's go, McQuinn. As you said, somebody must have seen that girl earlier tonight and, just maybe, the monster who killed her."

Eleven

Midnight had long gone when Madeleine walked with Daniel against the wind, past hulking mills and deserted warehouses toward his—their—Canal Street flat. They'd exhausted their search for witnesses who might have seen the murdered girl in the hours prior to her death. They should have exhausted themselves, as well, Madeleine thought. Instead, the farther they traveled from the Levee toward Bridgeport, the faster they walked, as though sparking one another not only toward a shared destination, but toward a shared destiny. Moreover, she had no doubt that McQuinn was also pondering this unexpected alliance between them, between two people who had begun the day in mutual contempt and had ended it in a cooperative hunt for a killer. Several blocks back, he'd fallen with her into taut and silent contemplation.

Then, she sneezed.

Without stopping, McQuinn removed his jacket and draped it over her shoulders. Wrapping his arm tightly about her, he drew her hard against his side. He said nothing. Madeleine would have clipped him if he had. Words would have defiled his gesture, poorly approximated the truth, which was that McQuinn had only to look at her, graze her with his touch, and she felt a shield form around her. Around them both. And between them, a bond she shared with no other soul. *Living* soul. They were indeed an exclusive society of two, joined by their profession and by the Red Rose story. And by something else.

Marriage.

Madeleine wondered when, exactly, the idea of being married to Daniel McQuinn had ceased to repulse her. Calling the events of the day and the longest night to mind, she couldn't identify a turning point. Rather, she saw that a series of moments had combined to reverse her contemptuousness of him: The moment in his flat when she'd held his books and felt love embedded in their covers. The moment she'd recognized him in that murderous alley behind Dearborn Street and instinctively felt safe. And then, when she'd heard him inform Lieutenant Grimm that she was his partner. She might not have believed her ears if he hadn't then proved, in so many ways, that he really did want her for a partner.

He'd proved it by refusing to spare her the findings of the victims' autopsies; by insisting that the story was hers to call in then laying his notes out before her; by deferring to her wishes and holding the phone to her ear while she, partially paralyzed, dictated the story to rewrite. She couldn't think of another man who would trust her to know better than he what was best for her, not even Rawley. She couldn't think of another man who could melt her by claiming she'd done as fine a piece of reporting as he could have done; by claiming that he, too, had been physically sickened by the grim sight of an unimaginable death. Now that she thought about it, she wasn't sure he'd been telling the truth about that. What she *was* sure of was that he'd been trying to lessen her humiliation.

Those moments alone would have endeared McQuinn to her. But in the midst of them all, he'd kissed her, and not endearingly. He may have given her equal status as a reporter, but when he'd kissed her, he'd only taken—her breath and the little that was left of her reserve. God forgive her, but he hadn't taken nearly enough.

Oh, she wasn't in love with him, not the way she was—had been—*was* with Delaney. But her love for that boy was—had been—always would be the pure, once-in-a-lifetime first kind of love. The kind that happens only to the very young and completely innocent. Well, she was no longer so young. And as for innocent, after lying, cheating, posing as a prostitute, and marrying out of the Church—after the unspeakable evil she'd seen in that alley behind Dearborn Street last night—she was innocent only in the maidenly sense. But she no longer wanted to be. She wanted to lose the last vestige of her innocence and to, of all the unlikely men, her husband. Strangest of all was her conviction, bolstered by the dream she now believed had been alerting her to a war within him, that by losing her innocence to McQuinn, she would be granting him the means—his last hope—of regaining his own.

Only Daniel McQuinn wasn't her husband, not in the eyes of the Church. And yet, in less than a day, they'd become wedded by a most binding power—a side-by-side journey through the streets of hell. And now, feeling the heaven of his solid warmth, of his ribs expanding and contracting with hers, she wanted—needed—to know what he was, if not her husband, in God's eyes.

Her own eyes narrowed on another question. Was God now looking with mercy on the soul of the girl who mere hours ago had agreed to sell her body only to lose her life? She hoped so and prayed there would be none for the girl's killer. Angrily, she kicked a tin can up the street.

"Roses," she said.

"Smelled like corned beef hash to me," Daniel replied, watching the can roll a few feet away then disappear in sooty darkness.

"McQuinn, I meant that I'm still convinced the key to this whole mystery lies with the roses the killer placed in his victims' hands." Madeleine drew up the left side of his jacket collar, nestling her cheek against its nubby texture, as abrasive—and as stimulating—as he. In her core, she felt the wrenching of desire. She laid the collar flat. "If we could just find the flower vendor who sold them to him—"

"My dear Babe, for the third and last time," Daniel began, sliding his hand over the back of her neck and lifting the collar up around her ears. He liked the idea of his clothing caressing her skin. Even better, he liked the idea of his flesh caressing her flesh. Best of all was the fantasy that she really was his dear Babe. She'd been to Hell with him tonight but hadn't let it take her soul. Not that she was like Madeleine, an angel. Maggie McQuinn was too real, too much of this earth and far too much of an earthly temptation to be an angel. And yet, he sensed that wherever Maggie went, there went his salvation. Reaching across himself, he held his jacket closed beneath her chin.

"How do we know," he continued, "that the killer didn't buy the roses at some flower shop on State Street or bring them from his own hothouse?"

In a hothouse was precisely where she could have sworn she was now, Madeleine thought as she flushed to McQuinn's radiating touch and cocooning scent. She took a deep, bracing breath of air. "McQuinn, I've done some gardening in the past—"

"I know, with Percy Teasedale."

Madeleine met his gaze, a tease, a provocative glimpse of the raw edges of his nature. At the core of her nature was the will to hone his edges, but only a little. "The rose I saw in that girl's hand last night was not the highly cultivated type."

"Unlike you."

Madeleine stared at him. He'd spoken the truth. She had been cultivated, bred for a life far different from the one she was leading, from the one she wanted. With him. "Not anymore," she said softly.

That's what worries me, Babe, Daniel thought, knowing that if he told her he still feared she might not survive the transplant from her sunny Southern garden to this cold Northern jungle, she'd only take greater risks to disprove him. He had but one choice. Brushing the backs of curved fingers down her cheek, he vowed to take care of her, certainly for the rest of the night and until they came to the end of the Red Rose story. If he was lucky, for longer than that.

Of course, he hadn't taken care of anyone since he was a kid, when he'd make compresses of comfrey tea to apply to the ugly bruises his father had raised on his mother's face and behind their locked bedroom door. Always behind that door. He remembered how helpless he'd felt to protect her, how he'd sometimes hated himself because he was just a kid. All he could do was to have the compresses ready when his father would finally open the door and, swollen-faced himself, stalk from the house. He'd learned then what it meant to him to feel responsible for someone.

Years later, when he'd grown tall and strong, he learned another lesson—what it felt like to want to kill someone. When Sean Delaney once again swaggered out of that chamber of untold suffering, Daniel clamped his fingers around the man's throat and began to squeeze the miserable life out of him. His mother, failing to stop him, called down for the patrolman on the corner, who did stop him— with a billy club over the top of his head. Daniel went to jail and then to trial and would have gone to prison if a Father Ralph Bianco hadn't intervened on his behalf, asking the court to remand him to St. Augustine's rather than to the penitentiary.

Wherever the judge had sent him, though, he'd have gone feeling betrayed. At his trial, his mother had denied her husband's years of abuse, strengthening the state's case against her son. At his release, she'd disappeared. The neighbors had said she and his father had left Chicago for points unknown, "to make a new start." He might have killed *her* then, if he could have found her, if he hadn't still loved her. He'd spent two years under the "tutelage" of "Monstrous Lucifer" on her account only to discover she'd abandoned him for the man who would surely one day kill her. From the moment of that discovery, Daniel had made a virtue of being responsible for no one but himself.

Until now. Now, he had a wife. True, the Babe was his wife in name only and the name wasn't the one he'd been born with. But for as long as she was willing to go by the name "McQuinn," he would be responsible for her. And at the moment, the responsible thing for him to do was to vanquish the false hope that a flower vendor would lead them to The Red Rose Killer.

"Listen to me, Babe, I've already questioned the flower vendors. I've followed every lead they gave me. Benny's followed the leads. None of them have produced a suspect. You talked to every one of the vendors yourself. Did you hear anything you haven't seen in my notes or read in my stories?"

"No," Madeleine replied. "But we didn't talk to *all* the vendors. There's still the old woman I saw Captain Carnation buy a stem from two nights ago. *She* may know something. We have to find her, McQuinn."

"Sure, and maybe while we're looking for her, we'll also find 'the little people.' "

Stepping from McQuinn's embrace, Madeleine turned to him. "Are you saying you won't help me find her?"

"I'm saying it would take a miracle to find her and, even then, would probably be a waste of a perfectly good miracle."

"Maybe it's time I start believing in miracles," Madeleine said, removing his jacket and laying it over his arm. "I'll find her myself."

"If you don't find your way into the morgue first," Daniel replied, angrily shoving his arms into the sleeves of his jacket. When she'd returned it, she might as well have slapped him. Again. "Do you have any idea how many rum holes and flophouses you'd have to search on the Levee alone?" Half-turning, Daniel paused to light a cigarette. Throwing the match to the ground, he exhaled a stream of smoke. "Even if you got out of those alive, you've still got your Bad Lands, Satan's Mile, Dead Man's Alley, Hell's Half Acre, the Black Hole." When he ran out of fingers on his left hand, he brought the list of Chicago's vice districts up short. "She could be living in any one of those swamps. Hell, she could be dead. Maybe that's why she wasn't around tonight," he said, turning back to the Babe.

She wasn't there.

"Babe?"

Daniel glimpsed a diminishing sliver of soft light above his head. A door was closing. Flinging his cigarette away, he quickly took the five steps ascending to the door, caught it, and dashed through its portal after Maggie. In degrees, he halted and looked around. Had he been blind, though, he would have known where he was despite not having set foot inside a church since he'd left St. Augustine's. There was no scent like that of altar candles, strangely sweet, embracing, otherworldly. Eternal. Though the candles didn't burn and no priest stood on the altar, when Daniel closed his eyes and inhaled the mystical aroma, he could see the ritual of the Latin sacrifice, hear the transporting chant of male voices. As a child, he'd been an altar boy. His mother had never missed a mass he'd served. He remembered holding the paten beneath her chin as she knelt for Communion, the way she'd gazed up at him with pride and at the Host with something like rapture. It was the only time he ever saw her truly happy.

At the stinging sensation behind his eyes, Daniel opened them. After removing his hat, he walked from the vestibule of the church up the main aisle, his gaze sweeping the pews for Maggie. Not finding her, he panicked and turned to the exit. Then he saw her, in an alcove toward the rear of the church, kneeling before tiers of votive candles flickering blue and white at the feet of a statue of the Blessed Virgin. Her head was bowed over her folded hands. Daniel softly approached. Standing to her left several feet away, he watched her, her eyes closed and prayer evident on her lips. He wondered what she was praying for. Forgiveness for a marriage that was sinful and to so great a sinner as he? Deliverance from it, from him?

He gazed at the statue of the Virgin, her expression serene yet strong. *Two things,* he told her. *First, the Babe has nothing to be forgiven for. By marrying me, she did what she had to do and not only for herself. And second . . .* He looked down at Maggie. *I'll never harm her. I'll never touch her until she tells me it's all right with her . . . and with you. All I ask is that if anything should happen to me. If for any reason I can't be with her, take care of her for me.* Daniel turned his gaze back to the Virgin. "Please," he said.

At the sound of his voice, Maggie turned her face to his. Their gazes met but Daniel's image of his wife soon dissolved in a shimmer of mist and candlelight. Maggie McQuinn was looking at him with the same expression of serene rapture he'd seen on the face of Kathleen McQuinn Delaney during the only times she'd been truly happy.

After making the sign of the cross over herself, Maggie rose and came toward him, her gaze transfixing him every step of the way. "Why, Dan'l McQuinn," she said. "Are those tears I see in your eyes?"

Daniel shifted his gaze to the Virgin, then looked down at Maggie. "As far as I know, Babe, all that's in my eyes is you."

Smiling up at him, Madeleine slipped her arm through his. McQuinn didn't know it, but she'd just prayed for the right to make certain that he never looked at another woman the way he was looking at her now.

Thank God, she'd received it.

Shivering and alone, Madeleine climbed the stairs to McQuinn's flat. She'd survived the cold trek to and from the necessary out back of the house by imagining the warm bath she was going to enjoy in the tub McQuinn had told her stood in a small room beneath the stairs. But the tub had been nothing more than a tin basin just large enough for her to stand in and to catch the cold water she ladled from a bucket over her soapy skin. Though she had bundled herself in the wrapper she'd brought with her, as she opened the door she shook uncontrollably— with both cold and foul temper. The least McQuinn could have done was warn her. She'd have gladly lit the kitchen stove herself and heated water to avoid taking pneumonia with her bath. Heaven help him if he met her on the other side of the door.

He did not. Instead, she was met by the warmth of the fire he'd built in the stove while she'd been gone. *Yes, Heaven,* she thought as she rushed toward the glow in the stove's belly, *do help the man all you can.* She held her hands over the heat for a moment, then in a chattering whisper, called, "McQuinn, are you there?"

"Over here," he said.

Madeleine heard his smoky baritone behind her. Keeping her gaze on the fire, she called, "Where's here?"

"By the bed."

Madeleine smiled. "I thought I was to have the bed."

"I have no plans to stop you."

Madeleine puzzled at the blaze and McQuinn's cryptic reply. "Are you there by habit, then, or by design?"

"The design leaves a lot to be desired, I'm afraid, but it will have to do."

"It?" Turning and gazing across the room, Madeleine saw, where the bed ought to be, a dingy sheet. It was one of several hanging over a rope strung diagonally from near the ceiling beside the bed to the corner behind his reading chair.

"Not the queen's bedchamber," he said, as he came from the corner. Holding back the edge of one of the sheets, he showed her the way inside the enclosure. "But it will give you privacy."

For a long moment, Madeleine simply stared at him. He'd removed his coat, shirt collar, even the suspenders from his trousers. His chest muscles were evident beneath the visible part of his long johns, which were unbuttoned nearly to his waist. Black hairs filled the opening she so desperately wanted to widen to admit her touch to his hair and the skin over his muscles, and the shoulders that were even more powerful than the cut of his jacket had suggested. Feeling a deep longing in her own divide, she tore her gaze from him and peered inside the little room he'd made for her. It was going to be a lonely room without him. She gazed up at him. "What made you do this?"

Daniel paused in thought. During the time he'd gone downstairs to borrow the sheets from Eileen Corrigan then hung them, he never questioned whether he ought to or not.

Shrugging, he said, "It was the right thing to do."

Madeleine fixed a puzzled look on him, finding no answer to her unspoken question in his extraordinary eyes, so bathed in the glow of the fire, they had turned to pure light. But she must have an answer. "Was it right because we married for other than love or right because I'm . . . not Mrs. Corrigan."

"I'll say you're not and she's none too happy with you for that reason." Daniel walked to Maggie's valises and lifted one in each hand. "When I told her I needed extra sheets, she rolled her eyes and said, "Oh, she was one of *those.*"

"She meant virgin, of course," Madeleine said as McQuinn passed her, setting her bags inside the room beside the bed. "She thought I'd, we'd, bloodied the sheets."

Stepping out between the two of them, Daniel gazed down at Maggie. With her back to the fire, her eyes were black, unreadable. But a soft light framed her head, turning her brown hair gold. "You're the strangest woman, Maggie McQuinn. Two nights ago you slapped my face because I'd thought you were the kind of woman you were pretending to be. Now, you talk about things . . . I can talk to you about things that I wouldn't think of discussing with any *but* that kind of woman."

"There ought to be only one kind of woman. The kind who's true to herself." Reaching up, Madeleine lightly touched the wound she'd given his cheek the other night. Already, it was disappearing into his encroaching stubble. She ought to cut him regularly, she thought, trim back the undergrowth that would choke his better nature. "One kind of man, too," she whispered.

Daniel clasped her hand in his. "With you, I feel truer to myself than I have in—"

No! In his entire life, he'd been true to himself with only two females and both had betrayed him. He would look after Maggie; he'd be responsible for her. She was, after all, his wife and a damn good reporter. But he would not let her inside him. He would not come to love her. Tearing away from her, Daniel went to the trunk beside his chair in the corner.

"If we're going to start looking for that old flower woman later today, we'd better get some sleep."

He set his typewriter on the floor then placed the trunk in front of the chair. Sitting, he pulled off his shoes then stretched out between the chair and trunk. He pulled his jacket up to his chin. "Good night, Babe," he said, then angled his back to her.

Madeleine sighed. While she'd been praying for the right to take McQuinn to her bed, she should have prayed for advice on getting him there. Still, he'd agreed to help her find the old flower woman. That was a step in the direction she wanted to share with him. The direction she'd set less than an hour ago, inside that church. After she'd promised she would never forget Delaney, never forget the ideal he had been, she'd prayed that he would release her heart for all time.

For the love of Daniel McQuinn.

He wouldn't be an easy man to love nor to make love her. But Madeleine had forsaken ease long ago and without regret. Besides, she sensed that in McQuinn, her time had once again come.

"And what am I to do when my time comes?" she'd asked Eleanor Barlow the day before she'd left Louisville forever.

"Risk your all, Madeleine," Eleanor had replied, her disfigurement her own badge of courage. "Nothing less will do."

Nothing less than abandoning the only life she'd known to live the only life she'd ever wanted had done for Madeleine then. Nothing less than being truly and completely married to McQuinn would do for her now.

The only difference was that when she'd left Louisville for Chicago, she'd merely risked starvation. She'd come terrifyingly close to it, too. And yet, as she gazed at McQuinn's dark figure and saw that he hadn't needed to build a room for her because he'd built walls around himself, she thought starvation nothing compared to what she was risking now.

Her heart and soul.

"Good night, McQuinn," she said. Then, with a glance at the fire that had dwindled to embers, she stepped inside the enclosure she had no fear—or hope—he'd breach tonight.

Indeed, she felt so utterly alone in the now cold and darkened flat that she disrobed without giving a thought to the silver-gray eyes she would have liked to pry. So alone that as she sat wearing the one item from her trousseau she'd brought with her, a lovely white cambric gown trimmed with satin ribbon and French lace, she removed her brown wig, unpinned her long platinum hair, and lingeringly brushed it out. Each stroke, from roots to the tendrilling tips, reminded her that despite her many incarnations, from Madeleine Faurest to Margaret Flynn to "Sadie" and now Babe McQuinn, she was one woman with one destiny. Half of it she'd met in Rawlston's office—was it only yesterday morning?—when he'd offered her a job as a city reporter. The other half lay just outside these mere cotton walls but far beyond her reach.

For now.

After she put her brush and wig away in one of her bags, Madeleine snuggled into McQuinn's bed, burying her cheek in his pillow and drawing his linens up over her mouth. She took a deep breath, hoping to become intoxicated on the mingled scents of his skin and hair. But her hope vanished at the sobering aroma of fresh air. McQuinn had put clean sheets on the bed and even changed the blanket. This one was too soft, she thought as she ran her palm over it, to be the horse blanket she'd seen earlier. He'd probably borrowed it from Mrs. Corrigan along with the other linens. *Damn.* She wished she hadn't made that insulting remark about the fleas minding a new tenant. She hadn't really thought there were fleas in his bed. But even if there had been, they'd be company now. And they'd have been nearer to McQuinn than she was going to be tonight. Perhaps, she thought as her eyes shuttered to a close, for many a night.

Then, remembering that nightfall brought with it the compensation of dreams, Madeleine held an image of McQuinn, not in his fedora nor with a patch over his eye. But the way he'd stood looking at her inside that church.

With innocence.

Hearing a woman's anguished moans, Daniel stirred from a deep and only recent sleep. *Compresses,* he thought. He had to get up and make compresses, and find the whiskey and a clean cloth in case there were cuts. His eyes still closed, he placed one foot on the cold bare floor and knew that the fearful moaning wasn't coming from behind his parents' locked bedroom door but from behind the thin wall he'd erected between himself and Maggie McQuinn. His wife. He bolted upright in his chair, his jacket falling from his lap, and listened.

The moaning had stopped. Or perhaps he'd just dreamed it. It wouldn't be the first time, he thought as he settled back into the chair, that he'd heard his mother's cries in his sleep. Usually, though, he wouldn't awaken. He'd merely continue dreaming until with his own two hands, he'd finished what he'd started over ten years ago. Until he'd killed his father and forever ended Kathleen Delaney's pitiful cries.

He wondered if he would dream that same dream when he fell back to sleep now. *If* he fell back to sleep now. Perhaps he'd lie awake as he so often had as a child, trying to understand what had gone on—what perversity, he now surmised—behind that locked door to turn his father into a madman. Unlike other men in the neighborhood, Sean Delaney hadn't touched drink. Nonetheless, there'd been a poison in him, one that had driven him to react to his wife like a rabid dog to water. He'd always said he couldn't live without her, but the sight of her, privately anyway, would enrage him.

Always, the sight of his mother after his father had finished with her would enrage Daniel. It had been a son's rage. But now, as he glanced in the darkness at the wall behind which the Babe slept, he imagined her face bearing the marks of a man's fist—God forbid, he saw her with her throat slashed from ear to ear and a blood red rose in her hand—and felt a husband's rage.

Troubled, Daniel laid his arm across his eyes. He didn't love his wife. Why, then, was he certain that he would hunt to kill any man who would harm her? Why kill, if not for love? Because she *was* his, because she belonged to him. But men like his father also thought of their wives as belongings. Was the seed of their brutality implanted in their possessiveness? Was it now being sown inside his?

No. Daniel knew his vices were many, but that he was capable of his father's particular evil he could not accept. The difference between himself and Sean Delaney was that he knew a wife was a man's not to use, but to defend, even from himself. When he refused, he ceased to be a man. Though Daniel knew he was still a boy in some ways—probably always would be—in this way, he had no doubt he was a man. His only worry now was whether his wife would ever want a man, would ever want him.

Maybe Benny had had a point after all when he'd warned him that a "new woman" was no kind of wife for him, even if his old pal had gotten the reasons all wrong. Daniel didn't care that the Babe would never knit him socks. She could weave one helluva a story. But he did mind that she didn't think she needed him, or even that she ought to need him. Maybe that's why she was the only woman—since Madeleine—he'd ever wanted to need him. Like Madeleine, she was self-possessed and brave. If and when she called on a man, neither one of them would doubt that he was a man tall enough for a woman like her to look up to.

Daniel recalled he hadn't been tall enough for Madeleine. She'd turned her nose up at him as though he were so much refuse and sashayed out of his life. But she'd left a proud though wounded adolescent determined to one day have her. He used to imagine her on her knees, begging him for his forgiveness, begging him for his touch. He'd always make her suffer the icy rejections of his cold heart until she was on the verge of brokenness. Then at that moment, he would raise her to him and, scooping her into his arms, take her to where they could break their bodies and souls on one another. To where they would drive themselves to the brink of death so they could return to life in love.

Daniel grew achingly hard now just thinking about what he'd wanted from Madeleine, with her. Over the crotch of his trousers, he rubbed himself to ease the pain and accepted once-and-for-all that he would never have her. She was an adolescent fantasy who, oddly enough, was fading into the reality of the woman sleeping within his reach now. He sat up and faced in her direction, his body preparing to follow his desires.

You made a promise, Daniel, remember? No, he'd made a vow, and in church. He'd vowed to keeps his hands off his wife until she blessed them, until she took them in her own and put them on her body. Clenching those hands of his, he groaned with thwarted pleasure. What had possessed him to make such a stupid vow?

Something that for the first time in years was more important to him than his pleasure. His duty, maybe even a thing called honor.

Unclenching his hands, he lay back in the hard chair and drew his jacket up under his chin. A man's honor, he realized, could be damned discomfiting. With a shiver, he closed his eyes and tried not to think about his bed, warm under the blanket he'd borrowed from Eileen Corrigan. Warm with Maggie's body. With . . . Maggie . . .

Pulling from the brink of sleep, Daniel shot out of the chair. No imagined moans had awakened him this time. This time, he'd heard a scream, real and terrified and coming from behind the wall between Maggie and him. Hurriedly feeling his way along it, he found the opening and dashed into the enclosure.

"Babe? Babe!"

She was a silhouette crouched in the far corner of the bed, her knees drawn tightly against her chest. He scrambled to her and, reaching out, found an ankle.

"No!" She kicked with both feet, striking the center of this chest.

Grunting, Daniel fell back. Quickly returning to his knees, he groped in the darkness for her feet going at him like a frenzy of bats, and soon cuffed her ankles. He dragged her to him on her back, then throwing his right leg over her midsection, caged her between his thighs. Lashing out at him with her fists, she made guttural noises, desperate cries that died in her throat.

"Stop it, Maggie," Daniel ordered as he clasped her wrists, holding her arms out stiff.

But she didn't stop. She thrashed her upper body, her chest heaving with cries it couldn't release.

Lowering to her, Daniel pinned her hands back beside her head. He felt the backs of his own hands sink into her thick, wilding hair. He'd never touched her hair before, so plainly brown and uninspiring that he'd never wanted to. Until now. Now it was like a match to the unlit torch of his desire. He stretched out atop her, released her hands and digging his fingers through her hair, clamped her head between his own hands. She grew strangely quiet. He brought his mouth to within a breath of hers and, opening it, dipped lower to kiss her.

Gasping, Madeleine held her breath. She was alive. She was safe. She was with McQuinn, his body covering hers with its heavy warmth and magnificent hardness. And he was going to kiss her. Opening her mouth, she started to raise her arms to embrace him.

Daniel tore himself off her. Sitting on his heels and rubbing his thighs, he breathed hard. Honor wasn't just discomfiting, it was damn near impossible, at least without sacrifice. "O-o-oh, Babe," he whispered on a ragged breath as with trembling fingers, he searched in the dark for her face.

Catching himself, he drew his hand back. "Are you all right?"

Madeleine still held her arms half outstretched, reaching for him, aching for him. "I thought I was," she barely whispered from a raw throat. She let her hands fall back beside her head, upturned and woefully empty. "I'm not sure now."

Ashamed, believing he'd compounded her terror, Daniel sat beside her. Drawing his knees up, he clasped them tightly to his chest. "You're safe, Babe. I promise." He grazed his chin over the back of the hand that he cupped over one knee. "You had a bad dream, that's all."

"That's not all," Madeleine whispered.

Clutching her throat, she sat up and faced McQuinn, who was no more than a presence in the darkness, a presence she wanted to bring nearer, to bring inside her, in the way Delaney had once dwelled inside her, but also in the only way he never had. She must, she would, in time. Wanting the time to be now, she reached out with her other hand, found his forearm—a strong, taut column of flesh and sinew and hairs that were both soft and resilient—and grasped it.

"McQuinn, he came at me with a knife and I couldn't run. I couldn't get away. I screamed and then he said that no one would ever hear my voice again because he was going to cut it out of my throat. And then . . ." Madeleine lowered her forehead to his arm. "It was horrible."

Daniel felt her own quivering touch and wanted to take her in his arms, hold her tight. So tight there'd be no room for nightmares, no room for anything or anyone who might try to come between them. Instead, he reached across with his left hand and cupped his palm over the crown of her head, so lightly all he felt was her hair, soft and radiant not to his eyes, but to his heart.

"I know," he said. "But listen to me, Babe. I won't let anything happen to you. I couldn't. I lose my mind just thinking about the possibility of anyone harming you."

Daniel's words raised Madeleine's eyes to his faceless form. "Since when? You didn't lose your mind the other night, when Captain Carnation was carrying me off like plunder."

Daniel lowered his head. "You weren't my wife then," he said softly.

"You mean you didn't own me then," Madeleine shot back.

Daniel looked up. "I don't now, not the way you're thinking. But you belong to me just the same, and what belongs to a man he takes care of. When he doesn't, when a lot of men don't . . ." Images flickered in Daniel's mind, of the streets he grew up on, streets with tenements where there were no fathers or the wrong kind of fathers. "Everything and everyone becomes prey. I don't want to live like an animal, but I swear to God, when I think about him preying on you, I feel I could kill him like one."

"*Kill* him? I won't deny he tried to silence me but I hardly think he deserves execution."

Her words chilled Daniel with memories of his mother's betrayal of him at his trial. "Obviously, I don't belong here," he said, getting up from the bed. "You don't need me after all. You don't need anyone. Or at least you think you don't." He turned to leave the tiny room.

Madeleine lunged across the bed, reaching for him. "Don't leave me, McQuinn!"

Daniel halted, his back to Maggie. He shouldn't stay. She was just like his mother, protecting her abuser, even if she'd only dreamed him; making her defender feel like a damn fool. Maybe he was a damn fool, because hearing the desperation in her voice, he couldn't leave her. He turned to her. "What do you want from me, Babe?"

"I . . ." Madeleine wished she could tell him that she wanted nothing *from* him and *all* of him. But she couldn't, because she didn't want the violence in his heart. "I want you to not want to kill."

"You women want the impossible!" On one knee, Daniel lunged at her. "You want to walk the streets safe from predators like The Red Rose Killer, but you don't want a hair on their sick heads harmed. If you ask me, I think *that's* sick and makes for a sick world."

"The Red Rose Killer?" Madeleine sat back, her legs curled under her. "Is that who you thought I was talking about?"

Daniel sank beside Maggie, facing her, his hip against her thigh. "Of course. After last night, who else would you be dreaming of?"

"My father, that's who else. At first, anyway. Then . . ." Inclining her head, Madeleine absently wove her fingers through her hair. "He turned into Roger."

Daniel tried telling himself the alarm clanging him to stiff attention was vigilance against a man she obviously feared would harm her and not jealousy of him. But he knew it was both. "Who the hell is Roger?"

Hearing McQuinn speak the name from her past, Madeleine suddenly sickened at her carelessness, but not at it alone. At the more immediate peril of which it reminded her. Her fingers still enmeshed in her hair, her own pale blond hair cascading down her back and over her breasts, she brought a thick strand of it before her face and saw . . . nothing. The darkness, fortunately, was total, and in it, her hair—a color so unusual it had always turned heads—was colorless.

Thank God, because now that McQuinn was here, in her bed, she couldn't risk his discovering he'd married not Maggie Flynn, but Madeleine Faurest. Not before she could convince him that whatever she called herself she was one woman with one heart and one mind, both of them genuine. And all of her genuinely wanted him. Needed him.

And McQuinn, she knew, needed her to need him.

Roger had needed her only to further his political ambition. Oh, he'd claimed he'd worshipped her and promised to lay the world at her feet—his world. But he'd never said he would lose his mind if harm ever came to her. Or that he would kill to avenge her. She wouldn't have believed him if he had. Roger simply wasn't the type to bloody his manicured, whist-playing hands.

McQuinn's hands weren't manicured. They were large and hairy and had long, strong fingers that could encircle a man's throat. And if he played cards at all, he played poker in smoky, back-alley dens like the Whitechapel Club. When he'd said he could kill, she'd believed him. But she'd also believed him when he'd said he didn't want to live like an animal. And she wasn't going to let him, not even on her account. Not even because she now understood the way in which she belonged to him and liked it. Men belonged to women, too, to be protected from the worst in themselves. She had to let McQuinn know that he belonged to her. Now.

Reaching out, she caressed his cheek, rough and warm and beautiful. "I'll tell you who the hell Roger is," she said. "He's someone I used to know who could never be the man you are, McQuinn." She palmed his jaw and neck, the breadth of his square shoulder, and his arm to his hand. "And he could never make me want him and need him as I do you right now." Taking his hand, she brought it toward her heart. "Stay with me, McQuinn. Come inside me."

Daniel halted their clasped hands. How easy it would be to believe she'd meant what she'd said, that she'd still mean it in a few hours, when the dawn would chase away the darkness and her fear with it. And how wrong. "If I did, Babe, the nightmare you just had in your sleep won't compare to the one you wake up to."

Madeleine tugged on his hand, but he held firm. "Doesn't a man need what belongs to him?" she asked.

Thinking of how her body had felt beneath his, so warm and soft, made Daniel shiver to hardness. "More than you know."

Feeling a give in his resistance, Madeleine brought his hand closer. When the backs of his fingers grazed a nipple beneath her gown, she inhaled a deep pleasure that stirred the need for a deeper one. "More is what I want."

Daniel pulled his hand back, away from the hard peak he knew his touch to the tip of her breast had aroused. "You can't be sure of that, Maggie, not yet."

"I'm sure that a woman needs what belongs to her, same as a man. And you belong to me, McQuinn. I'm sure because in that church tonight, I prayed for the right to make you mine and . . ." She felt his grasp relax. Opening his hand with both of hers, she took it to her and pressed his palm over her breast and her heart. "I received it."

Daniel looked up at the ceiling, unable to see the cracks and peeling paint. But seeing Heaven. With his pulse drumming in his ears and his lungs feeling close to bursting, he closed his fingers around his wife's breast. Its softness and roundness and weight drew his gaze to her dark shape, the shape of his future in the here and now.

"Thank you," he whispered to the Lady he hoped would hear him.

Kneeling, Madeleine flattened her palms against his chest. "You're welcome."

On his knees, Daniel took the Babe's face between his hands. "Believe it or not, it was another Virgin I was thanking." Lowering his mouth to hers, he kissed her, softly at first. Then unable to control the inferno her lips torched inside him, he inhaled her stoking scent and abandoned himself to his ravenousness. He opened his mouth over hers and plunged his tongue inside it, and when his hardness began to throb, he took his tongue to her ears and throat. When it met fabric and lace and buttons instead of flesh, he thrust his fingers into her hair, clenching them around a hank of it, and pulled her head back. With his other hand, he clutched her throat. He brought his mouth to hers and, hearing her gasp, hesitated. Maybe she'd changed her mind. Maybe she should.

"Damn you, McQuinn," she said.

His heart sank.

Then, Maggie laid her palm over the back of his hand on her throat and murmured, "What are you waiting for?"

Twelve

That was all the invitation Daniel needed. Unclenching his fist, he fanned Maggie's hair in his spread fingers. Then he combed along its silken path, letting the strands feather to her shoulder.

"You, Babe," he said. "I've been waiting for you."

And hooking his fingers over the neck of her gown, he ripped it open, baring her throat, her beautiful, precious throat. He wrapped one hand around it, his thumb grazing the delicate skin behind one ear, his forefinger the other. Then he slowly palmed the velvety column, and when he'd coursed its length, he bent and ringed it with kisses, protective kisses that turned hungry again when his lips reached the hollow between her collarbones. With his tongue, he filled it and exploded with desire to fill every hollow in her body.

Madeleine groaned, lifting her hands to his upper arms and digging her fingers into them. "You're killing me, McQuinn. I told you I didn't want you killing."

"I'll stop if you will."

She dug harder. "I can't stop."

By the crook of her arm, Daniel yanked her to his left, sprawling her on her back beneath him. Twisting to gaze down at her dark form, he felt her black gaze meet his, commanding him. To be himself. To be a man. Pivoting on one knee, he hiked the other leg over her and, pressing his hands into the mattress on either side of her head, tented her. As he lowered himself, bringing his mouth toward hers, he felt her reach into the opening in the top of his long johns.

Madeleine flattened her palms over McQuinn's nipples then spread her fingers around them like rays. "You're a hard man, McQuinn," she said. "Here . . ." She squeezed one muscle wall then ran her hand over his clothing down his chest and abdomen until her palm met the hilt of his manhood. "And here," she said, and slid her palm down the erect shaft to the bulge at its root. Cupping it in both hands, she fondled it. She'd had no idea what he would feel like, much less that her own throbbing need would cry out for what she was holding in her hands, or that he would shudder a gasp of pleasure at her touch then beg her for more. She trailed her fingers back along the column to the first button on the fly of his trousers and slipped it from its hole.

Then he backed away from her, off the bed, and rose. She heard the soft grating of fabric as his fingers went at the remaining buttons. Rising up on her elbows, she pictured each one sliding free, releasing more of his strength, a strength she wanted inside her. In her mind, she saw his hands over himself, where hers would soon be, guiding his power to her. Then she heard wool abrade cotton and saw him slide his trousers down his narrow hips and long, taut thighs. He was stepping out of them now. She drew back her legs, planting the soles of her feet on the bed, her knees apart, and waited to hear him start on the buttons on his long johns. She heard, instead, the bed creak and felt the mattress dip as he climbed onto it on one knee.

"That's not good enough, McQuinn."

Daniel paused, searching the darkness for Maggie's meaning. "But you can't see me."

"You can't expose just what you need to, not with me. I don't want just part of you."

"You want more than a man, Babe. You want a husband."

"I want a mate."

Peering into the darkness, Daniel pushed his palm over the bed until his fingers touched Maggie's. He sent them climbing over the back of her hand then with his whole hand, clasped the whole of hers. "Come to me," he said.

In McQuinn's tone, Madeleine heard neither a command nor a plea, but a promise. She sat up and he began backing away, guiding her toward him. When she reached the end of the bed, he raised her by her hands to stand before him. The space between them was a shaft of energy and heat she knew would fuse them if she allowed it to. "I believe in mating for life, McQuinn."

Joining their palms, Daniel meshed his fingers with hers. "I hope you know what you're saying. I intend to live a long time."

"You'd better get started, then," Madeleine replied. "Living."

Stepping nearer, she began undoing the last of his buttons securing the final barrier between her and his bare flesh. Then she reached up to his shoulders and slid the garment off them, grazing the backs of her fingers over his skin. She left his arms strapped and reached for his face. Closing her eyes, she cupped his cheeks in the palms of her hands, letting his stubble rasp her skin. Then she sent her fingers along the precipice of his jaw to his chin and down his throat. So many textures and angles and curves, but one scent. Commanding, compelling. She explored the prominent ridge of his collarbones, like sentinels guarding channels of taut, smooth flesh. Returning to his center, she drew curved paths with the heels of her hands over the mounds of muscle and hair surrounding his nipples. Hearing his chest hairs fuss, she smiled and lowering herself a little, soothed them beneath her cheek.

But McQuinn's scent was far from soothing. Aroused, she kissed his hair and skin and sent her mouth in search of his nipple, and finding the pebble, ran her tongue over and around it.

"Oh, Babe," Daniel murmured on a groan. He reached for her.

Madeleine opened her eyes. "Don't move."

He obeyed.

Madeleine freed first one of his arms, then the other, completely baring his torso. Hooking her arms under his, she laid her cheek against his shoulder, pressing him toward her with her hands on his blades. "I can hear your heart beating."

"Surprised I have one?"

"No. Are you?"

Cupping her shoulders, Daniel laid his head back and inhaled deeply. "Yes."

"Then I'll have to let you know what else I find in you."

Madeleine slowly lowered herself along his body, her hands coursing down his back, her cheek grazing the matted field of his chest and abdomen, her mouth stopping now and then to steal tastes of his flesh. As she came to her knees, she snagged his clothing over his hips and to the floor, exposing the long, erect shaft of his manhood. Laying her hands along either side of it, she pressed her cheek against it, feeling its burning smoothness. To her surprise, a tear coursed from the outside corners of her eyes. Delaney was dead and now his presence inside her was dying so that her completeness could be born in McQuinn.

"You're real and beautiful." She burned her lips on him. "And Daniel, you're mine."

With a cry of both agony and pleasure, Daniel thrust his fingers into Maggie's hair. No woman had claimed him, or had ever tried to. He'd never been with a woman who wanted him the way she did, completely. Kicking away the last of his clothing, he raised her to him. "Maggie, do you realize you've never called me 'Daniel' before? Just 'Daniel.'"

Madeleine felt a stab of regret. She'd loved calling him by his given name. She only wished she could hear him call her "Madeleine." Standing on her toes, she wound her fingers through the thick locks at the nape of his neck and raised her lips to his.

"Sometimes you're McQuinn, and other times, you're just Daniel. My Daniel."

Daniel took her in his arms. "My—"

Madeleine held her breath, wondering whether he would call her "Babe" or "Maggie." Neither would sound right. Or be right.

Turning her to one side, Daniel felt her long hair cascade over his arm and down his side. He shivered with delight, imagining he could feel each silky strand caress his skin. Feathering his fingers over her cheek, he brought his lips to hers.

"Mate," he whispered. Then, crushing her to him, he ravished her mouth.

Madeleine sank into his embrace. She felt as though the fire between them was melting her bones, turning her flesh liquid, forging an explosive new substance of their two separate beings. When she felt his hand course down her shoulder and find her breast, she noted the first eruption of that new substance in her core. It spilled from inside her, seeking him, seeking to ease his way to her.

Holding her breast, feeling her nipple erect and hard beneath her gown, Daniel knew he could wait no longer to feel it against his skin. He stood Maggie on her feet. Splaying his hands over the curves of her hips, he slid them up her body, lifting her gown toward her head.

Madeleine stood motionless, her arms at her sides, feeling the hem of her gown glide up her calves and thighs, over her hips. Soon, her soft, vulnerable womanhood was naked to his hard, probing manhood. She felt apprehensive, but wondrous. As he molded his hands to her breasts, she inhaled deeply then bowed toward him, softly kissing the skin below his shoulder.

That one kiss ended Daniel's patience with the time and distance that remained between Maggie and him. He took the gown over her head and, from behind her, ripped it down her arms. He threw it atop his own clothing, then scooping her in his arms, walked to the side of the bed.

Her arms about his neck, Madeleine clung to him even as he laid her down. She drew him atop her, opening her soft core to him.

Placing himself against it, Daniel began to pulse. He was ready, more than ready, but also afraid she was more eager than prepared for what was about to happen to her. She was going to make a magnificent lover, but only if he could protect her mind and heart from the damage he had to do her body. He moved to one side.

"Why are you stopping?" Madeleine asked, rising up on her elbows. "Where are you going?"

"Nowhere."

"But—"

"Will you trust me?"

Closing her eyes, Madeleine smiled. "You're going to share your notes with me again, aren't you?"

"Babe, I'm going to share the whole damn book with you," he said. And when she lay back down, he lowered his head and gently took one of her nipples in his mouth. He heard her gasp with pleasure, felt her hip graze over his aching need for her as she arched upward. Forming a V of his hand beneath her breast, he lifted it and took more of it into his mouth. With his tongue he circled the nub, and when she started to whimper, he expanded his hand, taking both her small, perfect breasts at once, suckling first one and then the other, turning her whimpers to moans.

Madeleine felt her soft inner space widen to a Daniel-sized need, her vulnerability become a vortex of demand for him that wouldn't be denied. To even think of him denying it was painful. She tossed her head from side to side, shaking off the thought. "Now, Daniel, please."

Daniel smiled. She was begging and he was loving it, not because he wanted to punish her but because he knew he would please her. Eventually.

"It's not time yet, Babe."

Audibly wincing, Madeleine buried her cheek in the pillow as she reached over her head and clutched a spindle. Why couldn't she declare this to be the time for him to relieve her of this burden of need she bore the way she'd declared other times to be turning points in her life? Because this wasn't her time alone. She wanted to give and be taken, but Daniel didn't want to take without giving. She knew he must give and she must let him.

"I trust you, Daniel," she whispered raspily.

Releasing her breasts, Daniel glided his palm down her torso, over her flat abdomen to the threshold of her femininity. With one finger, he glided over it, feeling its warmth and moisture. But he knew that if he stroked, her warmth would turn to a consuming fire and her moisture to a torrent of need that would recognize no pain but the pain of emptiness.

At his first touch, Madeleine released the spindle. Daniel knew what he was doing. He was going to take care of her, he was going to fill the need he'd created. As he laid his cheek over her heart, her fingers sought and found his hair. She raked as he raked her, until she could no longer hold on to anything but her sanity. "Daniel . . . I'm going to die."

At her declaration, Daniel covered her and, with one

massive, merciful thrust, was inside her. "No, you're not. You're going to live," he choked out. Then claiming her mouth, he began a cadence that was alternately driving and languid. With each new measure, he drove himself closer to release, to losing himself inside this woman, this miracle.

Madeleine clawed the sheets, searching for anything cool to quench the flaming tear in her soul and knowing nothing or no one ever could but Daniel. The pain of his entry was gone and now there was only the madness of the climb he was taking her on, toward a pleasure she'd never known with a man she never could have imagined, a man who was the answer to a prayer she never could have prayed.

With complete trust, Madeleine surrendered to his knowingness, allowing it to guide her to deeper intimacies, rarer pleasures. He was slow and tender and patient. With his touch, he paid homage to the mysteries of her body and, drawing her touch to him, revealed to it the magic of his. He held her in timelessness. Then, after bringing her to the pinnacle of need, he filled her neediness. And Madeleine knew the time, once again, was now.

Daniel could only brace himself. He'd driven them both beyond control, beyond the past and the future, to where there was only this one moment. When he could suspend it no longer, he gave himself to it, to Maggie, as he'd given himself to no other woman. Or ever would. This moment would last an eternity.

With a cry, Madeleine shuddered around him, then held him in the pleasure he'd given her. But he pleased her further, softly kissing her swollen lips as he left her, drawing the blanket over them, wrapping her tightly to him and gentling her trembling body. Then he smoothed her tousled hair back and Madeleine trembled in a way he could not gentle because he did not know she had deceived him.

Daniel held her quivering form against his, stroked her hair, hair he wanted so much to see free in the light of day. He recalled Madeleine's hair, the color of it, like light from Heaven. Strange, how Maggie had been the one to bring him Madeleine's name only to end his obsession with her. Maggie—slender, delicate, braver than she was big—was the one thing Madeleine could never be.

"You're so real, Babe. The most honest woman I've ever known, much less touched and held and . . ." Daniel wanted to say *loved*, but *love* seemed to him the biggest word in the language, a word whose meaning he'd never experienced with a woman—a grown, real woman. He wasn't yet ready to put that name to what he felt for Maggie. Not until he knew there was a chance she could feel love for him in return.

"Known," he repeated.

Madeleine felt her Heaven begin to slip away as a pang of guilt wedged itself between her and Daniel. She *was* real, but not honest, not totally. She trusted him with her body, with her life, so why shouldn't she trust him with her true identity? Now, of course, was not the ideal time to tell him who she was. But if she waited, she would appear to have been withholding the trust he'd earned, an insult she wouldn't dream of inflicting on him. Her hand on his chest, she rubbed several hairs between her fingers.

"Daniel, there's something—"

"Have you ever been in love, Babe?"

The question startled Madeleine. But she felt compelled to answer it honestly, to answer all his questions honestly from now on. "Yes."

Daniel felt the shadow of her former love come between them. Taking his arms from around her, he turned on his back. "With Roger?"

Madeleine sighed a breath of contempt both for Roger

and for herself, for the former self that had nearly married him. "No."

Daniel lifted his arm over his eyes. "What *was* his name?"

Madeleine hesitated. Strangely, though Daniel had helped her to recall Delaney's name, she didn't want the name coming between them, coming to their bed. Raising herself up on her elbow, she laid her hand atop Daniel's chest, over his heart. "Believe me, Daniel, when I tell you it doesn't matter. He's dead."

Daniel relaxed, a little. He turned to Maggie, propping his cheek on his hand. "Do you still think about him?"

She raked his hair back from his face, over his ear. "Yes. There's something I never got the chance to put right with him."

Daniel clutched a fistful of the blanket between them. "I don't like unfinished business, either." *Unfinished retribution.* He saw himself struggling with his father, his hands clamped around the bastard's neck. "Do you wish you could go back in time, make things right?"

Madeleine laid her open palm over his fist. "I like this time, Daniel. This moment. Things are right now." Almost right. They would be perfect once she revealed her true identity. "Daniel, I—"

"But if you could, return for just one day?"

Madeleine sighed. "I suppose, but why is this so important . . ." Suddenly, her eyes shifted toward the place outside the makeshift room where Daniel's copy of *The Divine Comedy* rested on a shelf. Perhaps there *had* been a Beatrice in Daniel's life, a love he still longed for. "Daniel, have *you* ever been in love?"

"Yes," he replied softly. Then, taking his hand from beneath hers, he ran his thumb over the seam of her lips. "And no."

Kissing the pad of his thumb, Madeleine paused. "How, may I ask, is that possible?"

Smiling, Daniel flicked his finger down her nose. "In a way you wouldn't know because you're not like her."

Suddenly, Madeleine wanted to tear the woman's hair out. "Is that bad?"

"That's good."

"That's a relief." Madeleine kissed the palm of his hand. "Tell me in what way I'm not like her so that I'll never make you . . ." She nearly said, *stop loving me.* But that would have been to assume he loved her now. Daniel wasn't the kind of man she could make assumptions of. "Sorry you met me," she said.

"I'm already sorry I met you."

"You're lying."

"True enough now. But my neck still hurts from the hours I spent sleeping in that chair."

Madeleine massaged the side of his neck, then gave it a pat. "If you don't tell me about her right now, I'll make you sleep in that chair until you do."

Daniel's heart swelled. She was going to stay, and let him stay with her. The walls he'd built around her, between them, would come down. Clasping her hand, he kissed the back of it. "She was two people. Or, I suppose she pretended to be one thing when all along she was something else."

Madeleine felt a shard of panic slice her joy. She withdrew her hand from his and sat up. "What do you mean?"

Daniel bent a leg, pushed off his foot, and sat back against his pillow. "When I first saw her, I thought she was an angel. With just a look and a smile she made me feel . . . clean, worthy of her." He sighed. "But in the end, she was just a spoiled Southern belle with a rich daddy and she let me know in no uncertain terms that I was beneath her contempt. I guess I was a fool for hoping she would turn out to be anything but a perfect specimen of her privileged and heartless class. But blaming myself had never kept me from dreaming I'd one day pay her back in kind."

Madeleine swallowed hard. "Meaning not kindly."

"Meaning I'd make her fall in love with me, then walk out on her the way she walked out on me."

Madeleine's heart plunged to its direst yet depths. Closing her eyes, she turned away from him and lowered her forehead to her fingertips. The confession her conscience had been demanding she speak lodged in her throat. How could she tell Daniel that the woman he thought was so real, so honest, was in all honesty and reality a member of the privileged class he so despised? She could easily argue, of course, that their lovemaking had proved that not everyone in her class was heartless, that she didn't feel contempt for him and never would. But "Beatrice" had apparently given him that same assurance only to betray it. And him.

Why should he believe you're different, Madeleine? Why shouldn't he leave you the way he'd wanted to leave her, with a heart he'd helped her to find only to break?

Running her hand through her hair, Madeleine knew she had no choice but to go on with her ruse until she was certain that nothing could drive him permanently from her, not even the truth. "Daniel, I— There are some things, personal things I need to—"

"Of course," he replied, a bit puzzled by her abrupt change of the subject. But he also understood that after her first time making love, she required soap and water as much as reassurance that she was like no other woman before her. As she turned away and moved toward the side of the bed, he stayed her arm. "I'll be waiting," he said.

Madeleine paused with both feet on the cold, hard floor. "I may be a long while," she said, wondering just how long it *would* take her to find a way out of this Hell she'd gotten herself into. Gathering up her gown and the valise that held her plain brown wig, she left him to wait for her, to wait indefinitely for Madeleine Faurest.

Awakening, Daniel smiled at the sight of daylight. He'd been dreaming of Maggie's hair, of it looking the way it had felt last night, long and soft and free. Now, he no longer had to dream. Eagerly, he turned toward her, but even before his gaze fell on her, his smile faded. He remembered that when she'd returned to him last night, she'd come with her hair once again pinned up, as if to signify that she was the same woman she'd been before he'd made love to her. Perhaps, when she had scrubbed away all traces of his lovemaking, the haunting remnant of her dead love had surfaced to reclaim her.

He studied her while she slept. Surely, she was more haunting, he thought, than haunted. Not that Maggie McQuinn was a ravishing beauty. Her features, except for her eyes which were now closed, and a lovely complexion, were unremarkable. And yet, he now felt ravished just looking at her, at lips that were sweet and plump to the taste, and concealed a tongue that could torture him as the beatings he'd taken in reform school never had. At a whole woman who needed him and had made him a whole man.

He didn't want to wake her, but he couldn't help reaching out for her, reaching for her plain brown hair, dull to the sight but glorious to the touch. For a moment, he lay with his hand hovering above a curl atop the crown of her head. Then, carefully working his fingers, he found the pin that held it in place and gently slid it out. The coil sprang loose and tumbled over her forehead.

With a terrified start, Madeleine opened her eyes. Behind the curl, she leveled an angry stare at Daniel. His eyes, two orbs of light beneath thick black brows and an unruly mass of black hair, were mesmerizing. But his understandable curiosity about what he thought was her hair was threatening to undo more than the style of her wig.

"Read any good poems lately?" she asked. *"The Rape of the Lock* perhaps? I saw that on your bookshelf, too, right beside—"

"The Taming of the Shrew?"

Sitting up, Madeleine snatched her hairpin from Daniel's fingers and began refastening the curl he'd undone. "Your library could stand with less of Shakespeare and more of *The Gentleman's Guide to Manners and Decorum."*

Grinning, Daniel sat up beside her. "All right, so you don't like mornings. But since when does a husband have to ask his wife's permission before touching her hair?"

Making a pout, Madeleine folded her arms. "I—I'm very particular about my hair."

"Yes, as I recall you were particularly creative with it last night."

Feeling a blush rise to her cheeks, Madeleine averted her gaze from Daniel's only to face what little was left of her scruples. When she'd returned to his bed a few hours ago, she'd thought she could continue to share it with him while continuing to masquerade as brown-haired Maggie Flynn McQuinn—only, of course, until she was certain she could safely reveal her true identity. Now she knew she couldn't—continue to share his bed, that is. Every moment she spent here with him would add another count to the charge of fraud he would have every right to level against her once he discovered that, by birth, she was all that he despised. If she wanted to keep Daniel forever—and she did, desperately—she had to give him up now. If she wanted to win his love later, she had to risk his hatred now.

"Daniel," she began. "About last night. It was—"

"More than I had any right to hope for." Taking Maggie by the shoulders, Daniel turned her to him. "My sweet Babe," he murmured and brought his lips near hers.

"No, Daniel," Madeleine said as she turned her face away. When Daniel released her, she looked back at him and, seeing his stunned expression, got up from bed.

Reaching out with both his hand and his heart, Daniel clasped Maggie's wrist. "What is it, Maggie? What have I done?"

Madeleine met his gaze and hoped that Daniel couldn't hate her any more than she now hated herself for the pain and confusion she saw in it. "Nothing, Daniel," she said softly, wanting to press his cheek to her breast, smooth back his riled hair, erase the creases from his brow with her fingertips. Kiss his mouth and love him as she had loved him last night. But she didn't dare take a step nearer to him. His fingers around her wrist was all of his touch she could resist, and that, only barely. "Please, Daniel. We—we have work to do. We have to find that old flower woman."

Incredulous, angry, Daniel let go of her. "Why don't you just say it?" Throwing off the covers, he jumped out of bed then, over his shoulder, cast a scowl at her. "The honeymoon is over!"

Madeleine started toward him. "Daniel, listen to—" She stopped, suddenly rooted to the sight of her husband, dark and naked, retrieving his clothing from the floor. Nothing less than enthralled, she watched the interplay of muscles along his expansive back and powerful haunches and long legs as he shrugged on his long johns, then his trousers. How it reassured her to see that all that her hands and mouth had explored and enjoyed mere hours ago was as real and beautiful in the light of day as in the dark of passion. She wished mightily she could give him the same assurance, allow her hair to tumble freely through his fingers and her heart into his hands. But all she could do now was to try to reason with him, and with a poor logic, at that.

"I only meant that we mustn't forget about the story," she said.

"Oh, by all means, let's not forget the damn story." Daniel looked up from buttoning his trousers. "What about the story we wrote last night, Babe, you and I, right here in this bed?"

Rushing to him, Madeleine grasped his arm. She fixed him with a gaze filled with all her being. "Daniel, I pray to God that what we wrote last night was only the first chapter."

Gazing down into her eyes, so large and dark and soulful, Daniel felt his defenses crumble. "So do I," he said and, taking her face in his hands, bent to kiss her.

Inhaling deeply, Madeleine parted her lips, eager for his kiss, then broke away. "Daniel, I can't. It isn't right!"

"*Why* isn't it right? Because you can't forget *him*?" Coming up behind her, Daniel pulled her against him. "If he's standing between us, Babe, tell me now. There's no man alive I wouldn't fight to win you. But I can't fight a ghost."

Her head light with a combustible mix of emotions, Madeleine laid it back against his shoulder. Feeling the breadth and warmth of him, she rejoiced that, for the moment, she could be completely truthful with him. "He no longer haunts me, Daniel. He's barely a memory now."

Daniel whipped her around. "Then why, all of a sudden, can't I touch you? Why isn't it right for me to kiss you?"

Finding his gaze unbearable, Madeleine looked down. She asked herself if the consequences of telling him who she really was could possibly hurt worse than the pain she was causing them both now. *No*, she answered. Cupping his elbows, she looked up at him. "Because, something *is* standing between us, something I must tell—"

"Daniel?" A demanding knock at the door accompanied a woman's insistent shout. "I know you're in there, Daniel McQuinn. I heard your voice as I was coming up the stairs."

"That's not Mrs. Corrigan," Madeleine said, giving Daniel a puzzled look.

"For once I wish it were," he replied, pulling on his shoes. "You'd better put on your wrapper, Mrs. McQuinn. We have company."

"Who?" Madeleine asked as she took the garment from atop her valise and hurriedly dressed in it.

Parting the sheets hanging around the bed, Daniel looked back at her. "The boss's daughter."

Madeleine's jaw dropped. "Pamela Hart? Isn't she being a bit rude, showing up at this hour without warning?"

"Pamela Hart is rude at any hour, so be warned."

Hastily, Madeleine finished buttoning the cuffs of her sleeves. She smoothed the fabric over her breasts and the curves of her waist. "How do I look?"

Daniel eyed her up and down. She looked delicious. But he'd be damned if he'd tell her so. He arched a brow at her. "At least your hair's done."

Lifting her chin, Madeleine passed by him as he held one of the sheets back. As she did, she said, "Obviously, Miss Hart had no difficulty finding your apartment."

"Miss Hart has no difficulty finding whatever it is she wants," Daniel said, taking Maggie by the arm to the door. "And right now, I imagine she wants a good look at you. Ready?"

Madeleine turned her mother's ring around on the third finger of her left hand, threw back her shoulders, and pasted a smile on lips. "Shall I tell her you snore," she said through her teeth. "Or does she already know that?"

With a wry smile, Daniel looked at her askance. "I'm afraid that's information she wasn't privileged to learn."

"Then again, she probably doesn't frequent the Levee."

"Where, as it happens, I met—" Responding to the battering on his door, Daniel opened it. "My wife," he said to the statuesque brunette glaring at him. "Miss Hart, meet Mrs. McQuinn."

As Daniel stepped to one side, Madeleine mirrored the up-and-down gaze of the other woman. She'd like to believe their mutual assessment had resulted in a draw, but undeniably, Pamela Hart had the advantage. Any woman who knew *haute couture* as well as Madeleine once had would recognize the Parisian flare of Miss Hart's wool suit and hat, both in a bright coral that enhanced her auburn-toned beauty. Her kid gloves, shoes, and parasol were a deeper shade of coral, the perfect frame around a figure that was a masterpiece of corseting. Altogether, Madeleine thought, she was a well-designed woman who was apparently unwilling to give up her designs on Daniel.

"Won't you come in, Miss Hart." Madeleine said, stepping beside Daniel and looping her arm through his. "I've heard so little about you."

Pausing as she entered, Pamela Hart cast at Madeleine a look as *haute* as her *couture*. "I beg your pardon?"

Madeleine smiled sweetly. "I meant *too* little, of course. As highly as Daniel's spoken of you . . ." He'd spoken of her in Rawley's office, which was on the second floor of the *Clarion* building. "I could never hear enough about the woman behind the *Clarion*'s presses." Especially if she were to be found beneath one of them.

"Nor I," Pamela Hart replied. "Hear enough about the woman behind Daniel, that is. She gazed around the apartment, then turning to Madeleine, gave a malicious laugh. "So far behind him, in fact, I didn't hear that he had a wife until late last night. Now why do you suppose that is, Mrs. McQuinn?"

Patting Maggie's hand, Daniel walked her toward

Pamela Hart. "Maggie wanted to keep our marriage a secret. She's a reporter too, you know, and she didn't want to trade on my name at the *Clarion*."

"I don't blame her," Pamela Hart replied. "Your name isn't worth much at the paper these days, is it, Daniel?"

Daniel returned the pointed stare of the woman who, in part, had turned his name to poison. "Through no fault of her own," he said.

Madeleine panicked. The whole point of hers and Daniel's marriage was to appease Pamela Hart so that Daniel could return to the *Clarion*. If he didn't control his temper, this scorned woman could see to it that he never returned to the newspaper under any circumstances. Madeleine herself would be out of a job. Worse, Daniel would slip out of the one tenuous hold she had on him, the marriage she wanted more than anything in the world—more, even, than she wanted to be a front-page journalist. With her elbow, she poked him in the ribs.

"Miss Hart, I'll just bet you didn't know that Daniel had to make the most painful little ol' confession to me on your account," she said.

"Oh?"

"I did?"

Madeleine gave Daniel another jab. "Why yes. He told me that he had all he could do to resist your charm and keep you from stealin' him right away from me."

"Really? How fortunate for you that Daniel was, I imagine, still a blushing bridegroom." Idly, Pamela Hart aimed the tip of her parasol at Madeleine's heart. "How long *have* you been married, Mrs. McQuinn?"

Madeleine stared at the sharp instrument pointed at her. "Long enough," she muttered, then looked up. "Six months."

Pamela Hart walked to the bed. She studied the hanging linens, parting them and peering inside the little enclosure, then turned to Madeleine. "And where you come from, is it customary to place sheets around the bed as well as on them?"

"Where I come from, we enclose our beds to keep out drafts and mosquitoes and . . ." Madeleine took a step forward. "Other pests." She entwined her arms. "Won't you stay and have breakfast with us, Miss Hart?"

"I've had mine, thank you," the woman replied abruptly. She crossed the room, stopping to look down at Madeleine. "I feel it's terribly important to rise early and get a good start on the day."

"How I envy you," Madeleine replied. "Daniel and I wish we could rise earlier, but our work keeps us up to all hours. Just last night, we were out well past midnight working on another Red Rose murder." For a brief moment, she saw the solid imperiousness in Pamela Hart's expression crack.

"Together, you and Daniel? I hadn't heard that part of the story."

Madeleine felt a grain of pity for the woman. Obviously, among her designs on Daniel had been one that called for the two of them to work side by side. How odd, she thought, to understand a rival's jealousy, to be able to put yourself in her shoes. On the other hand, she'd rather put a few of the cockroaches she'd seen in Louisville's Bug Alley in Pamela Hart's shoes.

"Daniel and I work as a team," she said.

"Yes," he said, stepping up behind Maggie and cupping her shoulders. "You could say that work is what brought us together." He bent over, bringing his lips to her ear. "And keeps us apart," he whispered. Kissing her on the cheek, he straightened.

Inwardly, Madeleine winced. Outwardly, she caressed her face where he'd kissed it. "Won't you at least stay for coffee, Miss Hart?"

"Thank you, but I really can't stay. I just wanted to meet

you, Mrs. McQuinn, and congratulate Dan—" Glancing at the kitchen, Pamela Hart frowned. "How long did you say you and Daniel have been married?"

Madeleine hesitated. "Six months."

"But there's still only—I mean there's just one stool at the—I presume that crate remains your dining table."

Madeleine and Daniel exchanged frantic glances. Finally, giving a laugh, Daniel shook his head. "This is so embarrassing." Stepping to Maggie's side, he hugged her to him. "Shall I tell Miss Hart our little secret, Babe?"

Madeleine paused, her eyes wide and wondering. "I can hardly wait."

Daniel took a deep breath. "The day Maggie and I were married, I did promise her I'd get another stool. But I've never managed to get around to it because the truth is, I just love having the little woman on my lap while I eat."

Pamela Hart gaped at him. "And does she spoon-feed you, too?"

"Only when he calls me 'the little woman,' " Madeleine replied. "I make him eat the spoon."

"Yes, I can see you two have been married awhile," Pamela Hart said dryly. She walked to the door, opened it, then looked at Madeleine. "I must give you credit, Mrs. McQuinn, for finally breaking the male lock on the city news room. I only hope you're prepared for the scrutiny you'll come under. Every newspaperman in this town will be watching you, waiting for you to prove that a woman is too frail and weak-minded to succeed in journalism. Even if you should last, they'll say you couldn't have done so without your husband's carrying you along."

"And what carries them along?" Daniel stepped forward. "It wouldn't be booze, would it? Or gambling? Or women who aren't their wives?"

Pamela Hart gave him a sly grin. "You ought to know, Daniel."

Daniel slid his jaw to one side. "All right. I deserved

that. But because I did I also know that, unlike me, Babe McQuinn is carried along by just one thing. Conviction."

Madeleine gazed at Daniel, who staring at Pamela Hart, failed to see the surprise in her eyes and the smile on her lips at the conviction she heard in his voice.

"At last I understand what attracted Daniel to you, Mrs. McQuinn."

Madeleine looked at Pamela Hart, who had straightened to her full, imposing height. "He sees you as Joan of Arc, and being a great sinner, he naturally . . ." She gave a chilling smile. "But saints eventually grow tiresome, especially to a man like Daniel." Bidding goodbye to "Mrs. McQuinn" but not to Daniel, Pamela Hart left, closing the door behind her with ominous control.

"She still wants you, McQuinn," Madeleine said, rubbing goose bumps from her arm. "And she means to have you."

"She means trouble," Daniel replied. Abruptly taking Maggie by the arm, he hurried her toward the bed. "Get dressed, Babe. We have no time to lose cracking the Red Rose case and hitting the front page with it."

Madeleine gaped at him. "What happened to the honeymoon you accused me of declaring over?"

"It's over."

"But—"

"Listen, Babe," he said, turning her toward him and pointing a finger at her. "Pamela Hart wants you out of the city room, out of her way, and probably out of the state. You already know she's capable of arranging whatever she wants. But if, as Rawley said, you and I can make headlines and win the heart of this town writing as—"

"The Sweethearts of the *Chicago Clarion*, then—"

"She'd have to fight not just you but our adoring, circulation-boosting public."

"And we'd get to keep our jobs despite Pamela Hart."

But what about keeping our marriage vows, Daniel? Standing at the sheets enclosing the bed, Madeleine ran her fingers down the edge of one of them. She wanted to tug on it with all her strength and bring the whole ridiculous divide tumbling down. But she knew that even if she did, she wouldn't topple the divide she'd erected with her deceit. Only the truth could do that.

Watching Maggie finger the sheets, Daniel clenched his fists at his sides. She had made it quite clear that she was a reporter first and a woman second. A wife, maybe not at all. But to him, she was all those things, and if he couldn't have all of her, he didn't want any of her. Much. No more than he wanted to go on breathing. And that was exactly why . . .

"Those will stay, of course," he told her. "As you said, we mustn't let anything distract us from our work."

You've got a vengeful streak in you, Mac, Madeleine recalled Rawley telling Daniel. He'd been right. She was reeling from Daniel's retribution—in the form of her own hurtful words—now. With a wounded gaze, she turned to him, but all she saw was his back—a towel hanging from his shoulder—as he walked out the door.

Looking down through pooling tears, she crushed a fistful of the sheet beside her. She realized she no longer owed Daniel the truth about her identity.

Daniel no longer cared that they lived in a house divided.

Part Three

Thirteen

Several weeks later, in Vernon Rawlston's office, Madeleine stood beside the city editor as beneath a circle of lamplight, he pored over hers and Daniel's latest copy on the Red Rose murders. She avoided eye contact with Daniel, opposite her on the other side of the desk, a task she found surprisingly difficult considering that in the last week they'd gone from sharing intense conversation—if only about their work—to snarling at one another to barely speaking at all. Ironic, she thought, their not talking, because they were certainly the most talked-about couple in Chicago.

Although Archibald Monroe despised Daniel and, in principle, the very idea of a woman writing hard news, the *Clarion*'s managing editor correctly calculated that the novelty and romance of a husband-and-wife reporting team would sell papers, especially to an increasingly powerful and demanding female readership.

"I don't care if the story is that there's nothing new in the Red Rose story," he'd told Rawley. "I want the 'Babe and Daniel McQuinn' byline on the front page every day. And in extra editions!"

Rawlston had gone further. He'd expanded the scope of the McQuinns' assignment from the Red Rose story to the far reach of vice throughout the city and city hall's protection of it. The daily exposés enthralled readers and won Madeleine and Daniel praise from no less than William Roger Hart, the *Clarion*'s publisher.

Their peers, however, shunned them. They'd been as disdainful of Madeleine as Pamela Hart had predicted they would be and treated Daniel as though he were a traitor both to his profession and to his sex. Madeleine recalled one scene, in particular, that had occurred a week earlier outside the Whitechapel Club. Finley Peter Dunne had stepped into the alley to inform Daniel that by just one vote, he'd retained his membership.

"You can come in, McQuinn," Dunne said. "If you don't mind leaving Mrs. McQuinn in the alley, that is."

"Oh, but I do mind," Daniel replied.

"Then you shouldn't have brought her here."

"Maybe you're right, Peter." Daniel lit a cigarette. "She's too good a journalist to waste her time with a bunch of hacks who are so busy keeping women from reporting the news they can't see that women reporters are the news." He flung his match at Dunne's feet. "Now that I think about it, so am I." After tendering his resignation, he took Madeleine by the arm and led her from the alley.

When they reached the street, she gave a triumphant shout. "McQuinn, you were magnificent! You certainly told him a thing or two. Oh, but—" She stayed his arm. "You needn't have resigned on my account, however much I appreciate the gesture."

"Appreciate it all you want," Daniel said, flicking his cigarette away. "But you should know I didn't do it on your account."

His tone, as coldly cutting as a slice of wind off Lake Michigan, momentarily stole Madeleine's breath. "Then why—"

"Because if I went in there without you, Pamela Hart would hear about it and realize that our much celebrated domestic bliss is much exaggerated. Quicker than you could say 'Daddy's girl,' she'd have me in her sights and—"

"How horrible for you!" Suddenly stung beyond bearing by his

reflexive loathing of the daughters of wealthy and powerful men,
Madeleine retaliated with scorn. "I can only imagine how
revoltin' it must be to know you're attractive to anyone so con-
temptible as to have been bo-wen to privilege."

"At the moment, Magnolia." Daniel said, opening the door to
the establishment behind them. "I'd like the privilege of enjoying
a drink without some damn argument!"

Peering inside the building. Madeleine saw that it was a tav-
ern. She squared her shoulders. "Then you'd better drink alone,
suh, because arguin' seems to be what we do best."

Daniel stared—right through her, she felt. "On one occasion.
at least, that wasn't so."

Madeleine watched him disappear into the tavern, behind his
bitterness. She closed her eyes but failed to end her vision of mak-
ing love with him. "No it wasn't," she conceded in a whisper,
then turned away.

For hours afterward, Madeleine now recalled, she'd
walked the streets, paying no heed to where she was while,
in her mind, she retraced every step of the path along
which she'd led Daniel to his inevitable resentment of
her.

And her maddening need of him.

Yet another irony, she thought as she struggled to focus
her attention on Rawley's words—her missing Daniel to
distraction even though he'd always been as near to her
as he was now.

So near that not once during the many times they'd
met with Benny Grimm about his investigation of the Red
Rose murders had she been able to steal a moment alone
with the detective. She would have asked him how he'd
forged a decent life for himself—she'd quickly gathered
he was a proud family man and the rare honest police
officer—after the horrors of a youth spent at St Augustine's. She would have asked him whether Delaney had

done the same before he'd died. That was all she wanted or needed to know about him, that he'd come to a better place. Then, she could have forever laid all that remained of him, the shade of his memory, to rest. But with Daniel ever physically present though emotionally distant, she hadn't dare risk confirming what she'd earlier denied, that her heart still belonged to her first love. That denial had been the one truth she'd been able to tell him.

Among so many that she hadn't, not least of them that every night this past week she'd lain awake inside her tiny enclosure in their small flat, listening to him toss and turn in his reading chair. Despite his not having spoken a civil word to her all day, she'd wanted him so desperately that she'd had to hold her hand over her mouth to keep from screaming with the pain of his absence. Each night, the pain had subsided a little as she'd seen a glow behind one of the sheets around the bed and known that he'd risen and lit a cigarette. A strange comfort, simply to know that he was conscious, stranger still to count the steps he paced while he finished his smoke. Strangest of all to hear the door click shut, the stark sound of aloneness. The strangest of comforts because all it had brought her was the freedom to voice her anguish, release her sobs as she imagined Daniel going to some woman who needn't hide her true identity from him.

Or her desire.

Madeleine's one consolation was that whoever the woman was—perhaps a different one each time—she'd given Daniel little comfort. In the morning, he would return in an even surlier mood than he'd been in the night before, giving Madeleine no choice but to sharpen her own tongue. Funny, though, how her barbs always cut her more than they seemed to cut him. But then, what was one more cut when she was already bleeding to death?

"We've already bled the Red Rose story to death, you

two. I don't care what Monroe says, I can't justify putting copy like this on the front page."

Rawlston's speaking the eerie confluence of their thoughts drew Madeleine's attention back to the here and now. "I told McQuinn you wouldn't run a story comparing the phases of the moon the nights the murders occurred."

Pressing his knuckles into the desk, Daniel leaned over it. "Rawley, would you please tell my wife to consider how many werewolves there may be in Chicago who would find that story fascinating?"

"Rawley," Madeleine said, turning Rawlston toward her. "Would you please tell my husband to consider that I consider him a complete idiot."

"Kindly remind Mrs. McQuinn, Rawley, that she didn't consider me an idiot when I suggested she give Benny Grimm a description of the old flower woman she's so sure can identify The Red Rose Killer."

Once again, Madeleine drew Rawlston's gaze from Daniel to her. "My instincts tell me she can."

Daniel laughed. "Too bad they can't also tell her where she is."

Madeleine tugged on Rawlston's arm. "Benny *will* find her."

"Assuming she's not a ghost," Daniel said. Though addressing Rawlston, he looked directly at Madeleine. "My wife tends to harbor ghosts."

Twining her arms, Madeleine returned Daniel's hard stare as she spoke to Rawlston. "Inform Mr. McQuinn that as I have already assured him, I do not harbor ghosts. But even if I did, better that than harboring a grudge."

"Tell Mrs. McQuinn—"

"Whatever it is, Mac, tell her yourself. That goes for you, too, Maggie. I know this may come as a shock, but when I looked in the mirror this morning a messenger pigeon did not look back." Throwing down his pencil,

Rawlston stepped from behind his desk and, reeling on his star reporters, riveted them both with the wrath in his one-eyed gaze. "Now lend me your ears, children, before I box them," he began, launching into a tirade at the pair that ended when a woman Madeleine had never seen before wandered into the office.

"Excuse me," she said, clutching a large, worn packet to her bosom. "I'm looking for the *Clarion*'s Sweethearts."

"What a coincidence," Rawlston replied. He shot Madeleine and Daniel a stern look. "So am I."

"Actually, I want just one sweetheart," the woman amended. "I want to talk to Mrs. Babe McQuinn."

Madeleine gazed querulously at the woman. She appeared to be in her late fifties, and was shabbily dressed but clearly resolute. "I wonder what she wants with *me*," she said under her breath.

"Maybe she wants advice on how to balance a career and marriage," Daniel whispered back, though his snide tone struck Madeleine with the force of a shout.

She lifted her chin. "That's easy. Any woman who wants a career shouldn't marry a man who's unbalanced." Dusting off her palms, she stepped toward the woman. "I'm Babe McQuinn. How can I help you?"

The woman glanced from Daniel to Rawlston to Madeleine. "Only you, Mrs. Babe."

"If you'll excuse us, gentleman—and others," Madeleine said, looking at Daniel, "this situation appears to require discretion and sensitivity. In other words, it's woman's work."

"Come on, Mac," Rawlston said, giving Madeleine a skewed smile. "Maybe we can find some ditches that need digging."

Daniel settled his fedora on his head. "And insult them while we're doing it."

After the two men had gone, Madeleine invited the

woman to take a seat. Inside of ten minutes, she learned that her visitor, a Mrs. Kozyck, had come to her for help because, for many years, she could get no newspaperman to listen to her story. It was over a decade old, they all told her. The judge in the case had died long ago. The witnesses' memories had all faded. Yet Mrs. Kozyck had never lost faith that the evidence that would acquit her husband of the murder he'd been imprisoned for so long ago still existed.

"My Tomas is innocent, Mrs. Babe. This I know the way I know my own soul."

Madeleine sat stunned. How rare, and perhaps miraculous, for a woman to know a man that way. She'd thought that kind of knowing was possible only in the innocence of youth. "Forgive me, Mrs. Kozyck, but I can't help but be struck by your devotion to your husband. It's remarkable that you've remained married to him all this time."

"You think so? But did you not stand before God and say to your husband as I did to my Tomas, 'till death us do part'?" The woman, whom Madeleine thought must have been quite pretty once, gave her a puzzled look. "I was sure *you* would understand."

Madeleine sank down atop Rawley's desk. She did understand the meaning of the marriage vows, and because she did, she was ashamed of herself for making a mockery of them. Ashamed that she had allowed invisible bars to stand between her and Daniel while the steadfast woman before her bore her own husband a love that transcended his real imprisonment.

You can bring the bars down, Madeleine. All you have to do is tell Daniel who you really are. Yes, that would bring them down, she thought, and he would walk over them and out of her life forever. He despised women whom he pronounced "pedigreed" with a contempt usually reserved for a different kind of woman. For that reason, when she'd returned to their Canal Street flat the evening

Daniel had resigned from the Whitechapel Club, she had panicked at the sight of the handbill stuffed through the handle of the front door to the house.

The circular had borne a fairly good sketch of her, her description, and the promise of a thousand-dollar reward for any information leading the Pinkerton Agency to her whereabouts. Feeling more like a fugitive than ever, she'd fled upstairs and burned the circular in the stove.

But even as she watched it turn to ash, she listened for footsteps on the stairs. Benny's footsteps. Of the likely thousands of circulars the Pinkertons had distributed throughout the city, surely a large number had been delivered directly to the police. Though he'd never been less than polite and cooperative, she sensed that Benny still didn't approve of her, either as a crime reporter or as his best friend's wife. Besides, what policeman with a growing family couldn't do with an extra thousand dollars?

Benny hadn't come that night, though, nor given any indication at their subsequent meetings that he knew her secret. She now believed he might never discover it among the layers of "Missing" and "Wanted" posters plastering the walls of police stations.

Still, it was only a matter of time before someone else found her out, and then Daniel. And when he did, she would wish the slow death she'd been dying would finish its work. Though living with him and not touching him had been torment, she'd rather the torment of not touching him than of living without him. For each night, when she parted the sheets around her bed and entered a world of indescribable longing for his kiss, for him to enter her body and make her whole again as he had before, she also faced an unbearable truth.

You, Madeleine Faurest McQuinn, are desperately, completely, and eternally in love with your imitation husband, the only real man you've ever known.

"Dear God," she whispered as she lowered her head to her hand. "What am I going to do?"

"Mrs. Babe?"

Madeleine looked up at Mrs. Kozyck, who was now standing before her.

"You'll help me, yes?"

Smiling, Madeleine rose from the desk. "I'll be only too glad to help you, Mrs. Kozyck," she said, patting the woman's shoulder. "Maybe I can see to it that your story, at least, has a happy ending."

That afternoon, outside the coffee shop several blocks from the *Clarion* building, where he'd agreed to meet Benny and Maggie, Daniel paced with his eyes lowered. His pride wouldn't tolerate his searching over the heads of passersby for that first glimpse of Maggie, for the thrill he felt every time she came into view. But to think about it was to want it, and soon he was standing still, sweeping his gaze and listening to his heart pound in expectation of her at any moment turning a corner or crossing from the opposite side of the street.

He must be insane, of course, behaving like a schoolboy over a woman who between her past love and her current one—her job—had no room for him in her bed. What other explanation could there be?

He'd taken a vow of responsibility for her, sure. But even though he'd had little experience with responsibility, he knew it wasn't responsible for the light that blazoned inside him at her appearance, then dimmed at her leaving.

Perhaps his working with her day and night for nearly a month was the sole explanation. But he'd worked with Rawley for years and had never wanted to take him in his arms and never let him go.

Then again, he had enjoyed watching her grow as a

reporter and grow lovelier as a woman on the regular meals that had fleshed her delicate bones. That explained why he'd been unable to sleep nights knowing that she lay within reach but no longer needed or wanted his touch. Still, he couldn't understand why the thought of touching another woman suddenly revolted him.

One thing was for certain, though he'd found one place where he felt closer to her than when she stood right beside him, he was getting damned tired of sleeping on a hard pew in the back of that church he'd followed her into so seemingly long ago.

No, there was one more thing he knew for certain, he thought as Maggie, her stride as bold as it was feminine, captured his gaze from half a block away. "You, Daniel Patrick Amadeus McQuinn"—he drew a breath—*"Delaney,* are deeply, eternally, and hopelessly in love with your wife."

Funny, he thought, that he'd spoken his true name at the same time he'd spoken his love for Maggie. But then she had a way of making him say unexpected things—in this past week, mostly cruel things that he knew would hurt her. Like his wisecracks about women with "pedigrees." He knew full well the Babe was no mutt, so by exaggerating his contempt of Pamela Hart, for example, he could reject her as she'd rejected him. To his surprise, however, his revenge hadn't eliminated the pain of her rejecting him nor diminished his powerful longing for her. For the lips he could now clearly see and ached to kiss, for the skin he yearned to caress, for all of her.

For all of that, as she approached, he turned away and pretended to watch a pretty woman having coffee behind the shop window.

Madeleine recognized a snub when she received one. McQuinn had seen her; he was merely letting her know he hadn't much cared for what he saw. Whatever had attracted him to her the night they made love, it couldn't have been her appearance because they'd loved in total darkness. And considering how resistible he'd apparently found her since then, she must have lost what little appeal she had. She'd once thought—hoped—that his bitterness was the result of the desire for her that she herself had frustrated. But the few times she'd accidentally touched him, brushing his side as she passed him in their tiny kitchen or grazing his knee with hers beneath a table, or joining her fingers to his as she took a pencil he was handing her, he gave her no sign that the contact jolted him as it had her. No sign that he noticed her touch at all.

Now, as he stood with his back to her, apparently fascinated by the woman inside the coffee shop, she wondered if her unexpected touch would reveal whether or not he'd truly lost all feeling for her. She lifted her curled fingers and lightly grazed the tips along the nape of his neck, beneath the tangle of his thick, black hair.

Daniel had been surreptitiously watching Maggie's reflection in the window. When he saw her raise her hand, he steeled himself for her tap on his shoulder, but when she fingered the nape of his neck, he nearly bit his tongue in two suppressing an agonized cry of pleasure. What the hell was she trying to do to him? Wasn't barring him from her bed torture enough? Did she have to brush and graze and finger him to death, too? Summoning the strength to contain both his pleasure and his anger, he reached for the back of his neck. She withdrew her hand. He gazed up at the sky as he turned toward her.

"Damn pigeons," he said.

Anguished, Madeleine gasped. At least she knew what her touch felt like to him. Pigeon droppings. "I'm sorry I'm late," she said. "I've been digging through the morgue for clippings about an old murder case. I think there might still be a story in it."

Daniel waited, expecting her to give him the details.

Finally, he said, "Are you going to tell me about it or do I have to interview you?"

"Forget about it, McQuinn." Madeleine looked away. "You wouldn't be interested."

Daniel shoved his hands in his pockets. "Meaning you want it for yourself."

"I just don't think it's your kind of story!" *A story about a love that lasted for more than a night.* "You wouldn't understand it."

"Why? Because I'm not a woman?"

"Don't you dare shout at me!"

"How can I help it? I'm indiscriminate and insensitive, remember?"

"What *I* remember," Benny Grimm said, his raspy whisper preempting Madeleine's rejoinder, "is that Alice and I didn't fight when we were still newlyweds." He hiked his pants over his round belly. "This is not a good sign, what I'm seeing here."

"You want to see a good sign?" Daniel asked. "There's a good sign." He pointed at the building across the street and the shingle hanging over its door that read HAROLD Z. BIXBY, ATTORNEY-AT-LAW. CONTRACTS. WILLS. DIVORCE.

Madeleine grabbed the lapels of Daniel's jacket. "I'll never give you a divorce, Daniel McQuinn, if only to keep alive the hope of one day sending you to jail for bigamy."

Looking down, Daniel came nose-to-nose with her. "Matrimony is the one mistake not even I would make twice."

Benny pried the pair apart. "Do you think you could continue this inside? I've been on my feet all day chasing down leads on that old flower woman."

Letting go of Daniel, Madeleine looked at Benny. "Any luck?"

Benny shook his head. "Sorry."

"But you have to find her, Benny," Madeleine said. "The last Red Rose murder occurred nearly a month ago and we've examined every angle of the story to death since. She's our last hope."

"I've got it!" Benny whisper-shouted. He drew Madeleine and Daniel close. "The old woman must be the killer. After all, none of the victims were sexually assaulted and nobody on the Levee's seen her since the last slaying. She knows we're looking for her so she's skipped out of town."

Daniel and Benny broke into laughter. Madeleine folded her arms and looked at the two of them as though she wanted to stuff rags down their throats, which she did.

"Laugh all you want, but I won't give up trying to find her. The question is, how?"

"I've done all I can, Maggie," Benny said. "I've even had my men pass out handbills with the description you gave me."

At his mention of handbills, Madeleine studied Benny's expression for the least sign that he'd seen the one bearing her own description and, to her relief, found none. "Something tells me handbills don't reach the greatest number of people," she said. Suddenly, her jaw dropped. "But I know what does! A newspaper."

Pushing back his hat, Daniel tugged his chin. "You know, Babe, you may have something. If we could get one of the *Clarion*'s illustrators to sketch your description of the old woman—"

"And talk Monroe into running it along with the offer of a reward . . ." Madeleine added.

"That's a great idea, Maggie," Benny said, "Except for one thing. Whoever the old woman is, she doesn't want to be mixed up in a murder case. Nobody does. She'll see herself in the paper and run."

Grinning, Madeleine shrugged. "How fast can an old woman run?"

Benny propped his hands on either side of his wide waist. "And I thought my Alice was determined. Listen,

Maggie, I didn't want to tell you this before because I didn't want to get your hopes up, but I'm really close to finding the old lady, so close I can smell the rum on her breath. Hold off running a sketch of her for just a few more days. I'll put more men on her trail, I promise."

Benny's face was so cherubic, Madeleine felt as though there were nothing she could deny him. Besides, she didn't want to do anything that might jeopardize his finding the old woman. "What can I say?" she asked rhetorically, then smiled. "You're the law."

In the dark at the end of the bitterly cold day that followed her meeting with Benny, Madeleine trudged along Canal Street toward hers and Daniel's flat. She hadn't seen him since early that morning, when he'd gulped down a cup of hot coffee and left without a word after they'd had an even hotter exchange. She'd fired the first shot, but then, he'd asked for it, monopolizing the one stool at the crate.

"Do you really need to sit down to drink a cup of coffee?" she asked, standing over him with a fork in one hand and a plate of fried eggs in the other.

"It's not my fault that coffee's all the breakfast I could muster. Somebody took the last two eggs in the house."

"How thoughtless of somebody," she said between clenched teeth. "Here, have one of mine." Using her fork, she shoved one of the eggs off her plate and into his lap.

The strange part was that by the time he had scrubbed up and stormed out minutes later, she'd lost her appetite for the remaining egg. And for her incessant and senseless war with Daniel because she'd already lost it. She'd already lost him. All that remained was for her to surrender. But when she laid down her sword, at least it would be the sword of truth.

"Tonight," she said, strangling a lock of her brown wig. "Tonight Daniel McQuinn will meet Madeleine Faurest."

"Tonight, Madeleine," she murmured as ten hours later she stood before the door to their flat, squeezing her key in the palm of her hand, "is now."

Fourteen

Standing at the window, his copy of *The Divine Comedy* in one hand, a twice-emptied glass of whiskey in the other, Daniel sighed his relief at the sound of Maggie's key in the door. Knowing she imagined no harm would come to her while she was searching for the Holy Grail of the story, for hours, all he'd imagined was the hell she'd found. Or had found her. And finding her, him.

But then, he'd been there all along. Tonight, as he'd paced and read and drank and worried, he'd also come to a stark realization and then a decision. His wife no longer needed him, if she ever had, not even professionally. He'd known it even before she'd refused to tell him about the story the woman in Rawley's office had brought to her. He'd known it because she'd learned everything he'd had to teach her and had taught him a thing or two herself. She was a damn good journalist and deserved the chance to prove that, without him, she was the match of any reporter in town. That's why he'd decided to leave town—just as soon as he finished the bottle on the kitchen crate. He wanted to numb himself for when he cut out his heart.

Madeleine shut the door behind her. "Hello, McQuinn."

Daniel downed what remained of his third shot. Maybe he could douse the fire that erupted inside him every time he looked at her. As he did, he chided himself for not realizing that alcohol would only fuel it. "Ah, the famous Mrs. Babe," he said, toasting her with his empty glass. "Back from a hard day's exposing crime and corruption. How are things at City Hall?"

Madeleine glanced from the glass in Daniel's hand to the bottle beside a lamp on his makeshift table. Unpinning her hat, she walked to the crate, laid her hat down on the stool beside it, and picked up the bottle. In the light, the amber liquid sparkled with a promise to ease her pain, but through it, she could still see the reason for her anguish. She could see that nothing remained of Daniel's feelings for her the night they'd made love, not even his claim of feeling responsible for her simply because she was his wife. Apparently, he'd never given a thought to her unusually long absence.

"For the record," she said, setting the bottle down. "I spent the day at the penitentiary talking to Tomas Kozyck, the husband of the woman who came to see me the other day."

Walking to the table and standing opposite Maggie, Daniel set down both his book and his glass. He filled the latter and lifted it to his lips, but couldn't drink. He knew he couldn't have got anything past the knot of anger in his throat. Since Rawley would never have sanctioned her going to the state pen, of all places, alone, she'd gone without Rawley's knowledge and without his protection. He banged the glass down on the crate.

"You're good, Babe, but not good enough yet to count on Rawley's overlooking shenanigans. I'd love to hear the cussing out he's going to give you when he finds out you went on a story without me."

Madeleine looked at her hands as she yanked off her gloves, angry, and mostly at herself. She couldn't bear to look at Daniel knowing that his concern about her striking out on her own was for the byline he wasn't going to share rather than for her safety. And to think that the moment the prison had loomed up before her, she'd missed feeling him at her side, feeling that as long as he was near, no harm would come to her. What a fool she'd been to fall in love with a man whose business, after all, was swaying people with words. He'd swayed her into his arms and then beneath his body with words that, however thrilling and beautiful, had been empty sounds.

She flung a glove down, hitting the whiskey bottle. "I'm sorry to deny you the pleasure of hearing Rawley curse someone besides yourself," she said, "but I have no choice. You see, he gave me his blessing." *After I harangued him for about an hour.* "After all, Mrs. Kozyck did entrust her story to me alone."

Alone. Of all the words Daniel had read and written, that was the one that haunted him now because, for the first time in his life, he feared aloneness while the woman he loved obviously considered it a virtue. Taking a swallow of whiskey, he picked up Maggie's glove, feeling its softness and recalling the soft feel of her breasts. Missing it. "You couldn't have gotten into the prison alone," he said, resenting his need of her. Resenting her not needing him. "What did Rawley have to do to get the warden to let you in?"

Watching him finger her glove, Madeleine wanted to give him her body in its place. But knowing he had no desire for her, she reached out and snatched the glove away, joined it to its mate, and set the pair beside her hat.

"He didn't have to do a thing. You said it yourself. I'm the famous Babe McQuinn."

Folding her arms, Madeleine gave a sad, self-derisive laugh at the recollection of how she'd wished her equally famous husband had been with her when she'd interviewed Tomas Kozyck. She hadn't realized how much she'd come to depend on Daniel's instincts as well as on her own until she'd worked without him. But working without him was something she would have to get used to.

"McQuinn," she began, looking at him and wondering how she was going to get used to never again gazing into the smouldering eyes that lighted infernos inside her. "I know you find our marriage as . . . *trying* as I do—"

"I don't know what it's trying to do to you," Daniel said, putting his glass down, half-full, and returning the bottle to the cupboard. He'd suddenly lost his thirst. "But it's trying to kill me." *Walking into this flat when you're not here, smelling your scent, touching the sheets you sleep on until I lose control is killing me.*

Madeleine held back the tears that were smarting her eyes. "Not *only* you."

His hand on the knob of the cupboard door, Daniel bowed his head a moment. What a fool he'd been to fall in love with a woman who, however much she denied it, had no heart, no love to give him. He'd give anything to have been her first love, to be her only love. Slowly, he turned to her, almost smiling at how, despite his anguish, seeing her afresh was still like seeing the sun after a long, sunless winter. But he was going to have to get used to living without sunlight, he thought. Without his wife.

"Maggie," he said after letting out a sigh, "I have something to tell you."

"I have something to tell you, Daniel." Reaching for the crown of her wig, Madeleine clutched a handful of lies.

"Sorry to bother ye, your ladyship, but your hoosebund has a phone call." Mrs. Corrigan's booming voice followed her booming knock on the door. "Urgent, the man says."

"Tell him to wait, Eileen," Daniel yelled back.

"Don't do it, Mrs. Corrigan!" Madeleine had kept her secret from Daniel for nearly a month, she could keep it a few minutes longer. "It might be Benny," she said. "I'll wait for you."

Daniel ratcheted a breath. How many times as a youth had he imagined Madeleine speaking those words to him? How he wished now that Maggie had meant them in the same way, as a vow of fidelity. "Don't worry, you won't have to wait long," he said with a hint of contempt—for himself—before leaving her.

After he'd gone, Madeleine picked up the book he'd left on the crate. She saw he'd been reading *The Divine Comedy,* that he was still searching for that one, true love. "I hope you find her, Daniel," she said. Then putting the book down, she removed her wig and dropped it in the ash can beside the cupboard. She unpinned her own pale blond hair and, fetching her hair brush, ministered to the truth that would end her marriage in fact but never in her heart.

Stunned, Daniel hung up the phone. Benny had said that this time, he was certain he'd found her. Kathleen McQuinn Delaney.

"She came back to the old neighborhood just like you said she would, Danny. I was standing on the corner, talking to a patrolman, when all of a sudden I see her going into a flophouse across the street."

"Any sign of my father?"

"No." Benny's whisper had gathered new breath. "She wants to see you, Danny. And from the looks of her, you don't have a minute to waste."

So she's come back to die, Daniel thought, *and she wants my absolution before she does.* Well, if she wanted forgiveness for betraying then abandoning him, he wanted explanations for why she had. He wanted the satisfaction of telling her that whatever they were, they weren't good enough.

As he rushed toward the door with the address Benny had given him branded on his memory, he bumped into Eileen Corrigan, her battering ram of a bosom preceding her. Daniel usually avoided the sight of it, but sparks from the lavaliere laying at the apex of her cleavage where a crucifix had always hung caught his attention. The piece was big and gaudy and Daniel wouldn't have given it another thought if he hadn't also known that it wasn't cheap.

"Finally win the Irish sweepstakes, Eileen?"

"I won all right," she said with a cackle. "I always do. One way or ta other."

Daniel's thoughts returned to Benny's phone call. He asked his landlady to let Maggie know that he'd had to go out and didn't know when he'd be back. "Tell her . . . tell her I've gone to write the end of an old, unfinished story. She'll understand," he said. And as he started up Canal Street, he couldn't shake the feeling that he was starting a long overdue journey to the past.

Inside their flat, after she'd received Daniel's curious message, Madeleine found the trunk beside his reading chair once again an object of her curiosity. She'd given it little thought since she'd first attempted and failed to discover its contents. She'd been too busy trying to unlock the contents of its owner's mind and heart. She'd failed at that, too, of course. Though she loved Daniel McQuinn undyingly, she didn't understand him; the reasons for his unforgivingness, for the vengeful streak Rawley had predicted would one day take him places no man wanted to go. Before she went from his life, she wanted to understand him. She wanted to take his story with her, his complete story, so that she could read it in the pages of her heart as she had always wanted—and still did—to read Delaney's. Whatever the ending of whatever story Daniel had gone off to write, her instincts told her that the beginnings of his own lay within that trunk.

Standing over it, her hair tumbling about her shoulders, she lifted the typewriter and set it on the floor. Then, as once before, she knelt in front of the trunk and tried raising its lid. She should have anticipated it would be locked. After scrambling to gather one of her discarded hairpins and a lamp, she returned to the trunk and set to work picking the lock. Daniel had taught her how, as he'd promised, claiming that no self-respecting reporter would let a lock stand between him and a story. Hearing the click of release, she sighed.

"Oh Daniel," she murmured. "If you only knew that, this time, the story is your own."

As Madeleine pushed back the lid, its hinges creaked like old joints too long unextended. From that sound and the musty odor inside the trunk, she guessed Daniel hadn't visited its contents in quite an age. Her heart beating wildly, she peered inside. Her immediate reaction was disappointment. At the bottom of the trunk, lying in a heap with half its collar and one cuff showing, was an old blue shirt that was certainly worth forgetting about. Still, there might be something of interest lying underneath it. Reaching in, she removed it and, as she dropped it to the floor beside her, gasped at an object that was not only of interest but came as a shock. A derringer. She recognized the small, one-shot pistol because Roger had carried one. She'd foolishly thought it a manly practice, but when she'd found him out for the back-stabber he was, she'd understood that, in his case, gun carrying was the practice of a rightfully fearful and completely cowardly man.

Something she could never say of Daniel. Though she supposed that in the course of his career he'd made his share of enemies, she'd never seen any kind of weapon on him. So why was he holding on to this one? Spying a small paper beneath the pistol, she thought it might provide a clue. She removed the derringer and laid it on the seat of Daniel's reading chair, careful to point the barrel away from her. Then she reached back inside the trunk and took out the last of its odd holdings. As she brought the slim card to the light, she saw something that astonished her even more than the derringer had.

A holy card, very old and tattered around the edges, and depicting the Virgin. That Daniel had probably been born into her faith shouldn't come as so great a shock, she thought, given that he was of Irish descent. But he'd hidden that information from her as deliberately as he'd hidden this holy card inside the trunk. More perplexed about him than ever, she sat to one side.

As she braced herself on her hand, she felt the course fabric of the old shirt beneath it. Laying the holy card down beside the derringer, she slid the shirt out from beneath her and, uncrumpling it, held it up by the shoulders. She looked at the back of it, a faded canvas of stains and wrinkles that was certainly too small for him, and wondered why he was saving an outgrown, completely unwearable garment. Getting to her knees and sitting back on her heels, she turned the front of the shirt around but still saw nothing that should have prevented Daniel from giving it to the ragman long ago. She started to wad it up again when something on one of the pockets caught her attention. It looked like writing, a label of some kind. Stretching just that portion of fabric between her hands, she held the writing to the light.

"No, it can't be. It can't *be.*" But recognizing the shirt once worn by a boy at St. Augustine's, the same kind of shirt—its label indecipherable—worn by the faceless man in her dream not long ago, she knew that it could.

Squeezing her eyes shut, she pictured Daniel McQuinn—tall, his shoulders a beam of strength—then saw a boy whose frame had held the promise of Daniel's height and breadth of shoulder. She saw Daniel's thick tangle of raven hair and then a boy whose shaven head had shown a smudge of new growth just as black. She saw the pride and defiance in Daniel's expression when he'd resigned from the Whitechapel Club, claiming he was too good a journalist to waste his time with hypocrites. And then she saw a boy whose face had been battered but whose expression had been every bit as proud and defiant when he'd said, "My mother's the one taught me to read." She saw Daniel's eyes, eerily light against his tawny complexion, telling her as a prelude to their first kiss that night on the Levee, that he could never harm her. And then the eyes—one pummeled shut and the other a window on his soul—of a boy who'd suffered at the thought he might have harmed her, even by accident.

Clutching the shirt to her breasts, she laid her head back, and as she rocked, she keened a torment of incomprehension and incomprehensible joy. He was alive, alive, alive.

He was her husband, the love of her life, the soul of her soul. "Dear God," she cried, gazing once again at the letters on the shirt through a bottomless well of tears. "Delancy. He's Daniel Delaney."

Madeleine arched her body over the shirt, touching her forehead to it in homage to a miracle. She lavished her tears on it and her deepest gratitude and her greater faith. She knew she could have found Daniel Delaney only by Loving Design. But she also recognized that only by that same design would she keep him.

She was the clearly spoiled Southern belle with a rich daddy who had seemingly humiliated Daniel and earned his contempt ten years ago. Now she must make him believe that she'd done so only to save him from the monsignor's wrath, to save him for herself. She must make him believe that ever since then she had carried his spirit in the core of her being as the best of her being. And when she'd strayed too far from herself and could no longer sense him inside her, she'd come to Chicago, she now realized, in search of them both. She must make him believe her, forgive and trust and love her as she loved him from the first. As she did now and would forever.

She picked up the holy card. Her words didn't come easily to her. Nonetheless, she spoke them fervently. "Please," she said. "Help me."

Hearing footsteps on the stairs, she laughed. "That was quick," she said, setting the card down on the chair atop the pistol. Then, still clutching the shirt, she dashed to the door and threw it open. "Daniel!"

Benny Grimm, short and round and his eyes—as Madeleine had always thought—too small for his cherub's face, stood opposite her. "Hello, Madeleine," he said, his whisper through a wad of gum unusually wet.

Instinctively, Madeleine's hand flew to the nape of her neck where it at last found the tell-tale strands of pale blond hair she had long feared would betray her. But it hadn't, because Benny had shown no surprise when she'd appeared at the door without her brown wig. "How long have you known my secret?"

"Since a few days after you asked me about St. Augustine's." He hiked his pants. "Of course, you've changed a lot since then and the brown hair threw me at first, but I don't forget a face. I knew you were the kid I'd seen in Father Bianco's classroom that day."

Lurching, Madeleine reached toward him, holding Daniel's shirt between them. "You haven't told—"

"Don't worry," he replied, his gaze fixed firmly on the shirt. "I didn't tell Danny. Knowing how he felt about you when you . . . I couldn't."

Slumping with relief, Madeleine smiled. "Thank you, Ben—" Abruptly, she straightened. "Maybe you didn't tell Daniel, but—"

"I didn't tell the Pinkertons, either. You can relax."

Madeleine did. "You're a good friend. I'm sure you could use the reward money."

His expression clouded, as though he were gathering an angry shout. Indeed, his voice, when it came, was louder than she'd ever heard it. "What's money compared to your self-respect?"

Making an L of her arms, Madeleine tucked Daniel's shirt beneath her chin. "I'm sorry, Benny. I should have known that if money were a temptation for you, you could easily take the offers of bribes you probably receive every day." Giving him an apologetic smile, she stepped back, clearing a way into the flat "Forgive me?"

His small eyes disappeared with his own broad smile. "You're forgiven, my child," he said, as he passed her by.

Madeleine laughed, then gazed quizzically after him. She might have imagined it, but she could have sworn she smelled alcohol on his breath. The only other time she had, she recalled, was when she first met Benny at the scene of the last Red Rose murder. Not that she blamed him for needing fortification every time he was called to view one of the fiend's victims.

"Benny?" Anxiously, she shut the door and followed him to the crate and one stool in the kitchen area of the flat. "The Red Rose Killer, has he claimed another victim?"

Benny removed his hat from a head of baby fine hair. "Not yet," he said, a sly smile on his lips as he laid his hat on the stool.

"Thank God."

"I did come to talk to you about the case, though," he said, reaching inside his overcoat.

"You angel!" Excitedly, Madeleine dodged the crate and spread her hands over his thick upper arms. "You found the old flower woman, didn't you?"

"Yes, I found her," he said.

His calm struck Madeleine as strange. "Well, where is she?"

"Right here, Madeleine."

His whisper, like wind moaning in a graveyard, gave Madeleine a chill. She didn't freeze with terror, however, until he withdrew his hand from inside his coat and she saw that in his pudgy fingers, Benny Grimm held a single, long-stemmed, blood-red rose.

Several blocks from the flat, Daniel waited impatiently for a streetcar, hoping the past would wait for him. Benny had cautioned he had no time to lose finding his mother. That didn't seem fair, he thought, considering it had taken her ten years to find him.

Still seeing no sign of the streetcar, Daniel took a cigarette from the pack in his pocket and placed it between his lips. As he tore a match from his matchbook, he reminded himself that he ought to be grateful for any chance at all of seeing her, of asking questions that might otherwise haunt him all his life. He had Benny to thank for that, he thought as he struck the match, for spotting her from across the street. Benny's eyes were small but his sight must be damn sharp and his instincts even sharper to recognize—from a distance, no less—a woman whom Daniel had described to him as she'd looked ten years younger. By now, her hair had surely gone from mahogany to gray, he thought as he brought the match to the tip of his cigarette.

Without lighting it, he looked up, his gaze unfocused. Suddenly, he wondered how it was that Benny could identify a woman he wasn't looking for and from a description that no longer fit, and yet couldn't find one whose current description he had—Maggie's old flower woman—even though he claimed he had men out combing the city for her. But then, he thought, dropping the match to the ground, that's just the way it went sometimes. Whether you were a cop or a reporter, trying to turn up a witness or a headline, you knew you sometimes had to depend on the luck of the draw. And from what Benny had said yesterday, he was confident of drawing aces. He'd said he was so close to the old woman he could smell the rum on her breath.

Daniel struck another match. Halfway to lighting his cigarette, though, he again paused. He remembered that, at the time, he'd wondered why Benny had depicted the old woman as a rumpot. A lot of them like her were, of course, and so he hadn't given Benny's assumption about her choice of intoxicant another thought. He didn't now, until, feeling a burn on the tips of his fingers, he dropped the match. He looked down at the ground where it had fallen and thought about the times he'd stood beside Benny, looking down at the victim of an incomprehensible evil. Those were the times Daniel had noticed the faint smell of rum masked by chewing gum on Benny's breath. The only times. He remembered once telling Benny to go home for some of Alice's hot apple pie and coffee. He'd especially meant the coffee. *Go home, you old woman,* he'd said.

Smiling around the cigarette in his mouth, Daniel thought how like an old woman Benny had always been, even as a boy. He was a natural-born worrier, an advice giver, a mother. Daniel had often poked fun at him, claiming that he didn't know why he was so intent on finding his mother when he had Benny to harp on him about finding a nice girl and settling down. Taking the cigarette from his mouth, Daniel laughed out loud. Hell, Benny even looked like a fat old hen, never more so than when he'd clucked his disapproval of the woman Daniel *had* married.

Seeing the streetcar, Daniel threw his cigarette away. He climbed aboard, paid his fare, and finding a seat, thought about how happy he must have made Benny yesterday when he'd more than hinted he'd wanted a divorce from Maggie. At the time, of course, he'd only been trying to hurt her. Divorce was the last thing he wanted, the first being that just once in his life he'd be blessed with a miracle and return to their flat to find that she wanted him. That she loved him as much as he loved her. But Benny didn't know that. He only knew that his old friend had said he wanted a divorce from a woman who'd spitefully vowed she'd never give him one.

Suddenly alarmed and not yet knowing precisely why, Daniel sat forward. In his mind, a jumble of thoughts was trying to untangle itself and failing as surely as his marriage had failed. Burying his face in his hands, he picked at a thought here and another there until he had them all laid out like the pieces of a puzzle that were meaningless until joined in just the right way.

Benny. Rum. Old Woman. Fat old rumpot flower woman with red roses. Maybe she was the killer, Benny had said. And Maggie saw her. Benny can't find her. Found my mother, though. At least he'd said he did. Benny's mother was a prostitute. Prostitutes are dying with red roses in their hands. Maggie's hands are as soft as rose petals. Her tongue as sharp as the blade of a knife. I told Benny that if I ever needed help getting her out of my hair, I'd let him know. Benny heard her say no divorce. Unhappy Mother Grimm. Fairytale. Babe in the woods. Alone. Babe at home. Waiting all alone.

Daniel shot out of his seat. "Maggie!"

As Benny gripped Madeleine's wrist, she stared at the butcher knife he'd drawn from inside his coat after dropping the rose at her feet. The knife with which he'd committed the Red Rose murders and intended to commit hers.

"Why, Benny?" she said, her voice a whisper, like his, but of fear. "Why did you kill those young girls?"

"I couldn't think of any other way to stop them," he said. "If I didn't, one of them might have a kid, and then he'd have to watch her die a worse death, one sin at time, like my mother did."

All at once and clearly, Madeleine understood Benny's anger when she'd suggested she wouldn't have blamed him for turning her over to the Pinkertons for reward money. *What's money compared to your self-respect?* he asked as he must have asked his prostitute mother.

"Benny, I understand you meant well," she said, sickening at the memory of the sight of his last victim and the knowledge that she could be his next. "But no one has the right to play God."

"I don't believe in God," he said. "If you were me, would you?"

Clutching Daniel's shirt in her free hand, Madeleine hesitated. "I can't answer that. I'm not you."

Benny looked at the shirt then at her. "And you're not little Madeleine anymore, are you? You're Babe McQuinn and you're the only person who both saw the old flower woman on the Levee and can afford to admit you were there by describing her to an illustrator for your paper. Then the whole city would be on the lookout for her and I wouldn't be able to dress up and go the Levee and ask the girls to help an old woman home and then do the things I have to do. That's why I have to kill you. You understand that, don't you?"

Madeleine tried twisting out of his grip, but to no avail. *Help me,* she prayed and the moment she had, she recalled the derringer on the chair across the room. If pulling away, she could lead him to it, she had a good chance of exchanging Daniel's shirt for it.

"I'm trying, Benny," she said, backing toward the chair. He followed. "I'm trying to understand and I think I do.

Maybe you're right. Maybe you really are doing a good thing and I would be doing a bad thing if I described the old woman for the *Clarion*."

"I'm glad you understand," he said, then pulled her to a halt beside the chair. "But I'd have to kill you anyway."

"Why?" Madeleine asked, dropping Daniel's shirt behind her. "Tell me, Benny. What have I done to hurt you?"

"Not me, Madeleine. Danny."

"Daniel?" Groping to her left, Madeleine found the arm of the chair. She had to keep him talking and, when the time was just right, lunge for the pistol. "What have I done to Daniel?"

"You won't give him a divorce. But you should because you're not right for him. He needs a home. A real home. Every boy needs a home."

Dear God, Madeleine thought, *he's thinking of himself as a child*. As terrified as she was, she saw that child in Benny's eyes and felt sorry for him. "But I'm Madeleine," she reminded him. "He loved me once, remember? I can make him love me again, Benny. But if he finds out that you took me away from him before I had the chance, he'll be unhappy." She stretched her fingers toward the seat of the chair. "And you want him to be happy, don't you, Benny?"

"Of course. That's why I didn't tell him I knew who you really were. And why I'll make sure no one ever finds your body. So that he'll never know."

What happened next seemed to Madeleine more like a dance than a struggle, her lunging sideways for the derringer, Benny's yanking her back toward him. Then, with remarkable grace for a heavyset man, he quickly released her wrist only to collar her from behind and clamp his hand over her mouth. "This will be quick, Madeleine. I promise," he whispered, his rum-and-spearmint breath striking Madeleine as festive, in a macabre way.

But the party was over, she knew, when she saw the blade of his knife rise before her eyes. She'd always wondered what her final thoughts would be and now she knew. She hadn't any. She was merely an observer, a fact gatherer, a reporter to the end. Only this was one story she'd never get to write. Suddenly, she was very sad because neither would Daniel. Not the real story, anyway. He'd write of Babe McQuinn's disappearance and presumed death but not of Madeleine Faurest Delaney's life, not of their life together.

Hell if he wouldn't! After ten years, nearly four hundred miles, and a miracle, she'd be damned if she'd lose her life and Daniel Delaney, too. At least not without a fight. She clawed the arm Benny held around her neck, and scratched and kicked and poked. And when the hand clamped over her mouth gave a little, she dug her upper teeth into the fleshy pads beneath the fingers.

Yelping, Benny let her go. Madeleine dove for the derringer. The front door shot opened. Benny grabbed her, his thick arm garroting her neck, and pulled her with him as he backed toward the wall. Beneath his arm, he pressed the cold blade of the knife against her throat. "Don't come any closer, Danny," he said.

At that precise moment, seeing Benny and the woman he held at the point of death, the woman he'd expected to be Maggie, Daniel couldn't move at all. Standing there huffing from having run faster than he'd ever run in his life, he narrowed his sight on her. Hair as pale gold as moonbeams cascading over her shoulders and trapped beneath Benny's arm spread like strands of silk over her breasts. Hair that looked the way Maggie's had felt as he'd sifted it through his fingers when they'd made love. Hair so remarkable he'd seen the likes of it only once before. It had shone like a halo around the head of a woman-child whose features had been a blur, except for her eyes. Eyes like Maggie's, darkly brilliant and in whose mysterious depths he'd lost the child he'd been and found the man he was meant to be. He'd asked for a miracle, just one miracle in his life, but he never imagined he could deserve one like this.

He swallowed past the fist-sized lump in his throat. "Madeleine?"

Tears streamed down her cheeks, tears of joy. Whatever happened now, Daniel would always have their story, their miracle. Despite the blade at her throat, she smiled. Then, she spoke raspily through the thin siphon of breath—perhaps her last—the knife had left her. "More things in heaven and earth than are dreamt of in your—our—philosophy." Unable to speak another word aloud, she mouthed, *I love you, Daniel Delaney.*

Daniel blinked in disbelief. She knew his real name. But how? He darted a look at the trunk beside the chair and saw that the lid stood raised. A bittersweet smile flicked the corner of his mouth. He'd taught her how to pick locks never imagining she would free him from a lifetime of longing for the missing half of his soul. She knew who he was and who he had been and she loved him. Somehow, he knew she'd loved him always, through time and from afar. "Madeleine," he said, taking a step toward her.

Benny jerked her back. "I warned you, Danny."

Daniel fixed his gaze on Benny, whose small eyes wore the look of a frightened animal. "You don't want to hurt her, Benny," he said softly, taking small, slow steps, one of them on a red rose. "She is *She,* remember?"

"I remember *Her,*" Benny replied, hissing venomously.

"No, Benny. She's not your mother. She's Madeleine, my Madeleine." Daniel showed Benny his empty palms. "But I didn't know that yesterday when I said I wanted a divorce. Anyway, I didn't mean it. I was only trying to hurt her because I loved Maggie so much and I thought she didn't love me. So if you hurt her, you'll hurt me and I know you don't want to do that. You're my friend. You've always looked out for me."

"I'm looking out for you now," Benny said, his whisper a tremolo. "You think you love her but she's no good. She'll make you miserable and ashamed. You'll think you can change her, but she'll never change, Danny." Benny was crying now. Turning his face aside, he momentarily took the knife from Madeleine's throat and wiped his tears on the back of his hand.

Daniel lunged forward, reaching the chair before Benny, whipping his gaze and the knife back around, said, "She'll never change!"

The hope that surged through Madeleine as Daniel came within feet of her plummeted. Then rose again, if only a little. Daniel was beside the chair, his hand gripping the arm. And just inches from his reach lay the derringer partially covered by the holy card. But how could she let him know it was there?

"Please, Benny," Daniel said, his voice shaking. "I'm begging you now. Don't kill her. You'll kill me, too. Please." He started forward.

"Stop, Daniel!" Madeleine swallowed painfully. "There's only one thing you can do for me now. Pray."

"Pray?" He looked at her as though she'd lost her sanity. But then, he wasn't the one with a knife at his throat.

"I know you've probably forgotten how," she went on. "But there's a holy card on the chair with a prayer on the back of it. Say it for me, Daniel. Please."

Glancing down at the seat of the chair, Daniel saw the holy card his mother had given him after he'd been sentenced to St. Augustine's and, protruding from beneath it, the barrel of the derringer he'd bought when Rawley had given him his first assignment as a wet-behind-the-ears reporter. He'd thought it would give him authority and dash, especially with the ladies. But it had only given him a rash where he'd kept it tucked inside his boot. And the only "ladies" he'd met hadn't been impressed by it because they'd packed pistols of their own. So he'd put it away and forgotten about it.

Unfortunately, he'd also forgotten whether or not it was loaded. Madeleine had been right. The only thing he could do now was pray.

He looked at his poor, blubbering, murderous old friend. "Let me say it for her, Benny."

Rivulets of tears streaming over the mounds of his cheeks, Benny nodded.

Slowly, keeping his eyes on Benny, Daniel reached down to his right. When his fingers brushed the face of the holy card, he slid it aside. Grasping the small handle of the pistol, he swept it up and, with lightning speed, aimed it at the lump that was Benny's shoulder, just visible above Madeleine's. He saw Benny look at the gun as he pulled the trigger.

Nothing happened. Nothing.

Then, Benny spoke softly. "You let me down, Danny." Shoving Madeleine into Daniel's arms, he made a waddle-run across the room and out the door.

"Benny!" Righting Madeleine, Daniel released her. He threw the pistol away then dashed after Benny Grimm. The Red Rose Killer. He pounded down the stairs, Madeleine on his heels. At the open front door, he saw, with great relief, Benny's knife on the threshold. He turned to Madeleine. "Get on the phone. Ask for Captain Grady at the Twenty-sixth Street station house. Tell him what happened and to get every patrolman he can muster out looking for Benny." Cupping her cheek in the palm of his hand, he gave her a smile. "Are you all right?"

"I am now."

Pulling her against him, he kissed her. He kissed his Madeleine then let her go. They turned in opposite directions but got no farther then a few feet from one an other when a sharp, reverberating blast halted them.

They looked at one another with alarm and then horror as each knew the other had recognized the sound.

A single gunshot.

Daniel ran toward the unpaved street. There in the pale moonlight, with one hand groping for the sidewalk as though he didn't want to die in the dirt, Benny Grimm lay facedown. His police revolver lay a few feet from his side. Squatting, Daniel turned him over. Though blood was staining Benny's shirt near his heart, he was still breathing. Opening his eyes, he looked at Daniel. "It's so hard, living a lie your whole life."

"Don't talk, Benny," Daniel said, tearing off his jacket and pressing it over the wound.

Benny winced. Then, in a voice strangely more audible in death than it had been in life, he said, "But I didn't lie about her, Danny. About your . . . mother." The last of his breath rattled from his broken throat.

Daniel felt the artery on the side of Benny's neck for a pulse. Then with a sigh, he closed his old friend's eyes.

Squatting beside Daniel as neighbors aroused by the shot straggled out from behind their doors, Madeleine stretched her arm across the back of his shoulders. "Is he dead?"

Daniel nodded. Standing, he raised her beside him and walked her away from the gathering crowd. "A good reporter is supposed to question assumptions," he said, "but I never questioned that the old flower woman and The Red Rose Killer were two separate people, even when Benny kidded that they weren't. I never doubted that the old woman was a woman."

"Neither did I. We were too busy doubting one another."

"That's all over now."

"I want to make sure of that, Daniel. I want you to know exactly who I am." Madeleine told him that she was the daughter of Judge Matthew Faurest, a politically ambitious man who had put the Pinkertons on her trail, offering a thousand-dollar reward for information leading to her whereabouts.

"He must love you very much."

"No, Daniel. He loves just one thing. Power." She lowered her eyes. "Do you remember I told you about a man named Roger? I fled Louisville just a few days before I was to have married him. My father's plan was to get Roger elected to Congress and, through him, extend his grasp to Washington. But even before I discovered what they'd both been up to, I knew deep inside my soul, where you were, that I was making a mistake." She clasped his arm. "I never loved Roger Mabrey or any other man. I swear it."

Daniel put his forefinger to her lips. "Don't you think I know that? We've always belonged to each other, Madeleine. Neither of us could have truly loved anyone else."

Madeleine smiled, grateful for his trust. "Yes, Daniel. But what you don't know is that I changed my name to keep my father from finding me, because I believe he'll stop at nothing to realize his plans. Not even at murder."

"Mine," Daniel said.

"If he finds me, he won't hesitate to threaten it to force me to succumb to his will." Tilting her head, she gazed up into his eyes. "And I would, Daniel. You must know I would."

Daniel plunged his hands into her hair. "I'd find you and give you that spanking I almost gave Sadie." He kissed the tip of her nose. "But he's not going to find you, Madeleine. And he's not going to find me."

Madeleine took hope. "You could change your name back to Delaney," she suggested.

Daniel frowned. "No. That's a name I wouldn't want to give you."

"Any name you give me is good enough for me," she said softly. "But why did you change it?"

"One of the priests at the reformatory thought that by taking a new name, I could bury my criminal record, make a fresh start."

"Father Bianco," Madeleine said.

"You remember him?"

"I went to see him, looking for you. Now I understand why he told me you were dead." She took her hands from his arms. He released her and she turned aside. "Daniel, there's something I have to know." She looked back at him. "Is it true that you were sent to St. Augustine's because you tried to kill your father?"

Taking a step back, Daniel shoved his hands in his pockets. "He'd been slowly killing my mother for years, body and soul. One day, I discovered I was at last strong enough to stop him before he finally succeeded. I know you won't understand this, but sometimes I think that if I ever found him, I'd be tempted to finish what I started."

Rawley's prediction of the toll Daniel's vengeful streak would one day exact sounded a knell in Madeleine's mind. "Daniel, leave the past behind. If not for your own sake, for mine."

"I'm not about to dismiss the past so quickly," he replied. Then with a wry smile, he rubbed the cheek she'd slapped twice.

Madeleine understood. "I slapped you the first time because I had the notion I could keep that devil of a monsignor from beating you to death."

Daniel smiled wider. "And the second time?"

Madeleine tossed her head. "Because I wanted to." Then, sobering, "I know I've hurt you, Daniel. In the past and—"

Daniel took her face in his hands. "I love you, Madeleine-Maggie . . ." He smiled softly. "Babe. I always have and always will. What more do you need for me to say?"

"That you forgive me."

"You haven't said you're sorry."

Madeleine wrapped her arms around his neck. Standing on her toes, she brought her lips to his. "I'm sorry, Daniel McQuinn. Or whatever you're going to call yourself from now on."

"So am I," Daniel replied and, clasping her arms, broke their hold of him. "Because as much as I want to kiss your mouth off, there's something we have to do first."

Sighing, Madeleine lowered to the soles of her feet. "I'm beginning to think, Daniel, that there are times when the story isn't all that matters."

"And matters, my dear wife," he said, his arm around her as he headed back to the house to call the *Clarion's* night city desk, "have never been more right."

At his words, words that should have comforted her, Madeleine felt a foreboding. But it was so sudden, so fleeting, she dismissed it as superstition.

Or tried to.

I don't believe in silly superstitions, she'd once told Daniel. But she'd nearly lost her life tonight because she hadn't followed his advice—she hadn't questioned everything she'd seen and seen the possibility of everything she questioned.

Still, the one thing she would never question was that from now on, she and Daniel would forever be inseparable.

Fifteen

Some hours later, after Daniel had called in the story with Madeleine at his side, and the police had questioned them and taken Benny away to the county morgue, Daniel sent her back up to their flat alone.

"The story you said you needed to finish?" she asked.

"Another. I won't be long."

Wrapped in his tight embrace, Madeleine opened her mouth to his kiss. She claimed his tongue and gave him hers, and knew they were combusting a fire that could never be extinguished. "Don't be," she said.

She returned to their flat, the place she had once thought barren, devoid of the least of the trappings that make a house a home; bereft of the evidence that in it, people live and love and fight and forgive so that they can love again. When she first saw it, she never could have imagined it would become the stage for the greatest drama of her life, and very nearly, the scene of her death. She looked at the crate and the one stool beside it, and smiled. How often she'd needled Daniel about getting another stool. She could have found one herself, of course, but their arguments over the matter had become something of a ritual. Rituals, more than pictures on the wall and rugs on the floor, made a house a home. Sometimes, even a sacred place.

She walked to the bed. For a long moment, she looked

up at the sheets walling it off then reached up and with one, powerful tug, pulled one down. Rounding the bed like a cyclone, she pulled them all down and flung them far from sight. She stood at the foot of the bed, staring at it as it stretched out before her. She'd shed a little of her blood on it the night Daniel had taken her virginity and given her an entirely new life, a life that was only beginning.

As she slowly unbuttoned her shirtwaist and then her skirt, she recalled the feel of his skin beneath her hands, smooth and taut here, a ripple of muscle there, hardness and hair and strength and vulnerability. Removing her corset cover, she tried to picture all that her hands had touched. The images that came to mind quickened her desire for him. And as she unbuttoned her corset, she felt his hands on her shoulders and breasts; as she stepped from her shoes and drawers and stockings, she felt them on her thighs and so exquisitely in between. She gasped a breath only to feel it snatched by the sound of Daniel's key in the door. She turned toward it.

Holding a sack in one arm, Daniel paused in the doorway. His breath caught in his chest as his eyes took in the sight of Madeleine standing at the foot of the no longer imprisoned bed—their bed—her naked limbs testaments to the inadequacy of his imagination. Closing the door, he walked toward her, and when he stood opposite her, he ran his gaze lingeringly, longingly, from the pale aura of her hair to the eternal mysteries in her eyes to her body, a true vessel of womanhood.

"I adore you, Madeleine," he whispered.

Reaching up, she began to comb back his hair, wild and raven, then withdrew her hand. She smiled. "Did you finish your story?"

He grazed his fingers down her face, then staring at her lips, plump and pink, he ran his thumb over and around them. "That all depends."

Parting her lips, she licked the pad of his thumb. "On what?"

"On you." Walking to the crate, Daniel set the sack down. "Stay where you are and close your eyes. Don't open them until I tell you to."

Madeleine gave him a puzzled look but, trusting him, did as he asked. She stood naked and sightless, feeling nothing but air that had chilled with the dying fire in the stove, hearing nothing but Daniel's footsteps and what sounded like the striking of matches.

Then she heard nothing at all. A moment later, something thudded on the floor not far from where she stood, then another something, followed by soft rustling.

And then, she felt Daniel's presence over her like a blanket between her and cold aloneness.

"You can open your eyes now," he said.

Blinking, Madeleine gazed up at him, his face a tawny interplay of soft but intense upward light and angular shadows. In it, his eyes were two orbs of blue-white fire melting dark cores of mistrust. Leaving them to burn, she lowered her gaze to the broad transept of his shoulders, the deep nave of his chest, the font of his manhood. It was then she saw the source of the light that bathed him, the candles on the floor at her feet, more than a dozen of them, all votives of his love.

"Oh, Daniel," she murmured, overcome and breathless. "I don't know what to say."

"I know what I'm praying you'll say. And if you do, the story will never end." He got down on his knees and, gazing up at her, saw the beauty of her otherness and worshipped it. "Madeleine, will you marry me?"

Inquiringly, she laid her head to one side. "We're already married."

"I meant . . ." He lowered his lids, the sudden, tender beauty of his dark lashes on the plains above his cheekbones rending her heart. He looked up at her. "In church."

Her heart now torn in two by the love that alone could heal it, Madeleine lowered herself to the floor, the candles flickering between Daniel and her sending up warmth and light. Reaching out, she placed the palms of her hands over the center of his chest. "Yes. In a cathedral if that's what it will take to assure you I'll never leave you again."

Daniel cupped her elbows and together they rose. Madeleine turned to the bed and Daniel, stepping over the candles, to her side. For a moment, they stood holding hands, their gazes joining them in a silent hymn to their love. Then, without a word, they climbed onto the bed and into each other's embrace as though for the first time. As though time and distance and, later, masks of falsehood had never split them into two desperately yearning halves of the same whole. Indeed, all yearning for what they had missed ceased, leaving only desire for what they'd miraculously found.

The candles had burned dangerously low when, for the second time, Daniel poured himself into the soft, warm cradle of Madeleine's love. He could feel a trembling in her thighs raised up on either side of him. Gently, he unsheathed himself and, lying beside her, covered her with the blanket and his arm. "You need rest," he whispered.

"I need you."

"I'm here."

Closing her eyes, she snuggled closer. "You tell good stories, Daniel."

Smiling, he stroked her hair back from her forehead. *"We* do, Babe."

"Does that mean . . ." Madeleine yawned. "You'll help me with the Kozyck story?"

Daniel wrapped her tightly in his embrace. "I thought you'd never ask."

He held her until she fell soundly asleep, then getting out of bed, put out all the candles but one. By its light he quietly dressed then penned a note to Madeleine and placed it on his pillow beside her. Going to the door, he opened it and took one last look at his wife.

Then, blowing out the candle, he prayed the flame of his mother's life still burned.

As fingers of daylight reached around the window shade and touched the bed, Madeleine turned over. Grinning, she reached for Daniel. In his place, she found a note with her name written on it in his hand. Disquieted, she opened the note.

"Dearest Babe," it began. "I had to go after that other story. I was afraid it wouldn't wait. I don't think I'll be able to either—for you to make me an honest man of me, that is. You can start, though, by declaring your intentions to the archbishop. Meet me at Holy Name Cathedral at ten. And Madeleine, every step of the way there, remember that I love you.
Daniel.
P.S. Bring your notes on the Kozyck story."

Madeleine grinned. But as she touched her lips to his name, another premonition, stronger than the one she'd felt the night before, sent a shiver of fear up her spine. Sitting up, she turned her mother's initial ring on her finger, the ring she'd worn as a wedding band. Telling herself her baseless, undefined fear would vanish once Daniel placed his own ring on her finger, she climbed out of bed.

But before she walked far, she looked back. Seeing the indentation left by Daniel's head in his pillow, she returned to the bed. Leaning over, she plumped his pillow, readying it for his return.

On Halsted Street, in the shadow of a bridge over the south branch of the Chicago River, Daniel stood outside a grimy, dilapidated building that had once warehoused goods bound for trade. Now, it warehoused only people, human detritus bound for nowhere. Somewhere inside was Kathleen McQuinn Delaney, his mother. Flinging away a cigarette, he entered the building.

Knowing that all that was required to "register" in a flophouse like this one was 25 cents for a bug-infested bed in a five-by-seven cubicle, Daniel didn't bother asking for his mother by name. He merely asked the manager of the place if in the last few nights he'd rented a bed to a woman in her fifties. She was a small woman, probably in frail health.

"Take your pick," the manager replied, smelling no better than the dump he ran. "I got a warehouse full of hags like her."

At the crude if impersonal affront to his mother, a remnant of an old, familiar rage shot through Daniel. Some instincts, he discovered, never died. Releasing a pent-up breath, he unclenched his fists. "Mind if I have a look around?"

The foul-smelling man shrugged. "Why should I?"

Daniel started for the doors on his right and the cribs beyond them then abruptly halted. "Any of the women here a reader?" he asked the man, who answered with a perplexed look. "Books. The woman I'm looking for always carried at least one book with her."

The man took the stub of a fat cigar from his mouth. "Top floor."

Slowly, Daniel climbed the stairs. With each flight came a memory of a childhood shuttled between Heaven and

Hell, between a place in the pages of his mother's books where men strove to understand the human soul to a place where men like his father crushed souls they couldn't begin to understand. All these years, Daniel had striven to understand why his mother had taken her husband's abuse. Once, he'd thought her devout faith had been the reason. Divorce was a mortal sin signifying the loss of grace. But he knew that couldn't have been the sole reason. Fear of eternal damnation hadn't prevented her from damning her son to a reformatory.

Climbing the final stair, Daniel stood at one end of a vast space crowded with beds, thick with dust, discordant with snores, coughs, and senseless jabber. Bed by bed he combed the rows, searching for the remnant of one particular life among the ruins of so many. At the end of the final row, he glanced down at a reed of a woman who was asleep on her side. She wasn't his mother. Swallowing a lump of old hurt and fresh disappointment, he started for the stairs.

"I knew you'd come," a soft, cracked voice behind him said.

Daniel looked at the woman in the last bed. With great effort and evident agony, she pulled herself to a half-sitting position. It was then that he saw her smashed left cheek and the newspaper she'd been sheltering beneath her thin chest—the *Clarion*. Warily, he approached her. He'd expected age and hardship to have changed her, of course, but he'd never expected this. Little more than a skeleton. Yet, her gaze was a vibrant blue, holding him as it once had, with a mixture of pride and joy that was jarringly out of place. Grabbing the iron rail at the foot of the bed, he lowered his head, squeezed back tears.

"I've been reading your stories, yours and your wife's."

Daniel looked up.

She gave him a wan smile. "I'm glad you're not alone."

"Since when?"

Her smile disappeared. "I . . . was happy you still thought enough of me to take my maiden name."

"For years I tried not to think of you at all." Daniel rounded the foot of the bed. "But then I couldn't help myself, if only out of curiosity. Why, I kept asking, did you lie at my trial? The one answer I kept getting was that you *wanted* to see me locked up."

His mother turned her waxen face to his. "I did, Daniel. You were so filled with vengeance, I knew you would have killed him. I couldn't let you do that."

Daniel sneered. "Because you loved him."

"Because I loved *you.*" Her words came slowly, breathlessly. "That's why I went away with him before you got out of reform school. I knew your hatred of him had only grown stronger and that you meant to finish the killing I'd stopped."

Daniel gave her a puzzled look. In the two years he'd spent at St. Augustine's, she hadn't come to see him once. *"How* did you know?"

Looking down, she worried the edge of the dirty blanket. "Father Bianco used to write to me about you."

"I see. A conspiracy to save my soul." Daniel laughed pitilessly. "Too bad you didn't care as much about my body. Did Father Bianco also tell you how many times I'd been beaten within an inch of my life?"

She lowered lids that were nearly transparent. "Six."

Daniel's lips parted in surprise.

"I won't ask you to forgive me for that," she said. "But Daniel, please know that I never wanted you to pay for my sins."

Daniel straightened to his full height. "You should have thought of that before the judge sentenced me."

Kathleen Delaney fixed her son with a fevered gaze. "I should have thought of that long before then." Suddenly, she arched her back as her mouth gaped with a strangled cry.

Instinctively, Daniel came to her side. Removing his hat, he tossed it on the foot of the bed then, leaning over her, gripped her hand tightly in a counterassault of pain. She squeezed back with a strength that surprised him, fighting off total delirium. As the battle waged on and Daniel stroked her once-thick, once-lustrous hair back from her forehead, he remembered how he'd felt so long ago, making comfrey tea compresses for her bruises. Needed. Despite his bitterness, he was glad he'd found her now, when alone and dying she needed him most.

"I'm going for a doctor, Ma," he whispered.

Slanting her gaze at him, she moved her head from side to side. "Too . . . late. There's only one thing you can do for me now, Daniel. Promise me you will do it."

Daniel hesitated.

Her grip tightened. "Promise me."

Daniel promised. "What is it you want me to do?"

Words crossed her colorless lips so softly that Daniel couldn't hear them. Asking her to repeat what she'd said, he lowered his ear to her mouth.

"Your father," she said faintly but clearly. "Find him, Daniel."

A crease between his brows, Daniel looked at her. "Why, after all these years?"

Exhaling a great sigh, Kathleen McQuinn Delaney slowly lifted the hand that had been clenched over her heart toward Daniel's cheek. "I . . . was . . . wrong . . . to keep you . . . from him." Without quite reaching him, her hand fell, coming to rest atop her abdomen.

"Ma?"

Her eyes closed.

"Ma!"

Daniel checked her pulse, finding it all but nonexistent. With a boulder-sized ache in his chest, he turned away. When he knew he could look at her again, for what may well be the last time, he turned back. Bending over her, he tucked her right arm beneath the blanket then reached for the left. As he lifted her hand, he saw coiled beneath it a fine gold chain and oval locket which he couldn't remember ever having seen his mother wear. Curious, he picked it up, laying the locket against the fingers of his cupped hand, and saw that one side of it was unembellished except for the dullness and fine scratches that come with age. He turned it over. The face of the locket was also unadorned except for a small cross etched in the center.

Intrigued, he pried the piece open. As he did, something fluttered from inside. A downward glance revealed it was a folded square of cloth, no bigger than his thumbnail and yellowed. A dark stain was visible along the folds, which Daniel quickly undid. To his eye, the brownish stain in the center of the small square appeared to be blood.

But whose? How long had his mother had this remnant and why had she secreted it like some holy relic? Had she meant for him to find it? He looked down at her for answers. Plainly, she was going to take them to her grave, leaving him to fulfill a promise to find a man she'd spent the last ten years keeping him from.

But she'd said she'd been wrong to do that. Had she spent the last ten years regretting that she'd thwarted justice for them both? Perhaps the blood on the scrap was Sean Delaney's. If she'd once fought back, drawn his blood, Daniel could understand her keeping it as a vestige of a small but sweet retribution. He could understand her bringing it to him as proof of her change of heart, proof of her desire for the vengeance she now wanted him to seek.

Daniel replaced the bloodstained cloth in the locket, creating a talisman for his crusade. Bending over his mother, he brought his face close to hers.

"Don't worry," he whispered. "I'll find him." He kissed her fevered cheek. Then, he retrieved his fedora and, with a last look at Kathleen McQuinn Delaney, settled it low over one eye and walked away.

Downstairs, he strode to the manager. "Whatever she needs," he said, removing several large bills from his billfold, "see that she gets it."

Chomping on his cigar stub, the man grabbed and counted the bills. "There ain't enough here for a headstone, because that's what she's gonna be needing."

Daniel felt a stab of premature grief. "Believe me, the thought of you picking one out for her is reason enough for me to make sure I'm here when her time comes." He paused. "But if I'm not, you buy nothing less than marble, you hear me? I'll settle up with you when I get back. Daniel gave the man his name and told him he could be reached at the *Clarion*. He moved toward the exit, then paused. "One more thing," he said. "Get a priest for her."

"She done asked me that herself," the man replied, stuffing the bills into his shirt pocket. "He was here last night."

Daniel lowered his gaze. As he turned and walked away, he felt the weight of sorrow in the center of his chest diminish. The knowledge that his mother would die happy, absolved by her two great loves, was no small comfort.

As Madeleine left the flat, she checked her watch brooch. Although it was nearly nine and Holy Name Cathedral was far across town on the North Side, she calculated that she had time enough to call Rawley before leaving to meet Daniel.

At the bottom of the stairs, she headed for the phone, passing the bath so luxuriously appointed with laundry tub and ice water. The first thing she and Daniel were going to do when they got home tonight, she thought as she picked up the receiver, was to scour the classifieds for a new apartment. Well, maybe not the first thing, she thought, smiling.

Her smile soon turned to a look of consternation. As she waited while the operator connected her with the *Clarion,* she distinctly felt a hostile gaze on her back. Peering from the corners of her eyes, she saw Mrs. Corrigan's doorknob turn and latch. The sight struck her as a premonition, the third in less than twenty-four hours and closer to dread than the previous two. Biting the inside of her lip, she wound a pale blond tendril at the nape of her neck around her finger.

Stop it, Madeleine. She released the curl and reminded herself that only last night she'd narrowly escaped being brutally murdered. For a time, she was bound to imagine that evil stalked her, lurking in shadows and behind closed doors. Fortunately, in the coming weeks, between her wedding and the Kozyck story, she wouldn't have an idle thought to spare bogeymen.

Hearing Rawley's voice on the line, she took reassurance that all was right with her world. Happily, she told him of hers and Daniel's plans to marry at the cathedral.

"It's about time you two realized you belong together," he said.

Smiling, Madeleine shook her head. "You knew it all along, didn't you?"

"My dear Madeleine, don't you know by now what the 'G' in G. Vernon Rawlston stands for?"

She laughed out aloud. Then, "You called me Madeleine. How long have you known who I was?"

"I always knew there was more to Maggie Flynn than met my one eye. I found out what it was when a man came to me offering to reward me handsomely if I'd launch a search for a missing Louisville heiress on the front page of the *Clarion.* He showed me a handbill describing you. Naturally, I told him the *Clarion*'s front page wasn't for sale and threw him the hell out. Then I called every other editor in town and told him that if I saw the story on their front pages, they'd see their names in headlines on mine."

Madeleine breathed a relieved sigh. As astonished as she was that a Pinkerton had tried to bribe an editor, she was glad he'd approached Rawley first. "I wouldn't expect less of you, but thanks anyway."

"Listen, integrity had nothing to do with it. After everything I went through to turn you into a crack reporter, I wasn't about to help some bastard kidnap you."

Madeleine smiled. With trueborn heroes like Rawley and Daniel on her side, she wasn't afraid of anything or anyone. "Then I assume you want me to get back to work. I'm meeting Daniel at the cathedral at ten then we're going to start tracking down witnesses in the Kozyck case."

Silence.

"Rawley? Are you still there?"

"I'm here," he said, his tone solemn. "I was just thinking about your close call last night and trying to figure out how to tell you that if anything should ever happen to you, Maggie, like that, I mean, my heart would break."

Madeleine swallowed a lump. "You just did," she said softly.

"But don't let that give you the idea you can shirk," he barked. "Tomas Kozyck may have been in prison ten years too long, and though this may come as a shock to you, he doesn't give a damn about your love life. Now get going!"

Chuckling, Madeleine hung up the phone, left the house, and inhaled deeply of the crisp October air. For the first time in her life, she felt complete. She had Daniel and her work, and a future that was as bright as the sun over her head. To cloud it with doom was senseless. No, she thought as she turned a corner, heading for the streetcar, it was a sin.

So is kidnapping, she thought, as Roger Mabrey, leaping from a hansom, clamped a hand over her mouth and dragged her into the cab.

Strangely calm, the one thing she worried most about was that when she didn't arrive at the cathedral, Daniel might think the worst:

That she'd broken her promise to love him to the day she died and into eternity.

Sixteen

As Daniel anxiously paced outside the stone-and-stained-glass Gothic cathedral on the corner of North State and East Superior Streets, the farthest thing from his mind was that Madeleine had jilted him. He knew her as well as he knew himself. She loved him as he loved her and wanted an indissoluble Church wedding as much as he did. She, too, would be eager to begin making the arrangements. At nearly ten thirty then, where was she?

Though he thought it unlikely, there was a chance she'd awakened without seeing his note. If that was the case, she might have reasonably assumed he'd gone to the *Clarion* and followed him there. With that possibility in mind, he headed up State Street looking for a public phone and finding one in a drugstore. After moments of nervously pacing on the leash of the phone's wire, he was asking Vernon Rawlston if he'd seen Babe.

"What do you mean have I seen her? She told me she was on her way to meet you."

Daniel gripped the mouthpiece. "When did you talk to her?"

"Dammit, Mac. Almost two hours ago."

Daniel cursed. "Something's happened to her, Rawley. Something bad."

After a pause, Rawlston came back, his voice taut. "My guess is that the streetcar she was riding broke down, so

I don't know why I even mention this. But I suppose you know some character's advertising a thousand-dollar reward for information about her."

Daniel looked at the receiver, then slowly put it back to his ear. "You know who she is?"

"Hell, yes! She's a damn fine reporter and I can't afford to lose her."

"And you shouldn't even mention it, but you think somebody's sold her out for the reward money." Or spite. Pamela Hart crawled through his thoughts.

Rawlston paused longer than before. "I'm crazy about the kid, Mac, as though she were my own daughter."

"I'm crazy about her, too, but not like a father." Daniel lowered his head over the mouthpiece, then after a moment, looked up. "I love her, Rawley. I can't live without her."

"I know."

With a single laugh, Daniel ran the back of his hand across his forehead. "You probably knew before I did."

"What do *you* think?"

"I think you did, so if you know so much, why the hell can't you tell me where she is?!"

"Take it easy, Mac. You know as well as I do that streetcars break down every day. She's probably outside the church right now, wondering where *you* are."

Pausing, Daniel shoved his hand in his pocket. "I'm sure you're right. I'll head back there." He was about to hang up when he became aware that, inside his pocket, he was nervously fingering something as though it were a rosary. The locket his mother had given him. Suddenly, the image of another piece of a jewelry, a gaudy and expensive piece, flashed across his mind. He'd seen the lavaliere only last night on Eileen Corrigan's equally extravagant and tasteless bosom just after Benny had called him away from the house, away from Madeleine.

Finally win the Irish Sweepstakes, Eileen?

I won all right, she'd said. *l always do. One way or ta other.*

"Dammit to Hell!" Daniel pounded the wall beside the phone. Eileen Corrigan hadn't won the sweepstakes. She'd cashed in on Madeleine.

"Listen to me, Rawley. Don't ask me how I know all of a sudden, but I know that Madeleine's been kidnapped, most likely by her father or one of his agents. I've got to get to Grand Central Station, an hour ago."

"What will you do if her train's already left?"

"Get on the next one," Daniel replied. About to hang up, he froze at the realization that even if he were to get Madeleine back, the story of her abduction wouldn't end there. If her father wanted her desperately enough to kidnap her once, he'd try it again and again until he succeeded. Daniel knew he had to stop the bastard once and for all. But how?

"Mac, are you there?"

Hearing Rawlston's voice, Daniel suddenly knew how. "Do something for me, Rawley, will you?"

"What?"

"Pretend I'm you for a few minutes."

"You're crazy."

"Damn right. My wife's been kidnapped."

"Fire away."

Daniel did, shooting orders at Rawlston like bullets. When he'd finished, he dashed out of the drugstore, breaking bottles, spilling pills, and praying he'd find a cab waiting for him.

And when he did, he couldn't have been more surprised. Before yesterday, he'd have said that its being in the right place at the right time was mere coincidence. Today, he called it a miracle.

"You look like you need to get someplace in hurry, young fella," a grizzled but harmless-looking old man called down from the driver's seat.

"What I need is to turn back the clock."

"Then I'm your man. Get in."

Daniel sprinted for the vehicle, but a closer look at it told him it wouldn't survive a pace faster than a plod. Even worse, the old hack's nag of a horse was so sway-backed, his tail could damn near reach his mane.

"On second thought, I don't think you can help me after all," Daniel called up to the cabby, his faith in miracles wavering.

"Whippersnapper! Appearances aren't everything." The old man shook his bony finger at Daniel. "Old Vergil here's got a lot of life left in him. And he knows his way to Grand Central Station blindfolded."

Daniel shot a querulous look up at the old man. "How did you know that's where I need to go? Never mind. There isn't another hack in sight, so Vergil will have to do." Opening the door, he set one foot on the step. "He wouldn't have heard of Babe McQuinn, by chance?"

The cabby lifted a newspaper from the seat beside him. "That reporter woman?"

"Yeah. Tell him to hurry it up because she's been kid-napped."

"Ayah!"

As Daniel ducked his head inside the cab, thinking the old man's response had sounded more like a confirmation of Madeleine's abduction than a spur to Vergil, the horse shot away from the curb. The cab lurched, throwing Daniel forward then back. His left foot slipped off the step and he slammed around, nailing the open door to the side of the coach. He was barely hanging on with the fingers of his right hand and the ball of his right foot, facing State Street and watching it pass in a blur of speed. With a burst of strength, he propelled himself back around and barely hung on to the rollicking cab with both hands and feet while his rear end took a paddling from the door.

"Hey! Slow Vergil down a damn minute, will you?"

But the cabby ignored Daniel while Vergil, as though responding to the sound of his name, exploded with reckless speed. As the cab took a corner, it nearly tilted over, lowering Daniel's rump to within inches of the chuckholed pavement. At that moment, Daniel shot himself into the coach legs first. Sitting on the floor, he drew his knees up, letting his hands dangle over them, and puffed out his cheeks as he blew a sigh of relief. After he caught his breath, he looked up at the cabby through the opening in the roof.

"I can only save Mrs. McQuinn if I get to the station alive."

The old man laughed a codgerly laugh. "You'll get there alive and in time to find your wife. Vergil and me's been to Hell and back and we ain't lost a soul yet."

Daniel shook his head as if to shake the contents into place. He still couldn't recall telling the old man that Babe was his wife. On the other hand, given his obvious haste to find her, the old man had simply made a reasonable assumption.

Just as it was reasonable to assume, Daniel thought as he hoisted himself onto the seat, looked out the window, and saw familiar Romanesque arches beneath the tall tower, that he'd arrived at Grand Central Station. Only it wasn't the least reasonable because as surprisingly spry as Vergil was, he couldn't possibly have made it to Wells and Harrison Streets from the near North Side in mere minutes.

"What are you sittin' there for?" the cabby asked. "We're here."

With no time to ask questions, Daniel jumped from the coach. He looked up at the cabby. "What do I owe you?"

"I need time to figure."

How much could a three-minute gallop cost? Daniel wondered, taking out his billfold. "Whatever you think it is, I'll give you two dollars more. I can't wait."

"That's all right. Vergil and me's got nothing better to do. We'll do the waitin' right here."

Putting his billfold away, Daniel ran toward the nearest entrance.

"Hey, young fella," the old man called.

Beneath one of the arches, Daniel looked back at him.

"You'll find the train to Louisville on Track Three."

Daniel gaped at the old man but had no time to ask him how he'd known Babe McQuinn would be on the train to Louisville. As he rushed into the station, he only hoped that the old geezer had been as right about the track number as he'd been about the train. Like a pinball, he caromed off passengers and porters pushing baggage until he found the Departures board in the center of the terminal. Looking up, he quickly scanned it.

"I'll be damned." The old cabby had indeed been right about the track. Unfortunately, he'd been wrong about the train still being on it. It had departed at ten thirty. Daniel lowered his head to his hand.

"Excuse me young man. I'm not able to read the clock up there on the wall. Could you tell me what time it is?"

Daniel looked to his right and then down at a very little and very old lady. She was squinting up at him. He glanced at the clock high above them. Then his jaw dropped. He rubbed his eyes and looked at the clock again.

"It can't be. It was after ten thirty when I called Rawley."

"Young man, did you say it was ten thirty?"

"No, ma'am," Daniel said, a bit giddily. "It's ten twenty-seven and I love you!" Taking her by the shoulders, he kissed her on the cheek and sprinted for Track Three. Feeling as though some unseen power was propelling him beyond his own strength, he reached the platform in time to jump through a fog of gathering steam onto the last car of the train as it chugged to life. Puffing like the train's engine, he nevertheless wasted no time in climbing into the car and beginning a search of the compartments for precious cargo. For Madeleine.

As he passed to the next car, and the next and the next without spotting her, the edges of his sanity began to unravel. She had to be on board. Though he still couldn't believe it, he knew that time, by some miracle, had reversed itself so that he might find her. Besides, he could feel her nearness in every fiber of his being, hear her calling him, heart-to-heart.

Then, in the fourth car, he saw her sitting in the middle compartment. He quickly drew back, out of sight. Stealing a second look inside the compartment, he ascertained that the only other occupant was a man who was too young to be Madeleine's father and too dandified to be a private detective.

Roger Mabrey.

Mabrey held Madeleine prisoner between himself and the window, his right arm crossing his body, his right hand gripping her left, his knees pinning her legs to the far wall of the compartment. At a rush of blood and rage, Daniel took a step toward the door, then forced himself back against the wall. He cautioned himself to keep his head. Judging from Mabrey's posture, he had every reason to suspect that the son-of-a-bitch was pressing the muzzle of a gun to Madeleine's ribs.

"I should have known you were the man who tried to bribe Rawley," Madeleine said, breathing against the derringer Roger held against her side. "After all, you have a history of bribing newspaper editors."

Roger Mabrey's smile was self-congratulatory. "So you found out about my little arrangement with Crowley to keep you off the *Record*'s front page."

"In time to keep you from slithering into my bed."

Roger patted a yawn that expressed utter boredom. "I

was never interested in your bed, Madeleine. You don't imagine that I tracked you down for love, do you?"

"Of course you did, Roger. For love of the power you would have enjoyed as the son-in-law of Matthew Faurest."

"Correction, Madeleine dear. *Will* enjoy."

"You're dreaming. I'm already married and you know it."

"There's no record of your marriage, Madeleine. I've seen to that."

Madeleine gave a snort of derision. "Do you think that by destroying a piece of paper you can destroy my love for Daniel?"

"Quite to the contrary, I'm counting on your love of him to make you my wife. You marry me, he lives. It's just that simple."

"You bastard!" Her hands forming claws, Madeleine struggled to break free of restraint.

"I wouldn't if I were you, Madeleine," Roger said, pulling her forward and placing the muzzle of the pistol at the base of her spine. "I can arrange it so that you'll be dead from the waist down, which as you already know, is of absolutely no consequence to me."

Madeleine slowly relaxed. As Roger returned the derringer to her side, she sat back, thinking that he needn't have threatened her with paralysis. She was already paralyzed by her love for Daniel and the certainty that unless she married Roger, he would see to Daniel's murder.

Unless the man she'd just seen glance at her from the aisle outside the compartment really had been Daniel. A breathless moment later, she saw the door swing open and Daniel, grinning like the drunken sailors she'd seen on the Levee, step over the threshold.

"Sadie, it really is you! Only last night, Captain Carnation—you remember the captain—well, he and I were saying 'Whatever happened to Sadie?' "

Madeleine tamped down the urge to return Daniel's grin. He'd saved her virtue once before by playing this same scene. Only now, he couldn't do it alone. She had to equal his performance. She gave Roger a stagy look of horror-protesting guilt, then turned to Daniel.

"I . . . I believe you have me confused with someone else, suh."

"The hell I do," Daniel replied. Then, to Roger, "Pardon me, fella," as he squeezed his tall, broad frame into the compartment, shutting the door behind him.

Roger lifted his leg onto the seat across from him, blocking Daniel's access to Madeleine. "The lady said you were mistaken."

Daniel chuckled. "You haven't been around much, buddy, have you? Gals like her, they all say that when it suits them. Fortunately, for half the Merchant Marine, it don't suit Sadie here too often."

Madeleine held her breath as Roger took the muzzle of the derringer from her side, then holding it at his hip beneath the fold of his Chesterfield coat, trained it on Daniel. What worried her more was that he was laughing. Mirthlessly.

"You know, you're really quite a good actor, Mr. McQuinn. You might have fooled me if I hadn't been watching your lodgings for Madeleine and seen you leave without her this morning."

Daniel and Madeleine exchanged looks, hers fearful for him, his apologetic to her.

"I'm sorry, Babe," Daniel said. "I was counting on Shakespeare."

She gave him a wan smile. "I know. 'The play's the thing.' "

Though Madeleine sat with her right arm trapped behind Mabrey's left and the other in his grip, Daniel felt her embrace. "Yeah, well, what did Hamlet know, anyway?"

"Ghosts," Roger said. "Which puts me in mind of yours, McQuinn." He openly pointed the derringer at Daniel's heart.

"Roger, don't!" Madeleine shuddered with revulsion. "I'll divorce Daniel and marry you in the Church, I promise."

"Then you might as well let him shoot me, Babe," Daniel said. "Besides, once I'm dead, he loses his hold over you. Believe me, I'll die a happy man."

"You'll die, all right, McQuinn," Mabrey said. "But, I'm afraid, not happily. Once Madeleine observes that I really am capable of murder, she'll be more than willing to accommodate me. And I won't have to worry about you showing up to wreck our happy home."

Madeleine fixed a hard stare on Mabrey. "I promise you, if you kill Daniel, you'll never get me to the altar. You'll only make it necessary for me to cease to exist. Do you understand what I'm saying?"

"Suicide?" Keeping his gaze on Daniel, Mabrey inclined toward Madeleine. "Pious, my dear, you are not. But you won't risk your immortal soul."

"You can't be sure of that, though, can you, Roger?"

"No more than you can that I won't take the gamble." Still holding Daniel in his sights, Mabrey moved back to center. "Which one of us, my dear, do you suppose will prove to be the better poker player?"

Slowly, he squeezed the derringer's trigger.

Madeleine screamed.

The train lurched. Thrown forward, Mabrey released Madeleine. With both hands, she grabbed his left arm and yanked it across her body, aiming the pistol at the outside wall of the compartment. "Run, Daniel!"

Daniel had already launched himself at Mabrey. "Honestly, Babe," he said, as he struggled to extract the pistol from Mabrey's hand. "For an intelligent woman, that was a stupid thing to say."

As Mabrey, now recovered, struggled with Daniel for control of the gun, Madeleine threw herself into the fray. With a whirl of small, pounding fists, she assailed Mabrey and with a shout, Daniel. "And I suppose you weren't stupid when you walked in—" One of her fists accidentally found Daniel's nose. "Here."

Eyes tearing, Daniel sniffed. "As long as I was stupid enough to try to rescue you, do you mind if I do it my own way?"

At that, Daniel shoved Mabrey's arm straight in the air, forcing the pistol at the ceiling, then pinned it against an overhead shelf. Repeatedly, he slammed Mabrey's wrist against the edge of the shelf, trying to dislodge the derringer.

"Hold him, McQuinn!"

"Babe, will you stay out of this?"

"We haven't got all day. This train is moving, fast!" Getting on her knees on the seat, Madeleine reached up through the vent at the back of Mabrey's coat, grabbed with both hands what little there was of his manhood and squeezed as hard as she could.

Both Mabrey's scream and his firing of the pistol's one and only shot were silenced by a shrill blast of the train's whistle. As Mabrey doubled over in pain, Daniel stripped him of the weapon, slipping it into his own pocket.

Grunting, Roger Mabrey rotated his gaze at Madeleine. "You bitch. You'll pay for that." He looked at Daniel. "You'll both pay."

Daniel pulled Madeleine to her feet. Wrapping her in a tight, one-armed embrace, he hauled her to the door. "You're through making threats, Mabrey," he said, gripping the door handle. "In fact, you're just plain through. In less than an hour, an extra edition of the *Clarion* will hit the streets and newsboys all over town will be shouting its headline, 'BABE McQUINN FEARED KIDNAPPED!' Furthermore, the front-page story names you and Judge Matthew

Faurest as suspects in a conspiracy to abduct her for political purposes. Quote: 'Mrs. McQuinn recently admitted to fearing that her father would coerce her into a marriage to Mabrey with threats against the life of this reporter, her husband.' "

Beaming, Madeleine rose on her toes and kissed Daniel on the cheek. "McQuinn, you're not stupid. You're brilliant! From now on, if anything happens to either one of us, Roger and my father will be prime suspects." She looked down at Mabrey, who sat chalk-faced, defeated. "Get used to it, Roger. It's called the power of the press."

Daniel opened the door. "Let's go, Babe. We pick up any more speed and we won't be able to get off until Indianapolis." He pushed her into the narrow corridor ahead of him, then taking her hand, headed for the exit at the rear of the car.

Before they reached it, he came to so abrupt a halt, Madeleine slammed into him.

"Aw, hell! Wait here, Babe. I forgot something."

Madeleine gaped after him as he ran back toward the compartment. "What could you have possibly forgotten?" Glancing out the window, Madeleine saw the terminal rapidly shrinking behind them. "McQuinn, come back here. There's no need to be stupid now!"

He ignored her, as she'd expected he would. *She*, at least, had learned a thing or two, but not enough to keep her from running after him. Only several paces behind him, she saw him burst into the compartment. A second later, she watched him pull Roger to his feet, then draw his own arm back like a battering ram and slam his fist squarely into Roger's nose, flattening both it and its owner.

"That was for calling my wife a bitch," Daniel said, huffing and rubbing his knuckles.

Madeleine leaned into the compartment. "McQuinn, did you have to?"

Daniel looked at her askance.

"I know, that was a stupid question."

Daniel pushed her toward the exit. When they reached it, he stepped into the well ahead of her and threw open the door, letting in a blast of air. "I'll jump first," Daniel yelled, "so I can catch you."

"Catch me?" Gauging the speed of the train, Madeleine gulped. "But I don't think I—"

Daniel jumped. After landing safely, he ran alongside the train, caught up to Madeleine, and held his arms out to her. "Jump, Babe!"

Watching the rapidly passing terrain, Madeleine froze.

"Madeleine! Look at me!"

She snapped a wide-eyed look at Daniel and saw her whole world in his eyes, a world where she loved and was loved. And was safe. Before her heart beat twice more, she took a breath and hurled herself into Daniel's waiting arms. She clung to him, her feet off the ground. When the final car passed, he set her down. They stood holding one another, watching the last car until it disappeared from the horizon.

Madeleine looked up at Daniel. "How did you find me?"

Hugging her to his side, he started back to the station. "Babe, when I tell you, you won't believe me."

"You were right, McQuinn," Madeleine said. "I don't believe you."

Outside the station on the spot where he'd left the old cabby, Daniel paced back and forth, scanning the street for a glimpse of a swayback nag pulling an ancient hack. "I don't understand it. He said he'd wait right here for me."

Madeleine eyed him dubiously. "You didn't really believe he was going to sit idle for who knew how long?"

"I owe him the fare for the trip here."

"He let you get away without paying him?" Madeleine rolled her eyes. "Daniel, there isn't a hack driver in this city—I don't care how old—who wouldn't have tackled you to get his fare. I'm beginning to believe he and his horse—"

"Vergil."

Madeleine slid her jaw to one side. "All right. Vergil. At any rate, I'm beginning to think you imagined them both. You said yourself you were out of your mind with fear you wouldn't find me."

Taking her by the shoulders, Daniel turned Madeleine toward him. "One more time. I prayed I'd find a cab waiting for me outside the drugstore, and when I came out, there it was. The old man said he could turn back the clock and he did."

"Your watch must have stopped."

"I don't have a watch. The clock inside the terminal said it was ten twenty-seven when I hadn't even hung up with Rawley until well after ten thirty."

"The clock stopped, then."

"That doesn't explain your train being on the track when it was supposed to have pulled out at the time I was talking to Rawley."

Madeleine propped her hands on her waist. "Daniel, when you're being kidnapped, you'd don't stop to ask whether or not the train that's stealing you away is on schedule."

Daniel looked aside. "Maybe. Maybe the train was late and the clock just happened to stop." Pulling her into his embrace, he gently rocked her. "Still . . . how did the old man know that the train was behind schedule and what track I'd find it on?"

Gazing up at him, Madeleine gave him a wry smile. "Maybe he's a spiritualist, like Madame Blavatsky."

Daniel snorted. "That wouldn't surprise me. The old coot certainly read *my* mind."

"I see you found your wife, young fella."

In unison, Madeleine and Daniel looked to the curb and saw a hoary, bearded man atop a dilapidated hack and holding the reins to an even more dilapidated horse.

Madeleine met Daniel's gaze, her eyes wide and wary. "Oh, no. Don't tell me."

Daniel grinned. "Mrs. McQuinn, meet Mr.—" He broke off, realizing he didn't know the old man's name.

"Pleased to meet you, Missus." The cabby tipped his worn cap. "This here's Vergil. Sorry about not being here for you folks. Vergil's knees lock up if he stands still for too long. But he's rarin' to go now. Hop in."

"Wait a minute," Daniel said. "You still haven't told me what that first ride cost."

"That one was on me and Vergil. I don't know what the next one will cost 'cause you haven't told me yet where you want to go."

"The *Clarion* Building," Daniel said.

"I'll discuss it with Vergil," the old man replied, then laughed so genially, Madeleine and Daniel joined in.

"What do you say, Babe? Want to give old Vergil a try?"

Amiably, Madeleine shrugged. "What could we possibly lose?"

"Time," the old man said.

Both McQuinns gave him a querulous look.

"To go," he added. "Old Vergil's knees, you know."

But Daniel had no sooner helped Madeleine into the cab and gotten one foot on the step himself, than the horse shot off as he had before, like an equine cannonball. And once again, Daniel struggled to gain entry to the wildly oscillating coach as the flapping door swatted his backside.

"Daniel!" Jostled all the while, Madeleine got to her knees on the floor of the cab, reached through the doorway, and grabbed his lapels. With all her strength, she held on to him until he finally propelled himself inside—

this time, head first. As he drew his long legs in behind him, Madeleine reached over him and, after three attempts, finally hauled the banging door to a close.

She no sooner did, than Daniel pulled her down and beneath him. As he gazed at her, he felt a desire for her so intense, he wanted to crush her, liquefy her, drink her. He feared he actually might.

Not even in Daniel's eyes had Madeleine ever seen such a look as this, one that devoured her. "Daniel, you're frightening me."

"I'm frightening myself." Then, inexplicably, the violence of his desire ebbed from the shores of his soul. He smiled at her. "You're a mess, you know that?"

"Who wouldn't be, what with you having me hurtle myself from speeding trains and Vergil tossing me like a salad?" She had barely begun to smile back at him when she saw the set of his mouth turn hard, bitter, and a shade descend over his gaze. "What is it, Daniel? Tell me."

Daniel breathed shallowly. "I don't know," he said, barely able to speak. "I only know that I need you, Madeleine. I need you and want you so much I'm afraid for us both."

Madeleine's stomach sickened as she saw the anthracite at the center of his gaze combust. Then, like a hellish, rampaging fire he swept away the hat that sat askew on her head. Tearing the combs from her hair, he cast them aside and, digging his fingers into her hair, clamped her head between his hands. She felt his gaze rip out her heart, then take her apart, bone by bone, and pile her into a pyramid. And with his kiss, he deliberately and savagely torched her.

When he released her and she lay smoldering in his arms, she searched the embers in his eyes. "Daniel, I don't understand. You've never kissed me like that before."

"And I never will again." He ran his thumb over her

swollen mouth, not gently. "But then, I'll never need to, will I?"

Madeleine inhaled sharply. "Now I see. You thought you might be kissing me for the last time, didn't you?"

"No," Daniel said, knowing full well he was lying. He'd never deliberately lied to her before. What the Hell was happening to him?

"You wanted to leave nothing of me for any other man to desire," Madeleine persisted. "Nothing of me with which to love another man." When Daniel turned his face aside, she drew his gaze back to hers. "You're going away from me, Daniel. I can feel it. Something's taking you away from me!"

"Madeleine, I swear, hell itself couldn't take me away from you." Nevertheless, he pulled back and sat up. Suddenly, he wasn't so sure about Hell itself because, suddenly, he felt It surround him like a pack of rabid hounds.

"But you're not sure, are you? Say it again, Daniel. Say it as though you mean—" Madeleine caught sight of something dangling over the pocket of Daniel's coat, a delicate gold chain. She slid it out, revealing an oval locket with a cross on its face. "Where did you get this?"

He took back the locket. "From my mother."

"When?"

"This morning." Looking at the locket lying in his palm, he turned the face of it over. "When she made me promise to find my father."

Madeleine felt a cold, sharp stab of terror. "Why, Daniel? Why would she want you to find him when she knows how you hate him? How you tried to kill him once before?"

"I don't know."

Madeleine yanked his arm. "You're lying. You do know. And you're perfectly willing to finish the deed that sent you to reform school, aren't you? Answer me!"

But Daniel couldn't answer. His teeth were chattering.

He was shivering, so hot he was cold. Then, everything went black. He rolled his unseeing gaze around the carriage. "Why is it so dark in here?"

"It's broad daylight." Rising on her knees, Madeleine took him by the shoulders. "The darkness is in you. Let it go, Daniel. Unless you want to destroy my love for you, let it go."

Suddenly, Daniel stopped shivering. His vision returned. The first thing he saw was Madeleine's face. As always, her timeless beauty took his breath away, but there was a resolve in her gaze that put him on notice. He was unworthy of her love, he knew, but paradoxically, he was also made worthy by it. He'd have to be a fool to risk losing her. Putting the locket away, he lifted her beside him onto the cracked and worn leather seat of the slowing coach. Wrapping her in his embrace, he pressed her to his chest and kissed the top of her pale gold head. "Have faith in me, Madeleine. I won't let anything come between us."

"You do and I'll track you into Hell, if I have to."

Daniel laughed. "And I'm sure Hell hath no fury like the Babe scorned."

Madeleine, too, laughed. The cab stopped and she saw the old man peer down through the opening in the roof of the carriage.

"We're here, folks," he said.

Madeleine sat up. She directed her gaze casually past Daniel to the scene outside the window. Abruptly, she lurched toward it, her eyes enormous. She looked up at the old man, but his face had disappeared. "Daniel, something's wrong here. *Terribly* wrong."

She was so suddenly drained of color, Daniel turned sharply and looked out the window. But he saw nothing that should have rendered her ghostly. "I don't know what you see, Babe, but I'm looking at the usual midday parade outside the *Clarion* Building."

"Look again. We aren't outside the *Clarion* Building. And even if we were, when was the last time you saw a parade of hoop skirts?"

Beneath a skeptical gaze, Daniel twisted a smile at her. "I think being nearly murdered and then kidnapped in less than twenty-four hours has done something to your mind."

Perhaps so, Madeleine thought. She took another look out the window, then deciding there was nothing wrong with her mind, just with the scene outside the cab, she slowly sat back. "Twenty-four hours, you said? And how many years?"

"Twenty-seven," the old man called down.

Thinking he had two asylum cases on his hands, Daniel leaned toward the door and scanned the scene outside it. Madeleine had been right about one thing. They definitely weren't stopped in front of the *Clarion* Building, six stories tall and in the heart of the city. The buildings here were short, squat, and constructed entirely of wood. Not a brick or a stone in sight. A typical neighborhood prior to the Great Fire that had destroyed the city in 1871.

There was something else Madeleine had been right about. Though he was no connoisseur of fashion, Daniel knew a hoop skirt when he saw one, and he was seeing dozens of them. Women hadn't worn hoop skirts for over twenty years. Hell, they didn't even wear bustles anymore.

Poking the roof of the carriage, he shouted up at Vergil's driver. "Where did you say we were?"

The old man's lined face suddenly appeared at the door. "Here, son."

"Yes, but where *is* here?"

Gazing at Daniel through eyes that were aged yet piercing, the old man scratched the top of his head. "Maybe I'm wrong, but didn't you promise your mother you would find your father? Well, this is where you can find him."

"No!"

Despite Madeleine's scream and her move to restrain him, Daniel burst from the carriage, ordering Madeleine to remain inside. Confiscating fistfuls of the cabby's jacket, he lifted him off his toes. "I don't know who the Hell you are and how you know things you couldn't possibly know, but you've gone too far."

"No, just twenty-seven years into the past," the old man replied. "Just far enough for you to keep your promise to your mother."

Daniel shook the man. "Skinny old geezer. You're lying!"

"Am I? Didn't I get you to Grand Central Station an hour *before* you discovered your missus had been kidnapped?"

"The clock stopped. The train was late. I got lucky, that's all."

"Was it your luck, too, that I just happened to know what train she'd be on, and what track her train'd be on?" The old man cackled. "Come on, now young fella. You know you don't really believe in mind reading or that phony Blavatsky woman."

His chest heaving, Daniel set the cabby down, though he held on to the man's tattered coat. "You, you couldn't have heard that conversation between Madeleine and me, about Blavatsky and mind reading. You weren't there."

"But I know about it, don't I?" The old man looked around. "Just the way that I know that this is Chicago in the fall of the year 1866."

Daniel let the old man go. A hellish heat, like the one that had assailed him inside the cab but hotter, much hotter, was rising from the pavement, engulfing him, dulling his faculties. He swayed.

"Don't listen to him, Daniel!"

Roused by the sound of Madeleine's voice, Daniel whipped toward her. Seeing her poised with one foot on the step of the cab, he spanned her waist with his hands. "Get back inside!"

Grabbing hold of the door's frame, Madeleine resisted his attempt to shove her back into the cab. She was surprised at how little resistance the task required. Since setting foot on the pavement, Daniel had lost a good measure of his formidable strength.

"Listen to *me*, Daniel, not him," she pleaded. "He's a crazy old man whom your crazy friends at the Whitechapel Club put up to a ridiculous prank."

Daniel peered at her, trying to steady her wavering image. "That would be just like Dunne and the rest of them, wouldn't it?"

"Of course," she replied.

"But you don't really believe that even they could put something this elaborate together any more than I do."

Madeleine's head began to tremble. "No."

"Paper, mister?"

Gazing over his shoulder, Daniel saw a newsboy, no more than six years old, several paces away. Daniel glanced back at Madeleine then, heaving a hot breath, walked to the boy and handed him a coin.

The boy bit it. "Hey, mister. Whadya call this?"

"A nickel."

"Don't look like any nickel I ever seen."

"Tell you what. Give me a paper and you can keep the change."

A moment later, Daniel stood examining the front page of the paper the boy had handed him. He read the masthead, then the date below it. Breaking into a sweat, he returned to Madeleine, each step taking all his strength and will. He handed the paper to her.

Reading the masthead, she squeezed his shoulder, but not because of the date. She hadn't found that yet. "Daniel, I thought I'd called on the managing editor of every paper in this city at least twice. But I don't recall once stepping foot inside the offices of the *Republican.*"

"That's because it ceased publication in 1872," he replied.

Her eyes wide, Madeleine now searched out the paper's date. When she found it, she slowly turned her head and met the old man's gaze. It was alight with something that was neither triumph nor mischief, something terrifyingly factual.

"Told you true, didn't I?" he said.

"What kind of truth takes two people back to the same date in October but nearly three decades back in time?" Madeleine flung the paper to the ground. "I wasn't even born until 1870." Suddenly, she wrung a handful of the fabric of her jacket, below her heart. "Daniel! When were you born?"

"August of 1867."

Madeleine stared at him for a moment, then closed her eyes. "Oh, dear God."

"I have the feeling God's not listening to anyone here," Daniel replied.

Madeleine opened her eyes. "What do you mean? *Here.*"

Taking a cigarette and a book of matches from his pocket, Daniel stepped away from her, into the throng. He looked up the street then down, then placed the cigarette between his lips and tore a match from the book. But before he could strike it, it erupted with flame.

He gave Madeleine a sly look. "You know, Babe. *Here.*" He lit his cigarette, dropped the match to the ground, then showed her his mother's locket. "Where I'm to keep a promise to Kathleen McQuinn Delaney to find my bastard of a father one month before she conceived me."

"And you will, before eight o'clock on the evening of November tenth, the time and date that she does," the old cabby said.

Hearing the old man confirm her worst fear, Madeleine saw her recent premonitions writhe like triumphant demons before her eyes. Earlier, she had dismissed them. Then, when Roger kidnapped her, she concluded they'd been uncanny predictions of her abduction. Now, she knew they had been warning her of something far more sinister, something that was literally a matter of life or death. Or more accurately, of life or never having been born. For Daniel.

Careful to maintain her foothold on the cab's step—one slip, one brush with the soil of history might leach the power of the present, her power to return Daniel and herself safely to it—she stretched her arm toward him.

"Listen to me, Daniel. Rawley said your vengeful streak would one day land you in Hell. But you have a choice. You can turn your back on your vengeance and come home with me." She stretched as far she could, her fingers straining toward him. "Please," she called, her voice raked with desperation. "I love you."

Daniel focused his gaze on her, surprised that despite her image wavering in a shimmer of intense heat and moreover, appearing suddenly distant, he had still heard her say she loved him. Stamping out his cigarette and putting the locket away, he made a move toward her. But something held him back. Memories. No, visions. Of living with violence, of tending to the flesh it had bloodied and bruised, of rising up to end it and failing.

"Daniel, I love you!"

He stretched his arm toward her.

There's only one thing you can do for me, now, son. Find your father.

Leaning as far out from the cab as she could, Madeleine groped for Daniel's hand, scant inches from hers. "Touch me, Daniel. Just touch me."

But his only response was to look at her as though she were a stranger to him, then lower his hand.

"He can't see or hear you now," the old man said. "His soul is in torment."

Hearing Vergil whinny as if in assent, Madeleine turned fiercely on the cabby. "In Hell, you mean. You've brought him to Hell, you and that devil of a horse of yours!"

"Hell for Daniel, yes. We had to." The old man hoisted himself one step to his perch, paused, and put his face in Madeleine's, his expression nevertheless kind. "You showed him Paradise, missus. Now he must visit Hell and choose between the two. All men must, sooner or later."

She grabbed his sleeve. "But you don't understand. Daniel isn't the kind of man who deliberates for long. He acts before thinking of the consequences, especially in defense of the people he loves. He's capable of blind rage, of killing. That's his nature."

"Of course it is. He wouldn't be here if it weren't." Shaking his head, the cabby smiled—with pity, Madeleine thought—for what he obviously considered her ignorance. "Don't you know that the only difference between a man and an animal is that a man can choose to be other than what his nature orders him to be?"

Madeleine let go of his arm. "Now I know why you look like Methuselah."

"Ayah. I been to Hell and back, lots of times."

"Maybe *you* have," Madeleine replied. She turned her gaze on Daniel. "But I can't take the chance that Daniel will make it back the first time."

She lowered her foot to the ground, but before she touched down, Vergil took off in a burst of speed so explosive, it shot her back into the cab. The door slammed shut. Coming to her knees, she dove for the handle. She pumped it once, twice, then continuously and frenetically, trying to release the unyielding door. When that effort failed, she leaned back on her elbows and repeatedly rammed the door with her feet. That, too, failed. Looking up, she shouted at the cabby.

"Open this door, damn you!"

"Damn me all you want, young woman, but I can't. It's locked as locked can be."

Half-rising, she pounded the roof with her fists. "I have to save him!"

There was a pause, then, "When will you women ever learn that you can't save a man from himself? *He's* the one's got to do the work!"

Pondering what the old man had said, Madeleine looked out the window, back at Daniel. He'd grown small, distant. Still, she could see that he was holding the pistol he'd seized from Roger. Staring at the pistol. Probably wondering where to find ammunition for it.

And then, where to find his father.

Then he was gone.

Bursting into sobs, Madeleine buried her face in her hands and slumped to the floor. On her side, she drew her knees to her chest. Soon, she was beyond tears, beyond grief. Alive, but only in the sense that she was breathing, to which death would be preferable.

But not very helpful to Daniel.

Once again, Madeleine got on her knees, and this time, she prayed.

Seventeen

At Vergil's shrill whinny, Madeleine lifted her head. She hoisted herself onto the seat of the cab and peered out the window, surprised to see dusk encroaching on daylight. In shadows stood a familiar house inside which a familiar flat no doubt sat as she had left it hours—decades?—earlier. Hers and Daniel's. Hers alone now.

"Time to get out, missus." As the old cabby spoke, the stubbornly locked door swung open. "As you can plainly see, it's near dark. Old Vergil don't make a trip to Hell and back so quick as he used to. I'd best be gettin' him a rub-down and his feed."

Looking around the hack as though checking for precious belongings she feared leaving behind, Madeleine gathered memories of Daniel. Of the lanky boy with the battered face and shaven head and thirsting spirit that had refused to drink a reform school swill of brutality and humiliation. Instead, he had defiantly recited lines he'd imbibed from a forbidden book. She recalled the way he had looked at her then, as though she, too, were a book, not forbidden, but new and fascinating. A book he must have, must read. From that moment she longed for—desperately needed—him to read her and then to help write her, co-author of the rest of her life.

And he had begun the task. But remembering the midnight blue of his voice, the soft suede of his lips, the gaze that conjured both fire dances and hymns, she knew those were as mere pages added to a story that remained incomplete. Unless he returned, it would forever remain so.

No, worse.

Madeleine already understood that if Daniel were to lose this greatest struggle of his life, to fail to defeat his passion for revenge, then he would never have been born. What she just now realized was that her own life would then be purged of all trace of him. In that event, it would read like a string of nonsense rhymes, repetitious, incoherent, meaningless.

"You know where you are, don't you, missus?"

Madeleine looked up at the old man. "Yes. In Limbo." She moved to the door, and, hunching, looked back at the ancient leather cushion on which she'd sat locked in Daniel's embrace, perhaps for the last time. Then she glanced at the floor where they'd lain together and saw the hat he'd torn from her head just before he'd kissed her as though he'd already known he might never kiss her again. When she retrieved it, she found one of her mother-of-pearl hair combs lying beneath it. She reached for it, too, then stopped, wondering what good it would do, if any, to leave it behind, a trace of herself bridging Daniel's past and her present. An offering to their future.

"Remember when I told you a woman can't save a man, he's got to do the work himself?"

Hearing the old man's voice at her right side, Madeleine looked to him. He had stuck his head into the cab and was peering directly into her eyes, his nose nearly touching hers. "I remember."

"Well," he began, rubbing the side of his long, crooked nose with a longer and more crooked finger, "that wasn't to say that she can't help him at all." He glanced at the comb then looked back at Madeleine. "She can believe in him."

Her eyes narrowing in puzzlement, Madeleine suddenly heard Daniel's voice, less than real but more than a memory. *Have faith in me.* For a moment, she felt strong, sure. So sure that she picked up her comb and laid it on the seat.

She turned to old man. "Thank you." He nodded sagely, then offered her his hand. Her spirits buoyed by her own small gesture of faith in Daniel, Madeleine took it, finding it not so surprisingly steady. Having nothing more to say, she started up the walk toward the house.

But the farther she stepped away from the cab and the comb she'd left inside it, the more minuscule her gesture seemed, the less it sustained her belief in hers and Daniel's future. There had to be more to having faith, she thought, than performing symbolic acts or even praying. But what?

Anxiously, she turned back to the old man. He was seated atop the cab, Vergil's reins in his hands. Before she could ask her question, he answered it.

"It's knowin' the worst and expectin' the best," he said. "And livin' as though the best is already here."

He makes it sound so simple, Madeleine thought, gazing up the street, as though by standing here every day and imagining Daniel running toward her and waving to him, she could bring him back to her when, in all likelihood, she'd only get herself hauled off to the county asylum. There probably was a fine line between faith and madness. How was she to know when she crossed it?

She turned back to the old man, but found that he and Vergil had vanished, leaving no cloud of dust, no wheel marks in the road, no trace that either of them had ever existed much less brought Daniel to the brink of negating his life and undoing hers. For a moment, she believed she must have dreamed the pair of them and would find Daniel waiting for her inside, melting her with a lopsided grin even as he stubbornly refused to relinquish the one stool at the kitchen crate. She ran to the front door, but the instant she touched the cold, tarnished knob, she knew that she had come closer to madness than to faith. Madness was the denying of what had already been, as Vergil and the old man most certainly had.

And so, Madeleine entered the house, no longer mad but not yet possessing faith. Not even able to believe that she ever would. As she climbed the stairs to the flat she'd left only hours ago, bound for a rendezvous with Daniel at the cathedral where they had planned to one day marry, she had to summon all her strength to the task. Now, she understood why faith was likened to climbing a mountain.

And hearing Eileen Corrigan's shriek of surprise at entering her house and finding Madeleine Faurest McQuinn returned, why revenge was so great a temptation. Daniel had told her that it was their landlady who had sold the information that led to Roger's abducting her and, later, to his nearly killing them both. But revenge against a pathetic creature who had condemned herself to substituting lust for love would be redundant. Turning, Madeleine looked down at the woman, at her tufted body silhouetted in the doorway. She was clutching the lavaliere between her breasts.

"Don't worry, Mrs. Corrigan. You failed to rid Daniel of me but your reward is yours to keep. You earned it."

Shutting the door behind her, the landlady approached the stairs. She looked up at Madeleine, no evidence of remorse or even embarrassment in her mien. "I take it you'll be movin' out then, you and Dan'l."

The woman had made a reasonable assumption, though until now, Madeleine hadn't considered just how reckless it would be for her to remain under the same roof with someone who bore her such ill will. She looked up at the door to the bare little flat that was a palace because it had been home to her and Daniel. If faith was living as though the best had already come, then she would live in that flat as though Daniel had already come home.

"No, Mrs. Corrigan. I'll be staying."

"You'll be stayin'? Where's Dan'l?"

"Away. On a story." Clutching the banister, Madeleine once again climbed the stairs, finding them less steep than a moment ago. "The story of a lifetime."

"Aw, if you listen to him, they're all the story of a lifetime." Eileen Corrigan cackled. "You know he's as likely as not gone off with some whore, don't you?"

From the landing at the top of the stairs, Madeleine looked down. "I wish to God he had. You don't know how I wish it."

Leaving her landlady to stare after her in amazement, Madeleine entered the flat, locking the door behind her. She gazed around, then set steps to her visual journey, picking up Daniel's coffee mug from the side of the crate table where he always sat. Earlier that morning, with him gone, she'd laughingly left the stool on her side of the crate, imagining him snatching it back with exaggerated pique when he returned. Now, she brought it to his place. Another small, ineffectual gesture of faith, she supposed, but one that comforted her. So much so that she continued about the room, tidying here, readying there. Lighting a fire in the stove, putting on coffee, setting out his shaving mug and honing his razor on the leather strop that hung beside the cupboard, where he kept a small mirror and basin.

The bed, however, she left as it was when she'd run out to meet him that morning, very nearly as it was after a night of sometimes tender, sometimes rough, though ultimately indescribable lovemaking. She circled it several times, shedding her clothing among the stubs of the candles that still stood on the floor at the foot of it, remembering all they had done and said and vowed. Soon she was naked, the bed stretched out before her, Daniel's

reading chair and bookcase behind her. With no effort at
all, she saw Daniel and herself, half ghosts twining in the
light that tapered from the stove. Holding the image, she
reached out and stroked his untamable black hair, her
hand outlining the curve of his beautifully shaped head.
Then, with both hands, she sculpted his shoulders, running her palms flatly along the long, sleek, muscled line
of them then molding them to the thick, rounded corners. They were slightly damp with exertion, pleasantly so
to her touch. Closing her eyes, she buried her nose and
mouth in the crook of his neck, abrading her lips on his
stubble, gliding her tongue over it and tasting grains of
love, inhaling a scent that had no name but love.

And then she felt his hands on her. With her own she
followed their course, fingers limning her brows and
cheekbones, mouth, and neck; palms curving over her
breasts, spiraling her nipples into hard peaks, then lower,
down her ribs, over her hips, toward the apex of her legs.

Breathing hard, she opened her eyes. "This, too, Daniel,
I'll keep for you." Then, getting down on her knees, she
gathered her clothing and set it aside in a heap. Taking
the book of matches Daniel had left on the floor, she lit
the candles. Then she stood, and never taking her eyes
from the bed, found her wrapper, slipped it on, and curled
up in Daniel's chair. There she sat until long after the last
candle had swallowed its flame.

*Though fevered, Daniel knew he was not ill, at least not with
any malady a doctor might cure. Whatever was causing perspiration to stream down his back, his heart's pounding to reverber-
ate in his stomach, and his hands to quake was not something
he had, but something that had him. Something that drove him
unseeing and unhearing, something heedless of his prerogative to
choose.*

Not that he was exercising that prerogative. No, he'd not re-

sisted this dark passion that had compelled him to locate a gun shop because it was as much a part of his nature as his will was. For all that it strained his body, a part thta was tremendously pleasurable to his psyche, though he supposed the fact that his body and his mind were now disconnected, no longer communicating with one another, was as dire a warning as any that what felt good may not in the long run be good.

But if Daniel had ever had much concern for the long run, he wouldn't be standing where he was now, across the street from the house at the back of which, in a small flat on the second floor, Sean and Kathleen Delaney lived. He wouldn't be waiting for the short but powerfully built man who would in a month's time sire him, waiting with a loaded pistol concealed in a pocket in the lining of his jacket.

Still, he knew that despite his disregard for the ramifications of what he was about to do, it would change the future. He would not be born. But his mother would be free of Sean Delaney's blows to both her body and her spirit. She would marry again have another child, perhaps the large family she'd always wanted. She'd never said so, but he'd always suspected that, despite her devout faith, his own birth had been an accident and that, afterward, she'd been careful not to bring another child to live in so violent a household. So careful that she must have resisted his father more often than not, and those had been the occasions on which he'd staggered from their bedroom, red- and swollen-faced, cursing her, leaving Daniel to tend the marks his hands had left on her and vow he would one day still those hands forever.

Now, seeing his father step from the front door of the house, Daniel's own hands fell suddenly quiet, assured. As he crossed the street toward Sean Delaney, he no longer felt torn, body from soul, by his dark desire. He was his desire, the perfect embodiment of it. For several blocks, he effortlessly shadowed the man, his vision and hearing supernaturally acute, though only in the perception of his prey. All else, the crowd, the clatter of passing wagons was on the periphery of his existence and its single purpose. to pick the right time, the right place.

When Sean Delaney stepped into an alley that was deserted but for heaps of trash and woodpiles, Daniel knew his time had come. He followed, no more than six paces behind, hearing nothing now but his own breathing, like a hot wind inside his head. He drew up when his father did to light a cigarette. With his right hand, he reached across his body to the pocket inside his jacket. Silently, he unsheathed the derringer and, straightening his arm, aimed the muzzle of the gun between his father's shoulder blades.

Slowly, he pulled the trigger, able at last to render justice, deliver peace.

Madeleine heard a gunshot. "Daniel!"

Another silence-shattering crack, much closer, and she opened her eyes. Seeing hers and Daniel's bed, realizing she was still sitting in Daniel's chair, she shuddered a sigh of relief. She could have breathed it the instant she'd cried his name, however, had she been fully awake. She'd have known then that as long as she could think his name, speak it, he was still alive. Obviously, she'd only dreamed she'd seen him draw the derringer and take deadly aim at his father. She hadn't, however, dreamed the short, sharp blasts. A third came, at the door.

"Madeleine? Is that you in there? Are you all right?"

Rawley! As she hauled herself out of the chair, she couldn't have said how long she'd been asleep in it, but if her sorely aching neck and cramped muscles were any indication, all night. Tightening the belt of her wrapper, she shuffled to the door. After she'd unlocked and opened it, Rawley stood staring at her, holding a newspaper, one pirate eye wide and his mouth agape.

"When I didn't hear from either you or Mac again, I thought I'd better— My God, Madeleine. You look like you've been through Hell."

"Not quite," she replied, finger-combing her damp and

matted hair back from her forehead as she stepped aside for him. "Vergil took me to it but he wouldn't let me in."

"Ah yes, Vergil," Rawlston said, frowning worry at Madeleine as he closed the door and followed her into the kitchen area. "The greatest of the Roman poets, more widely known for having escorted Dante through Purgatory and Hell. Having nothing better to do while you were being kidnapped, I suppose you read *The Divine Comedy.*"

"*Read* it?" Madeleine hugged herself to contain her shivering. "I've been living it."

"Really? The Good Book must be in error on the subject of Hell, then." Dropping his newspaper on the crate, Rawlston seated Madeleine on the stool. "It isn't an inferno, it's an icebox."

Her teeth chattering, her knees bobbing like buoys on a choppy sea, Madeleine pointed to the woodbox behind Rawlston.

"Correct me if I'm wrong," he began as he set about lighting a fire in the stove, "but don't you have a husband who's supposed to see to it that you don't freeze to death?"

Madeleine grew still. "Daniel isn't here," she said softly.

"I gathered that," Rawlston replied. "Where, precisely, is he?" When Madeleine didn't answer, he turned to her, his hands on his waist, light from the fire in the stove dancing in the triangles his arms formed. "Madeleine, where's Mac?"

For a moment, she considered telling Rawlston the whole truth, then realized that there were some things not even this sage city editor, who had surely seen it all, would believe. "He's . . . following a lead."

Rawlston lowered his arms. "He's gone looking for his father, you mean."

Madeleine bolted upright. "How did you—how could you know that?"

"An obit in this morning's paper caught my eye. Kathleen McQuinn Delaney's." Rawlston slowly walked toward her. "I figured she'd come back to Chicago to see her son before she died."

"She did. She made him promise to find his father." Madeleine asked for forgiveness for wishing the woman had died just a day sooner. "How long have you known about Daniel's past?"

"Since he was tried for assaulting his father with deadly intent. I was a reporter then, doing a series on juvenile crime for the *Clarion*." Rawlston walked to the bed, glanced down at the candles on the floor, then taking a blanket, returned to Madeleine and wrapped it around her shoulders. "I knew he'd told the truth when he testified that Sean Delaney had routinely abused his wife. Kathleen denied it, but I believed she wanted Daniel sent away for his own protection. She knew the violence wasn't going to end and she was afraid that her son would become its next victim, if not by killing then by being killed."

Rawlston's words echoed in Madeleine's mind, delivering a horrifying epiphany. "Oh, my God," she murmured. "I've been so terrified that Daniel would kill his father, I never once considered that his father might . . ."

Slowly, she rose. The blanket slipped off her shoulders as she circled away from Rawlston and shambled about the flat, trying to absorb the full import of this newest ramification of Daniel's descent through time to his own, personal Hell. The fact that she was in their flat then, and still—to Rawley as well as to herself—Daniel's wife, was proof only that he had born, not that he was still alive.

"Why?" she demanded, turning to Rawlston. "If she'd lied to protect Daniel once, why after all these years did Kathleen return only to jeopardize him? It makes no sense."

"I'm not sure why," Rawlston replied. "I have something in the back of my mind, not a theory really, just

something . . ." He shoved his hands in his pockets.
"Daniel's the one who will have to come to terms with
the truth, whatever it may be."

"The truth," Madeleine said, rushing to him, "is that
he's so hell-bent on revenge against his father that, just
as you predicted, he's gone . . . where no man wants to
go."

"But must go." Rawlston took Madeleine by the shoulders. "Listen, Babe. You're his wife. You've got to have
faith that he loves you more than he hates his father."

"Faith?" Madeleine tore away. "I try, Rawley, but it's so
hard. From one minute to the next, I don't know if he's
alive or dead." *Or if I will never have known and loved him
because he will never have been born.* She looked back at Rawlston. "You don't know what it's like, living in Limbo."

Coming up behind her, Rawlston cupped her shoulders. "What are you going to do?"

Lowering her head, she picked at the knot in her belt.
"What *can* I do? Stay here in our home and wait."

"Of course, I understand if you feel you can't work."
Rawlston removed his hands from her shoulders. "But
what about Mrs. Kozyck?"

"Mrs. Kozyck?" Madeleine turned around. "What has
she got to do with this?"

"Nothing at all. But you did promise her you'd help
her find the evidence to acquit her husband of a crime
she believes he didn't commit. You talked to Kozyck yourself. You believe he's innocent, too, don't you?"

"Yes, but . . . ." Pressing her fingers to her temples,
Madeleine shook her head as though to shake off the
swelling pain. "I can't, Rawley. Don't ask me! I can't think
of the *Clarion* or Mrs. Kozyck and her husband . . ."
Through hot, biting tears, Rawlston's image blurred.
"Don't you understand? I can't think of anything or anyone but my own husband."

Heaving a sigh, Rawlston patted her arm. "Sure, kid, I

understand." He walked to the door then, pausing, looked back, his pirate gaze like a beam of light directed at her heart. "Just one more thing. Do you really think Mac would want you to make a shrine of that bed and a plaster saint of yourself on his account? He was—is—so proud of you, Babe, proud of the reporter you've become. What do you think he'd have to say about your walking out on the Kozyck story?"

For several moments after Rawlston had left, Madeleine stood stunned. Then, utterly uncertain of herself, she walked to the crate and sat down on the lone stool. Fingering the corners of the edition of the *Clarion* Rawley had brought, she thought about what the old cabby had said yesterday, that faith was living what you believed. She believed in the Kozyck story. Daniel had come to believe in it, too. He'd asked her to bring her notes on it to the meeting they were to have had at the cathedral yesterday morning. They would have worked the story together, Babe and Daniel McQuinn, the Sweethearts of he *Chicago Clarion*. And they'd have made headlines with it, too. With the truth.

But without Daniel, Madeleine had lost all desire for headlines, even for getting at the individual truths underlying untold stories. Without Daniel, "the story" wasn't any longer all that mattered. Indeed, it no longer mattered at all.

Propping her elbows atop the crate, she rubbed her throbbing temples, the *Clarion* beneath her unfocused gaze. Soon, however, the paper's bold headline captured her notice.

"BABE McQUINN FEARED KIDNAPPED," she read aloud. "That has it about right. I'm yesterday's news." Still, she'd hadn't had the chance to read the story Daniel had dictated to Rawley yesterday morning from a phone in a drugstore on State Street. Finding his byline, she began reading and, within seconds, was smiling broadly. In style and pacing and the ability to keep readers breathlessly reading, Daniel McQuinn was inimitable. She still marveled at him, especially since she knew—he'd told her so himself—that the entire time he was composing the story for Rawley, he was terrified he'd lose her.

Just as she was now, afraid of losing him and the life and happiness she'd known because of him. He could have surrendered to his fear, lost his head and his will. But he hadn't. The story he'd given Rawley had been a masterpiece of forethought and faith in their future together because it had not only told the news of her abduction but had eliminated the threat posed by her father and Roger.

Pushing away from the crate, she rose. *But how can I possibly continue with the Kozyck story?* she thought as she walked toward the bed. If Daniel were to murder his father, he would obliterate his own life and completely rewrite hers. She couldn't possibly say whether or not she'd ever have made her way to Chicago had she not known him. Even if she had, Rawlston certainly wouldn't have hired her without Daniel to act as her guardian. What was the good of beginning a story she might not be able to finish?

Of course, Babe McQuinn might very well survive. As Rawley had said, she had every reason to believe that Daniel loved her more than he hated his father, that he would forswear vengeance on the man and return from Hell. Still, he wouldn't do so before keeping his promise to at least find Sean Delaney, and as violent as the man apparently had been, she had every *other* reason to believe that, confronted by a hostile stranger, he would provoke violence. Perhaps he already had. At this very moment, she could be Babe McQuinn, widow.

"No!" Then, softly, "I can't believe that you're not coming back to me, Daniel. I won't." Refusing to believe that he wasn't returning was not, she knew, the same as believing that he was. But it was better than despairing.

Better yet, she thought, glancing down at the candles, was living as though he'd already returned. Bending down, she gathered the candles, carried them to the trash, then checked her three-quarter coat to make sure the Kozyck notes were still in the pocket. "After all," she said, finding them and smiling, "somebody has to keep the McQuinn name on the front page."

Releasing the derringer's trigger before firing its one shot, Daniel lowered his arm. In a confessional, he could turn a young priest's head white with an account of his sins. One thing he would never want to confess, however, was shooting a man—not even Sean Delaney—in the back. No one would ever know he had, of course, because if he did, he would have prevented his own birth. Still, he would know, if only for this one moment in time. But then, his whole life had come down to this one moment. How he lived it, as a murderer or a just executioner, was everything.

"Sean," he called, following his father a few more steps then stopping beside a woodpile and raising the pistol. "Sean Delaney!"

The man halted. Looking over his shoulder, he glowered at Daniel then, spotting the pistol, turned and faced him. "That'd be me. What the hell do you want?"

"You," Daniel shouted. "In hell."

As Daniel began to take the trigger back the fatal distance, perspiration dripped into his right eye, rendering him sighted only in the left. Instantly, an image of Madeleine came to mind, Madeleine as she had looked to his single-eyed vision the day he'd bumped into her at St. Augustine's. She was so young, so small and slender. Yet even then, she had evidenced promise of the woman she would become.

Unless, perhaps, he were never born. She'd said that she'd carried his spirit inside her, as the best part of her; that it had urged her to break with Mabrey and her father and come to Chicago. For his own part, Daniel believed she would have done so had he never lived. Still, he wouldn't have been there that night on the Levee to keep her from falling victim to Archibald Monroe's insane scheme to turn her into a stunt journalist and Captain Carnation's more carnal designs. Even if both she and the Clarion had survived that episode, Rawley wouldn't have hired her unless he'd been able to give Daniel his job back in exchange for acting as her bodyguard. She wouldn't have been assigned the Red Rose story. Without Madeleine and her insistence that the old flower woman was crucial to the case, Benny might never have revealed himself. He might still be savaging young prostitutes. Without Madeleine, Mrs. Kozyck might never find another journalist to listen to her husband's story. He might die serving a sentence for a murder he didn't commit.

Wiping the perspiration from his eye, Daniel once again focused on his target. But even with both eyes, he saw that he wasn't holding a gun only on his father, or even only on himself, but also on the one person he loved more than he hated his father, more than he'd ever loved anyone in his life. Madeleine. His wife. His soul.

He'd promised his mother he would find his father and he had. Whatever choices she'd made for her life for whatever reasons, he couldn't undo the consequences of them for her, not even as she lay dying. Whatever her regrets, she would have to take them up with her God and He with her. As for himself, he was looking forward to having a Maker to meet, though he didn't plan to meet Him for a long time to come. He had a life to live and a beautiful, loving woman to live it with. He was going to find the old cabby and his damned horse, Vergil, and go back to Madeleine.

Grinning now, he fired the pistol in the air then threw it down and headed out of the alley. Already, he could feel Madeleine's skin beneath his hands, taste her mouth and her tongue and—

"Umff!" As something massive struck him in the back, Daniel fell to the ground, the palms of his hands and one side of his

face leaving gratings of skin among the cinders. Behind him, he saw the tips of Sean Delaney's boots. Despite near paralysis, he rolled himself over.

Sean Delaney stood over him, his face pinched red with rage, as he poised himself to lower a six-inch thick log onto the top of Daniel's skull. "Bastard!"

Eighteen

To Madeleine, the perfectly polite knock on Rawley's office door was a skull-splitting blow. But in the last month, hardly a day had passed that headaches hadn't plagued her. She needed rest, Rawley had insisted again just before he'd been called to the city room. Her simultaneous work on one of the biggest stories of the year, the assassination of Mayor Carter Harrison on October 28, and the Kozyck story had taken a terrible toll on her, he'd said. But having exhausted the Harrison assassination for the time being and finishing the Kozyck story three days ago, she had taken time off. Still, the headaches came, so violently she often felt they would rend her in two. They came, as Rawley well knew, not because of overwork, but because of the conflict raging in her soul. Though her faith in Daniel had grown with the passage of time, her hope of his returning had dwindled.

The old cabby had told Daniel that he would find his father before eight o'clock on the evening of November tenth, the time and date he was conceived. Four hours from now. Of course, since as of this moment Daniel's byline still appeared on his old stories, he *had* been conceived and born. That meant that either he hadn't yet found his father, or he'd found the man and had chosen life over revenge.

In the latter case, however, he would have come home

to her. And still might. But if after eight o'clock tonight Daniel's name still appeared on his stories and he hadn't returned, only one explanation for his past existence would remain, one that would crush her very soul: Daniel had found not only his father but his killer.

Another knock came at the door. Grimacing, Madeleine dug her nails into her skull, "Go away! Mr. Rawlston isn't here."

"I'm not looking for Vernon Rawlston," a man said, his voice gentle and his speech refined. "I was hoping to find Mrs. McQuinn."

Sitting in a chair in front of Rawley's desk, Madeleine looked around at the man. He was nattily dressed, though perhaps a recent gentleman, and had a broad, youthful face and a genial, if pugnacious, gaze. "I'm Babe McQuinn," she said stiffly. "And you would be Finley Peter Dunne."

"Guilty as charged, ma'am," he replied then walked toward her, derby in hand. "I've followed your series on the Kozyck case. It was as brilliant a piece of journalism as I've ever read, as any which that husband of yours could have written. One I would have been proud to write myself." He proffered a well-groomed, gloved hand. "If I may be so bold, I'd like to shake the hand of the woman who won an innocent man's release from prison."

Madeleine stared at Dunne's hand for a moment, then accepted it, more for Daniel's sake than her own. "Thank you for saying that, about my work being as good as Daniel's. If you've been following the series, you know he's been away on assignment. I've kept myself going with the thought that wherever he is and whatever he's doing, he's watching me and he's proud."

"You don't mean you haven't been able to communicate with him?" Dunne appeared puzzled. "Where's he gone to? Hades?"

Madeleine swallowed the urge to scream. "I wouldn't be surprised."

Dunne laughed. "Neither would I. Well, if anyone can cover it with both skill and flair, McQuinn can." Smiling warmly, he gave Madeleine's hand a reassuring squeeze. "Don't worry. If I know McQuinn, wherever he's gone, he'll soon be back. His lifeblood is Chicago, this city room." He bent toward her. "You."

"I pray . . ." The fingers of her left hand trembling, Madeleine pressed them to the side of her head, trying to still what she'd come to think of as the maniacal creature incessantly pounding to get out.

Letting go of her right hand, Dunne began toying with the brim of his derby. "Mrs. McQuinn, Babe, the boys at the Whitechapel Club and I would like you to be our guest-of-honor tonight. We barred you once, because we didn't think a woman had any business being a crime reporter. We were wrong and McQuinn was right to wash his hands of us."

Madeleine recalled the night Daniel had resigned from the club, claiming he'd done so not for her sake but because he didn't want Pamela Hart to suspect the McQuinns weren't the happy, devoted couple they'd pretended to be. He'd only said that, of course, because Madeleine had hurt him terribly when she'd denied him her love. She'd done so because she'd feared his discovering her identity and concluding that she was just another willful, deceitful, spoiled heiress sent to humiliate him. If only she'd had the courage to tell him the truth sooner. How many more memories of loving him she would have had to console her these past weeks; how many more she would have if he never—

But he *was* coming home. He must. She gave Dunne a tense smile. "Thank you for the invitation, but some other time. As it so happens, I'm expecting Daniel home tonight."

"Of course, we'd be honored anytime," Dunne replied. He walked to the door. "But if for some reason, McQuinn should be delayed . . ."

"He won't be! You mustn't say that. I mustn't think it." Horrified and embarrassed by her loss of self-control, of rationality, Madeleine clamped her hand over her mouth and turned her back on Dunne.

"Give him our regards, won't you?" he said softly.

When Madeleine heard the door click shut, she released the demon that for the past month had screeched and clawed inside her head, released him to carry her soul to a hell all her own.

"Are you sure you don't want me to stay with you awhile?"

Unlocking her door and stepping inside her flat, Madeleine turned to Rawlston. "I'll be all right, I promise you. Thank you for seeing me home."

His one eye wary, he said, "You might faint again."

"I won't. Once was embarrassment enough for this reporter's lifetime." She curled her fingers around the edge of the door. "Besides, Daniel will be home tonight."

Inserting his hands in his pockets, Rawlston leaned against the doorjamb. "Madeleine, I've asked you every day for the past month to let me put a man on Mac's trail, and each time, you assured me it would do no good, that he was somewhere not even you could reach. So if that's the case, would you mind telling me just how you know he's returning tonight?"

Madeleine looked away. Less than two hours ago, she'd let the demon out, confronted her worst fear. And she hadn't been carried to a private Hell at all, only to a bench outside Rawley's office by the reporter who'd found her lying on the floor. When she came to, she knew—she couldn't have said how—that fear had lost all power over her, that her faith in Daniel was complete. Tonight, he was coming home. She was as certain of that as she was that her headaches had vanished, never to return.

"How do I know?" She looked back at Rawlston. "The same way Mrs. Kozyck knew that, one day, *her* husband would come home to *her*. It's a fact that just hasn't happened yet."

Rawlston straightened. "That's not much of an answer, but I'll say one thing for both Mrs. Kozyck and Mac. They're lucky to have you on their side." Giving her a pat on the arm, he bid Madeleine goodnight.

"Good night, Rawley," she replied. Then, locking herself inside the flat, she lit the nearest lamp, removed her coat, hat, and gloves, and set about readying the apartment for Daniel's return. She lighted the stove, then removed the plate containing her half-eaten breakfast from the crate to the basin on the cupboard. Returning to the crate, she grinningly moved the one stool to the side where Daniel had always sat, then picked up her mug of cold coffee and started for the cupboard.

Halfway there, she came to a halt so abrupt, coffee sloshed over her hand. Her eyes the size of the eggs she'd fried that morning, she turned and stared at the stool she'd placed on Daniel's side of the crate.

"One, two," she said, counting the extra stool. She squeezed her eyes shut then looked again. If she was seeing double, she should be seeing two of everything, but she wasn't. Just two stools where there should have been one.

"Daniel?" Madeleine dropped the mug, splattering coffee on the floor, the insteps of her shoes and the hem of her skirt. "Daniel!" She ran to the door, wrestled it open, then all but hurtled herself down the stairs in pursuit of him.

Before she reached the bottom of the staircase, however, she stopped. Where to begin looking for him? He'd obviously gone in search of her and, not finding her, would eventually return to the flat.

As she now did, to wait. To wait for Paradise.

At seven o'clock, Madeleine began checking the time every ten minutes until eight, when she checked Daniel's byline on the lead story in the *Clarion* extra headlining her abduction. It was still there, and at one minute and two and three minutes after eight. Madeleine gave a prayer of thanks. Unquestionably, Daniel had been conceived and born. He had gone to hell and defeated the worst in his nature but had not, except for the stool, given evidence of his return.

At eight fifteen, she went downstairs and phoned the *Clarion*. Assured that Daniel hadn't been seen anywhere in the building, she called Rawley at home. He'd hadn't talked to or seen Daniel, either. She started back up the stairs, then on a hunch, knocked on Eileen Corrigan's door. A man, a boy really, at least several years younger than Daniel, answered, his hair standing up like wheat stacks and his shirt-tails hanging out.

"Who is it, love?" the widow called from behind him.

"Some woman who says she lives upstairs. Wants to know if you seen her husband today?"

"Tell her I got better things to do than keep track o' her hoosbund." There was a pause, then, "But no. I ain't seen him, tell her."

Madeleine slowly returned to the flat. Sitting in Daniel's chair, she stared at the extra stool. Who else but Daniel, she asked herself at nine o'clock, could or would have brought it? Of course he'd come back, and any minute, he was going to walk through the doorway.

At ten, she wondered if she hadn't bought the extra stool herself—another gesture of faith—then, given the strain she'd been under, had understandably forgotten she'd done so. That meant, of course, that Daniel hadn't returned, after all. He'd lived, but he wasn't alive.

By eleven, she was certain that as great as her anxiety had been, she wouldn't have forgotten a gesture of faith, no matter how small and sentimental. Daniel had indeed been born. He'd returned. But perhaps not as a living man. Perhaps as a spirit, first making his presence known, then living with her from that moment on as he had before, in the deepest and greatest part of her soul. Daniel had honored his promise that not even Hell itself could keep him from her, that he would do nothing that would forever separate them. He just hadn't been able to keep his father from separating his soul from his body.

A sudden yet becalming sense of detachment from her own body overtook Madeleine. Then she felt a gentle power—Daniel, she imagined—take her hands and draw her out of the chair as though to lead her on a journey. Sometime later, when she found herself at Grand Central Station, then on the steps of City Hall—later still, roaming the Levee and then in front of the *Clarion* Building with no recollection of how she'd arrived at those places, she gathered that Daniel's spirit was guiding her back along the tumultuous, exciting path their love had taken. Lastly, when she looked up and saw a massive building looming over her fortress-like, turreted, haunting, she knew she had been right. Daniel had returned her to the place where their gazes had first met, the unforgettable place where their souls had been forever forged.

St. Augustine's.

Her journey back to the first stirrings of their love now complete, the full comprehension of the loss of that love struck Madeleine a merciless blow. When she'd married Daniel, she'd thought she'd mocked her faith, weak as it was. Now that it was strong, it mocked her. Both it and he were forever gone. Not even his spirit remained to comfort and guide her. No longer entranced, she buried her face in her hands, releasing sobs no less soul-wrenching and body-wracking for their silence. Daniel had last kissed her as though to leave nothing of her to survive him, but he'd failed. He'd left just enough of her to grieve for him until she took her dying breath. How she wished to God that breath would be her next.

Gathering her skirt, she turned and staggered away from the building. After a few steps, she halted then straightened her spine. Before she walked away from St. Augustine's for the last time, she would curse it and the day she'd first set foot inside it, the day that had begun her journey to this moment. This terrible moment of realization that her time had come and gone, never to return. Raising her fist, she turned.

"God—"

A guard opened the front door of the reformatory, letting a man out then relocking the entrance. The man, Madeleine noticed, was uncommonly tall, lanky, broad-shouldered. Cocking her head, she took a few slow steps toward him as he descended the stairs, then stopped when he did, scrutinizing his every move. Reaching inside his jacket pocket, he removed something, then turned aside, the brim of his hat obscuring his face. He brought his hands toward his mouth. Then, a single flame sparked, looking to Madeleine like a skyrocket on the Fourth of July. Though her heart was near launching as well, she held her breath, waiting, hoping, believing.

The man lowered his hand to the flame cupped in his hands, but instead of lighting his cigarette, he flung it away. Madeleine's expectant smile fell with her all but complete jubilation. Her pulse in abeyance, she continued watching the man who stood as if in deep thought while holding the match and its flame aloft. Finally, he dropped the still-lit match to the ground.

"Daniel!"

Hearing Madeleine cry out to him, Daniel whipped around, searching for her and, incredulously, finding her. After three strides, three long strides, twenty-seven years, and all the Hell he ever cared to encounter, he scooped his beloved wife into his arms.

"I'm back, Madeleine. I'm back and I'll never leave you again."

Everything about him, the coarse stubble beneath her palms, the scent of his skin above his collar, the eyelids and lashes and lips she kissed, the mouth that was now kissing her back—eyes and lips and throat—shouted, "Alive!" Daniel was alive and holding her, crushing her, loving her. He was so hard against her, so touchably hard and she so desperately needing to touch and bring his hardness inside her that she thought she might break her promise to herself and faint for the second time that day. With her remaining breath, she begged him for mercy.

"I was just about to ask you for some," he said breathlessly, his hands spanning her waist.

Laughing, Madeleine gently pounded his shoulder with her fist. "You'll get none from me, suh. Ah nearly had me a spell when I saw that extra stool."

"Complain, complain." Daniel smiled wryly. "Now if I'd come home after being gone for a month and hadn't brought you a little souvenir, you'd have moaned about that, too." Abruptly, he grabbed her upper arms and pulled her toward him, bringing his lips close to hers. "I love you, Madeleine. You're the reason I didn't pull the trigger on Sean Delaney. When I got back, I went straight to the flat, and when you weren't there, for that moment, all the life went out of me."

Madeleine sank against him. "Why didn't you wait?"

"There was someone else I had to see, even though I already knew I might be too late."

"Your mother. I'm so sorry, Daniel.

"So am I. There was something I wanted her to know

before she died." As abruptly as he'd taken her into his grasp, Daniel let Madeleine go. "I almost forgot. I brought you another present." From one of his pockets, he withdrew something he kept concealed in his fist. "The whole time I was in the hospital, even when I couldn't remember my own name, I knew somebody somewhere believed in me." Opening his hand, Daniel revealed the mother-of-pearl comb Madeleine had left on the seat of the old cabby's hack. He slid it into the pale gold hair he adored. "Thank you for believing in me," he murmured then, turning her in his arms, kissed her deeply and hungrily and, in Madeleine's mind and heart, unutterably sweetly.

Unlike the man who'd been on the brink of death, she thought. Instead, like a man on the eve of a new life. Twining her eager tongue with his, she regretted she'd been about to use it to curse the day she'd met him. Her faith had wavered, but it hadn't failed her. More importantly, it hadn't failed Daniel while he was—

In the hospital? Madeleine pulled away. "What were you doing in a hospital and without your memory?"

Daniel related his story to the point at which Sean Delaney attacked him with the deadly log. Daniel had escaped the blow, but a struggle between the two men nevertheless ensued. Still, knowing that if he took his father's life even accidentally, he would forever change the course of her life, he struggled only to get away from the man. Eventually, he did, only to stumble from the alley into the street and the path of a pump wagon speeding toward a fire.

"Yes, Babe, I'm all right now," he said, answering her question before she could finish asking it. Then, clasping the hand she was reaching toward his temple, he kissed the tips of its fingers. "I was out of the hospital in a week's time."

"A week?" Frowning, Madeleine propped her hands on

her waist. "You'd already fulfilled your promise to find your father, so what kept you in hell and me in Limbo all this time?"

"The old cabby and Vergil. I couldn't find them anywhere." At the appearance of sparse, whirling snow, Daniel slipped his arm about Madeleine's shoulders and walked her away from the reformatory. "After a few days, I started thinking that I wasn't supposed to return just yet, that there was still something I had to do. What, I had no idea, until it occurred to me that while I'd confronted the man who would become my father and found him to be as vicious as I remembered him, I hadn't seen the woman who would give birth to me. I wondered if my memories of her were accurate."

"Were they?"

"No. She was even more beautiful and high-spirited; quite a lady." Gracefully, Daniel moved Madeleine across his body to his left side so that he was now walking nearest the street. "Like you," he said, giving her a soft, reverent smile.

Wrapping both her arms around his one, Madeleine pressed her cheek to his shoulder. "Tell me more about your mother. The little I know about her puzzles me."

"She *was* a puzzle, even to me," Daniel said. "I always wondered why she'd married someone as different from her in background and interests as my father was. Whether my parents had ever really been in love and, if so, what had gone wrong between them. Back there, in the past, I realized I had the chance to find out."

"And did you?"

Daniel didn't directly answer Madeleine's question. Instead, he continued his story in a curiously objective tone, as though reporting it. He told her of the inquiries he'd made about the young Delaneys, discovering that in addition to his regular job at a nearby lumber mill, Sean Delaney worked several evenings a week tending bar. On those evenings, Mrs. Delaney had been observed leaving the house carrying an armful of books. She was known to read to children and the elderly in a nearby hospital run by an order of mostly Irish nuns. Daniel commented that he hadn't been surprised. His mother had loved both her children and her Church.

Nevertheless, one evening he followed her to the hospital and waited across the street from it while she performed her unsurprising act of charity. What he saw when she reappeared, however, did startle him. She wasn't alone. Obviously animated, she spoke with a man whose voice, features, and dress Daniel couldn't discern from a distance and in the dark. Whoever the man was, Daniel said, he appeared to be on familiar terms with Kathleen Delaney, familiar enough to walk her to her front porch carrying her books.

The same scenario played out on each of the next six occasions she visited the hospital. Though Daniel saw no evidence of a flirtation between his mother and her companion, it was clear to him that they were developing a bond.

Then, one evening, they failed to immediately return to the Delaney home. Not that they appeared to have another destination in mind. They'd been so deep in conversation, they hadn't paid the least attention to where they were headed.

On a dark street, they finally stopped before one in a row of shotgun houses. Daniel ducked to his right, hiding himself alongside the house's tall porch. In the stark calm and quiet, he clearly heard all they were saying.

"Madeleine," Daniel said, interrupting himself and turning her toward him. "What I learned that night was that Sean Delaney wasn't my father. He couldn't have been."

Through now steadily falling snow, Madeleine gaped at him. "What do you mean, *couldn't* have been?"

Daniel took a deep breath. "As my mother phrased it to her companion, Sean had been unable to perform the marital act since returning from the war. Hearing her say that was like getting hit with both barrels of a shotgun. I never guessed that Sean was impotent nor did I know that he'd served in the Union Army." Touching the first knuckle on his left hand to the right corner of his mouth, he gazed at Madeleine from beneath arched brows. "Of course, I can understand why he wouldn't want to discuss whatever injury or event that had literally cost him his manhood."

"I wonder what made her confess something so intimate to that man," Madeleine mused, once again falling into step beside Daniel. "Unless he was a doctor."

"I thought he might have been, too," Daniel replied. "But as I soon discovered, she wasn't seeking a cure for Sean's sterility. She was looking for a way out of their marriage."

Daniel told Madeleine of overhearing his mother's admission that she'd married Sean Delaney in haste before he went off to war, but had soon regretted it. Nevertheless, she'd been determined to honor her vows and make him a good wife. But since his return, he'd been making that task impossible. Unable to find conjugal fulfillment, as she had termed his problem, he had taken to blaming her and then striking her.

"She asked the man to help her obtain a papal annulment of her marriage," Daniel said. "Surely the Church, she argued, wouldn't keep her bound to a man who not only abused her, but could never father children."

Madeleine met Daniel's gaze with understanding in her own. "The man was a priest, wasn't he?"

"Yes." At a smack of an icy wind and stinging crystals of snow, Daniel turned Madeleine's collar up around her ears then pressed her to his side. "He gave my mother little pastoral comfort, though. I imagine she must have felt a chill as bitterly cold as this when he told her he would help her if he could, but she would never receive an annulment. Sad as her predicament was, her marriage had been consummated and was binding. End of story."

"Not quite," Madeleine said, coming to a better understanding of Kathleen McQuinn Delaney. "When your mother asked you to find your father, you thought she was giving you some kind of permission to avenge her by killing Sean. Obviously, she only wanted you to know who your real father was." With snow powdering her lashes, she looked askance at Daniel as she hastened to match his increased pace. "Did you learn who he was, Daniel?"

"Is." Daniel huffed a visible breath. "He's still living, here in Chicago. And it's long past time he acknowledged me."

Madeleine ratcheted in a series of cold breaths. "I know better than to ask if you plan to confront him," she said. "The only question is when?"

Daniel drew her to a halt. "Now."

"Now? You mean tonight?"

"I mean right now," Daniel replied, his voice trailing off as he turned to his left and gazed from one to the other of two stone angels flanking a cobbled path, a growing layer of snow outlining their wings. He stepped toward them.

Madeleine looked quizzically at the angels, then at Daniel. She came to his side, hugging herself, her teeth chattering. "Daniel, what is this place?"

He looked down at her. "A cemetery."

"I thought you said your father was living."

Before Madeleine had finished speaking, however, Daniel had taken off up the cobbled path, quickly disappearing in the dense snowfall. She followed him, but at a gait slower than his. Ice glazed the smooth stones, and several times, she nearly fell. To make matters more difficult, as she picked her way past the headstones, she was haunted by the realization that they served not only as memorials but as guardians, keepers of the secrets that surely lay buried with the bones beneath them. Secrets like Kathleen Delaney's. Madeleine felt as though she were trespassing. Soon, though, she knew she was lost.

Coming to a fork in the path, she looked around her for some sign of Daniel. Seeing none, she cupped her hands around her mouth and, in a loud whisper, called out to him. When he didn't respond, she arbitrarily chose the path to her left, following its winding course until, abruptly, it ended. There, she stood for a moment, gazing blinkingly through the blizzard, unable to see even the path along which she'd just come. Baffled, she simply chose a direction and set out on it. Fortunately, she hadn't gone far when the snow abated enough for her to see Daniel some twenty paces ahead. With his back to her, he stood as silently and rigidly as one of the sentinel-like headstones. Indeed, he did appear to be on watch, and as she approached, she saw that the subject of his intensely focused gaze was another man, who stood ten or so feet beyond Daniel. Unlike Daniel's back, this man's was hunched; his head was bowed. Though snow crunched beneath her feet as she approached the scene, he took no notice of her.

Daniel, however, did. Turning, he drew her into a one-armed embrace and held her at his side. Madeleine said nothing. She merely followed Daniel's gaze ahead, to the ground at the man's feet. Snow blanketed it; nevertheless, she could see that it was mounded like a freshly dug grave.

She clasped Daniel's free hand. "Your mother is buried there, isn't she?"

Silent, once again intently focused on the man before him, Daniel nodded.

"And that man is your father."

As it to confirm her statement, the man knelt down and

placed a sprig of evergreen—the symbol of eternal love—
atop Kathleen Delaney's grave. Then, crossing himself, he
rose and walked toward Madeleine and Daniel, head still
bowed, revealing only the crown of his hat. He was unaware of their presence until Daniel struck a match. Looking up, the man halted before the flame.

Seeing his face for the first time, Madeleine gasped.
She knew him, had been to see him not two months ago.
He was a gentle, soft-spoken man who nevertheless possessed a strong belief in the power of art and literature
to help mend the broken lives of wayward boys. Ten years
ago, at St. Augustine's, one of the boys he'd tended was
young Daniel Delaney. Or as Daniel would have been
called had he borne his father's name, Daniel Bianco.
Daniel was the son of the priest his mother had turned
to for help twenty-seven years ago, Father Ralph Bianco.
Monsignor Bianco, now.

"Hello, Daniel," he said, his eyes evidencing both his
grief and his joy at seeing his son. "How did you find
me?"

"It wasn't hard. I knew if I didn't find you at St.
Augustine's, I'd find you here."

"You must hate me."

On a large, wet snowflake, Daniel's match went out. But
he didn't need to light another. The snow suddenly
stopped falling and that which lay on the ground reflected the blue-white aura of the emerging moon. Dropping the doused match, he stepped toward his father.

Knowing neither Daniel's feelings toward the father
who had never acknowledged him nor his intentions,
Madeleine tensed. While she believed he had eliminated
his vengeful streak, he would never be predictable. He
might embrace his father or knock him down. Neither
would surprise her. However, when she saw Daniel remove
his fisted right hand from his pocket, she envisioned splat-
ters of red on the snow. She reached out as if to stay him,

then seeing him open his fist, lowered her hand. From his own, Daniel was dangling Kathleen Delaney's locket before his father's eyes.

"She gave this to me before she died," Daniel said. "I thought you might like to have it."

As though unable to believe what he was seeing, the priest took the locket in the palm of his hand. He stared at it for a very long time, then closing his eyes, also closed his fingers around it. A moment later, he looked at Daniel, his eyes moist. "I gave this to her on November tenth, 1866. We spoke vows. It was Kathleen's idea that we mingle drops of our blood on a small scrap of cloth. After we did, she folded the cloth and put it inside the locket. Nine months later, you were born."

"Did you love her?" Daniel asked.

"I worshipped her. I was prepared to leave the priesthood for her." Monsignor Bianco looked at Madeleine as if he were hoping that she, as Woman, would understand how deeply he'd loved one woman. "Kathleen wouldn't hear of it, though. She said that for me or any priest to leave God's service would be a worse sin than the one we'd been about to commit." He looked at Daniel. "But no one could make me believe you were conceived in sin, Daniel. No man loved a woman more than I loved your mother."

"Then how could you have let her stay with Sean?" Daniel asked. "He knew, of course, that she'd been unfaithful to him and he never let her forget it."

"He assured her that if she ever left him, he'd track her down and take his vengeance out on you. We both had every reason to believe that he would." The priest put his hands in his pockets. "From the day you were born, I neither saw nor heard from her again until your trial. You know the rest. She arranged things so that you would be remanded to St. Augustine's, where I could look after you while she saw to it that you'd never find her and

Sean when you got out. She thought of no one's welfare but yours, Daniel."

Daniel turned and, walking to Madeleine, drew her into his embrace. With her beside him, he returned to his father. "Right now, then, she's looking down from heaven and smiling."

One week before Christmas, on a night that was clear and bright and cold, Madeleine lay in Daniel's arms before a crackling hearthfire in the parlor of their new apartment, holding that day's edition of the *Chicago Clarion*. "Would you like me to read it again?" she asked.

"Let me," he replied, taking the paper from her. Raising it to his gaze, he cleared his throat and began reading. "At ten o'clock on the morning of December nineteenth, Miss Madeleine Marie Charbonnay Faurest, formerly of Louisville, Kentucky and Mr. Daniel Patrick Amadeus McQuinn, of Chicago, were united in matrimony at Holy Name Cathedral. Officiating at the solemn high mass was Monsignor Ralph Bianco. Giving the bride away was Mr. G. Vernon Rawlston. As the groom watched his beautiful bride walk up the aisle, he thought his heart would burst with love for her. He prayed he would always make her as happy as she was making him that day."

"It doesn't say that," Madeleine blurted, sitting up and turning to him.

He also sat up. "Oh, but it does."

"Show me where," she said, reaching for the paper.

Pulling it from her grasp, he laid it on the floor beside him. "Here," he said, touching his lips. "And here." He touched his heart. "And here." Taking her hand, he turned the gold wedding band on her finger. "For Madeleine, the story of my life."

Madeleine brought his finger and his ring to her lips. Gazing into the timeless light in his eyes, she softly smiled.

"The only thing that matters is the story, and what matters most about our story is that it will never end." She looked at his mouth with a sudden glint of hunger in her gaze. "However, there is one part I'd like you to read to me again." She touched her fingertips to his lips.

Taking her hand, Daniel laid her back. Her hair rayed about her head like a halo. But she wasn't a saint. Only a woman. And as he kissed her, he knew that because of the remarkable woman she was, he'd chosen, at last, to be a man.

HISTORICAL NOTES

Although Madeleine Faurest McQuinn is a fictional heroine, the obstacles she overcame in her quest for acceptance as a news reporter are a matter of historical record. It should be noted, however, that like many heroines, she was ahead of her time. Women journalists did not establish a significant presence in city rooms around the country until after the turn of the century, and it would be several more decades before they achieved equality with their male counterparts. As recently as the 1950s, for example, women were excluded from membership in the Chicago Press Club.

In that vein, it should also be noted that while the Whitechapel Club did exist as depicted in *Trace of a Woman,* Finley Peter Dunne's invitation to Madeleine on the club's behalf would have been outside the realm of possibility in 1893. Nevertheless, Dunne, creator of the Irish bartender and sage "Mr. Dooley," is legendary in the annals of Chicago journalism as is Eugene Field. Nora Marks, as mentioned in Chapter Four, was a stunt journalist for the *Tribune* and is best remembered for getting herself admitted to an insane asylum. The fictional G. Vernon Rawlston was drawn from two Chicago editors, James Keely and Walter Howey. Keeley was dubbed "J. God" after sending a reporter to cover a shooting *before* it happened. Howey was said to have lost the sight in one eye after falling on a copy spike while sitting at his desk in a drunken stupor. Each in his own era was a ruthless competitor who wasn't loath to invent the news. Interestingly, according to John J. McPhaul, author of *Deadlines and Monkeyshines: The Fabled World of Chicago Journalism,* reporters never used the term "scoop." "Beating the competition" was their jargon for breaking a story.

Finally, Daniel's recitation from *The Rubáiyát* is an incident borrowed from the life of Charles MacArthur, who with fellow Chicago journalist Ben Hecht, wrote the classic newspaper yarn, *The Front Page,* in 1928. Madeleine's pursuit of the Kozyck story is based on a famed case of wrongful imprisonment. In October 1944, Joe Majczek was serving a 99-year sentence for the 1932 murder of a Chicago policeman. A female reporter for the *Times,* Terry Colangelo, noticed an ad offering a $5,000 reward for the officer's killers. Discovering that the ad had been placed by Majczek's mother, who, believing in her son's innocence, had for eleven years saved her earnings as a scrubwoman, Colangelo initiated the investigation that led to Majczek's release. The story was later dramatized in the James Stewart film, *Call Northside 777.*

SAVAGE ROMANCE
FROM CASSIE EDWARDS!

#1: SAVAGE OBSESSION   (0-8217-5554-4, $5.99/$7.50)
Yellow Feather, Chief of the Chippewa, rescues Lorinda from an Indian attack and renames her Red Blossom. While they struggle through tribal wars they learn how to unleash their desires and commit to love.

#2: SAVAGE INNOCENCE   (0-8217-5578-1, $5.99/$7.50)
Tired of life in Minnesota, Danette leaves home to begin anew in the rugged frontier, where she meets the Chippewa warrior, Gray Wolf. Together they fight off enemies and begin on an adventure that will lead them to love.

#3: SAVAGE TORMENT   (0-8217-5581-1, $5.99/$7.50)
Judith McMahon is taken on a trip to visit Chippewa country, where she meets Strong Hawk and finds more than the land attractive. When love overcomes treachery and racial conflict, she is compelled to stay permanently and fulfill a new life.

#4: SAVAGE HEART   (0-8217-5635-4, $5.99/$7.50)
Traveling to Seattle, on a journey to riches, Christa and David lose their parents to cholera. Poverty-stricken, David forces Christa to marry a wealthy businessman against her will. Despite convention and a furious brother or a rival tribe, when she sets her eyes on the handsome Tall Cloud, chief of the Suquamish, she is joined to him forever.

#5: SAVAGE PARADISE   (0-8217-5637-0, $5.99/$7.50)
In the Minnesota territory, Marianna Fowler felt miserable and far from civilization. Then she meets Lone Hawk and the grass looks greener. Although they become outcasts, they both commit to a love that is taboo.

ALSO FROM CASSIE EDWARDS ...
PASSION'S WEB   (0-8217-5726-1, $5.99/$7.50)
Against the backdrop of sailing ships and tropical islands, a spoiled heiress named Natalie Palmer and a pirate named Bryce Fowler turn the Florida coast golden with the radiance of their forbidden love.

Available wherever paperbacks are sold, or order direct from the Publisher. Send cover price plus 50¢ per copy for mailing and handling to Kensington Publishing Corp., Consumer Orders, or call (toll free) 888-345-BOOK, to place your order using Mastercard or Visa. Residents of New York and Tennessee must include sales tax. DO NOT SEND CASH.